UNDER A NAMIBIAN SKY

A DESERT LOVE NOVEL

ANGELINA KALAHARI

FlameProjects

London

www.flameprojects.com

Under A Namibian Sky

ISBN 978-0-9954877-2-7

To the people and animals of Namibia

THANK YOU

For buying *Under a Namibian Sky*.

I hope you enjoy reading the novel as much as I've enjoyed writing it.

To receive occasional email notifications about freebies, new stories and novels, YouTube videos, podcasts, short stories and much more, you can subscribe to my Newsletter here – https://angelinakalahari.com/contact/. The first thing you'll receive upon subscribing, is an exclusive novella called *Diary of Naomi, a Desert Elephant* – it's the story of what happens to ellie Naomi.

Elephants in Namibia are the toughest in Africa. But orphaned elephants are the toughest still. And they need to be.

All elephants must travel great distances to find food to live on and they're renowned for their magnificent memories and deep emotions.

In this novella, discover what happens when they find the people responsible for making them orphans?

If you prefer, you can email me at angelina@agelinakalahar-i.com or please go to the end of this novel for more details.

ONE

"Naomi!"

Naomi knew that tone of voice.

She hurried barefoot across the cool, dark slate tiles. She sat down opposite her Auntie Elsa, the nickname almost everyone used.

Naomi crossed her long, bare legs. She eyed the menus and various email print-outs scattered on the coffee table that separated their two sofas.

Naomi sighed.

It looked like work... lots of work.

Elsa Smith's melodic voice had carried through the main house of the lodge.

Naomi's guardian, adoptive mother and boss, comfortable in her mid-fifties, was sitting in the guest lounge. Her reading glasses were balanced on the tip of her nose. The heat frizzed her short steel-gray hair. She was checking through the new menus Chef had prepared in time for their next guests' arrival and doling out tasks to her adoptive daughter and other staff.

The airy, shaded room, where the grand old house's thick

walls thwarted the afternoon's heat, was just about the best place to be. It also helped that the blazing Namibian sun threw its rays on the other side of the house at this time of the day.

Auntie Elsa was still busy sorting through the menus and, although aware of Naomi's presence, didn't look up as she spoke.

"Look at the email on top of that pile. Kerri printed it on pink paper, so I guess she must have thought it was important. Remind me to congratulate her. She was right."

Naomi knew what the pink paper meant.

"Is it another American wanting to 'observe' African elephants?"

Naomi made air quotes around the word, observe.

She picked up the sheet of paper, but before she could read it, Auntie Elsa snorted.

"No, this time it's an Italian 'prince'."

Auntie Elsa mimicked Naomi's air quotes around the word, prince.

Naomi sighed again.

She removed the sunglasses she had placed on top of her head and ran a hand through her long, straight, blonde hair.

Oh, no, not another spoiled, egotistical top brass from some fast-paced industry coming to 'relax.'

She'd be willing to bet he'd be the bane of everyone's life for the duration of his stay here, as they all were. But turning them away, Naomi knew, wasn't a choice as they paid well.

It had become a source of amusement among the staff who had made a game of trying to guess how much over the odds these guests would pay when they checked out.

Auntie Elsa had her photograph taken with each of them, and then the framed photos were hung on the walls in the well-appointed dining room for all to see. It worked. Every time. These rich guys clearly moved in similar circles, and even when they didn't know each other, they recognized the faces when they saw the photos. They seemed to want to outdo each other, even here.

Naomi ran her finger down the page as she read.

"Hmm... this is different. It says here he wants to photograph and paint elephants. I'm not sure he knows what he's talking about."

Naomi re-read the email just to be sure she'd got it right the first time. That's when she noticed the familiar logo.

"Oh, and he's not just any prince this time... he's the Armati prince, no less. From the supercar dynasty, if I'm not mistaken?"

Auntie Elsa looked up and smiled.

"Yes, he is. And I thought you would make the perfect guide for him, Naomi. You're very good with these types, and God knows we could use his money. We need to update the sanitation system for the entire lodge. The repairs and upkeep of this place seem never-ending, and the costs of doing so just go up year after year. This booking has come at just the right time. I don't know what I'd do without you, Naomi. What would we all do without you, my girl?"

Naomi returned Auntie Elsa's smile.

No pressure then.

Auntie Elsa checked her watch.

"Well, I'm almost done with these new menus, and I suppose you'd better get going. The new prince will be here within the hour."

Naomi's head snapped up.

"Really?"

She turned the email over and saw attached to it his arrival schedule sent by the private airplane company from Windhoek.

Auntie Elsa gathered the menus and the other emails and got up.

"I've allocated suite twenty-two for him as it's the biggest and most secluded, and suite eleven opposite, for his secretary, who is accompanying him. I believe Kerri has already arranged for the rooms to be thoroughly cleaned again, even though it was done just this morning. But perhaps it would be a good thing if you checked it, don't you think? We don't want to give him a reason to complain about any of the simple things, do we? And make sure Khwai brings all their luggage directly to their suites. He's getting forgetful in his old age."

PROMPTLY, on the hour, the sound of the small plane alerted everyone to their guests' imminent arrival.

Khwai was already waiting under the big camelthorn tree when Naomi got to the landing strip. It was on the other side of the grand main house with its gabled rafters. The old Khoisan man's face beamed when he saw Naomi.

He walked toward her, hand outstretched in greeting.

"Tjike."

Naomi returned his smile and greeting and stood by his side as they watched the Cessna plane flying closer. Naomi and Khwai glanced wide-eyed at each other when the aircraft was near enough to identify. It wasn't the usual bush plane they'd been expecting. Instead, a small jet was flying toward them. Only a few guests could afford such luxurious transport to the lodge, and they were always the biggest pains in the butt.

Naomi's heart sank further at the thought of how much more challenging than she'd imagined her life could be over the next few days.

The Cessna jet came down on the hardened part of the long, sandy driveway created as a landing strip for the small planes. It stopped amid the tiny sandstorm it had generated.

Khwai walked toward it, and Naomi followed with trepidation. The jet's door swung open, and a man's head appeared. Naomi and Khwai stopped nearby to wait for him to disembark.

The man who came down the short ladder looked to be in his late twenties or early thirties, a good few years older than Naomi, at any rate. His muscular body was evident at once and further enhanced by his immaculate dark blue jeans and a tailored white shirt. Naomi glimpsed a scattering of dark hair on his chest, peeking out from beneath the unbuttoned shirt. A somewhat thicker coat on his forearms peeped out from where he'd rolled up the shirt's sleeves.

Naomi didn't know what she'd expected, but this was not how she imagined Mr. Armati to look.

Mr. Armati saw them, raised a hand in greeting before reaching back to take the hand of an older lady and leading her carefully down the ladder. Her short dark hair was in sharp contrast to her stylish white pants suit and flat white shoes. When she stood next to Mr. Armati, she ran her hand down her clothes, the other hand clutching a brown leather handbag. Then she looked up, and a beautiful smile lit up her face. She stood tall and straight, but he was a whole head taller than her.

Naomi wondered if it was his mother. They looked so much alike. But then she remembered the woman had to be his secretary.

Mr. Armati turned towards the plane and pushed the ladder back inside the body of the jet before he closed the door. He heaved a large black bag over his shoulder with such ease it appeared to be lighter than it undoubtedly was. Long strides toward them further showed his athleticism and easy, aristocratic bearing. The lady kept pace with him. Her confidence and fluid movements belied the fact that she was so much older than him.

"Buongiorno. I'm Luca. This is Santina. I'm okay to leave my jet here? You're not expecting any others to arrive soon?"

His voice was deeper than Naomi had imagined. Although his English was perfect, she delighted in the slight Italian accent that appeared so exotic to her ears. Experiencing all the different accents was one perk of working with so many foreigners.

"Yes. No. I mean, yes, it's okay to leave your jet here."

Naomi felt silly for having stumbled over her words.

"You don't have a pilot?"

Her question was such a superfluous one, even to her ears, that she felt herself blush at her clumsiness.

"No. I fly myself. Much more exciting and fulfilling, si?"

Luca didn't appear to need her response and instead offered his hand in greeting to Khwai. The old Khoisan man smiled and nodded and tried to take Luca's bag. But he held on to it and handed Khwai a much smaller, lighter bag to carry, leaving a reassuring hand for a moment on the old man's shoulder.

There was no way he'd be this kind to Khwai when no doubt he'd be demanding, rude and unreasonable, soon. Why would he be trying to impress them? How long would it take before his true colors emerged?

Naomi had seen this kind of behavior from other princes before. It never lasted. It didn't impress her.

Santina smiled and shook Naomi's hand.

"Buongiorno. How lovely it is here."

Her voice, though authoritative, was clear and carried the musical tones found so often in Italian voices. Her smile was even more engaging up close, and her eyes reflected her powerful spirit. Santina's warm personality and elegance made an immediate positive impression on Naomi.

Luca moved toward Naomi, his hand resting for a moment on Santina's back, and they smiled at each other - warm smiles. Their affection for each other seemed genuine. Then Luca's hand enveloped Naomi's.

He was gorgeous at a distance. Close-up, he was the most handsome man she'd ever seen, looking more like a model than a spoiled, rich, Italian prince. His smile displayed straight, white teeth from a full, sensual mouth. Tall, much taller now he was in front of her, his physical presence crackled with energy. His hair was so black it shone blue in the sun, and intense eyes, like pools of the darkest water, rooted her to the spot and robbed her of her ability to think, much less speak.

Feeling foolish and like a peasant in front of this dazzling man, she almost tripped as she stepped back when he leaned forward to kiss her on both cheeks. It was the European way. She'd forgotten.

He grabbed her elbow with his free hand and pulled her upright.

"The sand is so soft here."

He smiled again.

For moments, Naomi stood dazzled by his beauty. The soft, erotic, expensive fragrance of his cologne, and his gorgeous dark eyes, with lashes so long they touched his cheeks when he looked down, was overwhelming. It felt as though she was continuing to fall. But his hand, hot on her elbow, kept her steady.

He may look like a God, but she knew at some point he'd behave like one, and not the good kind either.

Naomi felt the minor victory of taking back her power, as she extricated herself from Luca's grip on her arm.

She could feel her hair flick as she turned to lead them to their suites.

"This way."

Ahead of them, Khwai, carrying Luca's smaller bag, was already rounding the corner of the house on his way to the guest suites.

Naomi glanced at Luca from beneath her eyelashes.

He was chatting and laughing with Santina as they walked side by side.

He wasn't what she'd expected. But she was prepared for the inevitable change in character. Perhaps Santina's influence will keep him from becoming too demanding. He seemed very respectful of Santina.

All the same, thank goodness he'd be here for only a few days.

TWO

Desert Lodge rose from among the dunes surrounding it.

The figures of people waiting to welcome him and Santina became clearer as Luca maneuvered the plane towards the landing strip.

The sight of the tall young woman standing next to the old native man was a welcome surprise.

Luca hadn't expected to find such feminine beauty here, in the desert. But only when he'd landed and walked closer to her, did he see she wore no makeup. Striking, without it, she didn't need any. Hers wasn't the in-your-face kind of beauty. Instead, it was her powerful spirit shining through her green eyes that were instantly attractive. Her long, straight, blonde hair formed a halo around her head, casting her as a goddess in this desolate place.

Her casual clothes, a uniform of sorts, exposed as much of her gorgeous body as was decent. The curves of her breasts peeped shyly over the vest top. Luca drank in her long, toned legs clad in tight green shorts ending in sturdy walking boots, a killer combination for him.

Even more alluring was that she seemed unaware of her

beauty. She seemed so different from the models he sometimes had to work with in advertising campaigns for new Armati supercars. Luca hoped she wasn't the superficial, vacuous sort those beautiful models often turned out to be, in his experience, at least.

It had always confused him. How could such a lack of depth live in such beauty? Some were rather manipulative. He'd experienced their ulterior motives while they'd pretended to be in love with him. All the while, what they'd craved was the small amount of limelight his name, wealth and lifestyle could give them. He'd developed radar for those kinds of women.

But as he stood before this woman, the intensity, the intelligence, the innocent sincerity and the sensuality that shone from her eyes, was what struck him most. She was young, yes, but no pushover. Her strength was clear in her eyes.

Luca couldn't resist getting closer to her and was grateful that the European way of kissing her on each cheek allowed him to do so. He breathed in her scent of honey and apples and sunshine.

Did he imagine the increase in her breath at his quick, soft kisses?

When she stumbled back, he touched her elbow. He found her skin soft under his hand. But such electricity coursed through his body at their touch, he almost snatched his hand away. Somehow, he couldn't refrain from continuing to touch her, though. She was his flame, and he was the hapless moth circling closer and closer.

What was he doing?

Luca shook his head.

What was he thinking?

He had no time for this kind of thing. He hadn't come here looking for romance or love. Yet, he couldn't deny his response... his body's response to her.

He'd known many beautiful women and bedded several too, but none had ever affected him in this way, and so quickly. He wasn't ready. He wasn't here for some kind of vacation romance, either. He would photograph and paint elephants.

But he couldn't deny that what he'd sensed in this young woman had made his pulse quicken at once. It hadn't happened for a very long time.

Her cool front presented a challenge he couldn't resist. It made him want to tease and flirt with her.

Thank God Santina was here to save him from any real madness. No, actually, Santina had forced this break on him, insisting he was working too hard, and complaining he was married to his work.

He'd smiled when he'd realized she was planning to join him.

Reluctantly, he'd agreed to her suggestion that Namibia would be the perfect place for capturing images of African elephants.

Canvases with images of Indian elephants decorated the walls of his massive garage, where he kept the many Armatis he owned. But Santina had known of his dream to paint the images of African elephants. When she'd seen him hesitate, she'd offered the journey as an early birthday present. It was her way of encouraging his more artistic ventures he so enjoyed.

Dear Santina... What would he do without her? She'd always been there for him.

Images flitted across his mind of the time his mother had left. He was eight years old. The pain of his father being a stranger to him from that day always stayed raw. Even now, after they'd become friends as adults.

Santina was the only person who'd always been there. He loved her like a son and was grateful for her in his life every single day.

Only when he became older, did he discover why his father's grief and despair had consumed him so. How could it not? His mother was the love of his father's life.

Had he been in his father's shoes, would he have got over her leaving him for the Greek tycoon? One who could afford her the lifestyle she so craved? Or so the rumors went.

Even though they'd never discussed it, Luca knew his father continued to be tortured because his wife had left him for another man.

Depressed, Enzo was incapable of dealing with his young son at the time when all his energy had gone into mourning the loss of the woman he'd loved more than life.

Luca understood that now. But in his young mind, it wasn't a reason for having been packed off to boarding school and losing everything he'd known.

In typical Italian style, Cecilia's disappearance became a drama. No one knew what had happened to her. There were no notes, no body... nothing. But it was a media frenzy all the same.

When Luca caught himself remembering that time, it still amazed him that it went on for only three weeks before word came of her whereabouts. It was excruciating and felt like forever.

He was sure he'd loved his mother, but she was never the warm, kind, generous soul that Santina harbored. Cecilia never read stories to him at night. She didn't tuck him in and made him feel safe and wanted. She didn't make sure that the light in the hallway was on and his door was ajar, so the scary darkness of the night wouldn't envelop him.

But the room Naomi showed him now was the opposite of dark. It was everything Luca had imagined a suite at Desert Lodge would look like - large, bright, with high ceilings and beautiful African decorations everywhere. Simple but effective. That's how he liked things. A clean white en-suite bathroom and clean white sheets on his double bed looked inviting after the long journey from Italy.

He did his best to be patient as Naomi showed him around. But once he knew Santina was happy with everything in her suite, he closed his door.

As soon as he was alone, he got rid of his clothes and allowed the warm water of the shower to wash away the stresses of the journey.

He wished it could wash away the stresses of his job. He'd promised Santina he'd relax and enjoy his brief break, and he intended to keep his promise to the best of his ability. But he knew he couldn't ignore the emails and messages he'd receive and which he could access on his phone. It was the secret he intended to keep from Santina.

How thoughtful that the lodge staff had allocated Santina's suite opposite his. The pool that separated their rooms looked inviting. He was looking forward to an early morning swim. He might as well enjoy himself. A packed schedule seldom allowed him the opportunity to use the staff swimming pool at the Armati headquarters.

And perhaps Naomi would swim in the morning? He hoped so.

———

NAOMI HAD NOTICED the way Luca had eyed the pool. She realized it meant he'd want to swim. But was he a morning swimmer or an evening swimmer? She didn't want to bump into him during her customary early morning swim.

After Naomi left Luca's room, she walked to the end of the pool and waited for Khwai. He'd helped Santina to her suite. Naomi could hear them talking and laughing, but it wasn't long before he came striding toward her. Together they walked back to the main house. Khwai opened the back door, and they entered the kitchen, he to have an early dinner, and Naomi to get ready for her sunset safari.

But Naomi was still busy with the conversation in her mind about the swimming when Auntie Elsa appeared and snapped her out of it.

"Everything went okay? Our newest guests happy?"

"Yes, I believe so."

"So why the frown?"

"Nothing. I was just wondering if Luca was an early morning swimmer."

"Oh, for goodness' sake."

Auntie Elsa's face became an alarming shade of red.

"I'm sure he won't bite if you are in the pool at the same time. You should give people a chance. I won't be here forever, you know, my girl. You must face the world on your own at some point."

Auntie Elsa had never spoken to her like that before, not even when she was younger and perhaps in need of guidance.

It shocked Naomi.

"Oh, I... I'm sorry."

She felt even sillier for having stumbled over her words.

"I didn't mean-"

Auntie Elsa ran a hand through her mop of unruly hair.

"I'm sorry, Naomi. I'm just... I don't know. I'm just feeling out of sorts. I'm sure it's nothing, and I shouldn't take it out on you, of all people. I'm so sorry, my darling girl."

Auntie Elsa gave Naomi an apologetic hug and a kiss on her cheek. Then, she walked to her room without a backward glance.

Naomi didn't know what to make of the strange behavior. She'd never seen Auntie Elsa in such a state, or mood or whatever was going on with her.

Perhaps it was just money worries, as usual? All the more reason to see that everything ran smoothly for their new guests.

Luca and Santina were the only guests at the lodge this evening. According to the bookings, a German family would join them tomorrow, and the day after, another 'prince,' this time from America. Over the weekend, they were expecting some hunters from South Africa to check in, although they wouldn't be joining any of the safaris. As a result, Naomi was free to take Luca anywhere he wanted to go this evening. Santina had already said she wouldn't be joining them as she'd wanted to rest after the long flight from Italy.

Naomi couldn't help being excited they didn't have to follow the regular route. She loved taking individual guests to places and animals they may not visit again when others joined them.

She made her way outside to check that the cooler bags contained drinks and snacks Luca would like. Everything was ready and waiting for the staff to load onto the safari truck. Auntie Elsa had trained them well. Things ran like a well-oiled machine. Kerri had been clever in getting a list from Santina of snacks and drinks Luca liked.

Naomi checked the charge on the walkie-talkie she was taking with her and that the rifle was loaded, its safety catch on, and that it was stowed safely behind her seat in the truck.

She'd never needed to use the walkie-talkie. But she always took it along just in case something went wrong, and she needed help to get their guests back out of the desert. There was no mobile phone satellite reception in the desert.

She'd never needed to use the rifle, either. But the thought it was at hand for protection in case they came across big predators like lion was comforting. A pity those were woefully scarce in the desert these days.

Satisfied that everything was in order, she went to her room to get a light jumper in case the evening got cooler.

Just as she came out of her room, she bumped into Auntie Elsa, who seemed much more her old self again.

"I was just looking for you. I've been thinking... perhaps we can get Gerhard to take the other guests on safari. I'd like you to concentrate on Luca and Santina only."

"Sure."

It wasn't unusual for Naomi to look after only one or two guests, and Gerhard was an accomplished guide. She trusted him with their other guests as much as she knew Auntie Elsa did.

By the time Naomi got back to the safari truck, they had loaded everything to her specifications, and care taken for easy access when the time came for refreshments.

She was just about to walk to the front of the main house to wait for Luca there when he came around the corner. He was carrying a camera with an enormous lens and a case, which no doubt contained other lenses and photographic paraphernalia.

His smile lit up his face.

"Hello again."

Naomi couldn't help noticing how white his teeth were, how sensual his mouth, how mischievous the glint in his gorgeous eyes, and how yummy he looked in a new navy t-shirt and jeans. He'd showered, and his ruffled, damp hair screamed to be touched. She felt her throat go dry, but managed a smile and a "hi" of her own. She could feel his excitement pumping through his body and jumping to hers.

Her smile loosened.

Luca was so uninhibited and energetic, she had a glimpse of what he must have been like as a boy. She was glad he'd kept his boyishness. None of the 'princes' ever did but it suited him.

Luca leaned into the truck and arranged his bag and lenses

at the foot of his seat before coming around the vehicle and helping Naomi up into the driver's seat. It was a first. None of the other 'princes' had ever bothered to treat her like a lady.

What was he up to? Someone like him couldn't be this courteous and charming as well? She'd have to watch him.

She waited for him to get into the truck, but he stayed there, instead, looking at her, his hand remaining on the open door. His excitement was still palpable. That, at least, was refreshing. But was he waiting for her to say something?

"It's just you and me this evening. So, I can take you to see things not on the usual route. That way, the safari won't bore you."

"Oh, I'm positive I won't be bored."

Luca's voice caressed the air, and his eyes held hers for a fraction longer than she'd expected. Finally, he broke contact, and with a smile touching the corners of his mouth, he closed her door. Long strides took him around the front of the truck, and he slid into his seat beside her.

What was he playing at? Was he flirting with her? Perhaps that was just the way he treated all women. He was handsome and glamorous enough. Women most likely jumped at the chance to be wooed by him. Well, if he thought she would jump when he snapped his fingers, he had another think coming. Okay, so he was stunning. But he was just another spoiled brat, wasn't he? Acting all gentlemanly was most likely just an act on his part. She wouldn't let him get the better of her.

But if she was honest, he didn't feel like just another spoiled brat. There was something more substantial about him, and he seemed like a genuinely nice guy. Even though she hated to admit it, she felt more comfortable with him than she'd ever felt with any man she'd met before.

Naomi started the truck and drove into the desert in the direction of the setting sun. Its huge disk already projected glorious orange rays over the red sands of the Namib Desert, turning everything it touched to gold.

Luca whistled under his breath as the beauty of the desert raced to meet them. He aimed his camera at the dunes.

Naomi was used to guests getting carried away taking photos and videos. She didn't want to disturb Luca or break his concentration, so she remained silent.

Usually, the atmosphere would feel strained with these types of guests. She'd get the message loud and clear that she was but an employee and they were the boss. They said nothing. Instead, their actions and attitude clarified that the world revolved around them.

But it felt different with Luca. Somehow, it felt comfortable, like she'd always known him. He must have felt the same because soon, a companionable silence settled over them.

After traveling for a little while, Naomi turned off the path they'd been following and drove into the unspoiled dunes. Above them, oranges, reds, and pinks from the sun's palette, was lacerating the blue of the sky. The last of its rays were dancing a battle in beauty to stay with them. The line of dark green trees was getting closer, and with it, a shaded coolness descended around them.

Luca's voice carried a note of concern as he continued to click feverishly with his camera, unwilling to miss even the slightest thing.

"Will we see the sunset from here?"

"Oh, yes. Beyond the line of trees is a slight opening. I plan to take us on top of the dune, just there. Can you see it?"

Naomi pointed towards the opening among the trees where a dune nestled and formed a hill higher than the surrounding dunes.

"But I'll stop over there for a moment, first. It will give you great shots of the zebras and giraffes grazing under the trees."

Surprised, Luca looked up from his camera.

"I didn't even see them. Their camouflage is perfect."

As they drove nearer, Naomi sucked in her breath and whispered to Luca to stay still.

He did what she asked without debate. But a questioning look told her he hadn't yet noticed the elephant bull standing under one of the big old acacia trees. It was a massive animal with huge tusks. He stood there like a silent, giant gray ghost. Only the slight movement of his ears showed he was cooling himself. His trunk plucked the small, juicy leaves from among the thorns with such gentle dexterity that they didn't seem dangerously sharp at all.

Naomi touched Luca's arm to focus his attention where she was pointing at the elephant. She let go the moment she knew he'd seen it. But not before she'd felt the tense excitement in his arm.

His emotions had to be contagious, as a sudden happiness suddenly washed through her. She was glad she'd followed her instincts and brought him here, to his first sighting of an African elephant. It was worth seeing the delight and joy on his face.

Luca was all concentration as he focused his camera on the elephant. Click after click told Naomi he was taking many pictures before he swapped the lens for an even bigger one. The bigger lens was to shoot close-ups of the enormous animal.

When Luca had the pictures he wanted, he sat back in his seat and blew out a soft breath, smiling all the while.

He leaned towards her.

"That was amazing. Thank you."

His whispered breath lifted some strands of her hair from her ear, and she gave a slight shudder. It was a new sensation. The tiny tickle felt too intimate for her liking.

She moved away from him. Perhaps being out here alone wasn't such a good idea.

She would try to get the safari over with as soon as possible.

"Are you ready to move on?"

He nodded.

Slowly, so as not to spook the animals, she turned the truck and drove to the dune she'd pointed out earlier.

Once they reached the top, they could see the line of trees with the animals below and behind them, and ahead, the miles and miles of dunes, in part, cast in shadow, as the sun was busy setting spectacularly.

Luca's voice told of his awe and reverence.

"Oh my God, how beautiful."

Once again, Luca aimed his camera at the dunes and the sunset.

"Italy is so beautiful, but this is..."

He seemed unable to find the words to describe what he was seeing.

Naomi understood and remained silent. Instead, she watched as he took photo after photo and expertly changed the focus on the images he wanted to capture. It gave her the perfect opportunity to study him.

His was a proud profile with a straight nose and full lips. The shadow of designer stubble on his square jaw gave him an even more handsome, manly appearance. But it wasn't just his physical beauty that was blinding. His energy was sizzling, his spirit like a vibrant bright light, illuminating the darkness and chasing away the bad.

Naomi loved her job with a capital L but was grateful for it anew, for making it possible to meet someone like Luca. She couldn't imagine any other circumstances under which their paths would have crossed. He was plainly someone special. She'd felt an inkling of it upon meeting him, but now, in the confines of the truck, she knew she was right.

When Luca finished and saw her looking at him, he grinned.

"It's been a hobby for some time. I love beautiful things."

His eyes roamed over her in such a way when he said it, that it brought heat to her cheeks. No man had ever looked at her like that before, and a man like Luca... She didn't know what to do.

Her heart was hammering in her chest. Could he hear it?

She had to get away from him, even if just for a moment.

"I'll get your drink. What would you like?"

She clambered down and opened the back of the truck where the drinks and nibbles were being kept cold.

Luca joined her but wanted nothing to eat. He didn't want to spoil his dinner.

Perhaps it was one way of keeping his body in such great shape.

When each had a drink in hand, they went to sit on the dune in front of the truck.

Luca's sigh was throaty and filled with contentment.

"I think I have fallen in love..."

Naomi couldn't look at him, but concentrated instead on the sunset in front of her. She cursed her heart for beating so fast and so loud. What was wrong with her?

"... with Africa. Thank you for this."

When she looked at him, his gorgeous smile and mischievous eyes were only inches away from hers. He clinked his glass against hers before taking a sip, his eyes never leaving hers.

THREE

When the sun set behind the dunes and the sky turned a dark velvet blue, Naomi felt herself relaxing even more in Luca's presence. There was something secure about the dark, something safe that protected her from his piercing eyes, which made her feel as though he could see deep into her soul.

She let out a sigh.

"Isn't it beautiful? Is Italy like this?"

"Yes, and yes."

She could hear his smile.

"Italy is a different kind of beautiful. Just as old perhaps, or not... I read somewhere that the Namib Desert is the oldest desert in the world. But yes, Italy is beautiful in another way. This is so raw, so naked and..." He stopped, evidently searching for the words to describe his feelings. "... massive, huge. It makes one feel so small, so insignificant. Do you feel it?"

"Yes."

Naomi felt surprised and relieved that he'd said things she could relate to so well - surprised because she didn't expect it from someone like him and relieved because it was a way to connect with him.

He'd described exactly the effect that sitting in the desert had on her day or night. But this time was her favorite. Dusk brought such magic when owls flew on silent wings, and night animals awoke. She was glad she could spend this time with Luca, just this once. She knew no matter what else happened in her life, this moment, with this man who was so beautiful he seemed unreal, would live in her memories forever. She could feel the beauty of his soul, although he was, no doubt, a spoiled brat. She decided to forgive him for trying to flirt with her earlier. It was probably just his way. Besides, she wasn't interested in him. Her body just needed to understand that, too.

"What are you thinking, amore?"

"Luca's voice was so close, his question so unexpected.

When Naomi turned to look at him, she realized his face was only inches from hers.

What was he doing?

She felt a kind of panic, but the warmth of his breath on her lips felt natural and right, somehow. Just as his kiss seemed inevitable, he appeared to change his mind. He leaned away from her, sat back on his elbows, and crossed his long legs at his ankles.

Why does he persist in trying to spoil things?

She didn't mean about the near-kiss. She was perfectly clear she meant that he insisted on flirting with her.

Perhaps he thinks she would like it? Maybe it worked with other women? Well, he was in for a big surprise with her. Yes, he was charming, and because of that, his physical nearness was disturbing. Yes, she had a sense of the beauty that lived inside him. But that didn't mean he could assume anything with her. She didn't want or need complications with amorous guests in her life.

Thank God he'd be gone again in a few days.

Beside her, Luca sighed again.

"This is heavenly. I could stay here all night."

But just then, his stomach growled so loudly that they both burst out laughing.

Naomi was still laughing when she collected their glasses.

"Well, you may want to stay here, but your stomach obviously disagrees."

Before she could move, Luca quickly stood and helped her up. The touch of his firm, capable hand sent tingles throughout her body. She shivered, and he took it to mean she was feeling cold. He slid an arm around her shoulders, and the heat from his body penetrated hers.

She didn't correct him. How would she explain it?

Luca spoke near her ear.

"But perhaps, after dinner, if you're not busy, we could come again?"

She wasn't sure it would be a good idea. But Luca was the client. How could she refuse?

"Of course. I'll see what I can do."

She extricated herself from his arm as naturally as she could and walked to the back of the truck to deposit their used glasses and to lock up so they could return to the lodge. He waited for her and helped her up into the vehicle again, before walking around the front to slide into his seat beside her.

Her body was still tingling from the intimacy of their touch, but Luca seemed unaffected by it. Instead, he commented about how dark the desert was at night, how you could hardly see anything, but for the extraordinary starlight. He took more pictures of the Milky Way and pointed out star constellations. It intrigued her. He seemed to have another hobby other than photography and painting. He told her about the stars over Italy and regaled her with tales from his home as they made their way back to the lodge.

It confirmed her earlier thoughts that he'd only been flirting with her and it had meant nothing. She felt relieved. Or did she?

Luca's voice was soft, as though he didn't want to disrupt the magic they'd experienced.

"That was great, thank you again."

He helped Naomi down from the truck. Again, he hesitated, standing very close to her, their bodies almost touching, his head lowered as though he would kiss her. Then, he seemed to change his mind and walked away with a smile, a wave, and a "Ciao, see you later."

Naomi stood rooted to the spot and watched as his broad shoulders disappeared around the corner on his way to the dining room and a much-needed meal. Then, she quickly went into the kitchen and to her own dinner.

Chef had prepared a fantastic feast, but Naomi wasn't hungry and nibbled at the food on her plate.

Why did she allow Luca to disturb her so? He was just a guest and would be gone again in a few days. Guests did that all the time. Why was it different with him?

She willed herself to imagine her life as it was before he came on the scene. It was peaceful. She'd been content. She wanted that again.

Auntie Elsa cast anxious glances at Naomi but said nothing. Instead, she concentrated on her food.

It was Auntie Elsa's habit to get to her guests as soon as possible after dinner to inquire if everything was to their taste and to solve any problems, should there be any. Naomi watched for the moment as her adoptive mother got up from the table.

She followed Auntie Elsa out of the kitchen.

"He asked for an after-dinner outing into the desert. Maybe I can ask Chef for some dessert and coffee to take along?"

"An excellent idea. Take what you need. I'm sure Luca will love it.

A frown appeared between Auntie Elsa's eyes.

"Hmm... perhaps it's something we should offer, anyway?"

Without waiting for Naomi's response, Auntie Elsa continued on her way towards the dining room.

Naomi stared at her beloved adoptive mother's retreating back.

What was she to make of Auntie Elsa's sudden, peculiar behavior? Again, Naomi hoped it was nothing serious. She'd talk to Auntie Elsa at the earliest opportunity to find out what was going on.

Naomi returned to the kitchen to find Chef.

Behind her, a commotion broke out, and she turned around to find her best friend holding court.

Kerri's eyes glittered with excitement.

"Oh my God, that's a great idea!"

She'd overheard Naomi talking to Chef about refreshments for Luca for their after-dinner excursion into the desert.

Kerri interrupted their conversation.

"We should definitely offer it as an extra, and charge for it."

Naomi had to smile.

Kerri was always thinking of the business, how to expand it, and how to make it more attractive to their guests. Kerri had been working hard to make a favorable impression on Auntie Elsa when the time came to put in her request to become Desert Lodge's next manager.

Naomi had no doubt that Kerri would succeed, and she supported her friend's every effort.

"Yes, Auntie Elsa said the same thing when I asked her about it a moment ago."

Kerri continued as though she hadn't heard Naomi, her mind on her prize.

"I can't believe we've never thought of doing it before. I'll bet Ilze at Solitaire and Hein at Waterspruit have never thought of it, either. I can't wait to see their faces when they realize what we're doing. Not that they'll hear it from me."

Kerri tapped a forefinger conspiratorially against her nose.

Everyone in the kitchen was smiling. They all knew how competitive Kerri was with the other lodges in the area. Her sometimes wacky ideas to outdo the others was a source of great amusement.

Kerri left the kitchen talking to herself, evidently on a mission.

"I wonder... maybe we could build a watchtower at the waterhole... and how cool that Luca is here now. Maybe we could make a deal with Luca and Armati for..."

Naomi knew that Kerri would most likely be in the office until the early morning hours again, perfecting her proposal for this new scheme of hers, whatever it was.

Naomi had finished the arrangements for refreshments and for the truck to be adequately supplied. Once again, she checked the walkie-talkie's battery and the rifle behind her seat. She was gone for only a few minutes, but by the time she arrived back at the truck, she found Luca in conversation with Santina and Auntie Elsa.

"Luca raved about his excursion earlier, so Santina and I have decided to come along. I've arranged for extra refreshments for us."

It was good that Auntie Elsa seemed to be back to her old self again. But relief and disappointment washed through Naomi's body in equal measure. She surprised herself when she understood she'd been looking forward to more time alone with Luca. Why? Perhaps she'd enjoyed his attention more than she'd realized.

Hmm, perhaps it was for the best that Santina and Auntie Elsa went with them. Luca would have to behave himself with them there.

Naomi smiled, nodded, and went to the driver's side. Luca walked to her side and, as before, helped her into the truck. Then, he took long strides around to the other side to help Santina and Auntie Elsa up. When he was satisfied that they were sitting comfortably, he slid into the seat next to Naomi, his camera equipment already stored at his feet.

Naomi enjoyed the conversation between her three companions but didn't feel pressured into contributing. Instead, she focused on driving the vehicle into the black night and staying on the well-worn tracks. The further she drove into the desert, the more she knew she didn't want to take Luca back to 'their' place with the others there. She took another direction to other dunes. She knew it was a good place to enjoy the vastness of the desert by the weaker light of the half moon and marvel at the sight of the Milky Way above their heads.

When they'd reached the right spot, everyone clambered down onto the soft sand. Luca was once again taking pictures of the surrounding night. He had some serious equipment that allowed him to take photos at night, and Naomi wondered if she'd ever see the photos he took.

After she'd lit a small campfire, for warmth and protection against any predators, she leaned against the bonnet of the truck. She could hear the deep silence of the desert. The silence didn't last long as Santina and Auntie Elsa's, voices joined the night sounds around them. But they spoke in whispers. The vastness seemed to inspire their reverence.

Each found a spot on the dune in front of the truck and leaned back to admire the stars that lay like jewels the Milky Way had strewn above them through the black sky. Only Luca was still standing with a camera pointed towards the dunes ahead of them. After a while, he found a spot beside Naomi and sat down, his camera balanced on his thighs.

"Thank you, amore. This is beyond anything I've ever experienced. I have no words to describe the beauty of this place."

He spoke with such sincerity that this time, Naomi believed him.

Moments later, Santina sighed.

"This is the closest to heaven I think one can ever get on earth."

Her voice told of her awe.

"I want to come back here for my birthday in July."

Auntie Elsa, as always, was genuinely interested in her guests.

"That would be wonderful. What date is your birthday?"

Naomi knew Auntie Elsa was already thinking about how to make Santina's birthday special. She was only half listening to the two women planning the party, but caught the fact that they shared a birthday. She could believe it. Auntie Elsa was such a warm, kind and generous soul, and Santina appeared to be the same.

Luca spoke near her ear, giving Naomi a little fright. When he saw her hand clamped over her heart, he took it in both of his.

"Oh, sorry for frightening you. I was after some dessert and coffee."

The heat from his hands flowed through her body once again, but she pulled her hand from his in such a way she hoped didn't offend him.

"Of course."

She got up and walked around to the back of the truck to unlock the compartment that housed the lovely goodies Chef had prepared for them. But when she looked up, she realized Luca had followed her and was standing very close to her.

She had to admit she felt flattered by all the attention he was paying her, but she wasn't an idiot. She wouldn't let his little game affect her. He was no doubt used to doing this with other women. She wouldn't allow him to play with her like this and then, when he'd had his fun, cast her aside to carry on with his life. Who did he think he was?

Luca held the tray for Naomi to load their desserts and coffees.

"Ah, Chef has prepared a scrumptious dessert for us, I see."

Naomi followed as he carried the tray around the truck to where Santina and Auntie Elsa sat. Luca unfolded the tray's legs and placed it on a harder, smoother piece of ground that was part of the track for the desert vehicles. Soon, everyone was enjoying a lovely dessert and strong hot coffee, each having made a little hole in the sand to support their coffee mugs.

Sounds of appreciation and the usual night sounds were all that disturbed the magical quiet.

Naomi noticed Santina and Auntie Elsa throwing occasional glances towards her and Luca, before smiling at each other. Their eyes were twinkling in the light from the crackling fire.

She hoped they weren't thinking what she thought they were thinking. It was clear Luca was just playing a little game with her. She had no interest in him, other than enjoying somewhat the attention he was giving her, and appreciating and savoring his exceptional beauty. But that was all. A frown appeared between her eyes. What she did not need was their meddling.

In the distance, a zebra barked.

Luca spoke with melodramatic alarm.

"Quick, let's finish. It seems we're going to have company and I'm not sharing this delicious dessert with anyone."

Luca followed his statement by making exaggerated sounds of eating faster. It was so funny that all three women burst out laughing.

Everyone helped to pack up, while Luca put out the fire with sand.

They filled the drive back with more laughter as Luca entertained them with tales of his own failed attempts at cooking, and Santina chipped in to elaborate on the details.

Naomi dropped Luca and Santina off as close to their suites as she could get before driving to park the truck under the porch outside the back door. That way, it would be easier for the kitchen staff to reload the vehicle for the next morning's sunrise safari.

Auntie Elsa leaned towards Naomi and gave her a kiss on the cheek.

"That was wonderful, thank you, Naomi. You did well. They seem like lovely people. I'll see you in the morning, darling. Night, night."

Naomi watched as Auntie Elsa let herself in through the back door before following her. Whatever was the matter earlier in the day seemed to have gone. Naomi breathed a sigh of relief.

As she walked down the corridor to her room, Kerri came out of the office, a thumb and forefinger pinching the top of her nose.

Naomi stopped in front of her friend.

"Tired?"

"Uh-huh, it's later than I thought."

Kerri's sudden bright smile belied her clear fatigue.

"But I think I've got it. I may even have thought of some fab new ways to grow our revenue and promote the lodge. It involves Luca. I'll tell you all about it tomorrow. Night, night."

"Wait. You can't say that and then just leave."

But Kerri winked at Naomi and waved as she turned.

"Tomorrow. Nighty, night."

Naomi knew there was no point in pursuing Kerri. She

could be stubborn. Instead, Naomi walked to her room, closed the door, and leaned against it.

What a day! How was she going to cope with Luca for the rest of his stay? Why did Auntie Elsa have to appoint her to look after him?

FOUR

She should have known.

Naomi cursed under her breath as she walked around the side of the building to the pool, only to hear the sounds of someone already swimming there.

Luca.

She'd forgotten about him. Well, actually she'd been thinking about him all night, wondering what to do with him today, where to take him to see more elephants. She ignored the little voice in her head that insisted it wasn't the only reason she'd been thinking of him, of his gorgeous body, his lovely smile, his dark eyes... She'd been concentrating on where to take him so much, in fact, that she'd forgotten about the possibility he might swim early this morning.

It was the best time for it. When some stars still twinkled in the lighter blue sky, the ghost of the moon faded, and the birds sang their welcome to the new day.

Damn. It was too late to turn back.

Luca had just finished swimming a length and was leaning on the side of the pool closest to where she was standing. His muscled shoulders and arms were as gorgeous as she'd thought they'd be.

He was wearing a wicked grin on his handsome face. He'd seen her.

"Buongiorno. What a vision you are, amore."

His eyes traveled down her body, admiring her usual pink bathing suit, and rested momentarily on her pubis before traveling up again to her breasts. The mischievous glint was undisguised as his eyes sought and held hers.

His gaze was so bold and so shocking that she felt heat traveling up her neck despite her best intentions.

What? Was he flirting first thing in the morning? Does the man never stop?

Naomi forced a smile to connect with her face. He was a guest.

"Good morning, Luca. You're up early."

"Habit, I'm afraid. Come on in. The water is lovely. Ah, but you probably already know that. I'm guessing you swim every morning, or did you come to join me this morning especially?"

"At the risk of sounding petulant, I'm not even going to answer that."

Luca pulled such a face of supposed disappointment that Naomi couldn't help giggling. She shook her flip-flops from her feet, dropped her towel over them, and dived over his head into the pool. She swam underwater for a while before surfacing and swimming freestyle in the opposite direction. But he surprised her by touching the side of the pool next to her at the same time her hand landed there.

"You're fast."

Luca's grin was one of sheer joy.

"I know. I love swimming."

"And flying..."

He was still grinning, his eyes staying on hers.

"And flying."

"And driving fast cars?"

His grin became wider as he wiggled his eyebrows at her.

"And driving fast cars."

"So, what's with the photography? You seem such a man of action otherwise?"

"It's just one of my hobbies. The other is painting. I told you I love beautiful things."

She was determined not to fall for his flirting yet again. Yesterday it was new, but now it was old news.

"Like beautiful cars, you mean?"

"I don't create them myself, unfortunately. There are far more talented men to blame for those. But now and then I get to have some input on color or interior design or something small like that. Not enough to satisfy my creative urges."

He moved closer to her, his eyes still fixed on hers, a smile emphasizing the contours his designer stubble created on his handsome face. He spoke just above a whisper, taking his cue from Naomi in order not to wake the other guests.

But unbeknownst to him, the only other guest at that moment was Santina.

"But how about you, amore? What are your hobbies? What stirs your passions?"

What was it with him? Did he even know another way of conversing than without flirting?

When she didn't answer, he moved even closer until their arms touched. It sent an electric shock through her body. As though paralyzed by his physical presence, she couldn't move away from him. Perhaps he'd experienced it, too. She didn't miss the slight widening of his eyes at their touch. No, she must be mistaken.

Before she could say or do anything, Luca spoke.

"No, don't tell me. Let me guess. But let me ask you this first. Will you join me for breakfast?"

Another first. No other guest had ever invited her for a meal with them. She couldn't deny that she was enjoying her time with Luca more than she'd imagined she would. But she was still alert to the personality change she was sure would happen at some point further down the line. It always seemed to follow that pattern with these wealthy types of guests.

She had to think quickly. Luca was waiting for an answer. Fraternizing with the guests wasn't allowed. But Auntie Elsa had asked her to look after Luca and Santina and Auntie Elsa herself had joined the after-dinner excursion last night. It was something Naomi had never seen her do in all the years she'd known her.

Naomi was just about to answer when Khwai suddenly appeared at the opposite side of the pool. He seemed to be distressed and used her childhood nickname.

His voice was soft with restraint.

"Nonna, you must come quickly."

Naomi knew well the old man wouldn't approach her directly when she was busy with a guest unless something serious had happened.

She turned to Luca.

"Please excuse me? And would you take a rain check on the breakfast invitation? If you'd like, perhaps we could have a sunrise safari breakfast tomorrow?"

Luca couldn't hide his disappointment. Again, his reaction amazed Naomi, because she hadn't realized it mattered so much to him. To her mind, he was just being polite, flirty again, and looking for company while having his breakfast.

Meanwhile, two other young native Herero men had appeared soundlessly next to Khwai. Both sported the dark green uniforms of the anti-poacher patrol unit. Both carried rifles.

"I'm really sorry, Luca. I have to go."

But before she could get out of the swimming pool, Luca's hand caught her arm. His touch was firm and sensual.

"I'd love to come along. Please."

Naomi knew with members of the anti-poacher unit there so early in the morning, it could mean only one thing. Poachers had killed an elephant, and it could get dangerous if the poachers carried guns, which more often than not, they did.

"I'm sorry, Luca. It may be too dangerous. I can't let anything happen to you."

"I'm a big boy. I won't get in the way, and I know how to take care of myself."

Naomi could see he was determined, and there was no time to argue, not if they wanted to catch the poachers. Besides, she'd pay good money to see who could resist those eyes when they implored with such intensity.

"Okay. But please do exactly as I say. I won't be held responsible if anything happens to you."

"Deal."

Luca got out of the pool quickly. He grabbed her arms and pulled her out behind him. A wide smile of happiness lit up his eyes, and he jogged to his room to get dressed. He waved to her as he opened the door to his suite.

"I'll see you at the truck."

Naomi nodded, went to retrieve her towel and flip-flops, and arranged to meet Khwai and the two guards at her truck parked near the kitchen. Then she ran to her room to get changed.

Moments later, she came running through the kitchen, walkie-talkie in one hand and keys in the other. She almost collided with Luca as he came running around the corner, carrying his camera equipment. Both had thrown clothes together, and their hair was still wet. His dark blue t-shirt and jeans looked expensive, and she had on her usual vest and shorts uniform. They spoke in stereo and laughed at their synchronicity.

"Oops, sorry."

But their laughter died as everyone got down to business. Everyone knew time was of the essence. Khwai and the two patrol guards got up from where they'd been sitting at the wrought-iron table just outside the kitchen door. Everyone jumped into the truck, and Naomi floored it towards the gate that took them into the Namib Desert. One guard leaned forward and gave her directions to the dead elephant's position.

It was a bumpy ride, but Naomi drove as fast as the tracks would allow her to go, trying to avoid the deepest potholes. She didn't want to deal with a flat tyre.

Luca was silent, but Naomi could feel the excitement pouring off him. Now and then, he lifted his camera to his eyes. But the bumps and holes in the road didn't offer the ideal scenario for great pictures. She'd take him somewhere later where he could get wonderful pictures and, hopefully, that would make up for this missed opportunity. She was trying to remember that he shouldn't be her priority at the moment.

After about five miles, they arrived at a sandy riverbank with trees on both sides.

Khwai pointed a little further to their right.

"Just there, Nonna."

How he could see so far and so clearly at his age was something that had always amazed Naomi. No wonder he'd been their best tracker for years. He was popular with the tourists who returned to Desert Lodge year after year for walking excursions into the desert with him.

As she drove closer, Naomi could see the towering gray hulk

of the dead elephant. The two guards, on extreme alert, held their rifles at the ready, looking out for the poachers, or for any big predators already near the kill. But apart from a few birds of prey that took flight as Naomi stopped the truck near the elephant, no vultures had yet announced the carcass to any other predators.

Naomi saw Luca going for the door handle. She laid a hand on his arm to stay him. His arm felt toned and hot beneath her fingers, and she became acutely aware of his nearness. In case he was about to protest, she lifted a finger to her lips, asking him with her eyes to remain still and silent.

A strange sound had everyone on high alert, but nothing stirred except for the trees in the slight early morning breeze. Otherwise, an unnatural quiet surrounded them. No birds sang, no cicadas announced the heat of the day. It was as though the desert was holding its breath. Only the weird sound came from somewhere nearby.

Luca cast a questioning look at Naomi. She shrugged her shoulders in response as if to say, "I don't know what it is, either."

But Khwai and the guards obviously knew what it was. They remained calm but seemed very anxious.

Naomi had stopped the truck behind the elephant, but she already knew what they'd see as they moved to its head and the enormous holes where the tusks used to be. It incensed her it was all the poachers ever took, that they would kill these gorgeous animals just for their tusks. But apart from trying to make things difficult for the poachers, it seemed to be a never-ending war with them.

Naomi sighed.

When Khwai gave the signal by nodding, Naomi released Luca's arm and opened her door, trying to make as little noise as possible. Luca followed her example. Camera strap slung over one shoulder, he too proceeded with as little noise as possible, following behind Khwai and the two guards.

The source of the strange sound they'd heard became plain as they reached the elephant's head. Between the dead animal's front feet, which had remained stretched out in front of her as she fell, stood a tiny baby elephant. It still had baby elephant fluff all over its body. Its miniature trunk was touching its dead mother's face repeatedly. Sounds of deep distress came from the little creature, as tears were streaming from its eyes and clinging to its eyelashes.

Naomi's hand went to her mouth, and tears sprang from her eyes. She stopped in her tracks as sobs tore from her body. No matter how many times she'd seen this scenario, it always killed her inside. But this was the smallest baby elephant she'd ever seen. It must've been only days old.

She felt Luca's arms slide around her as he pulled her into his body. Holding her head against his chest ever so gently with one hand, he stroked her back with the other as he tried to soothe her. She was grateful for his kindness, and after a moment, she held his torso as she cried on his chest. His body felt hot and hard, protective and comforting, his toned muscles discernible beneath his light t-shirt. She accepted the handkerchief he'd pulled from his jeans pocket, dabbed the tears from her eyes, and blew her nose. Instinctively, he seemed to know when she'd need it.

As she stepped away from him, embarrassed at the display of emotion, she noticed that the front of his t-shirt was wet with her tears. She wiped at it with her fingers.

"Oh, I'm sorry. I'll make it up to you."

She felt so silly and clumsy. What must Luca think of her?

But for once, he didn't respond as he had been doing since his arrival. He was serious and seemed as upset as Naomi felt, his face tense and white, his eyes dark and unreadable. A small tick along his jawline further showed his deep distress.

His voice sounded deeper, more authoritative.

"It's nothing. The heat will dry it soon."

It was Naomi's first glimpse of Mr. Armati. She liked his realness and wished he was always this way with her. Yes, he could be funny and made her laugh, and his incessant flirting was rather endearing, but she preferred the real man.

Khwai had asked them to stay where they were. He and the two guards tried to find the tracks left by the poachers, so they could follow them. The young guards who'd found the dead elephant earlier had followed the strict protocol not to go after the poachers on their own. Soon, more guards arrived, appearing from among the trees as though they were phantoms. Naomi counted. There were twenty. All carried guns, and all stood silently after having nodded a greeting to Naomi and Luca.

When Khwai found the correct spoor among all the many footprints in the sand around the elephant, he signaled them. Two of the younger guards stayed with Naomi and Luca while the others followed Khwai at a fast trot, disappearing quickly through the trees.

Luca had remained still until then, but as soon as Khwai and the guards had left, he went about photographing the dead elephant mother from every angle.

Meanwhile, the two guards tried to win the baby elephant's trust so they could get it into the back of the truck.

Luca came to stand next to Naomi as they watched the guards battling with the tiny baby.

"What are they doing?"

She couldn't tear her eyes away from the ellie as she responded.

"They're trying to get it into the truck. We can't leave it

here. It would die horribly, starving to death. At least at the lodge, we can feed it, get a vet out to look it over, and send it to an elephant orphanage nearby."

When the guards finally coaxed the ellie away from its mother and got it on to the truck, Naomi and Luca quickly clambered on board. The subdued atmosphere on the drive back to the lodge showed the sadness everyone felt by what they'd seen. That the little elephant was still deeply distressed and crying for its mother, concerned everyone.

Luca elected to sit in the back with the baby elephant and the two guards. He seemed unable to stop himself from fussing over the little ellie and couldn't resist taking loads of pictures.

His decision to sit there gave Naomi the space to experience her sadness without having to consider him. She breathed out a grateful sigh as she turned the truck onto a different track, one that didn't have as many potholes as the one they'd come on. She wanted the ellie to be as comfortable as possible. How scary it had to be for such a tiny animal?

As she looked back to check that her charges were comfortable, vultures were already circling the elephant carcass they'd left behind.

FIVE

Back at the lodge, the ellie enthralled everyone. It wasn't an everyday occurrence, even here, to meet such a young baby elephant.

Luca went to find Santina so she too could experience the ellie. Auntie Elsa and the kitchen staff came out to coo over the little creature. But Kerri, ever practical, took one look at Naomi's face and ordered sweet tea for everyone to help ease the shock of the morning's events. Then, she went off to call the vet and arranged with the elephant orphanage for someone to come to the lodge to recommend what to do with the ellie.

Reluctantly, everyone left to get on with their day when it became clear there was nothing more they could do while they waited for the vet to arrive.

Although it was still early in the morning, the sun was already hot. The experts at the elephant orphanage had advised the ellie should go into a cozy dark room at once with only one person attending it. They also suggested the mixture of milk for the ellie and confirmed someone would be at the lodge within the hour to assess the ellie.

Luca had taken many pictures of the little creature on the

way back to the lodge and was showing Santina the images on his digital camera. Auntie Elsa came to Santina's rescue, suggesting an early breakfast which both Santina and Luca welcomed. But as they followed Auntie Elsa to the Lapa, Luca remembered he'd invited Naomi for breakfast and went to look for her.

Naomi had been so vulnerable in front of him. He could still feel the softness of her body against his as he'd held her. He touched the faint white salt marks her tears had left behind on his t-shirt when it had dried. It felt good that she'd needed him, that he could comfort her. He had a feeling she didn't allow many people to see her vulnerable side. Nor did she appear to need anyone.

What could have happened to her that she carried herself with such dignity and restraint at such a young age? She must be what? Around twenty-four, twenty-five? She was an enigma, a puzzle to solve. It was fun flirting with her, teasing her, witnessing her embarrassment and confusion. But she was invading his thoughts more and more. Was he falling for her? He'd only known her for less than a day, and already she'd unlocked emotions inside him he never thought possible to feel. He'd have to watch himself with her.

He found Naomi leaning on the bottom half of the storeroom door behind which sheltered the baby elephant. One guard had assumed the role of a surrogate mother, and although the ellie was still crying and wouldn't take the bottle from him, the guard kept trying to get it to feed and to soothe it. It was heartbreaking to see.

When Luca touched Naomi's shoulder, she turned to look at him. She'd stopped crying, but her eyes were the saddest eyes he'd ever seen.

"How about that breakfast you'd promised to join me for?"

"I never-"

"Yes, you did. Only you didn't realize you did. Come, join me?"

With one last look at the elephant baby, Naomi allowed Luca to pull her away. He didn't remove his arm from her shoulders as he led her towards the dining room. She felt soft against his body, and he liked it.

But the question uppermost in his mind would no longer be silenced.

"Does it happen often?"

"Does what happen often?"

"You know… That poachers kill the mother, and leave the baby behind?"

Naomi sighed.

"It happens more often than you can imagine. All over Africa. That's why there's an elephant orphanage near here. They're great at taking in the ellies, nurturing them and introducing them to other orphans when they're ready. That way, they grow up in a ready-made herd. But elephants are such special animals. They grieve their dead as we do, and they never forget."

Luca could feel the little elephant's plight had had a bigger impact on Naomi than he'd imagined. He couldn't blame her. It was awful to see the small animal's distress.

Naomi's mind seemed to be elsewhere, and Luca wanted to comfort her but wasn't sure how to do it, other than with his questions.

"What happens to the poachers when they're caught?"

Naomi sighed again.

"That's the real sadness, I suppose. They're often just poor people from the area being bribed and paid just enough so it would tempt them to continue doing their masters' bidding. The big money doesn't go to them. It goes to untouchable kingpins somewhere in the Orient. The money goes back into the massive and very well-organized wildlife trade and is often used to fund larger scale activity, including militia. It's a vicious circle for these people."

Naomi sounded so sad.

Luca squeezed her shoulders.

"My God, I had no idea this was going on. I suppose it's such a big problem. Where to start to fix it?"

"Some people are fighting back. There's a guy who's into rhino conservation big time. He believes poaching will stop when the rhino horn is no longer available. He has over eight hundred rhino on his property, and he has dehorned them all. He may have a point because there is no poaching on his property, other than the usual."

Luca's eyes had asked before he formed the words.

"The usual?"

"You know... Poor natives killing the odd animal here and there to feed their families."

The way she'd said it, Luca realized it was a usual way of existence here, one he had never even contemplated.

An idea formed in his mind, but before he could give it too much room, he needed food.

"Talking of feeding...

He took her hand and pulled her along as he lengthened his strides, smiling at her. It had the desired effect of lightening her mood a little, and she gave him a small giggle for his efforts.

In the shade of the Lapa, Santina was already enjoying her usual light breakfast in the company of Auntie Elsa when Luca and Naomi took their seats at the table.

Auntie Elsa glanced at Naomi but said nothing. Luca noticed the glance and guessed at it. He was an employer himself. He realized that no matter how much he enjoyed her company, Naomi was a member of staff here. Perhaps it was frowned upon for a staff member to join guests at mealtimes?

He didn't intend to allow their rules to hinder his enjoyment of Naomi's company, and that included mealtimes.

He smiled when he spoke.

"I had to follow Naomi into the desert and help to bring back a baby elephant before she agreed to have breakfast with me. I can't imagine what I'd have to do for a dinner invitation."

Much to Naomi's dismay, the ladies laughed, and the serving girl snickered behind her hand at Luca's unexpected statement.

Heat spread up Naomi's neck into her cheeks. She kept her eyes down as an embarrassed smile hovered on her lips.

Her reaction only encouraged Luca, who took her hand under the table and gave it a friendly and conspiratorial squeeze.

Taking their cue from Luca, breakfast became a light-hearted affair.

When Kerri joined them and brought along Johan from the elephant orphanage, Luca realized his assessment of staff taking part in meals might have been incorrect. He liked Johan and Kerri at once. Johan was a gigantic man and obviously had a kind heart. He left no one in doubt about his passion for elephants as he answered all Luca and Santina's questions and provided interesting elephant titbits. His booming voice reverberated off the dining room's high ceiling.

It was a joy listening to Johan's stories. One could hardly miss hearing him. Johan had a habit of laughing about something before revealing the source of his mirth. This occasion was no exception. His infectious laugh rang through the entire lodge before he told them the reason.

"One guy over in Lesotho has trained his elephants to search out the poachers. So, the hunted has become the hunter, and they're bloody good at it, too. Their pads are so soft. The poachers can't hear them coming. He's a clever bloke, that guy."

Just as breakfast finished, the vet arrived. He and Johan went to inspect the ellie in the storeroom where it had been made as comfortable as possible. They didn't want too many people there to upset it, so everyone went about their business, but with an eye on the storeroom, in case any news came from there.

Kerri retreated to her office. Auntie Elsa took Santina to the veranda for coffee. Luca went to his room to download his pictures, and Naomi went to sit at the wrought-iron table beside the kitchen door with her mug of coffee. Everyone was on tenterhooks, hoping for the best outcome for the poor little ellie.

It wasn't too long before Johan and the vet reappeared talking while they walked back to the lodge. Their body language said everything seemed to be okay with the ellie.

As though they all had a sixth sense, Kerri, Auntie Elsa and Santina, Luca and several of the kitchen staff appeared as Johan, and the vet reached the lodge.

The vet declared the baby well enough to travel, and Johan readied his special truck to transport it to the orphanage.

Luca took his place beside Naomi and placed his arm around her shoulders as they watched Johan load the ellie into his truck. Johan took special care to make sure the baby elephant was comfortable. The vet had sexed the baby, and Johan had named her Naomi.

Tears welled up in Naomi's eyes as Johan drove the little elephant, Naomi, slowly down the road to her new home. At least this little Naomi would have a better start in life than her namesake had.

Johan shouted his invitation to everyone to visit the little ellie as he drove away, his elbow resting on the truck's open window.

After watching the truck until it disappeared around a bend

in the road, everyone went on their way to do whatever their day dictated.

Luca's arm was still around Naomi's shoulders.

He turned to her.

"As it's too late now for a sunrise safari, would you like to see the pictures I took of the elephants, instead?"

She nodded and together they walked to his suite. She sat down on a lounger near the pool while he went inside to get his camera and laptop.

Luca was happy and proud that his photos were so clear and professional. Silently, he thanked the fantastic new equipment he'd bought for this trip and that he took the time to learn how to use it properly.

There were gorgeous pictures of the huge elephant bull from the evening before and touching photos of the dead elephant mother with her baby. But the videos he shot of little Naomi were beyond adorable.

"I've been thinking..."

Naomi looked up when he didn't continue.

"I'd like to help with the poacher problem. I want to highlight it."

"How?"

"I'm thinking of writing an article and submitting it to National Geographic with some of these pictures. What do you think?"

The expression on Naomi's face spoke of her happy surprise and excitement.

"Oh, that would be fantastic, Luca. You would do that?"

"Of course. The editor is an old family friend. I'm sure he'd be delighted to help such a worthy cause."

"I don't know what to say, how to thank you?"

Naomi's eyes became guarded when Luca's eyes took on an instant mischievous glint.

He closed the laptop and sank onto the lounger next to her, his hands behind his head, feet crossed at his ankles.

"Hmm, let me see... How can you thank me?"

"Oh, no. I won't do anything silly or foolish, so you can just stop right there, mister. I've got your measure now. I'm grateful for your help, but not that grateful."

Luca pretended to be hurt, but the glint in his eyes and the smile lurking around the corners of his mouth betrayed him.

"I can't imagine why you'd think I had anything silly or foolish in mind?"

"Okay, then. Give it your best shot."

"How would you like to accompany me to an authentic Italian restaurant tonight?"

Naomi giggled.

"I won't do anything silly or foolish. Where do you see an Italian restaurant around here, never mind an authentic one?"

"I mean it. We could fly to Windhoek, have a lovely dinner, and be back before midnight. What do you say? It'll be fun, I promise."

Luca was sitting up on the lounger, his eyes full of hope.

He took her astonished smile as affirmation and opened his laptop to book a table for them and to arrange transport to and from the restaurant in Windhoek.

"I'll book the table for seven. Would that work for you?"

Naomi eyes still betrayed her thoughts that he was being mischievous and playing with her.

"Sure. What time do you want me to meet you for our flight there?"

"You think I'm joking, don't you? I never joke about food. Or flying. And I'll never joke about inviting you somewhere with me."

Luca could see her hesitation and wasn't surprised by her next question.

"Will Santina and Auntie Elsa be joining us as well?"

"No, Naomi. I'd love it if it were just us for dinner. Wouldn't you?"

The way her name sounded on his lips made him feel all wobbly inside.

SIX

Dinner was even more perfect and wonderful than Naomi had expected it to be.

Luca had been waiting for her in the guest lounge. His eyes widened when Naomi walked through the door, the effect she had on him immediately clear in the dilation of his pupils.

"Wow, you look stunning. I mean- even more stunning than usual."

Naomi felt the heat of her blush on her cheeks. She seldom dressed up and wasn't much of a dress girl. The few dresses in her wardrobe were gifts Auntie Elsa had brought back from trips to Windhoek. The strappy silk dress Isabelle had chosen for tonight's dinner felt lovely on her skin as it flowed over her curves. She'd always thought turquoise was the perfect complement to her coloring.

Naomi returned Luca's smile.

"You don't look so bad yourself."

It was a massive understatement because Luca took her breath away in tailored black trousers and a black shirt unbuttoned at the top.

How could he be that beautiful?

He quickly got up.

"Shall we go?"

He indicated for her to go ahead of him through the French doors that opened onto the patio. But when his hand contacted the small of her back, she almost gasped at the heat that flowed through her body at his touch.

His voice was like a hot desert breeze on her neck when he spoke so near her ear.

"We'll have a problem with you walking over the sand to the jet in those strappy heels of yours."

Naomi was only half listening to Luca's words. His presence and the nearness of him entirely overwhelmed her senses. So, it came as a complete surprise when he suddenly scooped her up in his arms and carried her towards the jet. She squealed with delight. His laugh reverberating from deep within his chest felt amazing against her body. The fresh scent of his musky, manly aftershave assaulted her nostrils and made her head spin. All too soon, they were at the jet, and he helped her up the stairs.

Luca made sure she was comfortable before he started the engine.

"Are you strapped in?"

Naomi nodded, as eager as Luca to get going. She'd never been inside a small jet before, like this one. It smelled expensive, of leather and Luca and money. Four seats in the front separated the small area at the back. There, two sofas opposite each other, a toilet and a kitchen/bar offered a further touch of luxury.

As Luca prepared to take off, his cheerful smile stretched over his handsome face, his excitement tangible.

"I know we've missed the sunrise safari this morning, but

the ellie more than made up for it. And we've missed the sunset safari, but this will be the best sunset you'll ever see."

The small craft lifted into the air with power and finesse. Luca handled the jet with such capable confidence that Naomi wasn't nervous at all.

As they climbed smoothly higher into the sky, the vastness of the Namib Desert lay beneath them. In the distance, the faint blue line of the Atlantic Ocean was just visible on the horizon.

Luca was right. It was the most beautiful sunset Naomi had ever seen. That she was seeing it from this perspective and sharing it with Luca made it even more special. Naomi watched awestruck as the darkening ocean slowly swallowed every spectacular ray of sunshine.

An immense velvet sky, strewn with the jewels of the stars, greeted them when they landed at Eros Airport in Windhoek.

Luca had arranged for a table on the roof of the Namib Sands hotel. Hollywood A-listers and other celebrities there on vacation often frequented its grand, world-renowned restaurant. It was something Naomi only ever read about, but now, it's opulence impressed her. Her eyes widened as the Maître d' ushered them up an imposing staircase, into a lift that wouldn't have looked out of place in a palace, and on to the large roof area.

The sight that met them seemed like something from a fairy tale. Candles in tall holders, medium-sized holders, smaller holders and a sea of tea lights surrounding their table, rivaled the light of the stars above their heads. Towering palm trees on either side of their table furthered the illusion of intimacy.

Luca pulled out Naomi's chair for her. When he was satisfied that she was sitting comfortably, he took his seat next to her. His actions surprised Naomi because she was brought up with the idea that people usually sat opposite one another for dinner.

But she loved having Luca so much closer, especially when he angled his chair more towards hers.

He took both her hands in his and gazed deep into her eyes.

His lovely smile lit up his face.

"Thank you so much for accepting my invitation to dinner, amore. I hope it will be the first of many."

Naomi sat transfixed by his beauty and nearly forgot to answer.

She kept her response light.

"You didn't give me much choice. You practically bullied me into coming out, remember? But how could I refuse such a sweet invitation?"

She wanted to add, how could she refuse a man such as him, but couldn't muster the courage for such honesty, even if it would sound flirty to him. Perhaps when she knew him better...

Being dined by Luca was the most incredible experience of her life so far. He seemed to know her taste in food, wine, music, everything. It was all perfect.

When their starters arrived, Naomi realized she was famished, and tried not to gobble down the delicious baked goat's cheese with cranberry sauce served on delicate salad leaves.

Luca had ordered a glass of Louis Roederer Cristal Brut Champagne for her, and mineral water for him. He was flying, he explained. The champagne's bubbles danced in the candlelight.

Naomi scrunched up her nose as she took a sip.

"It tastes like a little piece of heaven."

Luca smiled at her antics and clinked his glass against hers. She knew he thought she was only humoring him.

By the time their lobster dinner arrived, Naomi had a handle on her hunger and could appreciate more the care and attention that had gone into preparing the delicious meal. The butter sauce was sublime, the creamy mashed potato and the crispy seaweed an unrivaled complement to the scrumptious lobster, cooked and seasoned to perfection. Naomi was in food heaven. Or she would have been, had it not been for the nearness of Luca. Even how he ate was exotic and sexy. His habit of putting the food on his tongue and then squashing it against his pallet first before chewing was mesmerizing to watch. He seemed oblivious to the effect he was having on her.

Although he was clearly enjoying his dinner, his eyes remained on her or found hers again as soon as he lifted them from his plate. Luca remained ever the gentleman, making sure Naomi was comfortable and had everything she wanted.

After a divine chocolate dessert and coffee so rich it could have been a meal in itself, Luca escorted Naomi away from their enchanting table. He took her hand and laced his fingers through hers. She felt herself blush at the intimacy of the act.

They walked to the other side of the roof. The city lights blinked to their left, and to their right, the deep darkness of the desert loomed.

Luca took Naomi in his arms and held her gently against his muscular chest. His arms felt warm around her, and his heart beat powerful in her ear. She sighed against him and wrapped her arms around his torso in response.

Could the night be more perfect?

If this was just dinner with Luca, she couldn't imagine what it felt like to be wooed by this man. But is it what she wanted?

She couldn't allow herself to believe that this was anything other than just a vacation romance for him, a brief fling. But he differed from the other princes she'd met before, and she couldn't stop herself from liking him more than she thought was good for her.

Just before he escorted her away from the rooftop, he lifted her head and gave her a soft peck on her cheek. At the touch of his lips against her face, Naomi felt her pulse quicken even more than it had been doing all evening. His hand lingered in her hair for moments before he took her hand once more and led her back through the door, into the belly of the restaurant and out the front door. It seemed to happen so quickly, Naomi felt the dinner had been a dream.

The Armati supercar, in which Luca had driven them to the restaurant from the airport, had drawn a small crowd of admirers. He smiled at them, opened the door for her, and helped her into the low seat. It was so quiet inside the car that Naomi felt safe from the bustle of the small crowd around the vehicle.

When Luca opened the door on the driver's side, Naomi noticed the applause the crowd had given Luca. He was waving at them and laughing as he got into the car.

"Does it happen often?"

"You mean the reaction to the car? Yes, everywhere I go, especially for the newer models, like this one."

Naomi couldn't deny the car felt very luxurious, the drive to the airport uncommonly smooth. Once again, she wondered about Luca's life in Italy. The supercars, the glitz and glamor. She couldn't even begin to imagine it. But he seemed to enjoy his time with her and Desert Lodge, so perhaps her life was refreshingly different from his.

Back inside the jet, the tower asked for Luca's patience, informing him it would be a few hours until his take off.

"What is this 'Africa time' everyone boasts about? It just means everything moves slower, si?"

Naomi laughed at the pained expression on his face.

"Yes, that's exactly what it means. But we're here now, in this lovely, cozy, comfortable jet. Why not relax and enjoy it, right?"

She looked around at the soft white leather sofas and the

plush carpet underfoot and felt there were worse places to spend a few hours. As she looked up, she caught the devilish grin on Luca's handsome face. He winked at her.

"Oh, I intend to enjoy myself. Can I get you a coffee or something?"

SEVEN

Luca went to open the door.

"It's hot in here. I'll leave it open for now."

Naomi nodded. Taking off her shoes, she folded her legs underneath her, sat down and leaned back against the soft white leather sofa.

Luca got soft drinks from the small bar, offered Naomi one, and sat down next to her on the sofa. He took a sip of his mineral water, his eyes on hers.

"So, tell me about yourself. I take it you're related to Auntie Elsa, as you call her?"

"She's my adoptive mother."

Luca turned his body and leaned back against the armrest of the sofa, ready for her story.

Naomi narrowed her eyes, wondering how much to tell him.

But as though Luca could read her mind, he nodded.

"I want to know everything."

Naomi took a sip of her drink and held the glass between her hands as she started.

"Auntie Elsa was my grandmother's best friend. She didn't have to do it, but when she realized what had happened, she and Uncle Wouter adopted me. I was five when my parents died in a car crash, you see. By then, I was alone in the world. I had several foster parents, but things never seemed to work out in my favor."

In her mind's eye, Naomi re-lived a scenario again with one set of foster parents. From the way they spoke to her at breakfast that morning, she knew something terrible would happen.

They'd told her that the social worker was coming to collect her. Naomi had to get her things ready after she'd finished her cereal. The woman had given her a black bin bag to put every-thing in as Naomi didn't have a suitcase. But she didn't have much, so it didn't take long. There was still plenty of room left in the bin bag. But the thing that couldn't fit into the bag was her pain. Her entire body ached from missing her mummy and daddy so much. The other thing that wouldn't fit into the bin bag was more immediate. It was her tremendous sense of loss, of another mummy and daddy no longer in her life, of sadness, of rejection, none of which she knew then how to process or express. There were just feelings. Feelings that weighed more than anything she'd ever carried before.

But she knew it was her fault that her new foster mommy and daddy didn't want her anymore. She was too quiet. She never smiled or laughed. There was no space in their lives for her or her grief. But they hadn't given her a reason. She was just a foster kid. When things didn't work out with one family, they simply moved her on to another.

Naomi was sitting on the steps to their front door when the social worker arrived. The couple had had to lock the door when they'd left for work that morning. It wasn't raining, but she'd needed the loo so badly. When she couldn't stand it anymore, she ran around the house and peed in the flower pot outside the back door. She'd told no one.

Similar experiences with several other foster parents locked up Naomi's tears. There was no point crying. It didn't help. She had failed again and again to be the daughter they'd wanted, the daughter they'd loved.

Luca put a hand on her arm, bringing her back to him and this reality.

"I'm so sorry, amore. I had no idea. You don't have to tell me more if you don't want to. I understand completely.

Naomi looked up. She appreciated the empathy in Luca's eyes.

"There's not much more to tell.

"I only found out later how hard they'd fought to adopt me. Uncle Wouter and Auntie Elsa were older than most couples seeking adoption, and they lived in Namibia. That counted against them as I had to travel to a different country, and a different culture. But the Smiths had a brilliant lawyer on their side and the adoption went through."

Naomi remembered the genuine sense of leaving everything, and everyone she once knew, behind. The adoption meant she could no longer go to her old school. She would never again see her friends and classmates, the only thing left from her past. It was the only thing that still somehow connected her with her parents. She'd lost that connection the day she'd boarded the plane that took her to Windhoek, to her new adoptive parents. She was so scared they would again find her wanting. The social worker had taken great pains to explain over and over that this new mummy and daddy would be her forever family.

Naomi shook her head as though she was shaking away the memories.

"But I was lucky. They loved me. I am loved. Over the years, Auntie Elsa and I have grown as close as two souls can. I love her with all my heart."

But Naomi couldn't reconcile herself with how much she owed

her adoptive mother. How could one ever repay such kindness, such love, such generosity, such selflessness? It wasn't dramatic to say Naomi felt she owed Auntie Elsa her life. She felt the love from Auntie Elsa she imagined she would've received from her grand-mother—comforting, accepting, inspiring, guiding and full of wisdom. She couldn't imagine anyone else loving her that way.

"It's sad, you know. They had no children of their own. I know Auntie Elsa carries a deep sorrow in her heart. I think that's why she doted on me so much. She never denied me anything. And when Uncle Wouter died, we became even closer. I know his death was unbearable for her. She'd always said he was the love of her life. She still goes to talk to him, you know?"

Luca's eyes stayed intent on her as she spoke.

"I cannot even imagine what it must've been like for you."

Naomi smiled at him.

"Oh, no, don't feel sorry for me. I had the most amazing childhood. I had so many friends among the San tribes. When I was a little older, they allowed me to go into the desert with them. That's how I learned most of my skills. I followed them on hunts. They showed me which plants were safe to eat and where to find water. I learned the moods of the animals and the desert from them."

"And you got your nickname from them?"

"I did."

"Your childhood sounds idyllic."

The moment the words were out of his mouth, Luca real-ized what he'd said.

"I'm sorry- I didn't mean-"

"I know. Don't worry. You're right. After I came to live at Desert Lodge, and with the help of Auntie Elsa, I slowly came back into myself. I had a wonderful childhood. But I would have given it all up gladly, for just one more day with my own parents."

She heard how that must have sounded to Luca.

"Not that I'm ungrateful. I don't mean it like that. I love Auntie Elsa deeply, and Uncle Wouter was a wonderful man. I couldn't have wished for better adoptive parents. I'm very lucky."

Yes, she was lucky, but there was something she'd never shared despite how wonderful her life had turned out to be. The crippling fear had never left her that everyone she loved would leave her. The fear accompanied her profound yearning for true belonging. But how could she expect anyone ever to understand those feelings?

Luca took Naomi's empty glass, placed it on the little table at the side of the sofa, and slid closer to her. He put a comforting arm around her shoulders.

"I understand why you say you'd give it all up for just one more day with your parents. I can relate."

He told her a little about the disappearance of his mother from his life and, by default, also the withdrawal of his father. From what she'd told him, Luca knew if anyone could understand his yearning for a 'real' family, Naomi would be that person.

"Oh, Luca, I'm so sorry. I didn't know. You're always so light-hearted and funny. No one would ever guess."

Overcome by her kind words, Luca kissed her cheek. But as he inhaled her fragrance, and felt her feminine nearness, he knew he wanted more. She inflamed him with a passion he'd rarely allowed himself to experience. It had been a struggle to keep in check until now. But this woman wouldn't be a fling, an easy conquest, for him. She'd engaged his emotions, his heart. He kissed her more firmly, and when she didn't pull away, he cupped her face in his free hand and kissed her lips. She felt warm and real in his arms, soft, earthy and womanly.

He felt her sigh against his mouth. It was such a sensual sensation. He had to restrain himself from pulling her onto his lap and devouring her in the way he'd wanted to do since their first meeting. The heat between them increased their breathing. Gently, he licked the inside of her bottom lip, drawing an erotic moan from her. It almost undid him. He had to fight for control over himself.

Running his hand down her neck, he cupped her breast, feeling the hard bud of her nipple against his palm. It was his turn to allow the moan that had built up all the way from his hardness since their first deep kiss, to escape his lips.

It took immense effort, but Luca eased up and pulled a little away from Naomi.

She seemed dazed, her hair in disarray, her eyes unfocused as she opened them to look at him.

Luca's voice sounded far away and husky with desire.

"I hope I have not been too forward, amore?"

Naomi had been drowning in this beautiful man, in the passion of his kisses, in the heat between them, and in the quickening of her heart. She'd lost all sense of self or time. But now, with some reprieve from her desire for him, she felt a little embarrassed. What must he think of her?

"No, I'm sorry. I shouldn't have allowed... I've never... I haven't..."

Luca's eyes couldn't conceal his feelings as he contemplated her.

"Don't say anything. You are so beautiful, and I am sorry, but I couldn't help myself. Did I embarrass you?"

Naomi thought for seconds.

"No. I... I liked it."

She had no idea where the courage came from to be so forthright, but the words were out of her mouth before she could stop them. To her surprise, Luca didn't seem shocked.

He sighed and cupped her face in his hands.

"Oh, amore mio..."

He moved closer. So, she had plenty of time to pull away if she'd wanted to. When she didn't, he kissed her lips again. Soon, their kisses were again a kind of frenzy. They couldn't get enough of each other.

Luca had somehow pulled Naomi down onto the sofa and was leaning over her. Their bodies connected in such a way there was no doubt about his passion. She could feel his arousal pressing against her pubis. He pushed her flimsy dress up around her waist, and only her panties and his trousers were between them. It felt exciting, but dangerous. She wanted him. But what that might mean, she didn't understand. She just didn't want him to stop kissing her, stop touching her, stop what he was doing. But she had to. This was leading somewhere she might regret in the morning.

It took all her willpower to push against his chest until he had to stop kissing her.

She had trouble controlling her breathing, but she knew if she didn't stop now, it could soon be too late.

"Luca, I've never... I haven't..."

Luca focused on her words.

"Naomi amore, you are a virgin?"

Naomi nodded, eyes down, too embarrassed to say anything.

Luca moved away from her, an unreadable expression in his eyes.

"I'm so sorry I have put you in this situation, amore. What must you think of me?"

"Oh, no. Luca, please. Don't be sorry. I'm not. I just... it seems... You're so experienced. I just... I wanted you to know that I am not. I'm afraid I'll mess this up. And I really don't want to."

Luca's dark eyes rested on her. It felt as though he could see right inside her heart.

How refreshing and wonderful that she was so honest with him.

"You can never mess up loving me. But I'm afraid I have scared you, si?"

"No. No, you haven't. I just..."

Luca moved closer to her again and took her in his muscular arms, holding her against his chest.

She could feel his heart pounding against her ear.

His breath was hot against her cheek.

"Naomi, amore..."

His whisper sent shivers down her spine.

They sat still like that for a while, with him holding her as she clung to him.

She waited for her heart to stop beating so hard. The strength of her passion had caught her off-guard. How could Luca be so calm about it when she had to fight so hard with herself to regain control?

When the radio sputtered into life, and the tower gave permission for them to take off, neither wanted to let go but knew they had to. The journey back to Desert Lodge was silent, but Luca held her hand on his thigh all the way there, now and then glancing at her, a secret smile on his lips.

Naomi couldn't stop staring at him. At first, she was apprehensive about what had happened between them but felt much more confident when he took her hand in his. She wanted to drink him in, to remember every little detail about him, and felt grateful he didn't let go of her hand until he had to land at Desert Lodge.

After he'd taxied the jet back into the hanger and parked it, they sat for moments in the silence and the dark.

"Thank you…"

Both had spoken in unison, and they laughed at the synchronicity. Their laughter broke whatever had locked up their voices until now.

Luca brought Naomi's hand to his lips and kissed her fingers.

"You first, amore mio."

"I just wanted to thank you for the most amazing evening. I'll never forget it."

"And neither will I, beautiful Naomi. I'm honored that you agreed to be my guest tonight. I just hope I haven't scared you, or put you off me earlier?"

Naomi couldn't take her eyes off Luca. He shone. Yes, that was it. She'd figured out what made him even more beautiful than he already was. His spirit shone through his eyes, through his being. No wonder he didn't seem real.

"You can never put me off you, Luca. I'm just not very experienced, and I didn't want you to be disappointed."

Luca sighed against Naomi's fingers still held against his lips.

"Oh, amore mio, you can never disappoint me. You're everything…"

When he said nothing further, Naomi pulled her hand back.

"I guess we'd better go to sleep."

Luca had been gazing into her eyes. When she spoke, it appeared he woke up from some deep thoughts.

"You're right. I heard Santina tell Auntie Elsa how much she was looking forward to her first sunrise safari, so I guess we'd better get you to bed."

For once, Luca didn't make the flirty joke Naomi had half

expected from him. Instead, he helped her down the steps and carried her over the soft sand back to the patio and the French doors for which she had the keys. His body felt hot and hard against her, and she couldn't get the picture of him on top of her, out of her mind. He put her down gently and stroked her hair from her face. Then he drew closer and kissed her.

When she parted her lips to let him in, he groaned against her, his arms going around her. He held her tight against him. She could feel him growing harder against her as their kisses once again became more ardent, more passionate.

But Luca broke free and took a step back from her.

Their breathing was coming fast and uneven as they tried to regain composure.

Luca growled at her, took her keys, and unlocked the French doors. Then, with a small kiss on her head and a gentle push on her back, he steered her through the doors. He returned her keys and watched until she'd locked the door from the inside.

With a wave and a mouthed "good night," he disappeared around the corner to his suite.

Naomi walked to her room in a daze, closed the door behind her and switched on the light. Everything looked the same, but everything had changed.

She flung herself on her bed and dared to replay the whole evening in her mind's eye. But as she thought about it, the smile faded from her lips.

What had she done? No other guest had ever invited her out. Perhaps she shouldn't have accepted. But who could resist Luca? What had she been thinking? His attention had flattered her. His beauty and otherness confused her. What would Auntie Elsa say? She would most likely be furious.

Naomi vowed never to tell Auntie Elsa, although they'd agreed not to keep secrets from each other. But this belonged to

Naomi only. It was her experience to treasure, to hold fast to her heart, never to share with anyone else.

Luca would be gone again in four days and twelve hours. Why not enjoy him while he was still here? Most likely, this was just a bit of vacation fun for him. Naomi had seen this scenario many times, although never experienced it herself. Often, these young princes would choose a waitress with whom to enjoy a vacation fling, which always ended in tears for the girl. The men never took such flings seriously, and the girls never heard from them again.

But Luca had awoken and unleashed such feelings in Naomi that she never imagined she harbored. She could still feel his hands on her body, in her hair, on her breasts. She could taste his lips on hers, and his scent was all over her and her clothes.

Dizzy with excitement and happiness, Naomi slid under her sheet without removing her clothes. She prayed Luca wouldn't regret what had happened in the morning or mistreat her.

Kerri, who'd had much more experience with the opposite sex than Naomi, had told her guys sometimes behaved badly once they got what they'd wanted. Naomi would deal with the heartache of not seeing Luca or ever hearing from him again, later.

Despite her fears, she fell asleep, wearing her dress that smelled of Luca, a smile on her lips.

EIGHT

Naomi couldn't keep the smile off her face the next morning, no matter how hard she tried and despite the severe talking to, she'd given herself. Her heart was singing, her soul happy.

Her mind had other ideas, however. It was doing its best to bring her down. It insisted on reminding her that Luca was a prince. He was the Armati prince.

Why would he want anything other than a vacation fling with her?

It was a first for her, and she wasn't sure what to do about it. One thing was for sure. She'd never imagined she'd be having a vacation fling with anyone, much less with a man like Luca. No doubt he had chosen her as they'd been spending so much time together, anyway.

Was she capable of having a vacation fling? She'd done nothing like this before. Oh hell, why not?

If Kerri knew, she'd only encourage Naomi. She was young. She deserved some fun.

Naomi couldn't get the previous evening's events out of her head. She'd had the most fantastic evening with the most gorgeous man she'd ever met. That he was kind and considerate was a bonus.

Kerri was wrong for once. Not all men were the same. Luca didn't invite her for dinner only so he could have sex with her. Yes, she'd never been kissed like that before and if she hadn't stopped it, who knows where it might have led. But Luca had remained a gentleman throughout their date. Was it a date? She had to get a grip. Luca would be gone again in a few days.

She liked Luca, but she barely knew him. It wasn't as though she was giving her heart to the man, was it? No, it would remain safe behind the iron doors she had created for it. It was enough that Auntie Elsa and Kerri lived there. A horrible cold-ness gripped her at the knowledge that one day death would tear them from her.

Her thoughts were so filled with Luca and guarding her heart that she had to check and re-check the truck several times. The kitchen staff knew the drill and had packed the breakfast goodies in the back. Naomi made sure the walkie-talkie had been charged before she walked to the guest lounge to meet Luca and Santina.

Only Santina sat in one of the big armchairs, a cup of steaming coffee in her hand.

A big smile lit up her face when she saw Naomi.

"Buongiorno, Naomi. I'm so excited about our sunrise safari. Shall we go?"

Santina exchanged the coffee cup for her floppy sun hat she'd draped over the small table next to the chair.

Naomi returned Santina's smile and walked further into the room.

"Should we wait here for Luca or will he meet us at the truck?"

"Oh, no, cara. Today, it's just you and me. Luca left very early with the anti-poaching unit."

Naomi struggled to keep a professional attitude. It was even harder to keep the smile on her face. Her heart beat suddenly very fast, and she had to fight the feeling of disorientation that threatened to overwhelm her.

Even to her ears, her voice sounded strained and despondent.

"Oh. Luca said nothing about it last night."

Santina got up.

Her voice sounded musical and soothing when she responded.

"I don't think he knew then. I only found his note under my door when I woke up this morning. Apparently, he went to the kitchen for something to ease a headache. There, he found Khwai and members of the anti-poaching unit. They were discussing tactics. He decided to join them. Don't worry, Naomi. Luca will be safe with them, I'm sure."

Santina must have picked up on Naomi's change in mood and interpreted it as a mere concern for one of her guests. Naomi was grateful Santina suspected nothing more.

She tried her best to sound normal and professional.

"You're right. Luca will be safe with Khwai. Let's have some fun. Chef has prepared your favorite breakfast."

The women walked to the truck. After Naomi had helped Santina up into the seat beside her, she got into the driver's seat, started the truck, and drove through the gate that took them into the Namib Desert.

Santina kept up a running commentary on everything she saw. Although Naomi did her best to respond and point out anything of interest Santina might have missed, her heart wasn't in the safari. Her thoughts were with Luca.

Why had he gone off like that without telling her? Was it a way of avoiding her this morning? Was he regretting what had happened between them last night?

But in her mind's eye, she saw his face as he waved her good night, the intensity in his eyes. She felt his kisses and his hands on her body again. Was it all a lie? Her heart and her head were at war. Even the stunning sunrise over the dunes couldn't distract her from her thoughts.

But she noticed Santina's questioning glances in her direction. Naomi knew she had to do better. She was being silly.

Luca would most likely explain himself later, and it would be something simple. Either that, or she was right about the notion she was just a bit of vacation fun for him. Damn, she was unused to feeling this way about a guy. Why did it have to be Luca of all people? Oh well, it was what it was. Better to just get on with her life.

Santina was easy to talk to. As they were having their breakfast against the backdrop of a stunning sunrise, they chatted about the desert, about life in Namibia, life in Italy, traveling, and every subject that cropped up. But neither mentioned Luca.

Naomi was aware of it and wondered why Santina said nothing. Then, she realized Luca was Santina's boss. She seemed very loyal to him. Naomi could see it would be foolish of Santina to discuss him with anyone. Naomi almost sighed out loud. It was good to know Santina wasn't keeping anything about Luca from her. Naomi knew she had to stop obsessing about him and get on with life. Luca clearly did.

The safari went without a hitch. Santina seemed to enjoy the drive into the desert. She commented about the sunrise over the dunes and the early morning animals they encountered. Naomi couldn't blame Santina. The desert was unfailingly spectacular.

Naomi tried, as she always did, to see it for the first time through someone else's eyes. It was a joy to experience their wonder and awe of it anew, each time. It was pleasant to share it with someone as warm and tender-hearted as Santina.

Luca was still not back by the time they returned to the lodge. But Santina didn't seem worried. Naomi took her cue from Santina, and from knowing Luca would be as safe as he could be with Khwai and the guards. She could just imagine him walking behind them, camera at the ready.

Auntie Elsa came to join them for morning tea in the Lapa. Santina and Auntie Elsa had become fast friends in the short time they'd known each other and talked like old confidantes. Naomi, not wanting to be in the way, made herself scarce and called the elephant orphanage to check on ellie Naomi.

To her delight, Johan confirmed that the baby was doing well and invited Naomi around to see for herself. It was the perfect excuse to get away from the lodge for a few hours. When Santina confirmed she wouldn't need Naomi as she'd just wanted to relax by the pool, Naomi jumped into the truck.

The elephant orphanage was about an hour's drive away, and Naomi arrived just in time for the ellie's feed. Johan's booming voice greeted Naomi the moment she stepped from her truck. He filled her in on the ellie's night and accompanied Naomi to where the ellie's surrogate father was feeding her with a bottle.

Johan laid a gentle, comforting hand on the ellie's back.

"She's much better, but cried through the night for her mother."

Johan had appointed the little ellie her very own surrogate father. He was one of the younger guards with the anti-poacher unit here, who slept with her in her stable, fed her and played with her. It was a delight to see how much the little ellie had improved since yesterday. It was almost miraculous. Her surrogate father had somehow got her to suck at the teat of the large bottle containing a special formula for her maximum nutrition. Now, baby Naomi sucked at the milk in the bottle, eager foam forming at the corners of her mouth, her little trunk curling this way and that, as she emitted tiny sounds of pleasure.

Naomi wished she could feed the little elephant, touch her and hug her, but it was too soon. Baby Naomi first had to get used to and comfortable with her surrogate father before she could meet more people in such an intimate way.

Johan showed Naomi the other orphaned ellies who were older, more settled and who seemed happier. Johan's enormous smile showed his fondness, and huge pride, in his baby elephants. There was such gentleness in the big man's voice that it brought a tear to Naomi's eye.

"Little Naomi will join this group when she is much better and a little older. This little herd will be her new forever family."

When Johan invited Naomi to join him and the surrogate fathers for lunch, she accepted. A simple meal of barbequed Kudu steak and mielie pap awaited them on the veranda of the big old house that also served as the orphanage's headquarters. It was the perfect place from which to observe the ellies. They frolicked with a massive ball and splashed around in their very own mud bath. Their comical antics elicited laughter and joy from everyone there and did much to lift Naomi's spirit.

She hummed a merry tune as she drove back to Desert Lodge after the lunch. It was good to see the ellies and to see how well Johan and his team were looking after baby Naomi. The little elephant would be all right. One good thing to come out of the tragedy that had befallen her the previous day.

Didn't Naomi know what it felt like to lose a parent at such a young age? She'd been older than this little ellie when everything in her world had collapsed. But she'd been only five years old when it had happened. It had seared the memory into her brain as it would for the baby elephant.

Back at Desert Lodge, there was still no sign of Luca, or Khwai, or any member of the Desert Lodge anti-poacher unit.

Naomi had to resist the temptation to contact Khwai via walkie-talkie. It would be out of character for her to do so and might alert Luca to her paranoid feeling that he was avoiding her. No, he'd be all right with Khwai. The old Khoisan man had never once lost a guest before. But then again, none had ever gone along on an anti-poacher patrol.

Naomi gave herself another stern talking to for the second time that day as she walked to her room.

The day had reached the peak of its heat. Everyone was sitting in the shade or had sought their bed for the afternoon's siesta. The shrill sound of cicadas and the soft, comforting cooing of doves mingled to further lull the day into a state of lethargy.

In her room, Naomi picked up the book she'd been reading before Luca had appeared and caused such chaos with her emotions. She plopped down on her bed.

NINE

The knock on Naomi's door startled her away from the oblivion of dreamless sleep. Her book was lying upended on her stomach. The clock on the wall told her she'd been asleep for an hour.

The knock grew louder and more insistent.

"Naomi! Are you in there?"

Auntie Elsa's voice held a note of panic, which was all the motivation Naomi needed to scramble off the bed and open the door. Auntie Elsa stood there, hair disheveled. Something had disturbed her siesta.

"Kerri has already called the flying doctor. But you need to go. Now."

"Why? What happened?"

But Naomi knew. She just knew something had happened to Luca. Even as she spoke, she turned back into her room, shoved her feet into her desert boots and grabbed the truck's keys from the bedside table.

Auntie Elsa seized her arm. Together they ran down the long corridor, through the kitchen, to the truck parked just outside the kitchen door. Naomi had to move at Auntie Elsa's slower pace, even though everything in her screamed to get to Luca's side at once.

It felt as though her breath was choking her, but she got the words out.

"What happened?"

But before Auntie Elsa could answer, Naomi saw one of the anti-poacher guards leaning against the truck. He looked ashen with exhaustion. Sweat was dripping down his face and arms, and large wet patches under his arms and on his chest, together with his rapid breathing, all signs he had run here.

Kerri was standing near him with a large pitcher of iced water and a drinking glass.

"Small sips, okay?"

He nodded and accepted another glass of water from her, gulping it down without a break to breathe. When he'd had his fill of water, he wiped his mouth on his sleeve and got into the truck.

Naomi didn't wait any longer. She jumped into the driver's seat, started the engine and skidded off towards the desert. The enormous cloud of dust behind the truck obscured Auntie Elsa and Kerri, who had remained standing by the back door.

Naomi had to raise her voice against the engine's noise and the vibration of the truck.

"What happened?"

The guard sighed. He was clearly exhausted. Like Khwai, he used her childhood nickname.

"We found them Nonna."

"The poachers?"

"Yes, the same ones from yesterday. They wore the same shoes. They killed another elephant."

Naomi's heart beat in her mouth.

"Go on."

"We tracked them, Nonna. And we found them. But they are clever. It was an ambush."

Naomi drove faster. She needed to hear what he had to tell her, but did she really want to know? She nodded, indicating for him to continue. The only word her mind screamed was 'Luca.'

"We fought them, Nonna. They fought hard, but there were more of us. But some of us got injured."

She had to ask.

"Is Luca one of the injured?"

He continued as though he hadn't heard her question.

"And Piet got shot. He was bleeding a lot. But I got away and ran hard to get help."

"When did you leave them?"

The guard pointed at the sky.

"When the sun was there, Nonna."

Naomi calculated that almost five hours had already passed. Knowing how fast these guys could run, it meant she had almost twenty miles to drive to get to Luca and the others.

"Where did you leave them?"

"The place with the iron trees, Nonna."

Naomi grabbed the walkie-talkie from the seat beside her.

"Kerri, come in."

The device crackled into life. Kerri's voice sounded distorted and far away, but still recognizable.

"I'm here, Naomi. Have you found them?"

"Not yet. But can you redirect the flying doctor to twenty miles east of Desert Lodge? They're near Gemsbokvlei. They'd shot Piet, and he's bleeding out."

"Oh my God, is he okay? What about Luca?"

"Don't know yet. I'll let you know when I see them."

"Okay. Anything else?"

"That's it for now. But keep your walkie-talkie close, okay?"

"Done. Gerhard is on his way with the other truck to pick

up the rest of the guys. I'll tell him to go straight to Gemsbokvlei."

Naomi felt grateful that Kerri had their backs. She was great anyway, but strong as steel in a crisis.

Naomi stepped on the accelerator. Why couldn't the bloody truck go any faster?

It felt as though they'd been driving forever when the guard tapped her shoulder. He'd seen them first.

"They're there, Nonna."

He pointed to the left.

Even though Naomi couldn't see anything yet, she trusted the guard's sharper eyesight. She slowed, swerved left off the tracks she'd been following and drove into the desert. When she was about two miles from them, Naomi could see the group of men meandering toward her. They were carrying someone on what looked like a stretcher, but she knew it was a makeshift one they'd produced from items found around them in the desert. It had to be Piet on the makeshift stretcher. Everyone else was walking by themselves.

She sighed with relief and drove as fast as she could. Meanwhile, she told Kerri to re-direct the flying doctor and Gerhard to their new position. Just as she stopped in front of the group of men, she heard the flying doctor's Cessna plane getting closer.

None of the guards had escaped the battle with the poachers without injury. But the poachers hadn't escaped injury or capture either. The guards had bound the poachers' hands and tethered their feet just enough so they could shuffle forward. Desert Lodge's anti-poacher unit followed behind them, pointing guns at their backs. Both groups looked exhausted, dusty and filthy with blood spatters over their faces and clothes.

Now they were closer, Naomi could see she'd been right about Piet lying on a makeshift stretcher. Even though she saw everything at once, her focus was on Luca. But she couldn't see him among the men.

"Quickly. Bring Piet to the truck. At least he'll be in the shade. Where are Luca and Khwai?"

An older guard, a contemporary of Khwai and someone Naomi had known since childhood, walked forward.

"We had to leave them there, Nonna."

Naomi's breath caught in her throat, and a sudden sweat made her body feeling even more sticky and clammy than the heat of the sun could produce.

Oh God, they'd left Luca behind? Why? Is he still alive?

The guard saw Naomi feared the worst.

He babbled.

"No, Nonna. The guest man is with Khwai and two other guards. We had to leave them there because the guest man got knocked to his head. It was bleeding, and Khwai said they had to stay there until he felt better."

The guard hadn't finished talking before a small sandstorm hit them as the doctor's Cessna landed nearby. The young man with the black doctor's bag and a stethoscope around his neck, who came running from the Cessna, looked too young to be a doctor. But he was all they had. Naomi hoped he knew what he was doing. She explained the situation with Luca and Khwai and left the doctor to deal with Piet's wound and the other injured men. The older guard jumped into the truck and gave directions to where they'd left the others.

Naomi drove as fast as she could, praying all the while that Luca was okay. She didn't want to investigate why her heart was beating at a thousand miles a second, or why her stomach was as tight as the string on a San huntsmen's bow. Instead, she focussed on the potential disaster for Desert Lodge if anything happened to Luca.

After traveling for over half an hour, the dark green of a line of trees came into focus. The guard tapped Naomi on the shoulder and pointed towards the left of the trees. She could just imagine what had happened. These dry riverbeds with trees growing on either sandbank could be dangerous places. Wild animals and poachers could hide there with no one's knowledge, though not much escaped the Desert Lodge guards. They must have stumbled upon such a hideout.

Khwai would have known someone from Desert Lodge would come by truck or Cessna. As Naomi drove nearer, she saw Khwai and another, younger guard, on either side of Luca. He was barely walking, slumped between the two men. There was blood on the side of his head and his t-shirt. His head was lolling from side to side as he was jostled between his two supporters.

Naomi drove as close to them as she could and jumped down from the truck. The two guards who'd accompanied her jumped down behind her. With her heart in her mouth, she approached Luca. Khwai and the guard supporting him stopped.

Before she could say anything, Khwai explained that Luca had tried to join in the fight, even though he didn't have a weapon, and got struck on the side of his head by a poacher carrying a gun. She could only thank heaven they'd struck him and hadn't shot him. But Khwai confirmed her suspicion that the poachers had run out of bullets and could use their rifles only to strike.

Stupid, stupid man. Naomi didn't know whether to yell at Luca or hug him. She focused instead on trying to remain as calm as she could and touched his face, skimming her fingers over his skin.

His head snapped up, and he glared at her. Then, he closed his eyes again and murmured, "amore mio," before his head dropped back to his chest.

The guards lifted Luca into the truck. Khwai held Luca's head and put a bottle of water to his lips. Luca's eyes flickered. He took a few deep drafts from the bottle, trying to hold it in place with his hands, but he was too weak. His arms fell beside his body.

Khwai lowered Luca's head onto a rolled-up picnic blanket Naomi had taken out of the safari compartment at the back of the truck. Between them, the four guards held another blanket to create as much shade for Luca as possible.

Naomi grabbed the walkie-talkie and told Kerri what had happened. Kerri relayed messages back and forth. The doctor would wait for them, but only if Piet's condition didn't deteriorate. Otherwise, he'd have to come back for Luca after dropping Piet off at the nearest hospital.

Naomi drove back to the Cessna as fast as she could. She didn't want to cause Luca more damage or discomfort, yet the urgency of the situation spurred her on. The forty minutes before the aircraft came into view was sheer torture. She could see the men sitting in the shade around the small craft. Piet was inside the Cessna, lying on a gurney.

While Naomi had gone to find Luca and Khwai, the doctor had assessed Piet's wound and given painkillers. The doctor had checked the other men, but apart from superficial wounds, no one else had been badly injured.

When Naomi arrived back with Luca, the doctor inspected Luca's head wound. Khwai and the other guards helped to get Luca into the Cessna.

Then, despite Khwai's protestations, the doctor examined him and the guards that came with him and congratulated Khwai on the tourniquet he'd used, so Piet didn't bleed out.

Naomi gave the truck's keys and the walkie-talkie to Khwai and told him Gerhard was on his way to help transport all the men to Desert Lodge. She knew she could trust Khwai.

"There's water for everyone in the back."

She waved to Khwai as she ran to the Cessna.

He was already talking on the walkie-talkie, and she knew he was arranging with Kerri to get the police out to Desert Lodge to deal with the poachers.

The doctor had helped Piet and Luca to be more comfortable, but Luca still seemed out of it, unable to open his eyes, much less to speak.

Naomi went to sit next to him and held his hand as they took off to the nearest hospital. She watched the Cessna's shadow following them on the dunes below. Her thoughts went around and around about what had happened between her and Luca the night before. It had been the best night of her life. But how fast can it all change?

Here was Luca, in trouble. What would happen if she gave her heart to him, and something happened to him? This scenario was already scary enough, even though the doctor had assured her Luca would be okay. What if something terrible had happened to him? Would she be strong enough to handle it?

All her life, people had been telling her she must be strong, that she was strong. But she knew otherwise. The scars on her heart of having lost her parents had not strengthened her. She was more sensitive, more vulnerable. It wasn't always true that the death of someone you love very much strengthens you.

Maybe it was true for some people, but not for her, and not for Auntie Elsa. She had seen Auntie Elsa go through hell when Uncle Wouter died. Her hair had turned gray almost overnight from the shock. Everyone knew they'd loved each other very much. Uncle Wouter always joked they should go together because he couldn't imagine a single second without his Elsa. Auntie Elsa said she felt the same. She always said they were forever soulmates.

Naomi saw it. She saw how Uncle Wouter's death made

Auntie Elsa softer, more fragile, less able to deal with the stresses of life.

Naomi's heart was already telling her it couldn't beat for any other man in the way it beat for Luca. There was no point denying it any longer. She'd known it last night and this morning, even though she was trying to talk herself out of it.

The thought of losing him before she'd found him hit her full in her solar plexus. Nausea traveled into her throat. Now, as she was holding his limp hand in hers, her silent tears wouldn't be contained and streamed unbidden down her cheeks.

An ambulance was waiting when they landed. The paramedics loaded Piet and Luca into the back. Naomi sat squeezed beside the doctor as he kept vigil over his patients during the short drive to the hospital. Once there, porters and nurses whisked the patients away. The doctor ran ahead of them, shouting instructions and orders.

Naomi sat alone in a waiting room. After several minutes, she got up and found a phone to call Desert Lodge. She had to let Auntie Elsa and Santina know where they were. But she was exhausted. At the sight of Luca's bloodied head, it felt as though all the life in her body had left her.

Despite what the doctor had told her, she knew head trauma could be very serious, and Luca had been so out of it. He didn't even realize she was there. He wasn't unconscious, exactly. He just wasn't functioning. That couldn't be right.

She wished she could locate the doctor. She needed assurance that Luca was okay. It was a small hospital. Would they have the right equipment here to help Luca?

There was nothing she could do but wait. She returned to sit in the waiting room. She should be concerned about Piet, too, but she couldn't think beyond Luca.

Auntie Elsa had arranged with a neighbor who owned a Cessna to fly Santina to the hospital. Naomi knew Auntie Elsa would accompany Santina. There was no way she'd let Santina fly here by herself.

Naomi sighed and leaned back against the wall. The plastic chair beneath her creaked as she forced it back on its hind legs. It was a comforting thought knowing the two ladies were on their way.

But as she waited, her thoughts once again turned to Luca. Today's events, if nothing else, had proved she absolutely couldn't give her heart to Luca. She just couldn't chance it.

No, much better to suffer for a little while when he left. She would get over him, wouldn't she? Eventually? Rather that, than to live a life with him in the full knowledge she'd lose him to death one day when she loved him more than life itself. She wouldn't be able to go on living without him then, she knew. It would break her utterly.

By the time Auntie Elsa and Santina arrived, Naomi had decided, her resolution set in stone.

TEN

Naomi sat with Auntie Elsa and Santina in the waiting room. They'd been there for what seemed like hours.

Naomi and Auntie Elsa weren't allowed to see Luca. But they joined in her relief when the doctor finally came to take Santina to see Luca.

Instead, they went to see Piet, who despite having lost a lot of blood, seemed in good spirits. He was lying with his leg up in a cast, a catheter peeping out from under his blankets, and a drip in his arm.

The nurses had cleaned his face, arms and hands from the blood and gore, and he looked recognizable again. He appeared well enough to crack jokes with the nurses who looked after him, and with the four other patients with whom he shared the small ward.

But as Naomi watched him, she could see he was tired. The police had already been to get his statement on the events that led to him being shot and to Luca being in the hospital. All the excitement had to have tired Piet out.

Meanwhile, Khwai had called to reassure Piet's parents. They'd visit him that evening.

Auntie Elsa held Piet's hand as she chatted to him. But they didn't stay too long after he yawned a few times.

Auntie Elsa went back to the waiting room, and Naomi went in search of some coffee for them both.

Auntie Elsa peered in the paper cup that held her coffee.

"Why does hospital coffee always taste so bad? It tastes like nothing close to resembling coffee."

Naomi smiled. She knew Auntie Elsa was trying to make light of what could've been something dire for Luca and for Desert Lodge.

Naomi didn't know how to express her gratitude that Auntie Elsa didn't blame her for Luca's condition. She could have done. Luca had been her responsibility. But Auntie Elsa knew very well these wealthy princes had their own agendas. Nothing could stop them when they had their sights set on something. Naomi wouldn't have been able to stop Luca going with the anti-poacher unit.

Only now did it dawn on her it might have been the reason he hadn't told her what he'd intended to do. He must've known she'd try to stop him.

When, at last, Santina appeared again, they watched with trepidation as she took a seat opposite them. For a few moments, she held her head in her hands. Then, as though she could feel their eyes on her, she lifted her hands away from her head and looked at Auntie Elsa.

Santina's voice was soft and serious.

"I was so afraid. Luca is like a son to me. I never imagined something would happen to him. It would have been my fault. I forced him to take this vacation. He was working too hard. He had no joy. I thought this would bring him release. He has wanted to paint African elephants ever since I can remember. Ever since he was a little boy."

She put her head in her hands again. Her shoulders shook with her silent sobs.

Auntie Elsa went to sit beside her new friend and put a supportive arm around Santina's shoulders.

Naomi felt her tears welling up. But she tried to hold on to what Santina had said, "... it would have been my fault..."

It must mean he's okay? Please let him be okay. Please. Please... She couldn't think beyond that.

After what seemed like an eternity to Naomi, Santina stopped crying. She took a tissue from her handbag, wiped her eyes and blew her nose.

Auntie Elsa still had her arm around her friend.

Her voice sounded strained as she addressed Santina.

"He's okay then?"

Santina nodded, a smile spreading over her face.

"Yes, thanks God. He is going to be fine. He's dehydrated, and the strike to his head caused some concussion. But he's going to be all right. I can't imagine what I would have had to tell his father."

Santina smiled, first at Auntie Elsa, then at Naomi, and beckoned for her to take a seat beside her.

She took one of their hands in each of hers.

"I can't thank you both enough for all you've done for us. It's such a blessing to meet such great new friends. I never expected it."

Santina's tissue lay discarded on her lap.

"If you ever come to Italy, you must let me repay your kindness."

Naomi understood at once Santina's tears had been those of relief rather than of sadness or grief.

She was careful not to show her relief, but couldn't help feeling much lighter, much less exhausted, able to breathe again. She hadn't been aware of the tension she was holding in her body. As she sighed and her entire being relaxed, she knew her muscles ached from holding on so tightly. She could only imagine how much worse Santina had felt. No wonder she had to cry from the relief when it came.

Naomi took Santina's hand in both of hers.

Auntie Elsa didn't have to be careful at all about sharing in Santina's relief. As tears brimmed in her eyes, she squeezed her friend's shoulders to show her joy at the good news.

"When can he leave?"

"They're going to keep him here for observation overnight. But he should be able to go back to the lodge tomorrow. I'll stay here with him tonight. I've asked that they give him a private room with two beds."

Auntie Elsa got up.

"Right. In that case, I'll get you some toiletries for tonight, and arrange with our neighbor to fly you both back tomorrow. I'll just check with the doctor what time he thinks Luca would be discharged."

Auntie Elsa, used to taking care of guests, went to find the doctor. Before Naomi could follow her, Santina put a hand on her arm.

"I hope you don't mind me asking, Naomi, but did anything happen between you two? Luca is delirious. He's said some crazy things."

Naomi felt her heartbeat increase as the heat of her blush crept up her neck to her cheeks. She lowered her head to hide her red face.

"No. We had a great dinner and came straight home. I didn't see him again until the guard came to ask for help this afternoon."

She didn't want to ask what Luca had said during his delirium, but she was burning to know.

Santina sighed.

"Well, perhaps he only imagines then."

Auntie Elsa, having spoken with the doctor, reappeared in the doorway.

"Let's go find a shop to get some things for Santina."

Naomi was glad to escape and followed Auntie Elsa out of the room and out of the hospital into the heat of the late afternoon.

Auntie Elsa glanced at her watch.

"I hope there's a shop still open."

The two women hurried down the road from the hospital to an intersection where they could see a few shops. The small supermarket was still open. Auntie Elsa bought some soap, deodorant, toothbrushes, toothpaste, and two packets with clean underwear for each of her guests.

"I hope these are the right sizes."

Their pilot, the neighbor who had flown Auntie Elsa and Santina there, was sitting in the café next door. Auntie Elsa arranged with him to fly them back to the lodge that evening, and also a time to pick up Santina and Luca the next day.

When they got back to the hospital, Santina was still sitting in the waiting room. She seemed much calmer and her old self again.

"Oh, but I can't thank you enough for your kindness."

"It's the least we can do. Regard it as a gift from Desert Lodge."

The friends smiled and hugged, and Naomi and Auntie Elsa watched Santina walk down the corridor to Luca's room. She waved at them before going in.

Then it was their turn to leave. Outside, their neighbor was waiting for them. Together they walked to his Cessna parked near the hospital to fly back to the lodge.

There, Kerri had turned the porch near the kitchen door into a kind of recovery area for the battered and exhausted anti-poacher unit. Water, food, plasters and kindness had been handed out, and the men resting there looked much better than when Naomi had found them in the desert. The police had been and removed the poachers from the lodge in the back of one of their vans, meanwhile.

Khwai came to ask after Luca and Piet at once.

"The boss man was very brave. He helped us a lot."

The old Khoisan man's relief was palpable when he learned that Luca was okay. A wide smile appeared on his wrinkled face. His joyous laughter rang clear in the early evening when Auntie Elsa told him about Piet joking and flirting with the nurses.

Naomi could see that he took his leadership of the men seriously. No wonder they all trusted him.

Kerri had arranged with Chef for a barbeque dinner for the men. As the waitresses brought the food out, Naomi excused herself and escaped to her room. She'd missed her swim in the morning. Now, while everyone was having dinner, was the perfect opportunity for a swim.

She donned her bathing suit and went to the swimming pool. This way, she had the pool all to herself, just the way she liked it. But as she got into the water, she couldn't help remembering her last swim here with Luca.

A sudden pang of sadness pierced her heart.

She'd feel lost without him and Santina at the lodge. But she'd have to get used to it. The Italians would leave in a few days.

Naomi swam length after length, as though she was trying to swim Luca out of her head and out of her heart. After about fifty lengths, she noticed Kerri standing by the side of the pool, watching her. She swam over to her friend.

Kerri put a hand on her hip.

"What's eating you, girl?"

If anyone could understand, it would be Kerri. But Naomi wasn't ready to share what had happened with Luca yet.

"Oh, you know. Just trying to get over the shock of today's events."

Naomi could see Kerri wasn't falling for it. But they knew other well enough to know they'd have that conversation when Naomi was ready.

"Hmm... yes, I can imagine. Aren't you coming to dinner?"

None of the staff ever dressed for dinner. Theirs was a casual, fun affair with diners coming and going as they came on and off their duties. The huge acacia wooden table in the generous kitchen away from Chef's domain was seldom unoccupied. But during dinner, it became the hub of the lodge for the staff.

Naomi didn't bother drying her hair, but she changed into a tracksuit bottom and t-shirt so as not to get everything wet in her bathing suit.

As always, Chef and his helpers had prepared a scrumptious dinner, and although Naomi felt hungry, she just didn't have the appetite for food. But she forced herself to have some chicken and salad and thought about how different this meal was from the one she'd shared with Luca.

As was Auntie Elsa's habit, she left after her dinner to visit with her guests in the dining room. But she returned a short while later because all the guests seemed satisfied and there were no egos to stroke or problems to solve.

It dawned on Naomi then that she wasn't the only one missing Santina and Luca. It fascinated her that in their short time at the lodge, everyone adored the Italians, and enjoyed having them around. Luca and Santina had felt like an extended family of sorts. Tonight, their absence created a strange tension in the air.

Naomi tried to remember what she used to do with her evenings before their arrival. Her mind drew a blank.

Usually, everyone would be on duty or gone to more leisurely pursuits. But tonight, even Auntie Elsa remained at the kitchen table, chatting with Naomi and Kerri.

It was almost a relief when several members of the anti-poacher unit entered the kitchen.

Khwai's presence among the group had a calming effect on everyone. He'd done his best to reassure the men, but even he needed to be comforted about the situation. The men stood around the table, unable to settle, their feelings of guilt about putting Luca in danger clear in their eyes.

Auntie Elsa relayed Santina's reassurances from an earlier phone conversation that Luca was doing much better and would return to the lodge in the morning.

The men stood around for moments, fiddling with their hats in their hands before bidding everyone good night and leaving as suddenly as they'd appeared.

Naomi stared after them as they closed the door behind them.

It would take a while for them to get over the shock of what had happened. They'd never taken a guest out on patrol with them before, and she had a feeling this might've been the last time they'd allow it.

Chef had their coffee mugs refilled again and again, and still, no one seemed eager to leave.

When the clock struck midnight, Auntie Elsa got up and with a yawn, wished everyone a good night, before disappearing down the corridor to her room. As though her leaving had given permission, one by one, everyone else left to go to their rooms where sleep would claim them and refresh them for the next day. Only Naomi and Kerri remained sitting at the enormous table, their empty coffee mugs in front of them.

Kerri pinched the top of her nose.

"I should turn in, too. It's been a long day. And tomorrow is going to be chaotic because the South African group will be here early."

Kerri put a hand on Naomi's arm.

"Are you okay?"

Naomi responded by covering her friend's hand with hers.

"Yeah, I will be. Don't worry about me. You have enough on your plate. Luca and Santina will be back tomorrow, and we'll take it from there."

Kerri sighed and pushed her chair away from the table.

"Okay. If you're sure? But you know where I am if you need me, hun. Do you think they'll leave straight away?"

Naomi knew Kerri was talking about Luca and Santina leaving. She didn't want to think about it, but knew she had to consider it.

"I'm not sure. It's a possibility. Why?"

"I still have my proposal that I'd like to put to them."

"What proposal?"

Kerri smiled, a mischievous glint in her eyes. She got up and rested her hands on the back of her chair.

"You'll just have to wait and see. I just hope I'll have time to put it to them while they're still here."

"You tease!"

"Yeah, but it's fun, right? See you in the morning, hun. Go. Get some sleep."

With Kerri's laughter ringing in her ears, Naomi watched her friend close the kitchen door behind her. She got up, pushed their chairs under the table, switched off the light and walked to her room.

When, at last, she fell asleep, images of a bloodied Luca dominated her dreams.

ELEVEN

Naomi's head felt thick with fatigue when the alarm buzzed.

She moved onto her elbow, intending to get up, but fell back onto her pillows as the pain in her head grew sharper with the movement. The alarm would go off every three minutes until she killed it. When it beeped again, she moaned. She sat up and pushed the off button.

She got to her feet and went over to her bathroom to find painkillers and to have a warm shower, hoping it would wake her up and ease the headache.

The sound of the shower mixed with the roar of the Cessna as it flew over the house, making the turn to land.

Naomi dried herself, pulled on her uniform, scraped her hair into a ponytail, and ran out the door just as the Cessna was landing on the strip behind the house.

Several members of staff, including Auntie Elsa, Kerri, and Khwai, were already standing near the big thorn tree waiting for the Cessna. When it came to a stop, everyone waited for its small sandstorm to die down before approaching the plane to welcome back Santina and Luca.

Kerri had arranged a wheelchair for Luca. Khwai hovered behind it, his hands on its back, unsure if they would need it.

Naomi's heart was beating in her throat, her hands clammy. How would it be to see Luca again when she'd decided that nothing further could happen between them? He had gone off with the anti-poacher patrol, so perhaps he'd come to the same conclusion. But would that make things easier for her? She prayed it would.

Their pilot neighbor disembarked and helped Santina down the ladder which he'd pulled from the belly of the Cessna. Then he went back inside to help Luca out.

Naomi's hand went to her mouth when she saw Luca emerging from the plane, looking pale and shaky. At least he was standing by himself.

Khwai, who had left the wheelchair under the thorn tree, hurried toward Luca. He lifted Luca's other arm over his shoulder, and between the pilot on one side of him and Khwai on the other, Luca walked slowly to his suite. Auntie Elsa and Santina followed, walking arm in arm. Kerri was busy giving orders and arranging a roster of staff to look after Luca.

Naomi stood rooted to the spot. Luca hadn't even glanced in her direction. Although she'd made up her mind about him, it was still a shock to realize he'd evidently come to the same conclusion. A big fist had clamped over her heart.

When everyone had gone, Naomi pushed the abandoned wheelchair back to its place in the storeroom behind the hanger where Luca had parked the Cessna. On her way back, she wondered if he'd locked it.

On a whim, she went inside the hanger and tried the jet's door. To her surprise, it opened with a click. Checking that no one saw her, she climbed on board.

The smell of expensive leather stopped her in her tracks. Memories of Luca burned in her eyes as tears rolled down her cheeks. It was both torture and rapture to be here. She sat down on the sofa they had occupied. It felt as though it had happened years ago, instead of only the previous night.

Naomi gave herself over to the memories and her tears. It would most likely be the last time she'd be able to be here.

It didn't feel as though much time had passed, but when she emerged from the hanger, the sun showed it was past noon already.

A member of the kitchen staff came running toward her.

"Nonna, you must come. He's been asking for you."

The woman hovered as though she was waiting for Naomi to follow her at once.

"He's all right, isn't he?"

"Yes, he is."

"Okay, I have to get something from my room first. I'll go to him soon."

The woman scurried off, no doubt to inform Luca that she'd found Naomi and passed on his message.

Naomi hastened to her room. Her face was blotchy from all the crying. She washed her face, applied a tinted moisturizer to hide the fact further, and combed out her hair. The face staring back at her from the mirror looked passable. It'll have to do.

Much more important was getting her head together for their meeting. Already her heart was beating faster than she felt comfortable with, and her hands were clammy again. She took a few deep breaths before opening her door. Then, she lifted her chin, closed her door behind her, and walked to Luca's suite.

Several members of staff stood outside his door. Laughter from within greeted Naomi when she arrived there. Luca looked much better than the last time she'd seen him. Cleaned and propped up against a gazillion pillows, he appeared as much a prince as anyone could.

Flowers, cards, chocolates, food, and drink surrounded him.

Santina and Auntie Elsa sat in two armchairs near his bed. All three wore smiles. The happy, light mood in the room brought the realization that Naomi had expected something more serious. For once, she was glad to be wrong.

Luca looked up as she entered. The smile on his face expanded.

"Here she is. I was beginning to think you'd forgotten about me."

Naomi smiled despite herself.

"I had some things to do first. But I'm glad you're being looked after so well."

She looked pointedly at all the goodies that surrounded him.

Luca's smile turned wicked, and he winked at Naomi.

"I know. I'm being spoiled, and I love it."

"I can just imagine."

She sat down on the edge of the chair opposite his bed, leaned forward, and smiled at him. She may as well play the game.

"Anyway, you called, my lord?"

Luca's eyes glinted.

"I did, indeed. I was hoping you would give me a foot massage."

Auntie Elsa and Santina burst out laughing as much at Luca's unusual request as the look on Naomi's face.

Santina got up and gave Luca a peck on the cheek.

"I don't think we're needed here any longer. I don't enjoy watching foot massages. Feet are such ugly things."

Auntie Elsa, laughing, followed her friend from the room.

Luca was still smiling at Naomi, expectation in his eyes.

"I'm serious. I walked extremely far yesterday. My feet are very sore and in need of some tender loving care."

"And you thought I could provide that?"

Naomi was more than a little annoyed for falling so easily

into Luca's trap. It was one thing to make a decision when he wasn't around, but he was apparently hell-bent on destroying her intentions. She should have known.

"Hmm... about yesterday..."

Luca looked suitably guilty.

"Yes?"

"I'm curious. Why did you go off with the anti-poacher unit?"

Naomi took some comfort in the fact that Luca was practically squirming against his many pillows.

"I know. I should have told you. But when I found Khwai and the guys in the kitchen in the middle of the night, I thought it would be a good idea. I really want to help."

Naomi wasn't smiling anymore.

"But it's serious, Luca. You could've been badly injured or even killed."

Luca was smiling again.

"I didn't know you cared, amore."

"It's no laughing matter, Luca, it really isn't."

Naomi got up and paced the room, her arms folded across her chest.

"Can you imagine what would have happened if they had killed you? What about Santina? Your father? Your business? Desert Lodge? Khwai?

"It was irresponsible, and I'm amazed that someone with your background would do something like that."

Luca contemplated her for a few moments before speaking.

"You're really mad at me, aren't you?"

"Yes. I am. You didn't think about anyone else, did you?"

"Actually, I did. I thought about you. I really wanted to help. I still do."

"Then why don't you use your photographs, instead, and do something with that article to National Geographic you spoke about. You may not realize it, and they'd say nothing to you, but you put Khwai and the guards in danger, too. They had to look out for you, instead of dealing with the poachers as they've been trained to do."

Luca held his hands up in defense.

"Okay. Okay. You've made your point. I'm sorry. It's true I hadn't thought about putting the guys in danger. But I can see that now. I'll do what I can to make it up to them... Main thing... we caught the poachers."

His smile was back, an indication of what he must have been like as a little boy, excited about the adventure that turned out all right, even though it could have gone so disastrously wrong.

"Smiling at me won't help your case."

"Then, amore, would you tell me what would? I don't want us to argue."

"I'm not arguing with you. I'm stating facts."

"Well, will you come over here and state more facts?"

Damn! Naomi knew this moment might come. What to do? Changing the subject might be safest.

"I thought you wanted a foot massage?"

Luca smiled like a winner.

"I do. But I thought you weren't going to offer."

"I'm not offering. You asked for one. Don't twist my words."

Luca pushed himself up against the pillows. He wiggled his eyebrows at her.

"Hmm... I'm loving fiery Naomi."

Naomi sat down on the edge of the chair again. She took a deep breath to calm herself.

"Stop it, Luca. Do you want a foot massage, or not?"

His smile broadened again.

"I'm yearning for a foot massage from you. Can't you see?"

He wiggled his toes under the duvet and pointed at them.

Naomi smiled despite herself.

"Fine. I'll get some oil. Do you like coconut oil?"

Luca reclined on his pillows making a dramatic show of it.

"Oh, yes, that would be heavenly, amore. The aroma of our first beach vacation together."

Naomi ignored that last comment and went in search of some coconut oil in the kitchen. A bowl of warm water and some gloves completed her arsenal of goodies. She'd use his shower gel in the water.

Luca was reading a newspaper when she returned, but set it aside at once.

"I can't thank you enough for doing this for me."

Naomi set the bowl and coconut oil down on the floor at the foot of his bed and pulled up a chair.

"You're a guest here, Luca. I'm happy to make your stay with us more comfortable if I can."

Luca was silent as Naomi went into his bathroom to retrieve his shower gel. She squirted a little into the bowl of water and swished it around to produce foam. Then, she donned the gloves and lifted the duvet away from his feet. She placed a towel under his feet and washed them.

Luca remained silent throughout. Naomi didn't look up from her work. She assumed his silence meant he was still reading the newspaper.

Luca's feet looked sore-red and swollen underneath. Naomi was gentle as she massaged them, not wanting to hurt him. She didn't know much about massages so imagined what she'd like done to her own feet and then did that for him.

Naomi meant it when she'd said she was happy to make his stay comfortable at Desert Lodge. He was a guest. But how was she going to get through the next few days without getting into a conversation with him about what had happened between them? Did she want to talk about it? It happened. It was a mistake. She should never have allowed it. And when Luca was injured, it only confirmed for her she couldn't get involved with him.

Luca's even breathing alerted her to the fact that he was asleep.

Naomi looked at him to seal him into her memory. His beautiful face with the high forehead over which black curls spilled, the long eyelashes that touched his cheeks with his eyes closed, the proud, straight nose, the full, sensual lips and his chiseled jaw sporting dark designer stubble. A plaster on the side of his head showed where the poacher had hit him.

Naomi's eyes traveled lower, to his neck as he lay with his head to the left. She remembered the skin there, so soft and yet so manly. One of his arms lay relaxed on the bed. A small plaster, the only sign he'd had a drip in his vein. Naomi could still feel the sensation of the soft hairs on his forearm beneath her fingers.

Slowly, so as not to wake him, she removed the gloves and pulled the sheets over his feet again. The smell of coconut oil and one last look at his sleeping form would be forever in her mind. The memory would be one more Luca keepsake tucked deep in her heart.

TWELVE

Naomi found Auntie Elsa and Santina sitting in the Lapa near the swimming pool. It was customary to have a barbeque dinner served in the Lapa over weekends. Today being Friday, staff were already readying tables in the cool shade of the structure behind the two ladies. A small table laid out with their lunches and teas, separated Auntie Elsa and Santina's armchairs.

Even though the sun was scorching, the German couple were in the pool. Naomi watched them chatting with South African guests nearby, who were wise enough to sit in the shade under the stylish large umbrellas that matched the loungers.

Naomi stopped near Auntie Elsa's chair.

"I hope the Germans are using sunblock. With their white European skins in this sun, they'll look like boiled lobsters by tonight without it, and no doubt will feel like it, too."

Auntie Elsa smiled at her adoptive daughter.

She put her hand over Naomi's resting on her shoulder.

"Yes, I believe Kerri gave them some sun lotions. I haven't seen them use it yet."

"Hmm... well, you can take a horse to the water..."

Santina smiled at Naomi.

"How is Luca? Did he enjoy his foot massage?"

"He's asleep. I don't think he even knows he's had one."

"Or it helped to relax him so much that he fell asleep? Thank you, Naomi. I can't thank you and Kerri enough, and Elsa, especially, for all you're doing for us. You must come to Italy. All three of you, so we can repay the kindness. Promise you'll come?"

Santina sounded so sincere.

Naomi returned her smile.

"I would love to go to Italy. And I'm sure Auntie Elsa would like to visit you. One day, when the lodge doesn't require so much attention. Thank you for the invitation."

Santina wouldn't accept 'one day.'

"Oh, no, come soon. Come, sit down. Join us."

One of Naomi's charges was asleep. Here was the other needing her, now. How could she refuse? She pulled up a chair and joined the ladies at the little table.

Just then, Kerri came around the corner.

"Ah, here you all are. Have you had lunch yet, Naomi? I'm starved."

Everyone laughed at her exaggerated performance, including the staff who were laying the tables behind them. Kerri organized lunch and tea for her and Naomi. In the same breath, she ordered more tea for the older ladies and asked a waitress to collect their empty lunch plates. Then she joined them. The four women sat facing each other making small talk until Kerri leaned forward.

"Auntie Elsa, I hope you don't mind, but I have a proposal for you and Santina. It's nothing formal, so perhaps I could tell you about it now?"

Kerri's request surprised neither Naomi nor Auntie Elsa. She was always thinking up some or other scheme, some great, some impractical and wild. But Auntie Elsa liked to encourage all her staff to take responsibility for their roles at the lodge. One way to have them feel more involved was to implement their suggestions when they were good ones.

She smiled at Kerri.

"Go on, then. Let's hear it."

As Kerri spoke, Santina's eyes grew wider with wonder and twinkled with excitement.

Naomi knew her friend was ambitious and creative, but even she had to take her hat off to Kerri. She had prepared her pitch well, even though she was trying to keep it as casual as possible. Naomi admired her clever friend, anew.

Even Auntie Elsa, fussy about which ideas she found useful for the lodge, was full of praise.

"I think it's brilliant. Well done, Kerri. You've outdone yourself. It's a win-win, both for Desert Lodge and for Armati. What do you think, Santina?"

"I just love the idea that Armati could supply your dune buggies. I agree... it's a brilliant idea. It's not something we've done before, but I know the guys back in Italy will be very enthusiastic about it. And it gives us an excuse, as if we needed one, to maintain our friendship. It's perfect. I can't wait to tell Luca."

"Tell me what?"

No one had seen Luca approaching. At the sound of his voice, the women's heads snapped in his direction.

Santina and Naomi got up at once.

"Luca, che stai fecendo?"

Naomi asked the same question in English in unison with Santina.

"Luca, what are you doing?"

Luca spread his hands out in a placating gesture, his smile lopsided.

"I was tired of lying in bed. And bored. I'm supposed to be on vacation.

Kerri arranged with staff members for a large armchair for Luca. Santina led him over to the chair, nodding her thanks to Kerri and the staff while continuing her admonishments to Luca in Italian. Once seated, he responded.

The passionate way in which they communicated sounded almost like they were having a massive argument. But when both had had their say, they smiled at each other and turned back to their hosts as though nothing untoward had happened.

Naomi thought the scene would have been funny were it not that Luca was still weak. He should have stayed in bed. But she couldn't blame him. He was on vacation, after all. It was such a lovely day. Who could stay in bed on a day like this?

After taking his order, Kerri arranged for lunch and coffee for Luca.

He had a sip of coffee and took a bite of food before looking at each of the women resting his eyes finally on Santina.

"What can't you wait to tell me?"

Santina indicated with her hand toward Kerri.

"I think Kerri can explain better?"

Kerri didn't need a second invitation and launched right into her pitch.

"I'm sure you've seen all the photos of Auntie Elsa with some of our wealthier clients in the dining room?"

Luca nodded and smiled at Auntie Elsa.

"I'm still waiting for my invitation to such a shoot with her myself."

Auntie Elsa returned his smile and nodded.

"Just say the word. It'll be my honor. Perhaps when you're feeling a little better?"

"It will be my honor, dear lady. Maybe tomorrow?"

Luca turned back to Kerri.

"Sorry, Kerri, I interrupted you."

Kerri didn't seem fazed at all.

"I'll be honest with you. As you can tell, our wealthier guests rarely come here to photograph elephants, Luca. They want excitement. They want to do something that will take them away from the stresses of their everyday lives. They want adventure. And they can afford to pay for it. As you know, we don't offer shooting adventures here, and our sunrise and sunset safaris aren't exciting enough for those guys. The most thrilling thing we can offer them is a walking safari with Khwai or one of the other guards into the desert. This can get hairy."

Luca snorted.

"Tell me about it."

Kerri reacted at once.

"Oh, sorry, I forgot-"

But Luca waved away her apology.

"Please. Continue."

Kerri watched him intently but took him at his word and continued.

"But even those safaris are sometimes not stimulating enough for them. As a result, we've lost out on securing bookings from that type of guest to other lodges that offer more exhilarating forms of entertainment. And we could do with their money."

Luca was still eating, his eyes riveted on Kerri.

Naomi could see she had captured his interest in the subject, and he wasn't merely polite.

"Such as?"

Kerri rattled off her list as though she'd rehearsed it.

"Well, apart from the safaris we already offer and the walks into the desert with Khwai and the fossil tours, there's wind gliding, dune gliding, shark fishing, diving to the many sunken ships around the skeleton coast, helicopter rides over the desert...

"But what if we could offer something the other lodges don't have? We are in a great position here, so near to some of the highest dunes in the Namib. What if we could offer them fun, adventure and excitement in the form of Armati dune buggies? We could arrange for dune races and camping trips further into the desert..."

Luca stopped eating and sat straighter in his chair.

Kerri took it as a good sign and continued with her pitch.

"These men are powerful in their own spheres. They want quality, even on vacation-particularly on vacation. They've worked hard and have earned the right to have their every need and every whim catered to. From experience with them, I'm sure that's how they see it. Special Armati dune buggies would be a great draw to Desert Lodge. Especially if we're the only ones supplying those buggies to our guests, don't you think?"

Kerri sat back in her chair, triumph already shining in her eyes. Luca leaned forward, placing both elbows on the table and lacing his fingers under his chin.

Naomi thought he was doing his best not to appear too excited, but she could see the effect of Kerri's proposal as his breathing had increased.

Luca cleared his throat as though he'd argue the point.

"It's a great idea for Desert Lodge, I agree. But what does Armati get out of it?"

Kerri was evidently ready for the question.

"The opportunity to create new, innovative products. And you never know where that might lead. With all the talk about people wanting to go to Mars, I can imagine your dune buggies will be perfect up there, don't you? It's fitting, too. The most prestigious car manufacturer on Earth branching out to another planet?"

Luca's infectious laugh bubbled up from his stomach. Soon, everyone, including the staff, had joined him.

"You had me until you started talking about Mars."

Kerri was the only person not laughing.

She'd been serious about Mars. She could see from their reactions it was another of her 'wild ideas,' as Auntie Elsa referred to them.

But she wouldn't give in that easily.

"Okay. Well, maybe it's far-fetched. But what about the financial benefits? These guys can pay. How about if we agreed on a special deal so that Armati gets their fair share of the hire costs for the buggies? Would that work for you? And it's an introduction to your Armati cars for them."

Luca's eyes were still laughing, but he could see Kerri had thought her proposal through.

"That sounds like a much better incentive for us, yes. I can see my dad agreeing to it."

Kerri could barely contain her excitement.

"You can? Oh, that's great. What do you need me to do next? I've prepared all the forecasts. But I would need your input regarding the costs."

Santina cleared her throat.

"Is this going to become a business lunch?"

Kerri remembered her guests were supposed to be on vacation.

"Oh, I'm so sorry. I got a little carried away. Perhaps, if Luca agrees, we could talk about it later?"

Luca leaned back, a smile on his lips.

"That sounds like a fantastic plan. Let's do it."

He glanced at Santina but continued to smile as he spoke.

"Santina practically dragged me out here because she was convinced I was working too hard. She probably didn't imagine I'd find more work here?"

He winked at Santina and took her hand in his.

Kerri got up.

"In that case, I wouldn't dream of dragging you back to work so soon, Luca. I apologize to both of you. You're right. You're here on vacation, and we'll see that you have the best, most memorable time with us."

Luca nodded at Kerri, but his eyes flitted in Naomi's direction.

"I'm already having the best vacation. Aren't you, Santina?"

Santina smiled, nodded, and reiterated Luca's sentiments. Their words placated Kerri, who excused herself from the company. She got busy with the evening's arrangements at once.

Lunch had gone on longer than anyone had realized. The sun had moved away from the pool. Long shadows licked over the lawn, the shade lessening the heat of the day.

Luca caught Naomi's eye.

"Would you like to join me for a swim?"

"Are you sure? Aren't you supposed to be recovering?"

He winked at her.

"I can recover better in the pool with you. My feet will appreciate the weightlessness of the water. They're still sore. I may need another foot massage later."

Santina and Auntie Elsa laughed at the exaggerated expression of pain on Luca's face.

But Naomi didn't smile. She wasn't falling for his charms so easily again.

"Oh, no. You've had your chance. You fell asleep and didn't even feel the last one I gave you."

"But that just shows you how good you are, doesn't it?"

Naomi could see she wouldn't win this argument.

She sighed.

"Okay, I'll see you in the pool."

She got up and went to change into her bathing suit.

By the time she re-emerged, Luca was already in the pool, waving at her, a big smile on his handsome face. They had to share the pool with several of the other guests staying at the lodge, but it didn't seem to bother Luca.

This time, Naomi didn't dive in. She went down the stairs at the shallow end and swam the length to meet him at the deep end on the opposite side of the pool.

"I can watch you swim all day, amore."

"I'll have you know I used to swim competitively for my school and later, at university."

Luca nodded.

"I knew it. Your form is perfect."

His eyes ran down her body.

She wasn't sure what form he meant, but decided not to pursue the matter.

"How about you? You're a pretty amazing swimmer your-self... very fast, as I recall."

Luca's smile was irresistible.

"Yes, I love swimming. I did it competitively too... at my boarding school. I always won."

"That I can imagine. Are you as competitive in everything?"

Luca pretended to be indignant at her suggestion.

"Of course, amore. Is there any other way to be?"

No. Naomi imagined losing at anything wouldn't even be in Luca's vocabulary. His world was all about being successful and winning, wasn't it? She had, frankly, been amazed that he'd even understood Kerri's concern about wealthy guests going to other lodges because Desert Lodge couldn't compete with their enter-tainment programs.

As though Luca felt Naomi had gone elsewhere in her mind, he touched her shoulder to redirect her attention to him. At his touch, such a thrill went through her body, Naomi was almost disappointed when he removed his hand from her shoulder.

Luca looked deep into her eyes as though he was trying to read her soul, but she couldn't read his eyes.

He moved a little further away from her.

"Did you mean what you said in my room? That I'm a guest and you'd make my stay here as comfortable as you could?"

Where was he going with that question?

Naomi squinted at Luca.

"I may have said that... I thought you were asleep?"

"I never miss a thing, amore. Did you mean it?"

"Of course, Luca. You are a guest here. It's my duty to make your stay good and comfortable..."

"Why do you do it?"

Realization dawned on Naomi.

She hesitated, weighing her words before speaking.

"So our guests would return... You mean, you're thinking of coming back to Desert Lodge? That's fantastic news. It means we've done a good job."

She said the words and heard them leaving her mouth. But would she be so happy for Luca to return to the lodge? How would she deal with it? It wasn't something she'd envisaged would happen.

Luca moved closer and lifted a stray strand of hair from Naomi's forehead.

"You already know we're coming back, amore. It's Santina and your Auntie Elsa's birthdays in July, si? I've heard a lot of plotting going on between the two. They're planning an extravagant party by the sounds."

The nearness of Luca affected Naomi's ability to breathe right. She moved away from him a little, but he followed right along, allowing the small waves created by the other swimmers, to bob his body toward her.

Naomi tried to focus elsewhere, other than on his gorgeous

muscled torso and his handsome face that was too beautiful to be real.

Other swimmers were getting out of the water and entering the Lapa.

Naomi registered the mouth-watering aroma from the barbeque that had wafted over the pool. She was suddenly ravenous, her light salad at lunch long forgotten. As though in a dream, she noticed steaming plates of food on tables in front of guests sitting on their towels to keep the chairs dry.

Before she could respond to Luca, Kerri appeared at the edge of the pool nearest the Lapa.

"You'll wrinkle like prunes, guys. We're serving dinner."

THIRTEEN

Naomi hadn't bothered drying her hair. Instead, she'd scraped it back, arranging it in a long plait that fell across her bare shoulder. She felt comfortable and stylish in her one-sleeved pink dress.

Evidently, Luca thought so too. His eyes locked onto hers and she could see his pupils dilate.

He got up as Naomi was walking toward the table where Santina and Auntie Elsa had joined him. He held out her chair for her and took his place next to her.

Naomi felt all eyes on her, but she knew it was for different reasons. She wished Luca's eyes didn't communicate his interest in her in such a bold way. Santina's raised brow was perhaps a sign she was thinking of the question she'd asked Naomi at the hospital about something happening between her and Luca. Auntie Elsa's warm, knowing smile was a sign of her consent to the couple.

Naomi squirmed in her chair.

But Kerri's appearance shifted the focus away from Naomi. She could have kissed her friend for her timely arrival.

There was no preamble from Kerri, who got straight to the point.

"Does everyone just want to help themselves, or would you prefer to place an order with a waiter?"

The dinner was a buffet affair and always turned into quite a social event as guests, queuing for the food of their choice, chatted and made new friends. It looked like fun and Santina, and Luca joined in the fray.

While they were away, the three Desert Lodge women placed their orders with a waiter.

Auntie Elsa would visit each table later, as was her habit, to determine her guests' level of satisfaction, and to fix whatever problems might need solving.

Auntie Elsa sat back in her chair and regarded Kerri.

"So? Have you arranged something with Santina and Luca about the dune buggies yet?"

"It's been a squeeze, but yes, we've arranged a working lunch on Sunday, so they can go on their last sunrise safari before leaving in the afternoon."

Naomi's head snapped up.

She'd known Luca and Santina would leave soon, but somehow, Sunday had seemed further away. She didn't know what to feel, other than emotional.

Pretending a need to use the bathroom, Naomi excused herself and went to her bedroom. She needed to get her emotions under control to face Luca.

How silly of her to feel like this. Hadn't she decided it was for the best to let him go?

It's precisely because he touched a place in her heart she'd long thought dead, that she couldn't allow him in any further. His experience with the poachers had made it more than clear. She didn't want to think about how it would feel if she'd given herself to him and anything had happened to him. She wouldn't survive it. Besides, she couldn't get the idea out of her head that she wasn't just a bit of vacation fun for him. She refused to be his plaything. What had happened between them, had happened. She couldn't retract it. But she could choose what happens now.

It took tremendous effort as she talked to herself in the mirror and stuffed her feelings of love for Luca back inside herself, locked in her heart.

When she again took her seat beside him, she felt much calmer, a deep serenity having settled over her. As though he could feel the change in her, he cast her a questioning smile.

Naomi, feeling in control of herself, gave him her most professional smile, and tucked into her dinner even though food was the last thing on her mind.

Kerri had left before they served coffee to respond to a phone call in her office. Auntie Elsa and Santina retired to the guest lounge for their coffee, leaving Naomi and Luca sitting at the table by themselves, albeit with a few guests still dotted at other tables.

Once again, the pool echoed with the sounds of enthusiastic after-dinner swimmers. Naomi focused her attention there. Much safer, in her opinion. But Luca had moved his chair closer to hers.

His breath sent shivers down her spine as he whispered in her ear.

"Are you okay, amore? You seem distant."

Naomi leaned away from him so she could look at him.

"I'm well, thanks. It's I who should ask if you're okay? You're the one who's been through the wars. Are you tired?"

Luca sat back in his chair, apparently satisfied with her answer.

"To be honest, I still don't feel one hundred percent myself. But I don't want to be in my room by myself. Would you sit with me... just until I fall asleep? Nothing funny, I promise."

Naomi smiled at him.

How could she refuse such a sweet request? Now her heart was intact again, she felt safe to be alone with him. But she'd have to watch him. No funny business.

"Sure, do you want me to read to you? It might help to block out the noise from the pool?"

Luca's eyes twinkled.

"The walls in my room are so thick, I'm sure the noise won't bother me. But yes, please. That would be great. I have my e-reader. I never travel without it."

When Naomi closed Luca's door behind her, she realized he'd been right. Quiet surrounded her. Other than faint screams of delight coming from the pool now and then, nothing penetrated the thick walls. She watched Luca walk to his bathroom to get changed.

How was it she couldn't imagine the days ahead without his broad shoulders in it? But she had to. It was for her own sanity.

She arranged his pillows, so he'd be comfortable, dimmed the lights, made sure he had some water on the bedside table. Then, she took a seat on the chair next to his bed.

Luca, dressed only in pajama bottoms, came walking into the bedroom. Naomi's heartbeat increased without her permission, and she struggled to get her breathing under control.

Luca was the picture of male perfection. His black hair mussed, his muscles rippling in the light from the bedside table, his long legs displaying his natural athleticism. He slid into the bed, a wicked grin on his handsome face.

Picking up and scrolling through his e-reader, he found what he was looking for and handed the device to Naomi, before making himself comfortable as he snuggled against the pillows. He must've known how gorgeous he was.

Naomi found it difficult to tear her eyes from him, but with a slight shake of her head, looked at the device in her hands.

"You are kidding!"

Naomi checked again the title of the book he wanted her to read. Yes, it was Delta of Venus by Anais Nin.

When she looked up, she saw that Luca was crying with laughter.

"Oh, so you think it's funny? Do you read erotica?"

He was laughing so hard, he couldn't answer, and when he did, he still couldn't stop laughing.

"You should see your face, amore. No, of course not. I just wanted to see your reaction."

"You're lucky this is a digital device, otherwise you would have more than just sore feet right now."

But Naomi couldn't keep a straight face. A smile tugged at the corners of her mouth. She had to fake scratching an itchy nose to keep him from seeing it. She wouldn't fall for his jokes so easily, or at least, she wouldn't show him she did. It might just encourage him.

Luca held out a hand to take back the device so he could choose the book he wanted her to read. With his other hand, he was wiping laughter tears from his eyes.

When he handed it back, his choice surprised Naomi. It was The Elephant Whisperer, a book she'd wanted to read herself. Now, she could share it with Luca, another keepsake.

She'd just started on the fourth chapter when Luca's even breathing alerted her he was sleeping. She closed the e-reader.

After watching him for a few moments, she sighed, got up and walked as quietly as she could to the door. There, she took a last long look at the exquisite man who'd crept deep into her heart. He would live there forever now, no matter what else life had in store for her.

IT FELT as though Naomi hadn't long been asleep when an almighty racket shocked her into jumping out of bed. She grabbed her dressing gown, and while running down the corridor, struggled to get her arms through the sleeves.

In the kitchen, she found members of the anti-poacher unit, Khwai and several male members of staff, all still half asleep. They had dragged two strange native men into the room who sat bound on the floor next to the kitchen cabinets.

Bright lights blazed inside and out, and everyone seemed to be talking at once, except for the two strange men. Their heads were down on their knees, their demeanor that of having been defeated.

"Who are these men, and what are they doing here?"

No one had seen Auntie Elsa enter the kitchen, but somehow, her voice penetrated the hubbub. Her hair was standing up, and her dressing gown was buttoned haphazardly, a sign they had awoken her from sleep and she had rushed to the kitchen.

Khwai stepped forward. He spoke to Auntie Elsa.

It transpired that the kitchen staff, who was on very early bread baking duty, had come upon the two men.

"These men were snooping outside the kitchen, Mrs. Elsa. The staff called us. We saw the men. They are from the same tribe as the poachers."

Auntie Elsa walked closer to the men, keeping her eyes focused on them. But they did their best to avoid eye contact with her, turning their heads this way and that.

"Naomi, call the police."

At the threat, the men's heads snapped up. They pleaded with Auntie Elsa and Naomi, and anyone else they thought might help.

Auntie Elsa looked fierce with her glasses balanced on the tip of her nose.

"Well, then tell me what you are doing here?"

The bigger of the two answered.

"We heard the ellie was here, Mrs. Elsa."

Auntie Elsa regarded the men, her eyes flicking over each.

"That's something I've never understood. When you kill the elephants and take their tusks..."

The men interrupted her.

"No, Mrs. Elsa, it wasn't us. We swear."

Auntie Elsa turned to Khwai.

"Is it true? These men weren't among the poachers?"

"It's hard to say, Mrs. Elsa. They were not with the poachers we caught. But they may have been there on the day of the kill."

Auntie Elsa refocused on the two who now regarded her with panic in their eyes.

"Hmm... well, I still want to know why you don't just eat the elephants you kill. Why do you sometimes afterward try to find the ellie for food?"

The men glanced at each other but realized they weren't getting out of this situation without some answers.

The smaller of the two who appeared older answered.

"It's like this, Mrs. Elsa. The men who kill the elephants have told us there is no time to take the elephant meat. Once they have the tusks, they have to leave very, very fast."

The man stopped talking. But Auntie Elsa made it clear she was waiting for him to continue and after a few minutes, he sighed, his body deflating before doing so.

"It's the anti-poachers, Mrs. Elsa. They're very fast. So, we have to come back another time for the ellie."

"Poaching is a very cruel thing you're doing -"

The men interrupted again, afraid of going to jail.

"No, no, Mrs. Elsa. We're not poachers. It wasn't us."

"Be that as it may, you can't have the ellie. But I will give you food. You're never to set foot on Desert Lodge ground again, and that includes the desert. Is that clear?"

The men, their eyes downcast, mumbled their thanks.

"Yes, Mrs. Elsa. Thank you, Mrs. Elsa."

By the time the men had eaten, more food packed up for their families, and the Desert Lodge guards had led them off the property, the faint pink of a new day was touching the horizon over the desert. There was no point returning to bed.

The dawn chorus crescendoed as Naomi made her way to the swimming pool for a quick swim before taking Santina and Luca out on a sunrise safari.

But when, after a quick shower, she went to collect them from the guest lounge, once again, only Santina was sitting there.

"Buongiorno, Naomi. What a lovely day. Will we see some elephants today, do you think?"

Naomi nodded.

"I don't see why not? I'll drive to the waterhole."

"Oh, is that the one where Kerri proposed to build a watchtower?"

Santina's question was a surprise. It wasn't the first Naomi had heard of it, but that Santina knew about it was amazing.

It was one of Kerry's better ideas. Naomi hoped Auntie Elsa would allow it.

She smiled.

"Kerri is full of bright ideas. Some work out, and some... not so much. Is Luca not joining us this morning?"

"No. I looked in on him before coming here. He is awake but says he has other plans this morning. At first, I thought he meant he was meeting with Kerri about the dune buggies. But he assured me the meeting is still scheduled for tomorrow. I want to be there for it, you see?"

Naomi nodded.

Whatever Luca was up to, it was none of her business.

When Santina didn't elaborate about Luca's plans for this morning, Naomi went to the French doors.

"Shall we go?"

Together the two women walked around the building to the truck parked outside the kitchen where the staff had loaded the breakfast things into the safari compartment. Naomi helped Santina up, got in, started the engine, and drove toward the gates that would take them into the desert once more.

Santina talked nonstop about the lovely day, how much she loved the feeling of the early morning's cool sun on her face, how she'd miss the expanse of the desert when they went back to Italy, and pointing at every tiny bird she saw. She didn't want Naomi to stop for breakfast, saying she'd prefer it back at the lodge.

Only when they stopped at the waterhole, and she'd finished admiring the animals there, big and small, did she turn to Naomi.

Her dark eyes fixed on Naomi's.

"I am looking forward very much to my birthday celebrations with Elsa here in July. I know Luca is also looking forward to returning here."

Naomi's heart beat faster at the thought of Luca returning. But she was also wondering where Santina was going with her statements. She remained silent, awaiting Santina's words.

"He's obviously interested in you, Naomi. I've never seen him so smitten. But I hope you will not hurt him. Can you promise me that?"

FOURTEEN

Naomi sat frozen. What could she say? It was the last thing she'd ever imagined Santina would broach with her.

Luca, smitten? With her? Really?

Her heart was thumping as though it wanted to break free from her ribcage. Her mouth was suddenly dry, her palms clammy with sweat.

So, his flirtatiousness wasn't just an act? The dinner wasn't just a wealthy prince's whim? What happened in the jet was...

Naomi couldn't get her head around Santina's words.

What if Santina was wrong? Could she really know how Luca felt? No one else could know what goes on in others' minds, their relationships, surely?

The silence from Santina filtered through Naomi's thoughts. She had to say something. It was rude not to respond. But she felt paralyzed. Had she already waited too long and given herself away in the process?

Putting her hands under her thighs gave her the confidence to respond.

"I don't know what to say... I... I'm shocked. Are you sure? About Luca, I mean...? He enjoys teasing me. I... I assumed it was just his way. We have to deal with very flirty guests here sometimes."

Santina fixed her dark eyes on Naomi.

Naomi squirmed a little under her scrutiny. It felt as though Santina could read her every thought, her every heartbeat.

"I am one hundred percent sure, cara. I know Luca as I would my own son. I don't know you. But you feel something for him in return, si?

Here it was again. The opportunity to deny Luca, to deny herself. What to do? What to say?

Panic was building up inside her. She couldn't allow herself to love Luca, to be loved by him. It was just too dangerous. She wasn't strong enough for it. It was one thing confronting herself, but it never occurred to her Santina would ambush her about this issue.

She felt cornered, trapped.

If Luca had feelings for her, this was the perfect opportunity to put a stop to any hope he might have in that direction. Santina would pass the message on to him.

Naomi struggled to get her thoughts together and her breath under control. A fist clamped around her heart at the thought of what she was about to do. Did she have the courage to deny herself the love, the happiness, the passion she'd allowed herself to feel for a few moments with him? Perhaps it was better not to be too committal?

She wanted to be honest with Santina. Well, up to a point. Auntie Elsa's voice sounded in her mind. "Don't burn your bridges..."

Naomi focused on the animals at the waterhole, but she wasn't seeing them.

Instead, she saw Khwai and a patrol guard supporting Luca between them, blood streaming from his head. Luca, lying inert in the flying doctor's Cessna, his limp hand in hers.

Luca, sleeping in his room after her attempt at a foot massage. Luca's black hair against the white pillow. Luca, laughing and smiling and playing the fool in the swimming pool. Luca relaxed and charming at the best dinner of her life. Luca, his dark eyes on fire, his kisses burning her skin, his passion consuming her. Luca... Pain in her heart. Pain as sharp and cold as death. But...

No! The alternative would be worse. She knew this pain. She'd felt it before. If pain for Luca were so bad now, it would be so much worse if she gave herself to him and then something happened. She'd be in hell. Worse than before, because now she was an adult. She knew what death meant, the finality. The despair, the darkness, the aloneness...

Naomi turned her head away from Santina. She shut her eyes, her breath escaping silently through her lips.

"I'm sorry if Luca misunderstood, Santina. If there was any way in which I might have led him on... seemed interested in him. He is a guest. You're both guests. We try to do the best for our guests at all times."

Santina wasn't letting it go so easily.

"But you accepted his invitation to dinner? You accepted his advances?"

Naomi knew she had to be very careful. She didn't want to appear heartless or insult either Santina or Luca, but she had to protect herself.

"True. I accepted Luca's dinner invitation. And even though it isn't something I'd normally do, as you know, Luca can be charming and very persuasive. It was just dinner. We could have had dinner at the lodge. But Luca wanted to go to Windhoek. It was difficult to deny him. He seems a very kind man. I think he just wanted to make it up to me for allowing him to come on the anti-poacher alert to rescue the ellie. It seemed to mean a lot to him."

Santina continued to stare at Naomi for a few seconds more. Then she sighed and stared off into the distance.

"You're right, Naomi. Luca has a very kind heart. And yes, it meant a lot you allowed him to help with the ellie's rescue. He has a thing for African elephants, especially."

Naomi saw her chance to shift the conversation to more comfortable grounds.

"Luca was so excited about the ellie and so shocked at what the poachers had done, he'd kindly suggested he'd send an article to National Geographic together with the photos he took that morning. He said he wanted to help highlight the plight of the African elephants. I thought it was such a compassionate and wonderful gesture. I hate to bring it up again, but it could have been one reason he went with the anti-poacher unit when they were tracking the poachers."

Santina sighed again.

"You are right again, Naomi. I'm sure that's why he went with them. I'm glad you can see his kindness and goodness."

Santina was silent for a moment. Then, she turned once again to face Naomi, her eyes glistening with unshed tears.

"I'm sorry if I made you uncomfortable before, cara. I had so hoped Luca had finally found love. Would you... Could you please be gentle with him?"

Naomi held the older woman's hand in hers.

"I understand. I wish it could be as you had hoped, dear Santina. I know you want the best for Luca. And when he finds the right woman, she'll be the luckiest woman in the world. Luca is an extraordinary man. But he is still young. There is still time for him to find the one, don't you think?"

Santina nodded, silent tears falling from her eyes.

Naomi's heart went out to the older woman.

It was a test for Naomi, too. Could she pass it?

"I am so sorry, Santina."

Santina let go of Naomi's hands and fished out a handkerchief from her pocket.

"No, I am sorry, Naomi. Sorry, I made you feel uncomfortable, sorry Luca feels as he does, and sorry you don't feel the same way. It will be such a blow for him."

Naomi had to ask.

"And you are sure he has feelings for me? He's said nothing."

Santina nodded and wiped her eyes with her handkerchief.

The journey back to the lodge was more serene than Naomi could have hoped. Santina seemed to have accepted Naomi's answer, and although sad for Luca, at least Santina didn't seem to blame her. Instead, Santina appeared eager to forget their conversation and move forward in her friendship with Naomi.

Back at the lodge, Santina thanked Naomi for the safari and returned to her suite.

Aware she still had to take care of Luca, and curious to see what he'd been up to, Naomi walked around the building to his suite.

She prayed things wouldn't be awkward between them. But to her surprise, his door was open, his room empty. The staff had already been to clean his room and make his bed. Everything was tidy and fresh. But where could Luca be?

Naomi walked to the end of the veranda in front of his suite and found him beside the building. Dressed only in shorts, his fantastic body glistening in the sun, he stood engrossed in the painting he was creating on the easel in front of him.

Not wanting to disturb him, Naomi stood watching him for several minutes.

Could what Santina had told her be true? Could this amazing man really have feelings for her? No, Santina had to be mistaken.

Before she could retreat, Luca noticed her presence. He looked up, his beautiful smile going straight to her heart.

"Buongiorno, amore. Don't come closer. It's a surprise."

Luca took long strides over to her, planted a kiss on her cheek and lifted a strand of hair from her forehead.

It amazed Naomi how much he appeared to be himself again. A good night's sleep had restored his vitality, and vibrant self, overnight.

His smile was dazzling.

"You're ready for our swim?"

He gestured to the easel and paint things.

"I'll just put these in my room. See you in the pool."

Luca packed up his painting things.

Even though Naomi had already had her morning swim, she felt it better to just go with the flow, especially after her earlier conversation with Santina. But she hadn't expected him to wait for her.

Would joining him encourage him to think she felt anything for him in return? Still, he was a guest, and it was just a swim.

When she arrived back at the pool, Luca was already there, talking and laughing with several other morning swimmers.

The man had formidable powers of recuperation. He seemed his old self again. No signs of his recent trauma remained.

The other swimmers who'd befriended Luca kept up their conversation while swimming lengths.

Naomi felt grateful to them. Their intervention meant she'd escaped a one-on-one with Luca. She was still reeling from Santina's words earlier.

The delicious aroma of coffee, toast and scrambled eggs wafted over the pool as the staff was getting breakfast ready in the Lapa. Everyone from the pool went straight there, sitting on their towels to prevent the chairs from getting wet.

Auntie Elsa, Santina and Kerri came to join Luca and Naomi. They'd chosen a table big enough to accommodate their friends. As had become his custom, Luca sat beside Naomi.

But Naomi's conversation earlier with Santina, her desperate vice on her feelings and Luca's nearness, resulted in a complete loss of appetite. She settled for rich coffee, instead, and watched as the others enjoyed a hearty breakfast.

Kerri gulped down her breakfast and left to see to her duties. Luca excused himself to finish his painting, winking at Naomi as he pushed his chair back. She watched him walk away until he disappeared into his room, no doubt to retrieve his painting things. Auntie Elsa and Santina were once again talking about the arrangements for their birthday party.

Naomi waited for a break in their conversation before checking Santina didn't need her for the rest of the day.

It was bliss to escape to the sanctuary of her room. Upon entering, she stripped her still-damp bathing suit from her body. Standing under the hot shower, Naomi could feel the tension leave her body. But her thoughts wouldn't let go of Luca.

If what Santina had said were true, was she making the biggest mistake of her life by letting him go? Was she condemning them both to lives without the love they could have had?

She knew with absolute certainty that no other man could ever occupy the space he had claimed in her heart. He was her forever soulmate as Auntie Elsa and Uncle Wouter had been for each other.

Suddenly, it was all too much. Naomi sank down the wall and sat in the shower with the water cascading down on her. Her tears joined the water as it dripped down her face. It felt as though her heart was breaking into a million pieces. Once she'd started to cry, to acknowledge her pain, she couldn't stop. She gave herself over to the sobs that wracked her body.

Deep inside, Naomi knew she was making the right decision. Better this short period of heartache, no matter how painful, than the inevitable annihilation down the road.

A knock on her door brought her back to reality. She wiped her tears and stuck her head out of the shower.

"I'm in the shower. Who is it?"

Kerri's voice came muffled through the door.

"It's me. Can I come in?"

"I won't be long. Can I come to your office when I'm done?"

"Sure."

Naomi got up, shut off the shower, and grabbed her towel.

Fifteen minutes later, when she walked into Kerri's office, she found Kerri arguing with someone on the other end of the phone. She finished the call and hung up when she saw Naomi.

Naomi contemplated her friend.

"That sounded serious. What's it about?"

Kerri shrugged.

"You don't want to know."

"Okay. Well...?"

Kerri cast a questioning look at her friend.

Naomi's smile wanted to ease the turbulent energy in Kerri's office.

"You wanted to see me?"

"Oh! Yes, I did. It's Luca."

Naomi's heart quickened at the sound of his name, but fear clutched it.

"That wasn't Luca on the phone, was it?"

"What? Oh, nooo..."

Kerri's eyes widened as she emphasized the negative, and she dragged out her "Nooo."

"That wasn't Luca. Absolutely not. No, it's something unrelated. No, Luca called to ask if you'd take him to see ellie Naomi. Apparently, he wants to take more pictures of her for an article or something. He got cagey when I asked him about it. Do you know what he's on about?"

Naomi gave a shrug and shook her head. She knew it must have something to do with the article and photos for National Geographic. But she'd leave the pleasure of revealing it to him when he was ready.

"When does he want to go?"

Kerri's gaze implied she wasn't sure whether to believe her friend.

"I think now. Can I come, too?"

"If Luca doesn't mind, of course."

Luca was already waiting in the Lapa. His photographic equipment was strewn on the table in front of him. Santina was leaning over one of his shoulders, Auntie Elsa over the other. He was showing them pictures of the little ellie on his digital camera.

All three looked up when Naomi and Kerri joined them. Luca smiled at Naomi, and she added Kerri to their outing.

"Kerri wants to see how little Naomi is doing. You don't mind, do you, Luca?"

He dropped his eyes briefly, perhaps to hide his disappointment, but his smile remained. He made an all-inclusive wave with his hand.

"The more, the merrier, as the saying goes."

Santina smiled first at Luca, then at Naomi.

"In that case, I'd love to see where she's ended up."

Auntie Elsa nodded.

"And me. I've never been to the elephant orphanage before. It's high time I showed interest. Goodness knows they've accepted enough orphaned ellies from us over the years."

They made their way to the main house and to the truck parked under the porch outside the kitchen. As was his habit, Luca made sure the older women were sitting comfortably before looking to help Naomi and Kerri. But they were both already in the truck, and Luca hauled his photographic equipment inside with him.

The hour's drive to the orphanage went faster than Naomi had expected. Auntie Elsa and Santina shared their birthday plans with the others. Everyone batted ideas back and forth, and by the time they reached the orphanage, the party sounded even more elaborate than the two older women appeared to have imagined.

Their high spirits matched Johan's. His booming voice preceded him as he came over to the truck to greet them and to help Auntie Elsa and Santina down.

Johan led the way over to the mud pool, now void of other members of the small herd. He explained they had gone into the bush on their daily walk. Only one little ellie played there with her surrogate father. She was pushing him into the mud and running around him as though she wanted him to chase her.

Everyone stopped in their tracks as a proud Johan introduced them to ellie Naomi.

The transformation in the little elephant was miraculous. Gone was the very sad, terrified, despondent little animal. In her place, a friendly, outgoing ellie Naomi greeted them, her teeny trunk touching each one as if to thank them for rescuing her.

Auntie Elsa saw Naomi's tears.

She put a comforting arm around her adoptive daughter, squeezing Naomi tight into her embrace. With her other hand, she held Naomi's head on her shoulder.

Her soothing voice traveled straight to Naomi's heart.

"No one stays lost. Love is the deepest healer of all, my darling."

FIFTEEN

Luca and Santina were as shocked as Johan when Auntie Elsa told them about the two poachers who'd come looking for ellie Naomi at Desert Lodge in the early morning hours.

Johan was particularly incensed, his nostrils flared and white.

"During the day, it's as if the orphans try to please us. You all saw ellie Naomi. They're so sweet, as if they are thanking us. But at night, these babies cry for their mummies for a very long time. It's heartbreaking to witness their tears and their sadness. They're often inconsolable. And we feel so helpless. There's nothing we can do. We can only try our best to make them feel better. We give love, and try to give their lives purpose and meaning, again. But make no mistake, it's tough going. These babies are as vulnerable, sad and depressed as human babies would be without their mothers."

Luca was bristling.

"So, it's not enough to kill the mothers for their ivory. And then these guys come to kill the babies for food. Oh my God, I can't even comprehend it."

Johan placed an enormous hand on Luca's shoulder.

"I know how you feel. That's why we have such powerful security systems here."

Luca looked in Naomi and Auntie Elsa's direction. His eyes asked about their security systems.

Auntie Elsa nodded.

"Yes, all the lodges have security. We have to protect our businesses, but the poachers can be very crafty."

Johan nodded.

"Another reason we have anti-poacher guards as surrogate fathers for the orphans and why they sleep with the ellies at night."

Johan led the way to the veranda and arranged for coffee and tea for his guests, while Luca stayed with ellie Naomi and her surrogate father.

Luca moved around her, taking many more pictures of her now she was more relaxed. She appeared to know she was the star and struck such comical poses, it had everyone laughing at her antics. But the attention only seemed to encourage her. She was so cute it was easy to fall in love with her.

Kerri winked at Naomi.

"I know she's named after you, but she couldn't be more different. I think she's more like me. I'm glad because it means we can share her. I hope that's okay with you?"

Naomi squeezed her friend's hand.

"The more parents she has, the better. We can make up for the horrible nightmare she's been through."

Naomi noticed Johan watching Kerri, and even though Kerri wasn't returning his gaze, her cheeks were pinker than usual. Naomi smiled to herself, glad for her friend. Johan was a wonderful man with a kind heart. Naomi knew Kerri had had her fair share of men problems. Johan would treat Kerri well.

A sudden commotion at the mud bath jerked her attention in that direction.

Luca was trying to fend off ellie Naomi. She was pushing him into the mud bath while he was trying to hang on to his camera. But just when it seemed he'd end up on his bottom in the mud, the ellie's surrogate father drew her attention to himself and away from Luca. It was so funny. Everyone, including Luca, roared.

After a delicious lunch of barbequed lamb chops served with baked potatoes and salad, Luca announced he wanted to stay and take more pictures and videos of ellie Naomi until she went to sleep. Johan agreed to get Luca back to Desert Lodge in time for dinner.

The drive back to the lodge with only the women in the truck was much quieter than the journey to the elephant orphanage had been. Naomi suspected it was because everyone was sated from the lunch, happy with ellie Naomi's progress, and ready for a siesta. But the journey without Luca in the car felt weird... empty.

No sooner had Naomi parked the truck under Desert Lodge's porch, than everyone deserted her, going to bed or, in Kerri's case, to check on her messages in the office.

In the kitchen, Naomi poured herself an iced tea to take to her room and walked down the corridor.

She could hear voices coming from the direction of the guest lounge.

Strange.

She was sure no one would be in there, but someone was, and it sounded as though they were arguing. As she neared the room, the raised voices became much louder. She recognized Kerri's voice, but the other belonged to a man.

He sounded very upset or angry.

"... a sorry excuse for a lodge I've ever seen."

As Naomi entered the lounge, the man looked up. He reminded her of the 'princes' that appeared at the lodge from time to time. A tall, large man with close cropped hair, he was dressed in a white shirt and jeans.

He glared at Naomi, his face red, both from fury and heat.

"And who might you be?"

His accent was difficult to pinpoint, but Naomi could hear a slight American diction in his speech.

Naomi walked farther into the room. She cast a quick glance at Kerri, who appeared very cross.

Kerri's breathing was fast and high in her body, but she was doing her best to stay professional.

"May I introduce Naomi Smith, Mr. Sawaski? She is our head guide here at Desert Lodge."

The man's hand swallowed Naomi's. His eyes ran up and down her body, apparently finding her wanting. A frown remained between his eyes, the color of a storm about to break.

He snorted a discontented greeting.

"Mph... Well, you'll have to do, I suppose."

Naomi glanced at Kerri, confusion in her eyes.

Kerri stepped forward, her hands up in defense.

"Oh, no, Mr. Sawaski. I'm sorry if I wasn't clear. Naomi is currently looking after other guests. I can get another guide, Gerhard, to take you on whatever excursions you would like."

The man's face went a notch redder. He threw his arms in the air in exasperation.

"Oh, for fuck's sake...!"

Auntie Elsa appeared in the doorway at the same time as the man swung back to yell at Kerri, a threatening finger pointing at her.

Auntie Elsa walked past Naomi, taking the glass of iced tea from her hand, and offering it to the outraged man. She took his elbow and steered him through the door that led to the dining room, which was empty and much cooler.

Auntie Elsa's soothing voice seemed to have an immediate

calming effect on the man who had allowed Auntie Elsa to lead him away.

"Mr. Sawaski, is it?"

Her voice grew fainter as they disappeared into the dining room, the thick walls of the old house the perfect soundproof.

Naomi blew out a breath she'd been unaware of holding.

Kerri slumped down into the nearest chair.

Naomi sat down opposite her friend, leaning forward toward Kerri.

"What was that all about?"

"I hope Auntie Elsa won't fire me."

Only now did Naomi notice her friend was shaking from head to toe.

"Why would she fire you? Are you okay?"

Kerri put her head in her hands.

"It's my fault, to be honest. I'd forgotten he was arriving today. We've had a few very heated phone conversations—"

"It was him on the phone when I came into your office earlier?

Kerri nodded, her head still in her hands.

"He was staying with Ilze at Solitaire..."

Naomi sighed.

She'd forgotten how appalling the behaviour of their usual 'princes' could be. Luca had spoiled them.

"And already he gave you a hard time before he even arrived?"

Kerri nodded again, then looked up at Naomi.

"I just pray he won't drop me in it with Auntie Elsa."

Naomi noticed that talking seemed to calm Kerri down. She wasn't shaking so much anymore. Naomi couldn't think of any reason her friend would be so worried. Her eyes and her arched eyebrow asked the question.

Kerri sighed, but a small smile played around her mouth.

"I went out last night."

"You did not. When?"

Kerri looked sheepish.

"When you all went to sleep."

"Now you mention it... I was wondering where you were when Khwai and the other caught those two poachers. I thought you were just asleep. But you weren't here, were you?"

Kerri shook her head, her eyes pleading at Naomi.

It was Naomi's turn to smile.

"You dirty stop-out, you! Don't tell me... you went out with Johan. Am I right?"

Kerri's mouth dropped open, her face a picture of astonishment.

"How did you-?"

Naomi had to laugh at her friend's reaction.

"I saw the way Johan looked at you and the blush on your cheeks."

Naomi got up, went to squeeze in on the chair beside Kerri, and gave her friend a big hug.

"I'm so happy for you. He's a lovely guy."

Kerri relaxed in Naomi's arms, her head on Naomi's shoulder, her voice smiling when she responded.

"He is lovely. I didn't know I could be this happy."

The two friends moved apart and looked at each other.

Kerri was smiling and patted Naomi's hand.

"Now we just have to sort you and Luca out..."

Naomi withdrew her hand and got up.

Kerri looked up at her friend, concern clear in her eyes.

"What? What did I say?"

Naomi shook her head, sudden tears burning behind her eyes as she lowered them to stare at her feet. She had to get away. Not even Kerri could know. Not yet, anyway.

"Nothing. I'm just tired. I think I'll have a nap before I have to take Santina for a sunset safari."

Kerri looked even more sheepish if that were possible.

"Sorry, I forgot."

"What?"

"She canceled the sunset safari today. She wanted to spend more time with Auntie Elsa, she said. I guess the two have become good friends. They probably want to chat more about their party before Santina leaves."

"Hmm... Well, I'll still have a nap if I can. I didn't get much sleep last night, seeing Auntie Elsa and I had to deal with the poachers by ourselves while you were out gallivanting with Johan."

Kerri knew her friend was only joking and blew her a kiss before getting up and going into her office.

Naomi walked further down the corridor to her bedroom.

THE KNOCKING on Naomi's door slowly penetrated her dreams and her consciousness. She felt groggy as she put her feet on the cool slate floor and walked to the door.

Kerri's voice came muffled from the other side of the door.

"Hun, are you in there?"

Naomi opened the door.

Kerri walked past her and plopped herself down on the bed where Naomi had been sleeping moments ago. She looked fresh and energetic in an emerald green top and black jeans. The green of her top was in perfect contrast to her red curls.

Naomi yawned and rubbed her eyes with the palms of her hands. She knew she had to wake up, but her body disagreed.

"What's up?"

"Luca's back. He's asking for you."

Naomi couldn't think. Why would Luca be back? Where did he go? Then she remembered he'd stayed behind at the orphanage to film ellie Naomi.

"Do you know what he wants?"

Kerri had started Naomi's shower for her, meanwhile. She returned to help Naomi to the bathroom.

"Come on, sleepy head. Let's get you into the shower. Luca wants to show videos of the ellie. He's asked me to arrange it so all the guests can watch the video before dinner in the Lapa."

Kerri put an arm around Naomi's shoulders and steered her toward the bathroom. While Naomi got rid of her clothes and stepped into the shower, Kerri went back to the bedroom and opened Naomi's wardrobe.

"What do you feel like wearing tonight?"

When Naomi didn't answer, Kerri put out the clothes on the bed. She knew Naomi didn't care too much about what she wore, provided it was clean. Naomi had lovely dresses, but she never wore them.

Kerri posed in the mirror holding Naomi's silver sleeveless maxi dress against her body. It was lovely. She laid the dress on the bed and took out silver flip flops from the shoe rack inside the wardrobe.

She waited until Naomi had the dress on and was sitting in front of her mirror before she brushed out Naomi's long hair for her.

"Are you more awake now?"

Naomi yawned again as she put silver hooped earrings through the small holes in her earlobes.

"Yes, thank you. I don't know what came over me. I guess I haven't caught up on sleep over the last few days."

The two young women walked to the Lapa together.

The moment Naomi laid eyes on the table, she understood

Kerri's nervous energy. Johan had joined the others. But so had the rude 'prince' they'd met earlier.

Naomi and Kerri glanced at each other, their eyes voicing their concern.

But he seemed much more relaxed, laughing and talking with Johan and Luca. Auntie Elsa and Santina sat at the other end of the table, deep in conversation. Luca and Johan looked up as Naomi and Kerri walked toward them.

Johan's friendly booming laugh greeted them as they reached the table.

"Ah, here they are. Have you met Stefan yet? Stefan, these are the most beautiful women and the best lodge managers you'll meet in Namibia or anywhere."

Kerri blushed at Johan's compliment and took her seat beside him. Naomi nodded at Stefan before sitting down in the empty chair between Luca and Auntie Elsa. Several empty bottles of the local Hansa beer stood on the table in front of the big man, who seemed more jovial now.

Luca took Naomi by surprise when he squeezed her hand under the table. He smiled at her before getting up and walking toward the wall at the back of the Lapa. His confident strides and tall frame drew appreciative glances from the guests seated at other tables. Stopping in front of a large screen Kerri had arranged there, Luca pinged a knife against a glass to get everyone's attention. People swiveled around in their chairs to look at him.

Luca smiled at everyone before speaking.

"I know you're all here on a wonderful vacation and you couldn't have chosen a better lodge at which to do so. But among all the beauty here, evil also lurks. I'm sure everyone here is at least familiar with the poaching problem in Africa of tusks from the elephants and rhino horn. I've experienced first-hand the horror of an elephant killed by poachers for her tusks.

What people talk about less is the fact that sometimes, the calves of the killed mothers are left behind to fend for themselves. Desert Lodge has a magnificent anti-poacher unit. I was lucky enough to meet them and to join them on an anti-poacher operation. I don't recommend it, but if you talk to them, I'm sure they will answer all your questions. Meanwhile, we placed the little ellie we found with the dead elephant mother at an elephant orphanage near here. Her name is Naomi, after Desert Lodge's brave head guide."

Luca extended an arm with an open hand in Naomi's direction. With so many of the guests looking at her, she could feel her cheeks burn, but Luca came to her rescue when he continued talking, drawing their attention back to him again.

"I'm fortunate Naomi was appointed to look after my secretary and me during our stay here. Anyone who inherits her services after we leave tomorrow will be extremely lucky."

Naomi noticed Stefan watching her and she shifted in her chair. But when Luca resumed talking, Stefan turned his head in Luca's direction.

Naomi breathed out a sigh of relief and listened to Luca's presentation.

"But, to get back to ellie Naomi... I was lucky enough to stay with her tonight until she fell asleep. I wanted to share my observations with all of you, and I hope it will inspire you to help protect these magnificent animals."

Luca stepped aside to appreciative applause. He pressed a key on his laptop connected to the screen.

Ellie Naomi appeared and was playing in the mud bath with her surrogate father. They were kicking a ball to each other. The image merged into the ellie going into her stable for the night. Her surrogate father went with her and offered her an enormous bottle of milk. The camera panned into her little face as she sucked at the teat on the bottle. Her shiny eyes were intently focused on her surrogate father as she drank, white foam bubbles appearing around her little mouth.

The guests in the Lapa made "ooh" and "aww" sounds as they watched the tiny elephant. Small, joyful noises accompanied the ellie's tiny trunk as it snaked this way and that over her surrogate father's hand and arm. She seemed to thank him for her meal. When the bottle was empty, her surrogate father laid down on the hay in the small stable and encouraged the ellie to join him.

At first, it looked as though she might do so, but she remained standing and walked back and forth. After a short while, heartrending sounds came from the small animal.

The camera panned into her face for a close-up, and people gasped when they saw the tears that streamed from her eyes and clung to her eyelashes.

Naomi looked around at the guests. Several were tearful as they continued to watch the ellie crying for her mother. Her surrogate father tried to comfort her, but she was inconsolable.

Naomi admired Luca's editing skills. He'd allowed them to see just enough of the sad ellie to make a lasting impression. The camera panned away, and the ellie's sounds grew fainter.

Luca pressed another key, and the screen once again became just a screen.

"It is heartbreaking to see what we humans do to animals, isn't it? I hope this inspires you to think of our animal friends in a different, more humane way and to help when they need us. Thank you."

Luca returned to his seat under thunderous applause, several people tapping him on the shoulder as he passed their tables or extending a hand to shake his.

Naomi's heart felt like it was jumping out of her chest from pride and love for this amazing man. She couldn't keep her smile from her face as Luca took his place next to her once again.

Everyone around the table congratulated him on his excellent film. Johan's voice boomed above the others'. Santina came to put a hand on Luca's shoulder, smiling down at him.

Naomi noticed Stefan was the only one not congratulating Luca. Instead, he scrutinized Luca from across the table, his cheerfulness diminished.

Naomi imagined he felt competitive toward Luca. It wouldn't be the first time she'd witnessed it among the 'princes.'

Much later, when most guests had gone to bed, Naomi excused herself and left the three men and Kerri sitting around the table talking and drinking beer and coffee, as she sought her bed. Auntie Elsa and Santina, and the staff had left the Lapa just after midnight.

Luca held on to her hand for a moment longer than she'd expected, his smile intimate, his dark eyes locked on hers.

"Good night, amore. See you in the morning."

SIXTEEN

Having checked the staff had loaded the breakfast things onto the truck, and having made sure the walkie-talkie had enough battery, Naomi arrived at the guest lounge.

To her surprise, Luca and Santina weren't the only people waiting for her there. Johan, who'd stayed the night, Kerri and Stefan, occupied chairs as they enjoyed steaming mugs of coffee.

Luca looked up when she entered, his smile breathtaking.

"Buongiorno, amore. As you can see, the party is continuing. You don't mind?"

How could she mind? But she was feeling a little disappointed at not having Luca to herself for the last time.

What was she doing? Hadn't she decided it was for the best?

Swallowing the slight pang of disappointment that refused to leave, Naomi returned his smile.

"Of course not. As you always say, 'the more, the merrier...'"

While she waited for her guests to finish their coffees, Naomi arranged with the kitchen staff to add to the breakfast offerings on the truck.

But she had noticed Auntie Elsa's absence and went to knock on her bedroom door.

It seemed like ages before Auntie Elsa opened the door. Her adoptive mother was still in her nightdress, her hair in disarray. She'd evidently only just awoken.

It struck Naomi how much older Auntie Elsa looked. When did she age so much?

She smiled at the older woman.

"Good morning, sleepyhead. Don't you want to join us on the sunrise safari? Santina is coming along too."

Auntie Elsa seemed disoriented.

She put a hand on Naomi's shoulder.

"Darling, you have fun with them. And please give my apologies to Santina. I'll see her later. I have a few things to see to here."

Naomi stared at the door for a few moments after Auntie Elsa had closed it again. It was unusual behavior for Auntie Elsa. Naomi put her hand on the door. She'd check up on her adoptive mother on her return.

The others were waiting. Naomi returned to the kitchen.

No sooner had the staff loaded everything onto the truck, than her guests came walking around the building. Luca helped Santina into the truck and then approached Naomi, but she'd beaten him to it and sat waiting in the driver's seat. He smiled at her, took long strides around the truck, and slid into the seat beside her.

Naomi started the engine and drove through the gate into the desert. Everyone seemed in a good mood. Conversation flowed as she drove to the waterhole where they could see the biggest concentration of animals so early in the morning.

Ahead of them, the sun was rising over the red dunes, obliterating the stars.

Luca had his digital camera around his neck and took

pictures of the dunes, the animals and the sunrise. Naomi had a sneaky suspicion he'd taken pictures of her. But each time she looked at him, he seemed to concentrate elsewhere when moments before she was certain he had aimed his camera in her direction. That's when Naomi noticed that Stefan was also snapping away as enthusiastically as Luca.

She felt a smile form around her mouth.

No matter how successful these men had become, they remained boys.

After about an hour at the waterhole, Naomi took a circuitous route back to the lodge, which she knew would take them to a special surprise for her guests.

Their reactions didn't disappoint when they neared the enormous old acacia tree that hosted a massive communal birds' nest. Khwai had once told her it was over one hundred years old, and quite a miracle. In the high heat of summer, these nests usually caught fire and didn't exist for very long. That this one had survived for so many years was astounding.

Her guests were awed and impressed, and Naomi felt it was the perfect place for their sunrise breakfast. But no one seemed hungry at that time of the morning. They wanted coffee and said they'd prefer breakfast at the lodge. Soon, everyone was standing around, a mug of steaming coffee in hand, admiring the enormous birds' nest from different angles as they walked around the tree.

Tiny birds, among a cacophony of twittering, flew in and out of the nest. It was amazing to see how each small bird found their own nest in such an enormous complexity of straw and mud woven together to create a veritable bird metropolis.

With their coffee cravings satisfied, they continued on their way back to the lodge, but Stefan made Naomi stop when he noticed abandoned ostrich eggs he wanted to photograph.

The morning sun rose higher in the cloudless blue sky as the symphony of animal sounds grew stronger.

Naomi took a deep breath as she leaned against the side of the truck, waiting for Stefan to satisfy his urge to photograph the eggs. Even though her heart felt heavy at the thought of Luca leaving later that day, the desert's healing powers buoyed up her spirits.

The drive back to the lodge went without more stops, but both Luca and Stefan continued their photographic endeavors.

By the time Naomi pulled the truck back under the porch near the kitchen, both Neil and Gerhard, the other two desert guides, pulled their vehicles alongside hers, back from their safaris.

Guests from all three vehicles disembarked, chatted and laughed, and shared their sunrise experiences as they went to their rooms, or to the Lapa. Some guests, having worn their bathing suits under their clothes, undressed at the pool's edge and jumped into the swimming pool.

In the kitchen, several members of the staff were enjoying an early breakfast around the large acacia wooden table.

There was no sign of Auntie Elsa anywhere.

Naomi went to knock on her door again.

"Auntie Elsa? Are you in there?"

After several moments, the door opened, and Auntie Elsa stood there, still in her nightdress, rubbing at her eyes. She had obviously gone back to bed since they spoke earlier that morning.

"Oh, I'm sorry. I didn't mean to wake you up again. Are you okay?"

Auntie Elsa yawned.

"What time is it?"

"It's time for breakfast."

Naomi led Auntie Elsa back into her room and sat her down

on the edge of her bed. She went to sit next to her adoptive mother. When she put a compassionate arm around her shoulders, she could feel the woman's bones under her nightdress. When had Auntie Elsa lost that much weight?

Naomi inspected the older woman. Something was ailing her adoptive mother.

"What's wrong? Are you ill?"

Auntie Elsa shook her head and ran a hand through her hair.

"No, I'm fine. I must be just exhausted."

It was as if the older woman suddenly realized Naomi was sitting next to her.

She turned her sharp eyes on her adoptive daughter.

"Have you just come back from the safari?"

Naomi nodded, her arm still around Auntie Elsa's shoulders, her eyes searching Auntie Elsa's as though to make sure she was still in there.

"I'll join you in the Lapa for breakfast. I take it that's what the others are doing?"

"Yes, they are. I'm on my way there now. But are you sure? If you're not feeling well..."

"No, no. I'm fine. I just overslept. It's okay. You go ahead. I'll see you there soon."

Auntie Elsa got up and shooed Naomi out of her room so she could get ready.

Outside the door, Naomi hesitated. She wanted to believe everything was okay, but a dark feeling lurked inside her body.

She gave herself a pep talk. They'd had a few late nights. Hadn't she overslept yesterday after her siesta when Kerri had come to her rescue? Auntie Elsa was tired. That was all.

Naomi decided the dark feeling was there because Luca and Santina were leaving later that afternoon.

With a glance at Auntie Elsa's door, Naomi made her way to the Lapa for a last breakfast with Luca and Santina.

Johan, Stefan and Kerri had also joined their table. Naomi felt relieved to notice Kerri and Stefan seemed to have buried their differences. They were chatting and laughing like old friends. Luca had leaned forward as he talked with Johan and Santina, but sat back in his chair when Naomi slid into the chair beside him.

His dark eyes were intent on her, and his smile lit up his lovely face. He seemed like a god among men. How was he even real? It was a thought that had often snuck into Naomi's mind.

Luca leaned toward her and his voice, when he spoke so near her ear, sent shivers down her spine.

"Is this our last breakfast together, amore?"

Naomi squinted at him. What could he mean?

"It is. Isn't it? Or do you mean you're staying longer?"

Her heart beat fast and loud as the words left her lips. The question had just popped out. She hadn't meant to ask it, but now it was out. Is it what he'd meant?

Luca took her hand. It felt warm and sensual and swallowed hers.

"Unfortunately, I cannot stay longer. But trust me when I say, I deeply wish I could."

His eyes burned into hers, his pupils dilating as they stared at each other.

Naomi felt goose bumps appearing all over her body. How could she forget his lips on hers, on her neck...? She lowered her eyes to break the connection.

Her voice sounded husky in her ears when she spoke.

"Oh. I see..."

Luca put a finger under her chin and lifted her head back so he could look into her eyes once more.

"I don't want it to be our last."

What was he saying? As she looked at him, her glance went to his arm and the small red spot where his drip had been just a few days ago.

The image of Luca slumped between Khwai and the younger guard flashed across her mind's eye. No, no, no. Whatever Luca was saying, she dared not imagine or wish it. It was just too dangerous.

Her heart was still galloping fast and loud, but for an altogether different reason. The dark feeling grew. The fear in her body squeezed a tight band around her torso.

"I... I'm sorry, Luca. I don't mean to be rude, but I need to check on Auntie Elsa. She wasn't feeling well earlier."

Luca released her hand at once, empathy shining from his eyes.

"Of course, amore. You must go to her. I understand. We'll talk later."

Naomi got up and hurried away as fast as she could.

Maybe Santina was right. Maybe Luca had developed a soft spot for her. Perhaps she was a little more than a mere vacation fling for him. If she understood him, his words seemed to imply it. Why else would he want to have more breakfasts with her? Surely, you only wanted more breakfasts with people you wanted in your life.

A maelstrom of emotions coursed through her as she fought to keep the tears that burned behind her eyes from spilling.

She blinked and wiped them away, feeling cross with Luca.

Why did he have to be so wonderful? Why did he have to be interested in her? Why did he have to make her fall in love with him? How was she going to live her life now knowing she'll meet no one else who could live up to him?

She fought hard to get her emotions under control. It won't be too long now. He'd be gone this afternoon and with him, gone also, the chaos and anguish he'd caused her. But she knew she was just fooling herself. Her feelings wouldn't disappear because he'd left.

As she came around the corner, Auntie Elsa came walking toward her.

The smile she gave Naomi was reassuring and calming.

"Have you come looking for me?"

Naomi did her best to ignore the pain and the constricted feeling in her chest.

She winked at Auntie Elsa.

"I had to check you haven't gone back to bed again."

Auntie Elsa laughed.

The cheerful sound did much to diminish some of Naomi's anxiety.

This was what mattered, this kind, strong woman who had become the most important person in the world to her. The love and the bond they shared and living here was all she knew as home.

Sometimes she'd still felt like an outsider, but it wasn't anything Auntie Elsa or anyone else here did or said. It was only her ghosts come to visit.

She stuck her arm through Auntie Elsa's and together they walked to the Lapa to join their friends.

Kerri's madcap ideas, Johan's booming laughter, and Stefan's new engaging persona helped to make, what could have been a sad affair, into an excellent farewell breakfast.

There was still something about Stefan... Naomi couldn't put her finger on it. But for now, he seemed fine.

Just as breakfast finished, a photographer arrived to take pictures for the dining room wall of Auntie Elsa with Luca, and Auntie Elsa with Stefan.

The photo shoot drew curious glances from other guests. Luca had made a huge impression on them with his video presentation of the ellie the night before. As he came to stand next to Naomi in the shade of the Lapa, several people came to shake his hand and thank him again.

Naomi stepped away from Luca to allow more people near him. Instead, she watched as Auntie Elsa and Stefan had their picture taken. That's when she noticed the expression on Stefan's face. Although he was smiling at the camera, it looked more like a grimace as his eyes narrowed and his smile looked like it was stuck. He seemed displeased by all the attention heaped on Luca. Again, Naomi got a weird feeling about him. But moments later, he was his jovial self and came to stand next to Luca, basking in his limelight.

Khwai and some guards appeared near the swimming pool. They were there to collect the guests who were going on a walking safari with them. Stefan, seeing this, joined the walking safari. As he disappeared around the corner, everyone let out a collective, and rather loud, sigh of relief.

Surprised by their reactions, everyone burst out laughing.

SEVENTEEN

A calm tranquility had settled over the lodge.

Most of the guests were away on the walking safari, or out with one of the desert guides. Some were sitting, talking, or reading in the shade of the Lapa or their rooms. Several sun-lovers were lying on sun loungers or swimming serious laps in the pool for that time of the day.

Naomi was helping Kerri. The dining room was to be the setting for her meeting about the dune buggies with Luca and Santina. But to maximize their time, it was also the last lunch before the Italians had to leave in the afternoon.

The staff had dragged four tables together to form a larger one and set the table for lunch. Auntie Elsa had arranged for a special last meal for her favorite guests and was fussing in the kitchen, no doubt to the annoyance of Chef. Kerri and Naomi had prepared bound documents for each of the five participants, and small notebooks and pens for everyone. A large whiteboard stood at one end of the table. Marker pens lay nearby.

Kerri rechecked her watch.

"Are we ready? Did I forget anything? They know to come here, don't they? Where are they anyway?"

Naomi looked at the oversized clock on the wall. Its chimes were imminent as the minute hand climbed to join the hour hand at one o'clock.

"I'm sure they'll be here any minute now. Don't worry. You've already sold it to them. This is just logistics. And you're good at that."

Naomi went to stand beside Kerri. She put her arm around her friend and gave Kerri an encouraging squeeze.

"Just remember to breathe. You'll be fine."

Kerri patted Naomi's hand on her shoulder.

"Thanks, hun. I'm so grateful you're doing this with me. It's my big chance, you know?"

The large brown eyes she turned on Naomi held a mixture of doubt, fire and hope.

Naomi nodded and smiled at her friend.

"And I'll be right beside you. You'll do just great. I believe in you."

As the clock chimed, Auntie Elsa led her guests into the dining room.

Luca smiled at Naomi as he walked toward the table. Her heart fluttered. She returned what she hoped was a professional smile.

Kerri stepped forward at once. An uncharacteristically shy grin played around her mouth. Her eyes traveled over everyone.

"Thank you so much for giving me this opportunity. Would you like to take your seats?"

Kerri pulled out a chair and indicated for Santina to sit facing the window.

Santina's smile, directed at Kerri, betrayed her excitement.

"This all looks wonderful, thank you, Kerri."

Naomi thought it brilliant of Kerri to seat Luca at the top of the table. This way, he was sitting opposite Kerri. It was the perfect place for him to be when Kerri delivered her presentation. Naomi also realized it was Kerri's way of acknowledging that Luca was leading the project.

Kerri might be full of madcap ideas, but when it came down to it, she was creative and flexible, yet single-minded. Her meticulous attention to detail and her formidable powers of organization complemented her outgoing personality that drew people to her upon meeting her. She made people feel safe, and as though she could handle any challenge.

Naomi didn't doubt Kerri would make a formidable manager for Desert Lodge. No matter what else went on in her life, Kerri had the enviable ability to focus on something when it was most needed. It was a gift not only for Kerri but also for Desert Lodge. Naomi always thought they were lucky to have Kerri working with them. Now, Auntie Elsa would have the perfect opportunity to see for herself what an ideal manager Kerri would be for Desert Lodge. Promoting Kerri could only be in their best interests.

Naomi sat down and crossed her fingers for her friend under the table.

Kerri waited until everyone had taken their seat before walking over to the whiteboard.

"Shall we begin?"

She took their silent nods as consent and rang a bell. Moments later, waiters appeared with food and drinks. While the waiters served lunch, Kerri wrote some figures on the whiteboard.

Satisfied that everyone had what they wanted for lunch, Kerri continued.

"I know you're leaving this afternoon, Luca and Santina. So, I'll keep this as brief as I can."

Naomi knew her friend well and could see how nervous Kerri was. But she also knew that no one else would see it.

Kerri was a masterful communicator and used that talent

alongside her discipline to run the administrative and house-keeping departments at the lodge most efficiently.

Naomi smiled and winked at Kerri in encouragement. It seemed to have the desired effect.

Kerri relaxed, and her brilliant smile returned.

"I'm grateful for this opportunity, and I'm more than happy to run all the logistics on this side."

Kerri looked to see if Auntie Elsa was in agreement before she continued.

"But since Naomi is our head desert guide, and she knows the desert like the back of her hand, I feel she should be our liaison with you in Italy. Naomi could tell you much more about the desert conditions and what would be required from the buggies than I could. Would that work?"

Again, Kerri glanced around the room for agreement from the others.

Luca looked pleased and nodded as he lifted a forkful of rice to his mouth.

Since there weren't any objections, Kerri continued.

Naomi tuned out Kerri's voice. She wasn't sure how to feel about liaising with Luca directly. Would contact with him not sustain and prolong the pain in her heart? But who else could do it, if not her? What about Gerhard? Maybe she could have a word with him?

The sound of Kerri and Luca's voices penetrated her aware-ness as they discussed some finer points of their agreement.

No, she must stop thinking of her own feelings. Her friend needed her. Auntie Elsa needed her. Desert Lodge needed her, needed this deal. She could be professional about this, couldn't she? These people, this place meant so much to her. Surely, it would be a sacrifice worth making.

The lunch meeting was over.

Naomi sighed.

How could an hour and a half fly by so soon?

The inevitability of their upcoming parting seemed to weigh on them all. Luca and Santina had both become important to Desert Lodge, even before the buggy deal. But now, Naomi sensed, it had sealed their fates.

She found it difficult to tear her eyes away from Luca as he talked with Kerri and Auntie Elsa. Although he seemed excited about the deal, a shadow had crept into his energy. It was the same shadow Naomi had felt in her body, the shadow that parting with loved ones always produced. But in Luca's case, maybe she only imagined it? She needed him to feel what she was feeling. Or did she?

With a smile and wave at her, Luca took long strides from the room on his way to check the jet for their return journey to Windhoek. Auntie Elsa left with Santina to help her finish packing, but clearly, the two friends just wanted to spend more time together.

Alone, Kerri and Naomi looked at each other. The dining room was suddenly quiet.

Both sighed in unison, then, laughed.

Kerri flopped down on the nearest chair.

"Wow, that was hairy. But I did okay, didn't I? We got the deal."

Naomi went to stand behind Kerri and put her arms around her friend, nuzzling her cheek against Kerri's.

"You did more than okay. I knew you'd do it, though. Congrats. We must celebrate later."

She let go of Kerri and went to sit opposite her, instead.

Kerri leaned forward, her eyes glittering even more than before.

"That's a great idea! I'll get some champagne to the Lapa before Luca and Santina leave."

Naomi held up a hand.

"Not so fast. Luca will be flying. He can't have any alcohol. You'd need to get him a soft drink or some mineral water. But yes, that would be lovely. A toast to our buggy future."

"Yes, and a toast to our future with Armati. Hopefully, now Auntie Elsa will be open to offering me the job as the manager, don't you think?"

Naomi knew Kerri was impatient to speak with Auntie Elsa.

"I'm sure. But just wait a day or two. Don't rush in there. You know she doesn't like change. And this would be a biggie for her. Even though we've never had an official manager before, she was always kind of the manager. So, she'd have to get used to the idea that someone else will do her job. And because she's preoccupied at the moment with Santina leaving, I'd wait a few days if I were you."

Kerri seemed to be turning Naomi's words over in her mind. But she couldn't contain her excitement about the possibility of her dream coming true.

Unable to sit still any longer, she got up.

Her smile lit up the room as she regarded her friend.

"You're right. I'll wait, and I'll make my proposal even better, so when I have my meeting with Auntie Elsa, she'll welcome the changes I'll propose. Thanks, Naomi, hun. You're so wise."

Kerri glanced around the room, at the whiteboard, the table with the remnants of their lunch, and crumpled pieces of paper here and there.

"Well, let's get all this cleared up. We can't allow anyone else to see our deals and figures. The staff can clear the lunch things later."

Kerri picked up the discarded pieces of paper while Naomi went to wipe their secrets from the whiteboard.

Naomi was aware that everything felt surreal. That Luca

had been here at all was beginning to feel like a dream. He was the man of her dreams.

As she was wiping the board, her eyes fell on the word, 'Armati,' that Kerri had encircled. Their deal with Armati sounded far-fetched to her rational mind.

She spoke without turning around, knowing Kerri was somewhere behind her and that they were still alone in the room.

"I must say, I'm astonished that no one else had ever approached Armati with a dune buggy idea like this. I was just thinking about the Middle-East and all those oil princes with their Armatis. They live near a desert. I'm sure they have dune races there, right?"

Kerri's voice came muffled as she was collecting paper from under the table.

"Yes, I've been thinking about that. I wondered why no one has ever approached them. Or maybe they had, but had been turned down? Perhaps Luca has only accepted our deal because of you."

"I don't believe that's true. No, this is a business deal. It has nothing to do with me. Why would you even say that? Yes, we spent some time together, but only because Auntie Elsa appointed me to look after him and Santina. I can't deny we got on well, but Luca is a businessman, and I'm sure for him, business is business. He's the Armati prince and heir apparent.

"Did I tell you how people surrounded us to gawk at the Armati the night we went for dinner in Windhoek? I'm sure he's surrounded by gorgeous women wherever he goes. With his lifestyle and money, he can give them anything they want..."

Naomi turned around at the sounds of Kerri banging her head on the table as she got up and cursed.

"Are you- Oh, Luca?"

Luca was standing in the doorway. But he may as well have

been standing on another planet, he seemed so distant. The look on his face was unreadable and serious.

Naomi realized he may have overheard her, and how wrong her words may have sounded to him.

"How long have you been standing there?"

"Long enough."

His eyes pierced Naomi's.

"I was going to ask you something, but since your duties regarding Santina and me are almost at an end..."

Kerri, sensing the change in atmosphere and eager that her friend's happiness and the success of their project not be jeopardized, she tried to come to the rescue.

"Luca, I'm sure Naomi didn't mean to upset you. Yes, Auntie Elsa appointed her to look after you and Santina. But you must know by now that you two have become friends if nothing else?"

Luca contemplated Kerri for a moment before his eyes returned to Naomi.

"I thought we were at least friends, si."

Naomi walked toward him.

"We are Luca. We're-"

But Luca had heard what he'd heard. Naomi's words had been like a punch to his stomach. He couldn't believe he'd been so wrong about her.

In his mind's eye, he experienced again all the wonderful times with her, swimming, sunrise and sunset safaris, finding and rescuing the ellie, laughing, flirting, the easiness of being with her, her willingness to put up with his most outrageous requests like the foot massage, her soft femininity and how eagerly she'd responded to his kisses.

He'd felt as though he'd found his soul mate in Naomi. Here was this beautiful, unspoiled, kind, strong woman - his perfect match.

How could he have been so wrong about her? Was it all in the line of duty for her? And those words... 'with his lifestyle and money...' How often had he heard those words? How often had those words led to rejection, pain and loneliness? Here they were again, just when he'd thought he'd conquered his demons, when he'd finally been brave enough to open his heart. But now, it felt as though an icy hand had seized his heart and was squeezing it tighter and tighter.

He had to get out. He had to get some air.

Luca waved a hand dismissing anything else Naomi might say and turned to leave.

Kerri went to him at once, taking his arm. Trying to douse the flames of the lurking friction, Kerri spoke with forced excitement, telling him about the small celebratory drinks in the Lapa.

As he followed Kerri from the room, his eyes flitted in Naomi's direction, but there was no warmth in them.

THE SMALL DRINKS party felt tense rather than congratulatory.

Naomi stood with Auntie Elsa and Santina. She was only half-listening to them, but their enthusiastic voices penetrated her brain. She knew they were talking about their upcoming birthday celebrations, but her mind was on Luca.

He stood off to the side with Kerri and Stefan at his side, who had gate-crashed the party when he saw the champagne. Luca's body seemed stiff as he stared off into the distance while Kerri and Stefan continued talking to him and each other.

Naomi couldn't understand it. He felt like a stranger. This Luca wasn't the man who'd held her in his arms, who'd kissed her, who'd laughed and flirted with her. But maybe this was the real Luca? Maybe he was reverting to his usual self now he'd finished his vacation? No wonder Santina had had to force him to have a break.

The sudden change in him made no sense. So, okay, he'd overheard her speaking with Kerri, but she couldn't understand what she could have said that would have had this impact on him.

The reassuring sounds of the other guests around them pulled Naomi back to reality. But she couldn't look away from Luca, even though he pretended to be unaware of her presence.

She saw him glancing at his watch and with a small, tight smile at Kerri and Stefan, excused himself as he walked over to Santina. He put a hand on Santina's back, alerting her it was time for them to leave.

Santina and Auntie Elsa led the way around the building to the jet, walking arm in arm, talking and patting each other's hands on their arms.

Naomi followed, dawdling, not wanting to be there. She knew Luca, Stefan and Kerri were behind her. She could hear snippets of their conversation here and there. It was just small talk from Kerri and Stefan. Luca remained uncharacteristically quiet.

As they neared the jet, parked on the runway ready for take-off, Khwai and the other members of the anti-poacher unit arrived to say goodbye to Luca. He seemed touched by their gesture, and for a few moments, he was once again the Luca Naomi knew. He spent time with each of the guards, shaking their hands and hugging them.

Khwai seemed almost tearful as he gave Luca a last hug and an elongated African handshake. Then Luca came over to Auntie Elsa and Santina. He kissed Auntie Elsa on both cheeks before turning to Kerri to do the same. He shook Stefan's hand, almost formally, wishing him a wonderful vacation at Desert Lodge.

But when he came to Naomi, she saw him becoming the distant stranger again. A quick, cold peck on each of her cheeks and avoiding looking into her eyes was her parting memory of Luca. It was such a different memory than the one she'd held of his arrival at Desert Lodge.

As she stood with the others, waving at the jet and its occupants, she could sympathize with the tears of the waitresses who'd been flung aside by some prince after their vacations here. She never imagined it would happen to her.

But she was grateful for Luca's sudden, unexplained coldness. It made it easier for her to say goodbye to him. If he'd been the Luca she'd come to know and love, it would have been absolute torture.

Naomi felt numb as she turned to follow Stefan, Kerri and Auntie Elsa back to the house. Auntie Elsa was sniffling into a tissue and wiping tears from her eyes. Kerri had a comforting arm around her, Kerri's taller size resulting in hugging Auntie Elsa to her.

Stefan, buoyed by the alcohol in his system, was ready to party more. His alcohol-fueled breath brushed over Naomi as he tried to get her to join him.

EIGHTEEN

Naomi didn't want to be rude to Stefan, but she couldn't face him or any of the other guests at the moment. She needed the sanctuary of her room, even if only for an hour.

She tried to extricate herself from his arm around her shoulders, intending to let him down gently about not joining him in a drink-fueled party. But the big man would have none of it. His voice became louder and more insistent.

Auntie Elsa and Kerri, hearing the commotion behind them, turned around just in time to see Naomi trying to push Stefan away from her.

Both women took a step toward Naomi.

All traces of her sadness gone, Auntie Elsa raised her voice.

"Stefan. Please stop. Naomi has work to do now. You must let her go."

But Stefan only grinned at Auntie Elsa and tightened his grip on Naomi.

He stuck out his chin in defiance, his voice slurring as he became even more insistent.

"I'll pay for her time. I can pay for her."

Auntie Elsa's eyes narrowed.

"That is not how we do things here, young man. This is a decent lodge. I don't know what you're used to, but–"

"But what? What can you do? As far as I can see, only you women are here. You have no authority over me. I will have what I want. And I want to know what Luca found so interesting about this one. I want to party with Luca's whore."

Naomi couldn't believe her ears. Her anger and humiliation spurred her on. She shoved at Stefan's iron arm around her using all her strength. But even though Stefan was much drunker than anyone had realized, the force with which he held her, was overwhelming. She couldn't escape him. By now, she was panting from the exertion, sweating, her hair in total disarray.

The state of her seemed to spur him on even more. He laughed and pulled her off her feet, threatening to throw her over his shoulder.

Naomi kicked hard but missed connecting with him.

It made Stefan laugh even louder.

"I see! Feisty kitty. That's what Luca liked, is it? Let's see how feisty you really are."

Stefan dropped the empty Hansa beer bottle he had in his other hand and heaved Naomi over his shoulder, using both hands to hold her down.

Naomi screamed.

"Let me go! Let me go!"

She pounded her fists on his back, but it was like steel - hard and inflexible. He appeared not to notice her efforts and ignored her protestations.

Auntie Elsa stepped in front of Stefan and grabbed his chin in her hands. As she was so much shorter than him, she forced him to look down into her eyes.

Her voice was firm and authoritative.

"I said, let her go. Now!"

For a moment, Stefan looked as though someone had slapped him, and he might come to his senses. Then he threw back his head. He laughed long before shaking Auntie Elsa off.

He took big, determined strides past her. Naomi's torso and head bounced on his brutal hard-muscled back.

Just as they reached the corner, Naomi heard the unmistakable sound of rifles being cocked. Through the curtain of her hair hanging over her eyes, she glimpsed the upside-down camouflaged trousers and scuffed desert boots of members of the anti-poacher unit.

Auntie Elsa's voice came again, firm and unafraid.

"Stefan. Put Naomi down this instant."

But Stefan just laughed again.

"Oh, this is getting better and better. A bunch of monkeys with pretend weapons? Let's see how that pans out, shall we?"

Naomi spotted Kerri's long legs among the camouflaged trousers that encircled Stefan. She knew what had happened. While Auntie Elsa had kept Stefan's attention on her, Kerri had gone to get the anti-poacher unit. They couldn't have been far after seeing off Luca and Santina.

Naomi breathed a sigh of relief for the first time since her ordeal with Stefan began.

Auntie Elsa addressed Khwai.

"Khwai..."

A single shot pinged. It kicked up the dirt near Stefan's sandal-clad foot. The ground was hard here, the earth compacted by truck tires over many rain-deprived years.

Stefan almost lost his balance as he jumped back.

"Hey! That's real ammo. Watch what you're doing."

Auntie Elsa stepped forward again.

"Let go of Naomi."

The seriousness of the situation appeared to penetrate Stefan's alcohol addled brain. But instead of putting Naomi down, he shoved her off his shoulder. Stefan stood at a solid six foot six inches, and Naomi tumbled to the hard earth at speed.

She tried to break her fall by putting out her arms. It happened so fast that no one could help her. She hit the ground with a sickening thud and a loud yelp.

The moment Stefan let her go, members of the anti-poacher unit swarmed him, pinned him to the ground and cuffed his hands behind his back. But they had their hands full as Stefan refused to give in without a fight. He was a big man, and the Herero and Khoisan men were slight by comparison, but tough. They struggled with Stefan, who kicked and head-butted anyone who came near enough. But when he tried to bite them, Khwai shoved a rag into his mouth and shackled his legs.

Meanwhile, Auntie Elsa and Kerri rushed to help Naomi up. She clutched her right wrist, which took the brunt of the impact. Her knees were bleeding, and the side of her face had connected with a stone when she fell.

Naomi felt as though she was in an alternate reality. What the hell happened? First, Luca turned into an ice statue before he left, and then this ridiculous situation with Stefan.

Tears burned behind her eyes, but not because she was feeling pitiful. She realized she was more than furious.

Before anyone could stop her, she walked over to where Stefan was still wriggling on the ground and kicked him hard.

Despite the rag in his mouth, he cried out when her boot connected with his arm.

"Ouch! That hurt! I'll get you, bitch! You hear me!"

Naomi walked away as fast as she could before the urge to kick him again overtook her.

She couldn't refrain from mumbling as she went, her jaw and left fist clenched.

"Bloody bully. Bloody coward."

All of a sudden, everyone was there. Staff members came

running toward them. More anti-poacher guards appeared like the ghosts of heat shimmers over the desert.

Kerri put a protective arm around Naomi while Auntie Elsa held up Naomi's wrist, scrutinizing it.

"Darling, Kerri has called the doctor. Let's get you inside and cleaned up. I'm so sorry, Naomi, that you had to go through this. I'll let the police deal with Stefan later."

Naomi was still too angry and feeling too out of it to respond, but she nodded, feeling a massive headache threatening as she did so.

Kerri was on her other side. She lifted Naomi's hair back from her face and tucked the strands behind her ear.

"I've called the police already. Johan will be here soon. Are you okay, hun?"

Again, Naomi nodded, slower this time, lest her headache got worse.

Auntie Elsa and Kerri helped Naomi into the kitchen. The kitchen staff, in a huddle at the door, shocked into silence, parted like the sands in a storm to let her through, concern for her clear in their eyes.

Satisfied his men had things under control outside, Khwai followed them into the kitchen. He got some tea towels from Chef and made a sling for Naomi to support her wrist while they waited for the doctor to arrive.

Chef pulled out a chair for Naomi and handed her a mug of hot sweet tea for the shock.

Naomi took a few sips of the tea and put the mug on the table in front of her. As she sighed, she felt the tension leave her body.

She leaned back in the chair and contemplated the worried faces around her.

"Well, that was a first. I thought I'd seen every prince under the sun. But this is the first time I've come across one that's completely crazy, and not in a good way."

Smiles and titters from those around her told Naomi they appreciated her attempt at lightening the gravity of the situation.

Naomi took her tea and got up.

Kerri went to her friend's side at once.

"Come on, hun, let's get you cleaned up. You'll feel better. I think you need to lie down, don't you?"

Naomi nodded again and grimaced. Her head felt like it wanted to explode.

Auntie Elsa saw her reaction.

"I'll get you some painkillers. Where does it hurt?"

"Everywhere. But yes, painkillers would be very welcome, thanks. I have the worst headache I think I've ever experienced."

Auntie Elsa's face was white with concern.

"That was quite a distance you fell. You may have a slight concussion. We won't know until the doctor gets here. So, yes, I agree with Kerri. Let's get you cleaned up and lying down."

Auntie Elsa and Kerri maneuvered themselves on either side of Naomi. They supported her and walked at her pace down the long corridor to her room.

Naomi inclined her head to look at Auntie Elsa.

"What will happen to Stefan?"

Auntie Elsa's lips stretched thin over her mouth.

"I'll have to leave that up to the police. But I hope he gets what he deserves. He can be jolly glad I'm not the one doling out punishments. I cannot believe what's happened. I've lived here all my life. I've worked here all my life, and I've never, ever experienced anything like it."

She stretched around Naomi to address Kerri.

"We have to put something in place to prevent anything like

this from happening again. It will have to go on all our marketing and must be repeated to each of our guests at the time of their check-in. That will be your first task. It takes priority as the new manager of Desert Lodge, Kerri."

For a moment, there was complete silence. Then Kerri gasped.

"You mean...?"

"Yes, Kerri. I'm sorry... I meant to have a more formal conversation about this, but with so much going on, there just wasn't the time. I was more than impressed with your presentation to Luca and Santina. I know you'll be a formidable manager for Desert Lodge. And I'd be grateful and honored if you'd accept the position. We can do all the formal things and sign your new contract tomorrow when we can discuss your benefits."

Naomi and Kerri spoke together.

"Oh, thank you, Auntie Elsa."

The young women giggled at their synchronicity.

Naomi's head threatened to knock her to the floor with the sudden pain that shot across her eyes. She slowed down more.

But Kerri smiled as though she'd never stop.

"It means the world, thank you, Auntie Elsa. I won't let you down. I think the first thing would be to call Ilze at Solitaire. Stefan stayed with them for a week. It would be interesting to find out what their experience of him was. And if I discover something similar had happened there, and she didn't warn me...!"

Auntie Elsa nodded.

"Yes, I agree. It's a great idea. Maybe Ilze knows something more about him. Where did he say he was from again?"

Kerri talked past Naomi.

"I checked him out after our first heated telephone conversations. He's the owner and CEO of a very successful tech company in Silicon Valley. A company called Sawaski Tech. I called them and pretended I wanted to interview him for the BBC. They confirmed he is who he says he is. And Luca seemed to know about the company and about Stefan when I asked if he'd ever heard of either. Although he'd never met Stefan until now. Isn't it amazing that someone as successful as Stefan can behave like this? It makes me wonder if he's always like this. How do his employees deal with him?"

The three women continued to amble down the corridor, their silence showing each was running her recent experiences through her mind.

Naomi wanted to get away from the memory of Stefan. It was horrible the way he'd treated her like a piece of meat. But there was nothing she could have done to get away from him. Scared at first, then feeling frustrated, only anger now remained. At least it was better than feeling sad and confused about how Luca had left. She didn't want to think about Luca either, but knew it would be impossible.

A sigh escaped her as they reached her room. She'd much rather just forget about everything that had happened and concentrate on those people here with her now. Auntie Elsa and Kerri were the most important people in her life.

Out of the corner of her eye, she could see Kerri still carried a huge grin on her face. Kerri wasn't thinking about what had happened with Stefan.

Naomi pressed her shoulder into Kerri's to get her attention.

"I'm so glad your dream has come true, Kerri. I'm so happy for you."

Then, she turned her head to look at Auntie Elsa.

"Thank you again, Auntie Elsa, for giving Kerri this chance. I know my friend will be the best manager you've ever seen."

Both women were smiling at her.

Naomi sighed again, and extracting her arm from Kerri's, put her hand on the doorknob, eager to get inside her room.

"I don't think I've ever longed for a shower more. I need the water to wash away every spot where Stefan touched me. And I hope neither of you mind, but I need time just to feel safe again. I can't remember ever feeling so violated. I can't handle any more shocks today, that's for sure."

But as Naomi opened her door, another shock awaited her.

On her bed lay the large painting of ellie Naomi Luca had painted. None of them had suspected he was such a talented artist. He'd captured the ellie exquisitely. Her little trunk was curled up, and her eyes shone with such hope, it broke Naomi's heart. The baby elephant looked as though she was smiling at Naomi.

Naomi's hand went to her mouth, and tears streamed down her cheeks.

Why had Luca left the painting here?

NINETEEN

Auntie Elsa and Kerri had been fantastic. They'd waited in Naomi's room until she'd finished her shower to make sure she felt safe.

She'd asked Kerri to close the windows and pull the blinds down halfway. She'd wanted as much privacy as possible.

Kerri had positioned the fan, so Naomi would be cool enough and comfortable. Like a saint, Kerri had brought ice in a tea towel for the swelling on Naomi's cheek, and fresh iced water and more hot sweet tea.

Meanwhile, Auntie Elsa had nursed Naomi's lacerated knees and made sure no small bits of dirt remained in the wounds. Then Naomi's guardian angels had left, closing the door behind them.

Naomi leaned back onto her pillows.

Alone, at last, ensconced in safe silence, she sighed. As she expelled the air from her lungs, it cleared the anger she'd held on to so tightly. Without it, sudden sobs wracked her body as she gave vent to her feelings... feelings of fear and frustration about what had happened with Stefan, mixed with the fear and confusion about Luca's strange behavior toward her when he'd left. Beneath those emotions was the fear that she'd lost him, even though she had decided she couldn't be with him.

But soon, it became clear that crying was a terrible idea. Each sob brought a new stab of excruciating pain that pounded her head relentlessly, reminiscent of the blistering sun as it struck the dry, cracked desert floor ceaselessly.

As Naomi stopped crying, an awareness of extreme nausea almost overcame her. Moving fast was out of the question. She just made it to the toilet bowl before everything she'd had that day came rushing out. Again, the sharp stabbing pain in her head almost blinded her, but she stayed put until she was sure everything that wanted to exit was out. Then, as carefully as she could, she crawled back to bed.

The chill slate floor beneath her felt good but was brutal on her sore knees. It took tremendous effort to pull herself up onto the bed.

She sank back against her pillows, just as someone knocked on her door. It wasn't a loud knock, but it may as well have been the deafening trumpeting of a bull elephant right next to her, the sound was so loud to her ears.

She didn't have the energy to respond, and moaned, instead.

Auntie Elsa's soothing soft voice ushered into the room the same young doctor who'd treated Luca. He was gentle, and Naomi appreciated more than anything, his cool hands on her face as he examined her.

"You definitely have a concussion. It doesn't seem severe at this stage and will most likely be gone in two or three days, but I feel it's better that we book you into the hospital to keep an eye on you. I can fly you there right now."

Naomi couldn't face leaving her room.

A sudden panic threatened to overwhelm her.

"No, please, I -"

But Auntie Elsa came to her rescue.

After many reassurances from Auntie Elsa and much humming and hawing from the doctor, he gave in and allowed Naomi to stay at Desert Lodge. With a diagnosis of concussion and a badly sprained wrist, he gave stronger painkillers and instructions that Naomi be awakened every three hours to make sure she wasn't getting any worse.

Naomi welcomed the silence once again, as her bedroom door closed behind Auntie Elsa and the doctor.

Despite feeling a bone-penetrating exhaustion, as though she hadn't slept for an entire month, Naomi knew she would recover physically. Her extreme tiredness was merely a symptom of her recent adrenaline dump.

Healing her thoughts and emotions was another matter altogether, however.

But despite her concerns, her eyelids grew heavier with each breath. When she could no longer fight it, she gave herself over to blissful sleep.

Too soon, she heard her name. Gentle pressure on her shoulder brought her back to reality.

Concern shone from big brown eyes looking into hers.

Naomi struggled to focus on the figure standing over her, but knew it had to be Kerri from the soft scent surrounding the person.

Was the immediate hammering headache the result of nausea, or was it the other way around? She couldn't tell.

"Naomi, hun, wake up."

When Kerri saw Naomi was awake, she added sheepishly, "The doctor said we had to wake you up regularly."

Naomi yawned and nodded, taking extreme care not to move too fast.

"Yes, I heard him telling Auntie Elsa. What time is it?"

"You did well. It's almost nine o'clock."

Someone had pulled the blinds over the windows all the

way down. Naomi realized Kerri meant nine o'clock at night. She sat up slowly. Kerri fluffed her pillows so Naomi was more comfortable.

"What's happened to Stefan?"

Kerri was just about to sit down on the bed next to Naomi, but at the question, she paced back and forth across the large room as she spoke, almost as though her words fuelled her movements.

"Johan arrived before the police got here. Can you believe that Stefan wanted to deny everything when Johan asked him what he thought he was doing? I've never been so mad in my life. He may be huge, he may be rich, he may be a bully, but I've never seen such a bloody coward. Johan didn't fall for his pathetic excuses. He gave Stefan a piece of his mind on how to treat and respect women. Stefan looked like he was going to cry when Johan asked how he would feel if some guy treated his sister in the same way he'd treated you.

I can't believe we allowed him such hospitality. He joined in our activities, for Pete's sake, and got to know us, and then did something so incomprehensible.

Johan was furious. As you know, the former Senior Superintendent, Nick, is Johan's cousin. He arrived with the police when they took statements from all of us, and will come to have a word with you tomorrow as well if you're up for it then?"

Naomi gave a thumbs-up, both in consent and as a sign for Kerri to go on.

But Kerri didn't seem to need any encouragement as she continued her tirade.

"Well, anyway... I've never seen such a miserable excuse for a human being. I wonder if he behaved that way because he's on vacation. You know we get all sorts here, and sometimes people behave uncharacteristically when they're on vacation. I've never understood it, but they do, don't they behave in ways they'd never do at home? But it says something about the man's character, doesn't it? It's true what Johan said, though. I bet he wouldn't like it if someone had treated his sister like that. I wonder if his mother knows her son behaves like this towards women. I'm sure she'd be appalled. I know he's American, but his surname is Sawaski. That sounds Polish, or at least Eastern European, doesn't it? Those cultures, as far as I know, don't tolerate this kind of behavior. They're usually very strict. I wonder if it's because he's so wealthy that he feels he's invincible, somehow."

Kerri stopped talking for a moment, before making a gesture as if to swat away a fly.

She sounded calmer when she spoke again.

"Anyway, the police have taken him away. They'll fly him to Windhoek tomorrow, as I understand it."

Kerri didn't need Naomi to respond. Both understood it.

Naomi's headache had subsided a little, and with it, the nausea had disappeared somewhat. But she still felt heavy with exhaustion, her mind slow to take in everything Kerri was saying, much less able to respond.

Kerri continued as though she could read Naomi's mind and knew her friend didn't want to talk.

"I'm just so grateful none of the other guests saw or heard anything. It would be challenging to rectify such a PR disaster. Not something I'd want to deal with in my first weeks as Manager."

Kerri came to sit next to Naomi, her eyes glittering with excitement.

"Can you believe it? I've done it. I'm the Manager of Desert Lodge. To be honest, I didn't think Auntie Elsa would ever promote me. And I never even pitched for the position. Well, indirectly, I suppose I did when I pitched to Luca. But I'm so grateful she trusts me. I have loads of ideas to make

Desert Lodge the most sought-after destination in all of Namibia."

Naomi couldn't help smiling at her friend's excitement and enthusiasm, but she still felt so tired. It was difficult to stay focused on what Kerri was saying.

Kerri seemed to read Naomi's mind and touched her friend's hand.

"Once you're better, we'll celebrate. Do you need anything? Are you hungry?"

Naomi checked in with herself. Apart from needing the loo, water, and more painkillers, she just wanted to go back to sleep.

After Kerri had helped her to the bathroom, brought fresh water from the kitchen, and closed the door behind her as she left, Naomi sank back into her pillows once again.

At Naomi's request, Kerri had pulled up the blinds and opened the windows. Soft night sounds, carried on a light desert breeze, floated through her room. Comforting sun-warmed scents of the geraniums in the window boxes wafted toward her through the mosquito nets over the windows. All was right in her world, again. Well, almost. There was Luca...

Just as she put her hand out to switch off her bedside lamp, she noticed the painting. Kerri had placed Luca's picture of ellie Naomi on a chair opposite Naomi's bed. The painting confused Naomi. Luca confused her. Luca must have given it to her before he became the Iceman. She couldn't imagine that cold stranger giving her anything as beautiful. But why? The painting was stunning. He could have sold it. But then again, he didn't need the money, did he? Perhaps taking it with him would have been too much of a reminder of her? Leaving it here would kill two birds with one stone, and put it, and her, out of his mind, wouldn't it?

A theory had been lurking at the edge of her mind. Now that Luca was uppermost in her thoughts again, the theory made itself known. She didn't like it but had to consider it. Perhaps underneath all that suaveness and charisma, alongside the ice, lurked a creature not dissimilar to Stefan? Did privilege and extreme wealth produce the character with which Naomi simply could not identify? Stefan had fooled her, why not Luca as well? These princes lived in a world she couldn't even imagine, and after her ordeal with Stefan, she couldn't imagine anything more distasteful.

What did she really know about Luca, after all? If it was true that Luca was more like Stefan than she'd suspected, banishing him from her heart would be easier, wouldn't it?

LUCA SAT BACK in his chair. A long, angry breath escaped his lips. His head was reeling. A maelstrom of emotions fought for supremacy in his chest as he tried to digest what Santina had just told him.

She'd been in touch with Auntie Elsa at Desert Lodge to discuss some or other detail of their upcoming joint birthday party. A distraught Auntie Elsa had broken down and cried over the phone at the sound of her friend's voice.

Minutes later, Santina was shocked into a low rage at hearing the incredible news of what Stefan had done to Naomi. She knew Luca would still be in his office, even at this time of the night. The brevity of their conversation belied the enormity of what she'd told him.

He ran a hand through his hair. There was no way he could continue working now. In his mind, he was already with Naomi.

Santina was right about Stefan, though. Someone had to do something. The man couldn't be allowed to get away with such behavior. Not toward Naomi. Luca wouldn't stand for it. But with how they'd parted, he was glad the buggy deal with Desert Lodge afforded him the excuse to go there now.

The image of Stefan's hands on Naomi made him see red. Would it have been different had he not been so deeply, madly, crazy in love with her?

Luca had never been so sure of his feelings for anyone before. Stefan would feel the full weight of Luca's wrath.

Luca suspected the depth of his anger had much to do with the fact that he felt guilty, as though it was his fault, somehow.

It didn't take long to realize Stefan was jealous of him. Luca was used to it. It was a fact of life he'd lived with since he could remember. There was always someone or other who felt moved to act on their jealousy, and Stefan was no exception. That Stefan would direct his resentment of Luca at Naomi was not only unexpected but unthinkable.

But a more profound emotion lurked. One Luca hadn't felt for a long time, not since his mother had left when he was a child. The sense of shame that washed over him as he contemplated the possibility Naomi might view him in the same light as Stefan was very uncomfortable. Luca couldn't bear the thought Naomi would tar him with the same brush as Stefan. But he realized she might do so because of the similarities as far as their financial status and privileged upbringing were concerned. She'd only known him for a week, and he'd behaved appallingly toward her before returning to Italy. He'd jumped to conclusions about her words in the guest lounge and not given her a chance to explain what he'd overheard.

His thoughts of Naomi had consumed him. He knew he'd not been wrong about her, about her goodness, her kindness, her strength, her purity. She was his perfect soulmate, and yet... he couldn't un-hear the words she'd spoken. '... Auntie Elsa appointed me to look after him and Santina,' and '... with his lifestyle and money, he could give women anything they wanted.'

Those words coming from her lips had brought all his fears to the fore, and the wound it made in his heart wouldn't stop bleeding. He'd heard that last phrase so often from women who'd wanted to be with him only for their own agendas and not because they loved him. He didn't care about them, yet it still hurt not being wanted for who he was, but for the wealth he could give them. His heart didn't want to believe it of Naomi, but his head wouldn't deny what his ears had heard.

Now there was some distance between that day and this, he wondered if what he'd heard was actually what she'd said. He was willing to consent there might have been a part of the conversation he'd missed that would make her words make sense. He'd wanted to believe so badly that the Naomi he got to know and love was still his Naomi. He'd wanted to believe that Naomi loved him as he loved her, that his depth of feelings had found its equal in hers.

He shook his head. Whatever she felt for him, he knew he loved her more than life itself, and he wouldn't allow someone like Stefan to hurt her. It was the least he could do. He wouldn't let Naomi face Stefan alone again should the man be stupid enough to return to Desert Lodge once he was free. Luca knew no African jail could keep Stefan for long, and he didn't underestimate Stefan. The man was dangerous, Luca now knew. He'd met Stefan's kind before. They always played dirty.

He picked up the phone.

After an hour of phone calls, Luca sat back, a smile tugging at his lips. The private jet that would take him to Windhoek would be ready in an hour. He had to get out of the office and pack a few things.

Satisfaction about the information he'd gathered about Stefan, stretched his smile into a wide grin. Stefan didn't know who he was dealing with. Luca had the perfect plan for avenging Naomi. He would have to be subtle about it, though. They could trace nothing back to him, or to Naomi. He intended to stop Stefan in his tracks, to teach him a lesson, if not humility. Luca was under no illusions that this would not have been the first time Stefan did something so despicable to a woman.

Well, this time, he'd picked on the wrong woman.

A frown appeared between Luca's dark eyes as he got up from his chair. He gathered his jacket and briefcase. He was eager to get to Naomi, to protect her, to love her. Time to go.

———

THE DREAM'S grip held tight, paralyzing Naomi, even as she knew she was dreaming. She was falling, falling... But instead of hitting the ground, the vortex of a vast, noisy sandstorm gripped her in its vice. She could feel her hair flying around her head, her nightdress ripped by the ferocious storm. Her consciousness floated higher as a sudden silence penetrated her senses.

Doors were banging, and soft, urgent voices spoke from somewhere, fading as they moved away.

Moments later, black, deep, dreamless sleep welcomed her back. But within minutes, she heard her name and felt a gentle nudging at her shoulder. A hazy reality pulled at her consciousness.

A man's voice...

"Naomi, amore..."

Her eyes wouldn't focus in the dim light, but she could have sworn Luca was standing in front of her, Auntie Elsa and Kerri just behind him. Luca kneeled down and put his head on her chest, his arms going around her, holding her gently, but firmly.

She sighed.

It felt so good. It felt so real. Please let this not be a dream...

ON THE THIRD DAY, when Naomi opened her eyes to the early morning sun peeping through her windows, she felt herself again, at least in body. Her mind and spirit might take a little longer to recover.

The sharp rap on her door belonged to Kerri, who entered without waiting for Naomi's consent.

Kerri's energy and enthusiasm were palpable as she came to stand in front of Naomi's bed.

"Good morning. How's the patient this morning?"

She held out a steaming mug of rich aromatic coffee toward Naomi.

"You look so much better, hun. Do you feel like getting up today?"

Giving Kerry a thumbs-up, Naomi took the mug of coffee with her uninjured hand.

She took a sip before responding.

"Thanks for the coffee. Yes, I feel myself again. I'd like to get back to work. I never thought I'd say this, but I'm bored from all this resting."

Kerri's voice retreated while she went to open the shower for Naomi.

"That's great news, hun. I mean about you wanting to get up today. But should you be going back to work so soon? Is your wrist strong enough to handle the truck?"

Kerri came back into the bedroom and bent over Naomi, touching the side of her face.

"Have a look in the mirror. I think we could probably cover the bruise with makeup. But I'm not convinced that driving a bunch of guests out into the desert is the wisest thing to do. Not after spending three days in bed recovering, do you?"

Kerri inspected Naomi's wrist.

She winced at Kerri's touch.

It was clear that her still-swollen wrist was going to hamper any ideas of going back to work. She had to hold the mug of coffee in her left hand, instead.

But she smiled at her friend.

"Are you going to start bossing me around now you're the new manager?"

"What do you mean 'start...?' Haven't I always been bossing everyone around, including you?"

"You have a point. Well, don't just stand there... help me up."

Kerri grinned, happy to have her friend back.

"Now who's bossing who?"

Kerri helped Naomi to stand and then let her go to see if she could manage by herself.

"How's that? Is the headache still there? Do you still feel nauseous?"

Naomi checked in with herself. She moved her head from side to side, rolled her shoulders, lifted her arms above her head and tried to intertwine her fingers, meaning to have a good old stretch. But her wrist wouldn't play ball, and a loud moan escaped her lips as she lowered her arms again.

"Nope, good as rain."

Kerri laughed at Naomi's joke and made herself comfortable on an armchair near the bookcase as Naomi walked to the bathroom.

"What happened to the painting Luca left for you? I put it on a chair so you could look at it while deciding where to hang it. I can't see it anywhere."

Naomi's voice came muffled from within the shower.

"I put it in the wardrobe."

"Why?"

Naomi's response came after a lengthy pause.

"I didn't want to look at it."

"Why?"

"It reminds me of Luca."

And there it was, the proverbial elephant in the room. The issue that wouldn't go away, the problem Naomi didn't want to deal with, didn't want to discuss with anyone, not even with Kerri. Not yet, anyway.

Naomi shook her head at the irony that the painting was of an elephant. The elephant in the room, for real.

Kerri was very diplomatic, or she didn't think Naomi's response was as weird as it sounded to Naomi's ears.

She was grateful when Kerri didn't push it.

"Talking of Luca... he's beyond furious. He's sworn to sort Stefan out. But Stefan is a slippery character. When the police took him away that night, Nick was with them and he was doubtful about Stefan's prosecution here. That's why they took him to Windhoek the next day. But you know how it is... Stefan is American, rich, and this is Africa... There will always be corrupt bureaucrats happy to help someone like Stefan who can buy his way out of any challenging situation."

Naomi entered the bedroom, a towel around her body, another on her head covering her wet hair.

"So, Stefan's already free. Is that what you're saying?"

Kerri nodded, a worried look on her face as she contemplated her friend.

Naomi shuddered at the thought of having to confront Stefan again.

"Well, he won't be coming back here, will he?"

"Oh, no. All of Stefan's belongings went with him. There's nothing here for him. I've rented out his room already, anyway."

Naomi sighed.

There was something here for him. Her. What if he wanted to take his revenge for not getting what he'd wanted from her and for being thrown into an African jail?

But she didn't voice her fears and toweled dry her hair.

"Well, I guess that's it then. There's nothing more we can do. It makes me so mad he'll get away with it. But I guess life isn't fair."

Naomi knew all too well how unfair life could be. Not only would the trauma of her early youth live forever in her soul, but now meeting her soulmate in Luca had turned into a disaster from which she didn't know how to recover.

Kerri shifted in the chair, a huge grin on her face, her eyes sparkling, and her excitement unmistakable.

She tapped a knowing forefinger against her nose.

"You're right, hun. We might not be able to do anything more about it, but I would eat Luca's painting if he doesn't pursue it to a very satisfying end for us all."

Naomi contemplated her friend. Kerri was hiding something. She could tell.

"What do you mean, Luca will pursue things to a satisfying end? How do you know that?"

Kerri smiled.

"He's back. He'll tell you himself at breakfast."

TWENTY

Thoughts of Luca dominated Naomi's mind as she walked toward the Lapa to have breakfast with him, Auntie Elsa and Kerri.

She couldn't get her head around the idea that Luca was back at Desert Lodge. It wasn't a dream as she'd thought at first, and yet...

Naomi had the sense her body was doing one thing, while she was somewhere else. Was this what people referred to when they talked about an out-of-body experience? It felt that way.

Within moments, she'd see Luca again. Her heart sped up. Images of him flitted across her mind's eye. How could she forget his gorgeous chest, wet and glistening in the pool? Dressed in jeans and a t-shirt, she remembered his excitement as he took pictures of the desert and the animals. The night in the Lapa, when he presented the heart-wrenching video he'd edited about ellie Naomi. Another image stirred in her mind of him sitting across from her, his lush hair begging to be touched, his beautiful lips curled in a smile, his dark eyes penetrating her soul, his presence overwhelming her senses.

As she came around the corner, there he was, dazzling, his

black hair glinting blue in the sun. Sunglasses covered his eyes. He'd bowed his head over papers in his hand.

Naomi stopped.

She tried to convince her mind she was actually seeing him. That he was here. Her heart was pounding. She wondered if he could hear it.

Luca looked up then, as though he'd heard her thoughts. He removed his sunglasses, his eyes moving over her face and body as he did so. The action was so sensual that a tiny gasp escaped Naomi's lips. She couldn't control the enormous smile that burst from her heart any longer.

Luca's face lit up with joy. Pushing the chair away, he took long strides toward her. His arms opened wide. Their hug couldn't get them close enough to each other. His body felt hard, comforting and sensual against hers.

Auntie Elsa walked past them toward the table Luca had just left, grinning at the couple clinging to each other.

Kerri winked at them as she followed Auntie Elsa moments later, a massive smile on her face.

"Shouldn't you guys be doing that in private?"

Luca's low, joyous laugh rumbled into Naomi's chest where their bodies were still connected. His lips felt soft, warm and gentle where he kissed her forehead. Then, taking her hand in his, he kissed her fingers as he led her to the table to sit beside him. He leaned toward her, his smile friendly, his eyes warm.

She'd forgotten how mellifluous his voice was.

"You look so much better, amore. How are you feeling?"

Naomi's voice wouldn't work. Her words stayed stuck in her throat. She gave him a thumbs up, instead, her mouth unwilling to relinquish the smile that wanted to live there permanently.

She was so happy to see him. All her doubts and fears disappeared like the early morning fog over the desert's dunes.

It was the best breakfast she'd enjoyed since he'd left.

KERRI TURNED out to be a far stricter boss than Auntie Elsa ever was. She refused to allow Naomi to take any guests, including Luca, into the desert until she'd recovered from her ordeal with Stefan. What was even more frustrating was that Luca sided with Kerri on the issue. He was supposed to be on her side, wasn't he? As far as Naomi was concerned, even though her sore wrist was still a bother, it was nothing she couldn't handle, having dealt with many sprained ankles and wrists throughout her life.

Naomi was as willful as Kerri, but when her protestations fell on deaf ears, Naomi made the best of a bad situation. She couldn't remember the last time she'd had a vacation. Now was as good a time as any to take one.

But how would she do that with Luca back at the lodge? She wasn't sure why he'd returned. She assumed it had something to do with the desert buggies, but there was no sign of them. And he hadn't explained himself. He was courteous, yet their former easy banter and intimacy, for the most part, was gone. But despite the shy awkwardness that had taken its place, each morning, they'd swim together.

Auntie Elsa and Kerri would join them for breakfast, after which Luca would excuse himself to get back to work. He spent much of his time working in his room, the same one he'd previously occupied. Apparently, according to Kerri, it felt like a home from home to him. He only reappeared again for lunch, groggy from concentrating in a world Naomi had never experienced.

After a few days, she was getting increasingly more bored. What began as a gift of time in which to swim and read as much as she'd wanted had now become tedium. What made it worse was that everyone else seemed inordinately busy. For most of the day, Luca was working in his room, a large area of which he'd turned into an office. Kerri had her hands full being the new manager and handling everything that entailed. Auntie Elsa was busy with Kerri or Chef, or she mysteriously disappeared from the lodge for long hours at a time, giving no explanation afterward. But everyone knew it had to have something to do with the birthday party she was planning with Santina.

There was only so much moping about the lodge Naomi could do before the desert called. The dunes beckoned like sirens. She could no longer ignore their ancient, primitive song. But even though she didn't want to admit it, the fear of bumping into Stefan somewhere in the desert, should he still be in Namibia, made leaving the immediate area deeply unappealing. She couldn't shrug off the feeling that he might lie in wait for her as a predator did its prey. But should he be hiding in the desert, surely he wouldn't be stupid enough to venture too close to the lodge, would he?

Naomi discovered quickly that Luca suddenly appeared if she moved too far away from the lodge for his liking. How he knew she'd walked through the gate that would take her into the near-desert within sight of the lodge, was beyond her. Did the man harbor some secret psychic ability?

No sooner had she walked but a half mile into the desert than she could hear him calling her name. She'd stop, smile and watch as he took long strides toward her. Grinning, sunglasses shielding his eyes, he'd take her hand and walk with her to the first big dunes.

Gratitude swelled in her heart that he understood how much her soul yearned for the unfathomable quietness. It was the desert's unique song that always revitalized her soul. Luca didn't make conversation. But his presence was more comforting than she'd wanted to admit, at first. Together, they'd sit against a dune, allowing the beauty of the wilderness to mesmerize them.

When Johan discovered Luca was back at Desert Lodge, he sent an invitation and truck around one morning for them to visit the orphanage.

Ellie Naomi was so much stronger and more confident than the last time they'd seen her. Her excited greeting filled both Luca and Naomi with joy.

This time, they could help with the orphans' breakfast feed, though Luca focused more on taking pictures of Naomi feeding them.

It was heartbreaking to think all fourteen of these gorgeous little ellies were orphans because the ivory from their mothers' tusks was so precious. But that time was a great healer was apparent in the antics of the boisterous bunch. Once they'd had their breakfast, their surrogate fathers took them for a long walk deep into the desert. As they walked away in single file, each ellie holding on to the tail of the one in front, silence descended on the orphanage.

Only ellie Naomi remained. She was too young yet to join the rest of the herd. Luca took more photos and videos of her.

By the end of the week, Naomi was desperate to return to work. She couldn't stand being idle any longer. Marching to Kerri's office, she was determined to get her way this time. Without knocking, she opened the door, ready to confront her friend.

She found Kerri with her back to the door, facing Luca sitting opposite her. They were evidently in the middle of a meeting. Luca had been reading from a paper in his hand, but when he heard the door open, looked up, and saw Naomi standing there. The pupils of his eyes dilated, and a stunning smile appeared instantly on his face.

Embarrassment coloring her cheeks, Naomi dashed backward, her good arm waving behind her to find the doorknob again.

"Oh, I'm... I'm sorry for interrupting. Hello, Luca. I didn't realize you guys were in a meeting. I'll come back later, Kerri."

She felt even more foolish for stumbling so awkwardly over her words.

Kerri turned her chair to the side, so she had both Naomi and Luca in view.

"Don't go yet, Naomi. Luca and I have nearly finished, and I think it's time for you guys to chat. Luca has some interesting questions about aspects of the dune buggies I couldn't answer. But I know you'd be able to give him all the information he needs."

Naomi felt her face flush.

Damn, she had chosen the wrong time to confront Kerri.

She moved to the other side of Kerri's desk to sit beside Luca so she didn't have to look at him. Perhaps that way, she could keep her mind on business and stay professional.

Being in such close quarters to Luca made Naomi nervous. It was one thing to be out in the open desert with him, or in the pool where she could swim away. But here there was no escape. There was no getting out of the situation. If she messed up now, it could damage their deal about the buggies, and she wouldn't be held responsible for that. No, there was no way out. She had known this moment would come, but she was unprepared for it now it was here.

She'd always imagined that they'd be communicating via Skype. Luca would be in Italy, and she'd be here, safe. But perhaps it was just as well it was happening this way. If she'd known beforehand, she'd be talking business to him today, she'd have had time to panic about it. Just the thought of it made her breathe higher and faster in her body, and her palms became instantly sweaty.

No, perhaps this was the best way. She was determined to stay competent and to have an effective and productive meeting with Luca about the buggies. She'd focus on that issue.

Naomi wasn't listening to Kerri and Luca's conversation. Instead, she tried to signal for Kerri to stay. But annoyingly, Kerri pretended not to understand what Naomi meant.

Instead, Kerri got up and smiled sweetly at Luca.

"Thank you for your time, Luca."

She winked at Naomi before closing the door behind her.

"He's all yours. I'll see you guys later."

Luca's nearness in such a confined space reminded Naomi of their time in the jet, and look what happened then. She pulled her chair away from his so there was a more comfortable space between them.

Naomi felt self-conscious suddenly. She was aware of the bruise on her face and that Luca was looking too directly at her. Her hand involuntarily went to her cheek, as though she was seeking reassurance that the swelling remained hidden. But her disobedient eyes wouldn't leave his face.

Luca waited, but when it became clear Naomi wouldn't say anything, he shrugged slightly and cleared his throat.

"Well, to business then, I guess."

Luca asked questions she could answer easily.

Naomi felt herself relax. Luca was still a stranger to her now, albeit friendlier than when he'd left, but a stranger. At least he wasn't quite the Iceman anymore. It was still difficult to believe that this dazzling man had held her in his arms and kissed her. She felt as though she'd been embraced by a dream that wouldn't let her go. The feeling was vaguely disturbing. It lived at the edge of her mind, half-formed. It wasn't the first time she'd thought of him as her dream man.

She sighed.

Immediately, concern showed in Luca's eyes as he leaned forward in his chair, placing a warm hand on her forearm.

"Are you all right? Have we tired you out?"

She knew she had to answer, but all her attention was on the heat from his hand on her arm.

"Oh, no. I'm... I'm okay, thank you."

"Good."

Luca squinted as though he didn't quite believe her, but he sat back in his chair again. He asked more questions about the desert conditions the buggies were most likely to meet on a day-to-day basis and seemed satisfied with the information she gave him.

"Right. I think that's all for now. If I need more information, we'll need another meeting."

She couldn't be sure, but the way he said it, she almost believed he was flirting with her again.

Luca lifted the small laptop on which he'd been taking notes from his lap onto Kerri's desk. He'd used a gorgeous picture of ellie Naomi as his screensaver.

Naomi hadn't expected it. It reminded her of the gift he'd left in her room.

"Thank you for the painting. I don't think I've thanked you for it yet."

Luca's eyes seemed to communicate something beyond his words. But perhaps she just imagined it.

"Do you like it?"

"Yes, it's stunning. Thank you. But why did you give it to me? Why didn't you take it with you?"

"Why do you think, amore?"

Once again, she couldn't think of anything to say.

But before she could respond, Kerri opened the door.

"Oops, I didn't realize you guys were still in here."

Luca got up, a smile playing at the corners of his mouth.

"We've just finished. Please take back your office."

His dark eyes returned to Naomi's. Once again, she had the

distinct impression there was more going on behind them than she could see. It was intriguing and annoying in equal measure.

Did he just wink at her?

"I'll see you later?"

Naomi nodded.

Luca picked up his laptop. Without a backward glance, waving at them with the back of his hand, he walked through the door.

Naomi continued to stare at Luca's back as he disappeared. She'd answered the buggy questions to her satisfaction, and his, apparently. Why, then, did she feel so upset? It was only right that Luca treated this as a business meeting because that's what it was. But her heart had wanted something different, something she couldn't have.

Not for the first time since Luca had left, did Naomi feel pity for those poor waitresses who'd experienced flings with one of these wealthy princes. The difference was they got over it quickly. So, it was just a fling for them.

But how would she get over her love for Luca? This wasn't just a fling for her. Luca lived in her heart. He lived in her soul. No other man would ever enter those places. It was not a decision. It was a fact cast in the hardest of Namibian diamonds. Yes, he was back. He was lovely toward her, and yet...

Naomi wished with all her heart she could undo this soul bond she'd experienced with Luca. It caused nothing but pain.

Kerri walked around the desk to place her hands on Naomi's shoulders.

"What's going on, hun? I know you. I can feel your pain. I know you and Luca had left on a weird note, but all relationships have their trials, don't they? Hasn't it helped to have him back? Didn't your meeting just now help to make things up with him again?"

Kerri massaged Naomi's shoulders while she waited for her friend to respond.

Naomi sighed as much from the pain in her heart as from the release of the tension in her shoulders Kerri's hands were massaging away.

"I don't know what happened. But it's for the best, you know. I'm just glad we have the buggy deal. That's all down to you."

Kerri's hands became still for a moment.

"You won't fob me off so easily again, Naomi. I don't like seeing you like this. How can I help if you don't tell me what's going on?"

Naomi put a hand over one of Kerri's hands resting on her shoulder.

"I'm not fobbing you off. I genuinely don't know what happened. All I know is Luca suddenly became so cold toward me. Yes, he's back. But he's here for the buggies, isn't he? He's said nothing to me or explained his sudden change toward me. And it makes me think it was just a vacation fling for him. We've seen so many of those here haven't we?"

Kerri grabbed a chair and sat down facing Naomi.

"I can't believe you'd think what you and Luca had was just a vacation fling. Are you serious? He flew you in his jet to dinner in Windhoek. Who does that with a fling?"

Naomi couldn't help smiling at the look of outrage on Kerri's face.

"I know what you're saying. But we're talking about Luca. That's just his lifestyle. I don't think he thought it was a big deal at all. I'm sure he does stuff like that all the time. And now he's back, he's... different."

Kerri frowned.

"But what about the painting? It's magnificent. If you were

nothing to him, why would he leave you a painting like that, one he'd put his energy into?"

Naomi didn't want to share her fears with Kerri. But she knew Kerri wouldn't let it go, not now they'd started.

"I don't know why he gave me the painting. I asked him, but he didn't reply. If he took it back to Italy, it would only remind him of me, and perhaps he didn't want that reminder? I don't know."

Kerri continued as though she didn't hear Naomi's last comment.

"And when he arrived that night, and you were still so out of it, he immediately went to you. Don't you remember how he held you? And the morning after, he hugged you so tightly I wondered if it was decent to do in public."

Naomi got up. She could feel herself getting upset now she was talking about Luca. She felt even more confused.

"To be honest, I don't want to think about it, and I don't want to talk about it anymore."

"Hmm…"

Kerri said it in such a way Naomi knew Kerri wouldn't rest until she understood it.

Naomi sighed and slumped back into the chair.

"Look, Luca is who he is, and I am who I am. We don't belong in each other's worlds. I'll get over him. It's just that I haven't allowed myself to feel this way about a guy ever before, that's all."

Kerri contemplated her friend.

"Hmm…"

"Stop it!"

"What?"

"Saying hmm… like that."

Kerri sat back in her chair.

"Okay. Look, you're more than my best friend. You're the

sister I've always wanted. I won't sit by and watch you suffer like this. Like I said, I can feel your pain. I also know you better than you know yourself. What are you trying to hide? What are you running away from?"

It was true, Kerri knew her like no one else ever had. Naomi remembered all the nights they'd spent sitting under the stars in the desert, talking their hearts out, sharing their secrets with each other.

Kerri knew of Naomi's indelible fear that death would claim those people she loved, as it had with her parents.

Naomi knew Kerri would put two and two together and come up with the answer Naomi was trying so hard to deny, even to herself.

Kerri seemed not to notice Naomi's hesitation.

"And don't deny it. Under normal circumstances, you would have had it out with Luca by now. But you haven't even asked him what this is all about, have you?"

Naomi shook her head, and Kerri continued.

"See? I knew it! I knew there's something about Luca you're running away from -"

A light bulb suddenly went on in Kerri's eyes.

"Oh, my God! You're petrified. That's it, isn't it? You love him so much you're terrified to lose him like you lost your parents. That's why you haven't talked to him about what's happened between you. Oh, Naomi, hun..."

Kerri kneeled down in front of her friend, her arms in a tight embrace around Naomi's torso as intense, unrestrained sobs tore from the very depths of Naomi's soul.

TWENTY-ONE

Naomi felt as though she'd never stop crying. The ache in her heart was a physical pain that no amount of tears could relieve.

But Kerri didn't seem to mind. She held her friend in silence and gave a safe space for Naomi to cry herself out.

An hour later, Naomi's tears stopped. Her face felt puffy, and she needed a tissue for her runny nose.

Kerri, who could feel the change in Naomi's body, knew the storm had passed, at least for now. She let her friend go and offered Naomi the box of tissues she kept on her desk.

"I'm so sorry I pushed it, hun. I should have realized what was going on with you. But you know you can always talk to me. You know that, don't you? God knows you've had to listen to my man woes often enough."

Naomi nodded and blew her nose in a tissue, taking another to wipe the tears from her eyes and face.

Her voice was hoarse when she spoke.

"I know. Thank you. But no one can help me. I have to deal with this myself."

Kerri stroked Naomi's hair from her face.

"I know you feel that way, hun. But you can ask for help,

you know. It's allowed. And I know a thing or two about men. So, believe me, when I tell you, you weren't just a fling for Luca. The man is besotted with you. You should have seen his face when I told him that Stefan was free and you worried he might show up here again. I swear, if he could, Luca would've climbed through the computer to get here. I don't believe he came here just to test the prototype buggy due to arrive next week. He was furious when he heard about what Stefan had done to you. I'm sure he's using the buggies as an excuse to be here so he could see you."

"Oh, I didn't realize you'd already told him Stefan was free... Do you really think he came here because of that?"

Kerri sat back in her chair.

"Yes, he woke me up in the middle of the night. Auntie Elsa and Santina had a late-night chat, and Auntie Elsa told her about what had happened with you and Stefan. Santina told Luca at once. That's when he called and called until I answered.

"Can you imagine my reaction when I found his face staring at me on Skype? And to answer your question, no, I don't think he came here because Stefan is free, although that might have put the jeebies up him. He came here to see you were ok, hun. Why is that so hard for you to believe?"

"Perhaps because he's changed so much toward me...?"

"Yes, it's puzzling. I don't understand it either, although I think it's just a blip. Your relationship is still new. All kinds of misunderstandings can happen, especially in the beginning. But I still think you should give him a chance. No, actually- Amend that... you should give yourself a chance, hun. You deserve it, you know?"

"Hmm... You engineered our meeting today, didn't you?"

Kerri's eyes glinted with mischief.

"I wondered when you'd notice."

Kerri's kindness and warm smile made Naomi feel much better. The tears had helped. Auntie Elsa's voice sounded in her mind, 'Things are always better out than in.'

Not for the first time, despite the unsettling situation with Luca, Naomi felt an overwhelming sense of gratitude for Auntie Elsa and Kerri in her life. They were her family, and she basked in the comfort of that knowledge.

Naomi closed Kerri's office door as she stepped into the corridor. She felt much calmer than when she went in there just over an hour ago. Her meeting with Luca had intensified her wish to get back to work. That Kerri was in her corner about her situation with him was comforting. Now, she didn't feel so alone anymore.

In her hand, she held the desert guide roster for taking guests on safaris. Kerri had agreed it was time for Naomi to get back to work. Work would get her out of the lodge and into her beloved desert. Naomi skimmed over the roster. Kerri had been kind. All the safaris under her name were sunset safaris, which Kerri knew she most loved. The schedule showed her first safari was today. She could hardly wait. With a spring in her step, she went back to her room. She needed to sort out her puffy-cried face.

It felt good to get back to her old routine. She chatted with the kitchen staff before checking her truck and making sure the walkie-talkie's battery was fully charged.

Naomi had not expected Luca to join the safari, but when she turned up at the truck, she found him leaning against it, his usual array of camera equipment in his hands. The other guests, beyond excited, had already taken their seats in the truck. Once again, Luca helped Naomi up to the driver's seat before walking around the vehicle to get into the seat beside her. It felt right to have him here, again.

Driving into the desert to the accompaniment of the excited

chatter from her guests, Naomi felt alive again for the first time in days. A spectacular sunset welcomed her back. Beside her, Luca's camera pointed this way and that as he took picture after picture of the ever-changing sameness of the dunes. Behind her, a symphony of "oohs" and "aahs" from the guests mingled with the sounds of the animals as she drove to the waterhole.

But it was the open space, the wind in her hair, the last of the sun's rays on her face, and the smells of the desert invading Naomi's being, that set her free. Here, she could breathe again, smile, feel the desert's ancient, wise energy fill up her body. She could be herself again. That the man next to her, whom she loved more than life itself, was here with her at all, completed her happiness.

Used to the unpredictability of nature and the desert, Naomi was the first to spot the pride of lions as she drove closer to the waterhole. It was rare to see the big desert cats in this part of the world. She slowed the truck and pointed with one hand, holding up her other hand to show that everyone had to stay silent. In her heart, Naomi gave thanks to the desert for giving her this rare opportunity to experience these magnificent animals. She was aware of Luca's excitement, jumping out of his body.

She turned to face her guests and whispered loud enough for them to hear.

"Don't make any sudden movements or noises. If everyone is okay with it, I'll try to get us a little closer. It's very rare to see desert lions here. In all the time I've been bringing guests here, I've only ever seen them once before. So, seeing them now is a fantastic opportunity. I know this truck is open and so it may feel unsafe so near the lions. But look to their left. You'll see they've recently killed and eaten a zebra. It means we're in no danger of an attack from them. Is everyone okay with us going a little closer?"

Smiles and eager nodding greeted her from excited faces. Naomi turned to face forward again and drove slowly towards the lions lying near their kill. Their tummies were huge from eating more than their fill. As she drove closer, the tiny figures of two small cubs became visible. They were lying on top of a female, fast asleep. Their little ears were twitching now and then, but had no actual effect on the flies that were pestering them.

Only the occasional growl and grunt of satisfaction from the lions disturbed the silence. The contortions their bodies adopted as they lay in various states of stupor and inertia belied their supremacy as the top predator. But it was clear in their level of contentment and complacency.

Naomi was aware her guests were holding their breaths, feasting their eyes on the wonder before them. Several guests and Luca had their cameras trained on the pride. Luca had swapped his lens on the camera. He was using the same one that produced the great close-ups of the bull elephant they'd seen on their first safari together.

One of the little cubs turned in its sleep and inadvertently slid off the female's body. Unable to stop, the cub performed a comical sand dive.

A guest laughed.

The sound had an immediate effect on the lions. They sat up. Their wild, predatory yellow eyes fixed on the truck. One female, presumably the mother of the cubs, gave a deep growl, her ears flattening against her head. Naomi took it as a sign they'd outstayed their welcome. She started the engine at once and reversed away from the pride as slowly as she could.

When they were several feet away, she breathed out her relief and heard the same from Luca and the guests behind her. Then everyone talked simultaneously.

Naomi knew it would be the major topic of conversation at

dinner that night. She smiled, grateful to have been the one to give Luca and her guests such an unforgettable experience.

The rest of their safari, although lovely, couldn't live up to their encounter with the lions. Several guests tried Googling more information about them until they realized there was no satellite reception in the desert.

Back at the lodge, her group of guests mingled with the rest who'd been on safaris with other guides and those who'd elected to stay behind. Her group talked up a storm about the lions they'd encountered.

Dinner became one huge affair. The waiters had pulled all the tables in the Lapa together. Everyone leaned forward to hear everything they could about the encounter with the lions. Luca was sharing his pictures with their fellow diners.

Although Naomi had looked forward to getting back to work, she had to admit the experience had been more tiring than she could have imagined.

When she excused herself and told Luca she'd see him in the pool in the morning, she could tell he was concerned for her. His reaction reminded of her earlier conversation with Kerri.

Did he really care for her so much that he would come to Desert Lodge just to see she was okay? It was difficult to believe, but she wanted to.

Luca stood up when she did, and he pulled her chair back for her.

His touch on her arm conveyed his concern.

"Sleep well, amore."

Naomi smiled and nodded at Luca. She could feel his eyes on her back as she walked away.

On the way to her room, she bumped into Kerri, who tucked a hand through Naomi's arm and turned toward the kitchen where her dinner awaited. Naomi allowed her friend to sweep her along. A few minutes in the kitchen won't make any difference to how tired she was.

"You look yourself again, hun. The desert agrees with you."

"It does. And you stopped me from going there. I may never forgive you."

Kerri giggled at Naomi's joke. The two friends took their places around the big old table where Auntie Elsa sat with other members of staff.

As was her habit, after finishing her dinner, Auntie Elsa excused herself to check on the guests and to solve any problems they may have.

As she walked toward the door, she turned to Naomi.

"Join me in the lounge after dinner?"

Naomi nodded and made wide eyes at Kerri when Auntie Elsa had gone. It was an unusual request and sounded more like a summons. Naomi couldn't imagine what Auntie Elsa wanted to talk about that sounded so mysterious. Having already had her dinner in the Lapa with Luca, Naomi asked a waitress to deliver coffee to the lounge. Then, winking at Kerri, Naomi left.

Although it was the guest lounge, guests seldom used the grand old room. Naomi sat down on her favorite sofa just as a waitress brought in the coffee. She poured herself a cup and settled back onto the couch.

It wasn't long before Auntie Elsa opened the French doors leading from the patio.

"Oh, good. You ordered coffee."

Auntie Elsa poured herself some and sat down in her favorite chair opposite Naomi. For moments, the women sat in comfortable silence, enjoying being together and drinking their coffee. Then, Auntie Elsa put down her cup, got up and came to sit next to Naomi on the sofa. She seemed very serious, but calm and waited for Naomi to finish her coffee.

She took Naomi's hands in hers.

"Darling, I have something to tell you. I'm sorry that I can't wait. Time is not on our side in this matter."

But before she could say anything more, Naomi had a sudden insight. Her heart beat faster. Her chest felt tight. It was as though her body already knew what Auntie Elsa would say even before the words had left her lips. Naomi's mouth went dry despite having just had coffee. She felt light-headed but focused on Auntie Elsa's face, instead.

How had she missed that Auntie Elsa looked so much older so fast? She was so much thinner. Her face had more wrinkles than Naomi remembered. Her hands felt bony in Naomi's.

Naomi glanced down.

Blue veins stood out against the pale skin flecked with age spots on her adoptive mother's hands. Hands that had soothed away her pain as a child, hands that had cared for her, hands that still cared.

She looked up into Auntie Elsa's eyes.

Tears brimmed at the lower lids of the older women's eyes. She stroked Naomi's hands as though trying to soothe the pain she was about to inflict on her daughter, the only daughter she'd ever known and loved as though Naomi was her own.

She brushed away Naomi's hair from her forehead, leaving her hand on Naomi's shoulder.

"I've been thinking and thinking about this moment, but there's no simple way to say it, darling."

Naomi's voice sounded shrill and desperate to her ears.

"Then, don't say it. Say nothing."

"That won't make it go away, my darling. It won't make it any easier. Not for either of us."

Naomi started to cry. The tourniquet that had squeezed her heart was squeezing tighter, making breathing more difficult.

Seeing how upset Naomi was, the dam that held back Auntie Elsa's tears, burst.

Despite tears streaming down her face, she tried her best to make this as easy as possible for Naomi. She'd held the information in her heart for the past week already. But she didn't want to burden Naomi with it on top of the trauma she'd had to deal with because of Stefan's actions. It was difficult enough getting her head around the verdict, and she knew her delay in telling Naomi sprung partly from denial, together with a desperate hope that the doctors had been wrong in their diagnosis.

But she had already lost one week. Further tests had confirmed she might be allowed only a few more weeks. She couldn't wait any longer, no matter how she prayed to spare Naomi this pain.

"It's pancreatic cancer, darling. The prognosis..."

She sighed.

"I have a few weeks..."

Naomi couldn't believe it. She shook her head as though to shake the words away.

"But... but..."

"I know, darling. There's nothing they can do. It's spread too far."

"But you didn't have any symptoms?"

Through the tears clinging to her eyelashes, Naomi squinted at Auntie Elsa. Panic had replaced a slowness, a numbness in her body.

"Did you?"

Auntie Elsa looked down.

"No, I didn't. I had some backache, but I thought I'd just been working too hard."

"That's why you made Kerri manager?"

"No. I didn't know then. I made her manager because I could see she would be excellent in the job, perhaps even better than me. And it was time. Now, I'm glad."

Naomi held on to Auntie Elsa's hands and wiped her tears on her arm.

"So, when...?"

Auntie Elsa had expected Naomi's questions. She'd do anything to spare her daughter this pain. In her experience, knowing the details of an unpleasant situation had always brought relief, somehow. It was all she could offer Naomi.

"I've been going to see the doctor in Mariental."

"But that's miles away...!"

"Khwai drove me."

Naomi sank her head onto Auntie Elsa's shoulder. The numbness that had invaded her body had reached her mind.

"So that's where you'd disappeared to. We all thought- Oh, Auntie Elsa... Is there really nothing...? How about going to Windhoek? Another opinion?"

Auntie Elsa moved closer to Naomi and held her, stroking her hair and back.

"No, my darling. There's nothing. It's too late. The scans and tests showed because of how it's spread, it's untreatable. I'm so sorry, Naomi. I truly am."

Auntie Elsa sighed again.

She'd known how challenging this news would be for Naomi, who'd already lost so much in her young life. All she could do was try to make the end as pleasant for them both as possible.

"But we have this time together now. Let's enjoy what we still have."

Naomi nuzzled her head into Auntie Elsa's neck, her arms around the woman who'd saved her life, the woman she loved like the mother she'd lost.

But even as she voiced the plea that flowed from her heart, she knew she had lost again, that death had won once more.

"Please don't leave me. Please..."

TWENTY-TWO

The days that followed were a blur, but Naomi was determined to be there for Auntie Elsa, to help her enjoy whatever time was left to them. Only in the privacy of her room at night did she give way to tears and wrestle with the all-consuming fear that death was claiming yet another important person in her life.

It was familiar territory. She knew only too well the devastating feelings of loss, grief and aloneness that would be her companions after Auntie Elsa's death. Would she be prepared for the pain that no pills could ease? Would she be able to climb out of the dark hole of despair once again? Last time she'd been a child, almost still a baby. She was an adult now. That made all the difference.

Ever practical, Kerri had called a meeting. She'd informed the staff of Auntie Elsa's illness and the short time the cancer had given her to enjoy the last days of her life.

Instead of the newscasting a heavy darkness over the lodge, everyone seemed to want to help Auntie Elsa enjoy every moment she still had on this earth. The news had pulled the staff together like nothing before. Many of them were grateful to Auntie Elsa, her father before her, and his father before him, for their employment through generations. They appreciated the love and fairness she'd always shown them. Now, it was their turn to repay her.

Kerri made sure the guests didn't know. It would make no difference to their stay at Desert Lodge.

Auntie Elsa had told Santina herself. As a result, they brought the date of their birthday party forward. Kerri had hired more staff, and the lodge was a hive of activity as preparations for Auntie Elsa's and Santina's joint party got underway. No one voiced it, but everyone knew it was more than just a birthday party. It was also a farewell to one of the most wonderful, kind souls they'd ever known.

Within days, Santina and her Italian friends and family arrived. It was clear Santina had told them about Auntie Elsa's situation. In their typical warm Italian way, they took her under their wings, advising how to be more comfortable and how to enjoy the last few weeks of her life best. They seemed to revel in their role.

Luca had arranged for another chef, who specialized in Italian cuisine, to work with Chef. Kerri had hired more kitchen helpers to cater to the sell-out lodge.

Luca became even more caring towards Naomi. His wonder of her had increased. She seemed so feminine, so fragile. How was she even coping with so many traumas following one after the other? He had to give her credit for being stronger than he'd imagined. His heart swelled with admiration and pride as he kept an eye on her. He so badly wanted to talk things through with her, to make things right between them, again. But now wasn't the time. Seeing her being so brave, despite the sadness he felt from her, tested his patience in every way. He wanted to hold her, love her and kiss away her sorrow. But not wanting to intrude on her grief, he spent most of his time with his fellow Italians. When he interacted with her, he kept things light. He felt grateful that she still observed their early morning swimming schedule each day, though he wouldn't blame her if she hadn't. Her commitment meant a lot. It was the only time he was alone with her these days.

NAOMI WAS SITTING with Auntie Elsa in her room. They sat together on the sofa every morning now, drinking tea and watching TV. Auntie Elsa liked to watch the news each morning and afternoon. But today, they were early. Twenty minutes remained until the news. It allowed them to talk about whatever crossed their minds, jumping from subject to subject.

Auntie Elsa smiled at Naomi, grateful for the time they were sharing.

"So, what's been going on with you and Luca? It's clear as daylight you're in love with each other. But I can see only shadows in your eyes, darling. I don't want to sound crass, given my current circumstances, but you know time is precious and so short?"

Naomi winced.

She hadn't expected Auntie Elsa to talk to her about Luca in such a straightforward way. But then, time was running out, wasn't it?

For the first time, it hit home. Auntie Elsa would die in a few weeks.

Naomi felt her face flush.

She wouldn't allow the tears that burned behind her eyes to spoil the time she was enjoying with this wonderful, inspirational woman. But a light bulb had gone off in her mind. The words Auntie Elsa spoke, '... time is precious, and life so short...' had always been only words, but now the truth of those words was impressed upon Naomi. Life was short. Time with those she loved was precious.

Before she could respond, Auntie Elsa continued.

"I do wish you and Luca would sort out whatever is the matter between the two of you. Seeing you together reminds me so much of Wouter and me when we were young. We were so in love. I'll be going home to my dear Wouter. He was the love of my life, you know. My soul mate. I'm not scared to die, and I don't want you to be afraid of death, either, my darling. Truth be told, I'm rather excited about seeing him soon. Life has just not been the same since he died. I want such happiness for you. You certainly deserve it. You brought such joy into our home and our lives. I'm more than grateful for you, my dear Naomi. I feel so blessed."

Auntie Elsa's smile conveyed her deep love for Naomi.

"I cannot imagine what my life would have been like without you or Wouter in it. Much poorer, I'm sure. Don't waste your opportunity, Naomi. Here is Luca, a wonderful man, deeply in love with you. Don't run away from love. Don't hide from it. It's all we have, you know. Love. It's all that matters. We come into this world alone, and we leave alone again. We bring nothing with us, other than love. And we can't take anything with us, but love. It's everything. It expands your life, your soul."

Naomi sat still. In the silence that followed Auntie Elsa's words, she understood with supreme clarity that this was the ultimate truth. This simple message from a woman on the brink of death. It was Auntie Elsa's last gift to her.

Suddenly, her reasons for not allowing herself to love Luca seemed so silly. Not only given Auntie Elsa's words but also in the glimpse Auntie Elsa had shown of an eternity of love that awaited her. Naomi felt comforted that Auntie Elsa seemed to take her death so much in her stride, as though it was just a part of her life.

Auntie Elsa, satisfied that Naomi understood what she meant, focused her attention on the TV just as the news came on.

"Oh look, isn't that Stefan? How did he make it on the news? Turn up the volume, will you, Naomi, please?"

The women watched in amazement as picture after picture of Stefan posing in front of a dead elephant appeared on the screen. He was beaming, holding on to a massive elephant gun. The elephant's tusks had been removed and were lying at his feet. The newscaster's voice became clearer as Naomi pressed the volume button on the remote control she held in her hand.

"... massive outcry against this man, Stefan Sawaski. The American allegedly paid one hundred thousand dollars for the privilege of shooting the elephant. Police in Namibia have said they urgently want to speak to the American Tech CEO on poaching charges, but his whereabouts are unknown..."

Naomi couldn't believe what she was seeing. Stefan had visited the elephant orphanage. They had introduced him to the orphaned ellies, and he had befriended Johan. He knew how hard everyone was fighting against poachers, and here he was, killing elephants.

She turned to Auntie Elsa, her eyes full of anger.

"I can't believe that man. How the hell did he get away with that?"

Auntie Elsa frowned.

"I'm wondering how it made the news. I'm sure Stefan wouldn't have shared it with a news channel. Not if he's disappeared, don't you think?"

The sharp rap on the door was Kerri's signature knock. The door opened at once, her face peeping around it. Behind her, Santina peered over Kerri's shoulder. Their smiles were the biggest Naomi had ever seen.

Something was up.

"Can we come in?"

Auntie Elsa smiled and nodded, patting the sofa beside her for Santina to sit down.

"Please do."

Naomi scooted nearer Auntie Elsa, making space for Kerri to sit beside her.

Something was going on. Kerri could barely contain her excitement. Naomi, who knew her friend well, could see how much Kerri was struggling not to blurt out whatever news they'd brought.

"Did you see Stefan? He's on all the news channels, all over the world."

Auntie Elsa's frown deepened.

"I was just saying to Naomi how amazing he made the news, especially if he's gone into hiding like they say he has. It makes little sense."

Santina and Kerri craned their necks around the other two women to share a conspiratorial wink. They made as big a show as they could.

Naomi couldn't suppress her giggle at their antics.

Realization dawned.

"Wait a minute... Don't tell me you both had something to do with this?"

Santina and Kerri spoke in unison, the innocence on their faces exaggerated.

"No."

Kerri could no longer contain herself. Fizzing with glee, she stood and took up a stance beside the TV facing her small audience.

"It was Luca. Isn't it clever of him? He found a private Twitter account that belongs to Stefan. Luca followed him and leaked Stefan's pictures to his contacts at several news agencies.

Stefan has had to go into hiding because the pictures on Twitter and other social media networks have gone viral. It's so cool!"

Kerri held her breath as she waited for the effect of her words on Naomi and Auntie Elsa. The air of expectation in the room reminded Naomi of Christmas when a treasured gift might summon similar behavior.

She had to ask.

"How do you know?"

Santina craned her head around Auntie Elsa to respond to Naomi.

"Just before I came here, Luca asked that I shred some papers in his office. I came across several with information that wasn't his usual work. As I didn't want to make a mistake, I called him to ask about it, and he told me. He asked that I keep it to myself until the news broke on TV. He's very clever, that boy."

Naomi had forgotten Santina was Luca's secretary. They looked so much alike. In Naomi's mind, they were mother and son. They seemed to care that way for each other.

Auntie Elsa was first to respond. She clapped her hands together, her eyes bright, an enormous smile on her face.

"I've wished no one ill, but after what Stefan did to Naomi, this is a better punishment than merely throwing him in jail. I don't think he'd be too fond of a public humiliation like this. Yes, Luca is brilliant. Where is he, anyway? I'd like to congratulate him."

Naomi's head reeled. She hadn't imagined Luca would come to her rescue so spectacularly. But Auntie Elsa was right. A worldwide humiliation would be far more devastating to Stefan. He wouldn't be able to bribe or buy himself out of this one.

Santina stood and helped Auntie Elsa to stand.

"We left Luca sitting by the pool. He likes the morning sun there."

Kerri went to Auntie Elsa's other side, and together the two women helped Auntie Elsa to amble from the room. Naomi followed, carrying her shrug, and took the throw from her bed for her legs. Naomi was mindful that despite the day's heat, Auntie Elsa's rapid weight loss meant she got cold quickly. The women made their way down the long corridor and went through the guest lounge's French doors out on to the patio that led to the pool.

Naomi's heart sped up when she saw Luca lying on a sun lounger near the Lapa. He had crossed his long legs at his ankles. Sunglasses shielded his eyes against the ferocious sun. He was in a relaxed pose, his arms by his sides. His naked toned torso had turned a deep golden brown from spending a few hours each day in the hot Namibian sun. The rhythmic movement of his stomach showed he was asleep.

Santina and Kerri helped Auntie Elsa into a chair in the Lapa, so she could sit in the shade. They made sure she had a view over the pool where a few people were swimming and chatting. Naomi draped the shrug around her shoulders and covered her legs with the throw.

Meanwhile, Santina went to touch Luca on the shoulder to wake him up. He pulled on the t-shirt he'd rolled up under his head and followed her to sit beside Auntie Elsa. Naomi and Kerri had pulled up more chairs to form a small circle.

Auntie Elsa put a thin hand on Luca's muscular, tanned arm.

"Thank you, Luca. We just saw Stefan's pictures on the news. Kerri and Santina told us what you've done. You are a good man. I feel comforted because you will be here to look after Naomi when I'm gone."

Naomi felt her face flush at Auntie Elsa's words. But Luca's dark eyes, now without his sunglasses, smiled at Naomi.

"I'll do my best if she'll allow me."

Naomi was aware of the double take Santina and Kerri gave each other. Did she just hear what she thought she heard? The blood rushing to her head made her ears ring.

Auntie Elsa patted Luca's arm.

"That's good to know, my boy. You'll forgive me, but your words sounded like a proposal. Am I the only one to think so?"

She looked around for confirmation from the others.

Santina and Kerri nodded, their eyes traveling between Luca and Naomi.

Luca grinned at Auntie Elsa.

"I haven't asked her formally, but I believe it's customary to speak to her parent first?"

Auntie Elsa's smile stretched over her mouth, her eyes brimming with happy tears.

"I couldn't wish for a better man for my Naomi, Luca. I know you'll look after her. And she'll be happy with you for the rest of her life."

Everyone, except Auntie Elsa, got up as though the excitement of the news had forced them from their chairs.

Tears were already streaming down Santina's face. She pressed her cheek to Auntie Elsa's and hugged her friend's shoulders.

"Oh, this is a lucky day. I'm so glad you're here to witness it, my dear friend."

Kerri and Santina took turns to congratulate and hug Naomi and Luca.

Afterward, Luca put an arm around Naomi's shoulders and pulled her close to his body as though he'd never let her go again.

His eyes traveled over the three women in front of him.

"Thank you, Auntie Elsa, for your consent and the good wishes from you all. Now, I just hope Naomi will make me the happiest man in the universe."

He turned to plant a gentle kiss on Naomi's cheek.

But before she could respond, Khwai and a Herero man appeared around the corner. They seemed excited and made a beeline for Luca.

"The truck with your buggy is here, boss man. It just arrived. This man brought it."

After Luca had shaken hands with the courier of the buggy, he, Naomi, and Kerri followed the two men to a massive truck parked near the kitchen. On it, a brand new, gleaming prototype dune buggy sat like a powerful shimmering desert insect.

Luca's excitement streamed from the enormous smile on his face. He walked around the truck to check there weren't any scratches on the buggy, even though it was only the prototype. The courier handed Luca the keys to the buggy before he lowered the truck. Meanwhile, Khwai helped to undo the strong straps that held the buggy in place during its long journey from Windhoek. Luca got up on to the truck and climbed into the buggy, ready to reverse it off the truck, grinning like a schoolboy.

Naomi couldn't help smiling at his obvious excitement. Boys and their toys. Did they ever grow up?

She was still reeling from what had happened in the Lapa. Luca wanted to marry her? Had he asked Auntie Elsa's consent to marry her? It felt like a fairy tale.

They hadn't fixed whatever went wrong between them yet. It was now more important than ever to have a heart-to-heart with him and find out what went wrong. Her emotions went off in different directions. She couldn't believe what he'd done. Was it just a spur-of-the-moment thing, or an impulsive action on his part? But the Luca she'd come to know didn't strike her as a man who'd do anything without thinking it through, first. So, she had to trust he'd meant to talk to Auntie Elsa about marrying her all along.

Kerri had her arm around Naomi's shoulders and gave her a squeeze, accompanied by a gigantic smile.

"So happy for you, hun. So, so happy for you."

Naomi returned Kerri's smile but was relieved and grateful for the interlude given her by the buggy's arrival. It felt as though she was walking on air, swept along by a whirlwind of events beyond her control. She just needed a little time to get grounded again.

After Luca had got the dune buggy off the truck, he bounded over to her, his smile dazzling, his eyes glittering.

He grabbed her hand.

"Come, amore, touch it. The special alloy we've sprayed it with will prevent the sand from scratching it, even in high winds. Isn't it clever?"

Naomi allowed him to lead her over to the buggy. Luca held his hand on top of hers as she glided her hand along the smooth form of the vehicle. Luca's grin widened as he saw the surprise in her eyes at the sensation under her hand.

"Let's go test it."

"What? Now?"

"Yes, now. Why not? Isn't it beautiful?"

Kerri and Naomi laughed as Luca moved from foot to foot, unable to contain his excitement.

Naomi touched his arm. It felt different, somehow, touching him now he was hers.

"Why don't we have lunch first and see if the storm will miss us?"

Luca looked up into the blue, cloudless sky.

"What storm?"

Khwai, having bid the courier farewell, walked over to them.

He, too, looked up into the sky, squinting, and angled a hand above his eyes to shield them from the intense sunlight.

The old man pointed toward the desert.

"That one, boss man. It's a big one. But Nonna is right. It may pass here."

Luca squinted in the direction Khwai and Naomi indicated, but he couldn't see anything that looked like a storm.

"Okay, since you both know more about these things than I do, let's have lunch first. I'm famished anyway."

He took Naomi's hand and led the way back to the Lapa where Auntie Elsa and Santina awaited them.

TWENTY-THREE

Naomi was fast beginning to understand why Luca was so successful in business.

He refused to accept 'no' as an answer. With his devastating good looks and massive amounts of charm, it was easy to see how no one could resist him. It was good to have her Luca back, but it concerned Naomi that they might get caught in the storm.

Khwai had confirmed the information Naomi had given Luca about the storm forming over the desert. However, he was adamant about taking the dune buggy out for a test. He pleaded with Naomi, teasing her, cajoling her, and pulling such comical faces, that he had everyone around the lunch table in stitches.

Luca made light of it, assuring her the test would be quick but thorough. He wanted to report back to Armati HQ as soon as possible. That way, production on the buggies could begin at once. If the storm got closer, he argued, couldn't they outrun it back to the lodge in the truck?

Against her better judgment, Naomi agreed.

Too many people and distractions at the lodge meant they couldn't talk properly. Perhaps being alone together in the desert, they'd be able to clear the air between them. It was important now Luca had asked Auntie Elsa for her hand in marriage.

As soon as they'd finished eating, the other women excused them from staying for coffee after lunch. Luca sprinted to his room to change his shoes into sturdier desert boots. Naomi went to check which of the trucks was resilient enough to carry the dune buggy and had an enclosed cabin in case they needed protection against the storm. By the time Luca reappeared dressed for the desert, camera in hand, Naomi had already driven the truck into the pit. It allowed Luca to drive the buggy onto the vehicle more easily.

She'd arranged for coffee, snacks and a cold dinner in case they got caught in the storm and couldn't make it back to the lodge. From experience, she knew these storms could be severe and last for several hours. The one she could see forming over the desert didn't look friendly at all. She'd made sure the walkie-talkie's battery was charged, though it would be useless in a storm, and packed torches.

Luca's broad smile revealed his excitement as he drove the buggy onto the back of the truck, and Naomi felt the vehicle give under the weight of the buggy. Luca secured it again with the sturdy straps the courier had left.

He was still grinning as he slid onto the seat beside Naomi.

Leaning over, he gave her a quick soft kiss on her cheek.

"You're the best. I guess that's why I can't help wanting to marry you."

"About that..."

Luca turned to her, his eyes serious.

"Say nothing yet. Let's get out of here first."

Realization dawned on Naomi.

"You didn't really want to test the buggy today, did you?"

"Oh, yes, I do. But I also wanted to get you alone so we can talk. We should talk, shouldn't we? Especially now? There are too many people here."

Naomi nodded in agreement and started the engine. She drove the truck out of the pit, used to lower the vehicles when required.

"So? How big does the dune have to be to test the buggy?"

Luca grinned, a wicked glint in his eyes.

"As big as you can find. I want to give it a proper workout."

Naomi couldn't help smiling at his boyish excitement.

They drove in comfortable, companionable silence for a while. The surrounding dunes were getting bigger and bigger. When they reached one the size of a small mountain right ahead of them, Naomi slowed down. She pointed at it.

"Will that do?"

A whistle of awe left Luca's lips.

"It's perfect. Can we get a little closer?"

Naomi nodded.

Driving closer to the dune, she turned the truck. Getting the buggy off the vehicle would be easier if she pushed the back into the sand. Luca got out and used the truck's sides to pull himself along, slipping and sliding through the looser sand. Climbing the sand hill, he got onto the back, undid the straps that secured the buggy, got on, and started the engine. The buggy roared its delight.

Naomi got out to get a better view of Luca and the buggy.

Luca reversed the buggy off the truck, its wheels spinning in the sand before they got proper traction. He drove along the base of the dune for a short while, then stopped.

Naomi smiled at the sound of Luca's jubilant whooping as he drove the buggy up the steep side of the dune.

At first, it slid around in the loose sand. But soon, Luca had the measure of the small vehicle. Naomi watched as Luca drove the buggy higher and higher until he reached the top of the dune. He stopped there. She knew what a fantastic sight met him from that height.

A light breeze had blown when they'd arrived, but it felt a little stronger now. Naomi squinted up into the sky. It was already a little darker. Thousands of tiny grains of sand were starting to obscure the sun as the wind picked up. But they still had time to test the buggy before the storm hit.

She reached inside the truck and grabbed Luca's camera. He'd brought the digital one, which was easy to use. She just had to point and press the button. The camera did all the work.

As Luca drove the buggy along the edge at the top of the dune, Naomi took picture after picture of the gleaming buggy against the orange dune with the blue sky turning a dirty light brown above it. The zoom button brought Luca and the buggy nearer and clearer in the viewfinder. Trying to capture the action shots as Luca maneuvered the buggy diagonally down the dune so it threw up streams of sand behind it, was a little more challenging. But by the time he roared back toward the truck, she felt happy with the shots she'd captured.

By now the wind had picked up. The grains of sand swirling inside the ever-increasing gusts were stinging her unprotected face, arms and legs. Naomi got back into the truck and closed the windows. Already a thin layer of orange sand covered the bonnet of the vehicle. Through the back window, Naomi watched as Luca drove the buggy back onto the truck and secured it with the sturdy straps once again. The wind was snatching at Luca's t-shirt as he worked and blew his hair into his eyes.

When he opened the door to get in, he brought with him a burst of wind, the smell of sand and the energy of his exhilaration.

Luca's eyes were glittering, and his smile stretched over his face.

"Phew! That was fantastic. Did you see?"

Naomi giggled as the infectiousness of his delight jumped into her body.

She showed him the pictures she'd taken, and his enthusiastic praise was her reward.

"These are great! Maybe we could use them in the marketing?"

"We?"

"Sorry, I didn't mean… I meant if you want my help. I'd be happy to help with the marketing for the buggies at the lodge. I meant it when I said your photos are great. But we could get a professional photographer to do amazing action shots."

"You'd do that? Oh, Luca, it would be lovely. Yes, please. But we may not need to hire a photographer. Have you ever seen Gerhard's photos?"

"The guide?"

"Yes, him. His photos have won awards in magazines. We're lucky to have him. He could have been a professional photographer and videographer, coming to think of it."

Naomi looked deep into Luca's eyes.

"Thank you so much for offering to help. I can't imagine Kerri having a problem with it."

Luca became serious as he put the camera away.

"Amore, I know Kerri is your friend, and she is now the new manager at Desert Lodge, but soon it will be yours, no? I know it's difficult to think about that now, but when the time comes, you may want to make different decisions than Auntie Elsa made?"

Luca was right. Naomi didn't want to think about the fact that soon she'd be the owner of Desert Lodge, the custodian of the generations of staff who'd worked there, and the keeper of long-held traditions. Her conversations with Auntie Elsa had helped her to understand that death was just a part of life, and yet... Would she be strong enough to face it? Kerri was the only other person left on earth who knew her, who felt like family.

"You mean get rid of Kerri? I'd never do that. Yes, she is my best friend, but I also think she's the best manager we've ever had. Auntie Elsa even said so herself."

Luca touched her arm to emphasize his point.

"Oh, no. I didn't mean getting rid of Kerri. I meant you might want to take a more hands-on approach to things, including the image and marketing of the place. And I'll help you and make available to you anything you may need or want."

She could see Luca was sincere, and he meant well.

"Thank you. That means the world."

They'd been so focused on each other they hadn't noticed the storm had been gaining in strength. A sudden loud rattle, as the wind tried to pull the buggy from the back of the truck, alerted Luca and Naomi to their situation. Together, they looked through the back window. Through the swirling orange and red sand around them, they could see the buggy remained tethered to the truck. It was being pummeled by the wind and sand and swayed like a tortoise drunk on fermented Marula fruit.

Naomi squinted through the dust-darkened windscreen. She started the engine and switched on the wipers to get a more unobstructed view. But sand poured onto the windshield faster than the wipers could remove.

When she spoke, she tried not to sound panicked.

"If we go now, we could still make it back to the lodge before the storm hits."

Luca pointed off to his left.

"How about sheltering under the trees over there? When I was on top of the dune, I saw a dry riverbed flanked by trees in that direction."

"That won't be a good idea. Many animals will head that

way. I don't fancy our chances against a herd of stampeding elephants. Or lions that might keep us captive for goodness knows how long while they shelter under the truck. And if this storm brings with it lightning, as these often do, then we don't want to be anywhere near trees, trust me."

Luca nodded, yielding to Naomi's superior knowledge of the desert.

Naomi eased the truck away from the dune, checking in the rear-view mirror that the buggy remained on the back. The volume of the storm increased as they left the soundproof the dune had afforded them.

When they were clear of the dune, Naomi drove slowly at first and then faster as the track became clearer in the full beam of the truck.

Suddenly, they heard a massive bang, followed at once by the truck's front wheel sinking into the sand on the right-hand side.

Naomi and Luca both looked back to check the buggy.

But Naomi knew what it was.

"Damn! I think we have a flat tire."

"I'll check."

Luca opened his door.

The wind tugged at it. He got out and had to push it shut.

Naomi watched as Luca checked the tire on the passenger side first. He gave a smile and a thumbs up. The lights illuminated his jean-clad legs as he walked past the truck's beam to the driver's side. His thumbs down gesture confirmed her suspicions. Then Luca battled against the wind to get back into the cabin.

"What now?"

"I'll let the lodge know we won't be able to get back tonight. We must stay here and wait it out."

Naomi switched off the engine and reached into the glove

compartment to retrieve the walkie-talkie. She pressed the button.

Kerri's voice crackled over the device, distorted by the storm.

"... you guys okay?"

Naomi raised her voice and spoke as clearly as she could.

"We're fine. But we're stuck."

"You... what?"

"Flat tire."

"Okay... Khwai... tomorrow morning... collect you... storm... over... then."

"Okay. Over and out."

Naomi put the walkie-talkie back in the glove compartment. Then, she lifted a panel on the seat between them. Their provisions were inside a small compartment underneath the seat, neatly stacked, each container wrapped with clingfilm to keep out any potential ants.

"Coffee? We may as well have some and enjoy the storm while we're here."

Luca nodded, but his eyes traveled over the darkening sky around them.

"And you're sure we'll be safe here?"

Naomi detected a note of panic in his voice. She wouldn't lie to make him feel better.

"As safe as we can be, yes. This truck is very heavy. I don't believe the wind will pick it up or throw us over. These storms aren't like the hurricanes I've seen on the news. We're more likely to suffocate from inhaling so much sand and dust."

Luca's head jerked in her direction.

Naomi smiled.

"Don't worry. I don't think we'll suffocate. While it's true it can happen, I only said it to reassure you."

The dubious look on Luca's face made Naomi laugh.

"We'll be fine. We might get a little hot and stuffy, but we'll survive. Coffee?"

He accepted the plastic mug she held out to him and took a sip, his eyes smiling over the rim. He winked at her.

"I can live with hot and stuffy as long as it's with you."

Naomi felt herself blush and knew she shouldn't. He'd be her husband. But she still had trouble getting her head around the idea.

Watching Luca, Naomi realized he had a sudden sense of just how isolated they were here, cut-off from the world, in a bubble of their own, as though they were the only two people in the world.

Luca put his empty mug on the dashboard and leaned back.

A soft sigh escaped his lips.

"We need to talk, don't you think?"

Naomi's heart sped up. She could feel her palms getting sweaty from anxiety. She'd been waiting for this moment. Now it was here, she was more apprehensive than she'd imagined. But she lifted her chin, squared her shoulders and looked into Luca's dark eyes.

Auntie Elsa's voice sounded in her mind, "... in for a penny, in for a pound..."

Naomi took the direct approach.

"You go first. Why did you change toward me so suddenly before you left?"

Luca moved around so he could face her head-on, his back against the door, his right arm resting on the top of the seat and one long leg bent in the space between them.

He held her eyes captive as he spoke.

"If you recall, I overheard you talking with Kerri. You said something that triggered all my insecurities. Two things, actually... You mentioned that Auntie Elsa had appointed you to look after Santina and me, and -"

Realization dawned on Naomi.

She turned her body to face Luca, pressing her back into the door on her side.

"And you thought our time together was just a matter of duty for me?"

Naomi's perceptiveness never ceased to surprise Luca.

"Yes, that's it exactly."

She lifted an eyebrow.

"Luca, I can't believe you'd even have thought it. Do you think if you were just part of my duties, I'd have spent so much time with you, swimming, going to dinner in Windhoek, and afterward, the jet...?"

Naomi felt her cheeks flush at her brazenness, mentioning the jet, but she refused to look away from his eyes.

Luca seemed embarrassed by his earlier thoughts. He lowered his eyes for moments, before looking back into hers again.

"I know. I couldn't work it out."

Naomi continued to look into his eyes as she spoke.

"But there is something else, isn't there?"

Luca loved their connection, even in their moments of discord. She was his perfect match. That phrase raced through his brain for the umpteenth time since he'd met her.

"Yes."

Again, Luca broke eye contact for mere moments before continuing.

"I heard you say something like... '... with his lifestyle and money, he can give women anything they want...' If you only knew how often I've heard that phrase and how women..."

Naomi had a sudden insight into the sadness that remained from the little boy who'd lost his mother to wealth.

She leaned toward him, putting a reassuring hand on his arm.

"No, Luca. I didn't mean it like that. If you must know, it was one of my insecure moments. Kerri had suggested you gave us the buggy deal because you cared for me. I found it difficult to believe.

"A man like you, with your lifestyle and your wealth and your privileges... That you would care for me? But now..."

Luca took her hand in his, intertwining her fingers through his.

"But now you know different. Now you know I love you, amore mio. I've loved no one as much as I love you. I didn't even know what love was until you. We don't know each other well yet, but I know one hundred percent you are the woman I've been looking for my entire life. Why would you ever think I wouldn't love you?"

It was Naomi's turn to lower her eyes as the heat of embarrassment crept up her neck onto her cheeks.

"Well, you know... You're an Italian god, and I'm -"

"You're my desert goddess."

Luca leaned forward and kissed Naomi ever so softly on her lips, lingering just long enough for them both to experience a physical reaction to the kiss. When he sat back, his pupils had dilated, his nostrils flared, and his breathing was uneven, matching Naomi's reaction. For moments, they stared into each other's eyes, in awe of their feelings for each other.

A slow smile played around Luca's lips.

"Now I've bared my soul to you, don't you think you should do the same?"

"What do you mean?"

"As I said, we don't know each other yet, and I can't wait to spend my life getting to know you. For now, though, I want to know why you became so wary of me after the poacher incident."

He picked up on that?

It surprised Naomi. He must've had feelings for her, even then, if he could be that sensitive to her.

"It's an old fear. Nothing to do with you."

"Well, I think it has. You say I changed toward you, but you changed toward me after the incident with the poachers put me in the hospital. Things were never the same between us after that. What happened?"

Luca stroked his thumb back and forth over her hand as though to comfort her even before she spoke.

His voice was soft as he encouraged her.

"Tell me?"

Naomi's sigh revealed her willingness to be vulnerable.

She had to be fair to him. He'd been open and honest with her. Now it was her turn. If they married, there could be no secrets between them.

As much as she could, she told him about her deep-seated fear of losing those people whom she loved, as she had her parents.

"I couldn't bear the thought of losing you, too. It would've been better, safer, not to love you to begin with."

A frown of concern appeared between Luca's eyes. But he listened in silence as he absorbed the information that had shaped so much of Naomi's life and personality.

Now, he understood how her fears had influenced her behavior toward him.

He brought her hand to his lips and kissed her fingers.

"Amore mio, that you love me as I love you is all I could ask from life. Death is just a part of life. It doesn't mean your love and your relationship with the person who has died, is over. Your parents still love you. They're still there for you. They're just in another dimension. Auntie Elsa will soon go there too, but it doesn't mean she'll stop loving you or caring about you."

Naomi's voice sounded a little sad.

"That's what she told me."

Naomi told Luca about how excited Auntie Elsa was to meet up with Uncle Wouter again, her soul mate.

Luca nodded.

"That's as it should be. At the end of our lives, we'll follow in their footsteps because you are my soul mate, amore mio. Nothing, not even death, can keep us apart."

Luca raised Naomi's hand to his lips and kissed her fingers.

Naomi thought nature had conspired to make this moment the most intimate and romantic. As the sand covered the truck, the sound of the storm diminished even more. It was the perfect soundproof against the cacophonous noise of the howling wind and the deafening claps of thunder. The lightning that followed sent shards of light across the sky that slithered through tiny gaps between the streams of sand running over the windows.

Naomi knew Luca had experienced nothing as terrifying, as intense, or as thrilling as this storm. That she could share it with him was beyond a bonus.

Luca interrupted her thoughts as he slid off the seat and maneuvered his tall body into the space between the seat and the dashboard. It was a tight fit, but he succeeded.

Naomi watched his unexpected and amusing behavior with a smile and a question mark in her eyes.

Luca managed to get himself on one knee, although he had to lean forward onto the seat in front of him.

"I know when I left, we were in a strange place and I wasn't sure if you'd allow me back in. But I took a chance anyway, Naomi, amore mio. I had to. I love you more than I've ever loved anyone in my entire life. I couldn't let you go. Now, I'm so glad I listened to my instincts because we've been able to come to an even better place.

"So, I called Kerri and asked her to check your size. I've had this made for you. I don't know of any better time to give it to you, amore mio. The wild, passionate storm around us matches my feelings for you one hundred percent."

Luca produced a small red box.

Naomi gasped. Her heart galloped at what felt a million miles an hour, and happy tears sprung into her eyes. Her hand went to her mouth, obscuring the enormous smile on her lips.

In the half-dusk of the cabin, the look on Luca's face was the most beautiful she had ever seen.

"Naomi, amore mio, will you please do me the honor of becoming my wife, forever and ever?"

Luca opened the box.

Inside, on the deepest red velvet, sat the most beautiful ring Naomi had ever seen. The ring was flawless and couldn't reflect more perfectly who she was. The diamond at its center wasn't big and ostentatious, screaming of wealth, but it was perfect both in size and style.

Luca held the ring out to Naomi, expectation and hope naked in his eyes.

Tears of happiness glistened in her eyelashes as she nodded, her eyes locked on the dark, intense eyes of the man she loved more than life itself.

The smile that lit up Luca's face outdid the lightning outside in its brilliance.

It was a perfect fit when he slipped the ring onto her ring finger.

But just as Naomi thought her heart would explode from happiness, she burst out laughing at Luca's contortions to extricate himself from the compact space, again.

He needed to sit on the seat for the kiss they both wanted to share so much, his entire body ached for it. The kiss that would seal their engagement.

When he returned to his seat, he took her face in his hands

and kissed her lips, and the magic of his sweet proposal swirled around them again.

At first, his lips were soft, but as their kiss deepened, so did their desire. Their breathing came fast and ragged, amplified in the small cabin. With a sensual groan, Luca pulled Naomi closer to him. But the confines of the cabin prevented any satisfying contact.

When they broke apart, their chests heaving, their lips bruised, Naomi had never wanted him more.

Luca's eyes burned into hers as his passion matched hers.

She loved how he showed his uninhibitedness by touching his arousal through his jeans, pinching the head of his penis to relieve the pressure and frustration. It was such a shocking thing, yet he handled it so matter-of-fact that it seemed natural. That he'd locked his eyes on hers, desire naked in them while he was doing it, was more surprising.

He growled at her, his voice deep and throaty. Then, a wicked grin curled around his mouth.

"Hmm, you taste just as delicious as I remember."

They laughed at their unusual situation, and then again, at their synchronicity.

Luca scooted nearer his door and pulled Naomi into his body, so she was lying across the seat they shared. His chest felt hard and safe under her head. His heartbeat slowed as his excitement diminished. After he'd kissed the top of her head, he leaned back against the window.

Outside, the storm had intensified. The ferocious wind howled around Luca and Naomi and pummeled the truck as it tried to get a grip on the vehicle. The buggy on the back was swaying faster as though dancing to a quick beat but remained where it was. Many-branched flashes of lightning followed the rhythm of deafening thunder. It was too dark to see if night had already fallen, and neither wore watches.

Curious, Naomi leaned forward and turned the key in the ignition. It was only eight o'clock.

Luca leaned against Naomi and peered at the time.

"Will the storm last all night?"

"Maybe. Are you hungry?"

Luca's eyes held a mischievous glint, but Naomi pretended not to notice. It could be very frustrating for them both, otherwise.

After dinner, they made themselves comfortable. Naomi snuggled against Luca's chest, again. He leaned back against the door, creating as much room for her as possible. His arms were around her, their fingers intertwined, and he held her as close as he could.

TWENTY-FOUR

Voices pulled Naomi from the deep unconsciousness of sleep. For a moment, she didn't know where she was. An awareness of being hot and stuffy in a tiny space became her first impressions. As her eyes got used to her surroundings, she realized she'd fallen asleep on Luca's chest in the truck's cabin. It wasn't how she'd imagined their first night together to be, but it was thrilling.

She sat up slowly, so as not to wake up Luca, whose rhythmic breathing showed he was still asleep. Turning her head left and right, she tried to iron out the stiffness from sleeping in such an awkward position.

Total silence greeted her. There were no signs of the storm, no howling wind, no shaking of the truck, but the sand had covered all the windows. She could see nothing through them. Yet, she was sure she hadn't imagined the voices nearby. She stretched her ears, holding her breath. At first, she could hear only babble, but the sounds became more distinct as they came closer. Naomi could make out some words in the Herero language.

Her first thoughts were of poachers. The increase in her

breathing and her heart beating faster were the only signs of her anxiety. She locked her door and sat still.

Luca was still asleep against his door, unaware of the danger they might be facing. She'd have to wake him up to lock his door. But it would be pointless. They'd be in real trouble if poachers had found them. Those guys usually carried guns and closed doors wouldn't stop them when they could shoot through glass and metal.

A scraping sound next to her alerted her that someone was brushing the sand from the window there. She continued to stare at the spot where the pink light of the breaking day was streaming in. When Khwai's smiling face peered at her through streaks of sand still clinging to the glass, relief washed through her veins and tingled in her fingers and toes. It brought tears to her eyes.

Beyond Khwai, stood several members of the anti-poacher unit. Soon, he'd scraped most of the sand from her window and door. She unlocked the door and opened it.

Luca was still sleeping. She held a finger to her mouth and pleaded with her eyes for the guards not to make a noise so Luca could continue to sleep a little longer.

She saw at once that Khwai had stopped the rescue truck, ready to take them home, a few meters behind hers.

Naomi got out and gently pushed the door closed again. She led the guards a short distance away from the truck where they formed a circle around her as she whispered to them.

"How will we get my truck with the buggy on the top back to the lodge?"

Khwai whispered back.

"Gerhard will bring the mechanic. He will bring the break-down lorry later, Nonna. The storm was still here two hours ago. So, we went to the waterhole to pick up Piet and Hans. But

Mrs. Elsa was worried about you. She wanted us to find you as soon as the storm finished."

It was unusual behavior for Auntie Elsa.

Naomi's pulse quickened.

"I see. Has anything happened to Auntie Elsa?"

"No, Nonna. She just wanted us to find you so you can go home."

Naomi prayed that was all it was, that Auntie Elsa was just concerned for her and Luca's safety. She looked back at the truck. It was recognizable as a truck, but the sand had covered it and the buggy on the back. Both vehicles would need a thorough wash. Thank God the buggy was only a prototype.

The passenger door opened, and Luca's dark hair appeared above the hood of the cabin. He saw her talking to the guards, closed the door and walked around the front of the truck to join them.

Khwai went to Luca at once, his hand outstretched in greeting. After their handshake, he and Luca joined the group. Luca put an arm around Naomi, giving her a squeeze and a kiss on her head. With his other hand, he greeted each guard.

Luca yawned, stretched and directed a sleepy smile at Naomi.

"I guess we'd better get going. I'm sure Auntie Elsa will be worried about you."

Khwai led his men back to the rescue truck, while Luca and Naomi went to collect their things from their vehicle. Khwai, meanwhile, had driven forward and stopped ahead of their vehicle to wait for them.

As Luca and Naomi walked the short distance toward their rescuers, they saw something on the back lying on a makeshift stretcher covered by canvas. The rest of the guards were already sitting on the raised sides of the truck facing inward, their fingers gripping the metal beside them, ready for the journey back to the lodge. They appeared unperturbed by whatever was under the canvas at their feet.

As Khwai drove off, he saw them glancing through the back window at the canvas.

"We found him by the waterhole, Nonna."

"What do you mean, Khwai?"

"The American man. The one who stayed at the lodge. When the boss man left, he got drunk and picked you up. We shot on the ground so he would put you down. Then the police came to take him away. That man."

Naomi gasped.

Stefan.

Luca and Naomi did a double take at each other, shock obvious on their faces.

Naomi stared at the canvas. Stefan was dead.

Naomi couldn't tear her eyes away from the canvas, even though everything in her screamed to do so. She should feel something. Relief, perhaps? Vindication? But all she felt was numb. Only two questions came to mind. How did it happen? How had Khwai found him?

Khwai was watching her. His response felt like he'd been reading her mind.

"The elephants trampled him, Nonna. So, we put him under the canvas.

Almost as an afterthought, he added, "I've already told Kerri on the walkie-talkie. She called the police."

Everyone was quiet for a long time.

Luca couldn't help feeling disappointed. He wasn't a vengeful man, but he would have liked the satisfaction he imagined he'd derive from bringing down Stefan for what he did to Naomi, and perhaps countless other women. But Luca was grateful the man would never again bother any other woman, including Naomi. He shuddered at the thought. He'd protect her with his life. That scum like Stefan had dared to lay his hands on Naomi? It still made Luca's blood boil.

Stefan had got his comeuppance, and what a way for it to happen. Luca should be happy. The man was dead. But should one ever delight in the death of another?

Luca sighed.

"It's the right punishment for what he did, don't you think? To you, and to that elephant he shot."

What could she say? Luca was right. The man was dead. But even in death, she didn't want to be near him. That day... what he'd done. It felt like it had happened to someone else.

Naomi was aware her detached feelings had everything to do with the trauma of the assault on her. It was as though her brain was protecting her by not allowing her to remember all the horrid details with any clarity. She was grateful for it. But it didn't diminish her distaste for having the man's body so nearby.

They drove in silence, Luca and Naomi both aware of Stefan's body lying under the canvas on the back of the truck.

As Khwai steered through the gate, Naomi noticed the flying doctor's Cessna parked on the small landing strip beside the house. Thoughts that something had happened to Auntie Elsa clawed their way back into her mind. Naomi couldn't wait to get out of the truck. As soon as she could, she excused herself and raced into the kitchen.

Auntie Elsa and Kerri sat at the big old wooden table. On either side of them sat the doctor, Johan and his cousin, Nick and Namibia's new Police Chief in his police uniform.

Naomi came to a halt.

"Oh. I... Are you okay, Auntie Elsa? I saw the doctor's Cessna."

Auntie Elsa's smile was warm and reassuring.

She understood Naomi's behavior.

"I'm as well as you see me, darling. The doctor, Nick and Chief Lucas Tumelo are here for Stefan's body."

Naomi almost cried from relief.

"Of course. Khwai said he'd called Kerri."

She went to press her cheek against Auntie Elsa's while hugging her bony shoulders.

Auntie Elsa put a hand over Naomi's on her shoulder.

"I'm so glad you're back. I was worried. It was a biggie this time, wasn't it?"

She paused as though to assimilate the information her fingers were giving her as her hand lingered on Naomi's.

"Is that a ring I feel on your finger, darling?"

Auntie Elsa pulled Naomi's hand forward so she could admire the ring.

"It's beautiful, Naomi. Congratulations. Where is Luca?"

The moment Auntie Elsa called attention to the ring, Kerri jumped up, and joined by several members of staff, they fawned over the ring, turning Naomi's hand this way and that.

Moments later, the light coming through the open kitchen door darkened as Luca's tall frame appeared there. An enormous grin lit up his face when he saw Naomi's admirers fawning over her ring.

Auntie Elsa beckoned him closer.

"Congratulations, Luca. Forgive me for not getting up."

The acoustics in the kitchen amplified Luca's deep voice as he spoke and took long strides toward Auntie Elsa.

"Please. Don't."

After he'd given her soft kisses on both cheeks, she introduced him to Nick and Chief Tumelo.

Luca shook their hands, and those of the doctor and Johan, whose booming voice was too loud for the kitchen.

"Good to see you back here, Luca. Congratulations, man.

Naomi is a cracking girl, but she's picky. You're a fortunate man."

Chef brought delicious freshly baked bread, jam and rich coffee.

Naomi took her place beside Auntie Elsa, and Luca pushed in her chair before taking his seat next to her. Everyone, except Auntie Elsa, helped themselves to Chef's offerings.

Auntie Elsa drank only coffee. Her appetite had diminished even more. But she appeared to enjoy the gathering that had turned into an early breakfast celebration of Luca's and Naomi's engagement.

Chief Tumelo and Nick popped out to check on Stefan's body and to take statements from Khwai and the guards before they left for the day on their duties.

Everyone's eyes were expectantly on them when they returned and took their seats at the table again.

Chief Tumelo nodded as he spoke.

"Yes, it's Stefan's body. The poachers we picked up yesterday were the men who'd helped Stefan track and kill several elephants in the desert. They were the same men caught here one night when they came looking for the ellie after they'd killed her mother. When we arrested the men yesterday, we didn't realize they had left Stefan alone in the desert. From the state of the body, I'd say it's clear he got caught in the storm. Most likely disorientated, he got in the way of the stampeding animals. I agree with Khwai. It looks like elephants trampled him."

Auntie Elsa sighed.

"I feel responsible because I gave those men food and sent them on their way that night, instead of having them arrested. What's even more disturbing is Stefan was so close to the lodge. Did no one suspect he was still in Namibia?"

Nick cleared his throat.

"Please don't feel guilty about the men you set free. You're a kind woman, Mrs. Elsa. But they're not honorable men. Even if we'd arrested them that night, we couldn't have held them for long because it would've been only on trespassing charges. We couldn't prove they were with the other poachers who'd killed the elephant that day. The moment they were free, they'd have continued to do what they wanted to do, anyway. Now, the charges are much more serious. They won't be killing any more elephants, for others or themselves, for a long time."

Everyone was quiet, hanging on Nick's every word, and turned to look at Chief Tumelo when he resumed where Nick had left off.

"To answer your question... yes, we knew Stefan was still in Namibia. But it's a big country with a lot of wildernesses. He could have been anywhere. We're lucky Khwai and your guards found his body at all. I guess we'll never know why he was so close to Desert Lodge."

But Naomi knew why. So did Luca, Auntie Elsa, Kerri and Johan. She suspected Nick and Chief Tumelo knew too, but they didn't want to cause more upset than was necessary - Stefan had wanted revenge on Naomi.

Her heart went cold when she thought about the number of times she'd walked into the desert during her brief break, first by herself, then with Luca. They would have been sitting targets for Stefan.

Chief Tumelo and Nick got up. The Chief put his cap on and pushed his chair back under the table.

"Well, folks, we'd best be on our way. Thank you for your hospitality, Mrs. Elsa. Once the Doc has finished the autopsy, we'll talk again."

With a wave and a smile, the Chief and Nick left, followed by the doctor.

Through the door, Naomi saw them lift Stefan's body from

the truck and carry it to the doctor's Cessna. It still felt surreal that Stefan had been so close, the way he'd died, and now they were taking his body away.

Luca squeezed Naomi's hand as though he knew what she was thinking. She was grateful for his support, for reminding her she was safe.

Feeling sticky and sweaty from their night's ordeal, Luca and Naomi left to go to their separate rooms to shower.

By the time Naomi re-joined the others in the Lapa, the sun was almost up, and most guests had yet to return from their sunrise safaris. She felt lightheaded as the events of the past few hours threatened to overwhelm her and was surprised to realize she was famished. Shock sometimes had that effect on her. Even though they'd had some bread and jam with their coffee earlier in the kitchen, her stomach growled at the delicious aromas of the breakfast. She took her seat between Luca and Auntie Elsa, as usual.

Around them, staff was readying the Lapa for Auntie Elsa's and Santina's party that evening. The big round table at the back of the Lapa already groaned under an avalanche of gifts for the two ladies. Stunning African rugs were being hung at three sides, leaving only the front of the Lapa open, offering a view over the pool. The staff looped thousands of Murano glass fairy lights Santina had brought from Italy through the rafters all around the Lapa. Massive African urns placed in the corners sprouted tall grasses, which lent a whimsical element to the venue.

In the cleaned pool, colorful lights secured to the bottom would add more magical light when the sun went down.

The day became a whirlwind of activity, not as desperate as the previous day's pandemonium in the storm, but just as intense.

Several members of the Italian party had commandeered

Luca to fly them to Windhoek for some last-minute shopping. It meant fewer people to cater to at lunch, which Chef appreciated.

The kitchen was hotter than the desert, even though several fans were whirring at full power and all the windows and doors were open.

After lunch, most of the remaining guests, Auntie Elsa and Santina, retired to their rooms for a siesta. Kerri had ordered coffee for her and Naomi in the refreshing coolness of the guest lounge.

Kerri poured two cups and handed one to Naomi.

"Do you think our gift to Auntie Elsa and Santina is enough? It seems everyone else's gifts are much more extravagant."

Naomi took a sip of her coffee and leaned back against the sofa, exhaling the tension from her body. She could relax now.

"I think our gift is perfect. Santina wanted an authentic Namibian experience. What could be more authentic than Namibia's ancient music? No one has ever heard this music outside of our country. And you know Auntie Elsa just loves it. She's always taken such pleasure in hearing the San people's voices sing in harmony. It's a shame we hear it so seldom. Someone should record them before their songs are gone forever. Speaking of which, it's the reason it's the perfect gift for Auntie Elsa. There's nothing we can offer that will give her more joy. And, as much as it hurts to even think about it, she'll be gone in a few weeks, and she can't take anything with her, can she?"

Kerri nodded.

"Hmm, if you put it like that... You know she's asked Santina to help get her ready for the party instead of us? Perhaps she doesn't want to remind us any more than she has to that she's so ill. I'll miss her so much. I can't even imagine how you must feel."

Naomi put her cup down on the coffee table beside her.

When she spoke, her voice sounded sad but intense.

"I feel lucky. Auntie Elsa is an incredible woman, and I feel truly blessed she's in my life. Of course, I'll be sad. I'm sad now. I'll be losing the only mother I've ever really known. I was too young when my mother died to remember her clearly. When I think of her, it's more the idea of her I remember, if you see what I mean? And I'm grateful we have this time left to get used to Auntie Elsa's leaving. She's told me how much she's looking forward to seeing Uncle Wouter again. Auntie Elsa has always talked about him as her soul mate, and I believe they'll meet up again. So, I'm happy for her. If I continue to think of her happiness, then my sadness won't be so overwhelming. Plus, I have you and Luca in my life. You're both pretty incredible, too."

Kerri winked at Naomi.

"Oh, stop it. You'll make me blush."

"Yeah, like you don't know it already. And I know I'm not the only one thinking you're wonderful. I saw how Johan could barely keep his eyes off you this morning. How are things going with him?"

Kerri's eyes glittered, and her smile got even broader.

"Funny you should ask... He's kind of asked me to marry him."

Naomi jumped up and rushed over to her friend. She plonked herself down beside Kerri and hugged her close.

"Oh, my God, that's amazing news. Congratulations! When?"

When Kerri could breathe again from being hugged so tightly, she giggled before answering.

"We didn't want to spoil things for you and Luca, but it happened the night before Luca asked Auntie Elsa for your hand. We'll wait a little while so we can decide the logistics. You know? Where to live, who'll be moving in with whom... That kind of thing."

"I'm so happy for you, Kerri. Just look at us. Both with the most amazing men."

A frown appeared between Naomi's green eyes.

"It feels kind of strange, though, doesn't it? In a good way, I mean. It's like Auntie Elsa is leaving us, but we won't be alone. Do you believe in coincidences?"

"I know what you mean. I had a similar thought. But, however it's happened, coincidences or not, I'm so happy for both of us."

"You'll still stay on as manager of Desert Lodge, though, right?"

Kerri hugged her friend back.

"You just try to stop me. All my dreams have come true. My dream job, my dream man..."

THE RAP on Naomi's door awoke her. She got up to let Kerri in. The large bag she dragged behind her nearly got stuck in the door, but she yanked it through as she spoke.

"I'm glad you could sleep a little with all the noise going on today."

Naomi yawned and stretched.

"Yeah, I guess I needed it. Sleeping in the truck in the desert during a storm wasn't the most restful sleep I've ever had."

"Well, I'm glad I came to wake you. We have to get ready. It's almost six o'clock. The rest of Auntie Elsa's friends will be here soon. Some have already arrived. They're in the Lapa having drinks."

Naomi yawned again, struggling to shrug the last vestiges of sleep from her body.

"What are you wearing tonight?"

Kerri plonked her bag on Naomi's bed.

"My green dress. It's in here. I've already had my shower and thought it would be fun to get ready together. That's okay, isn't it?"

Naomi smiled at Kerri and went to look through the clothes in her wardrobe. Kerri's bag was so large Naomi had wondered if she'd brought along her entire wardrobe. It contained enough beauty products to open a store.

A frisson of excitement coursed through Naomi. It had been so long since she'd shared a getting-ready event with her best friend.

"Sure, it'll be fun. We won't get many more chances to do so, now we're both nearly married women."

Kerri put on some music while she did her makeup at Naomi's vanity table. Naomi had a quick shower, dried her hair and got dressed so they could swap places.

Kerri's dress, the green of desert aloes, was the perfect contrast to Naomi's sky-blue dress. Arm-in-arm, the two friends walked to the Lapa to join the party already in full swing.

Luca's Italian chef had worked with Chef to create a fusion of food from the two cultures that produced the most delicious canapés Naomi had ever tasted. The guests thought so too, as they stood around the tables in the Lapa, on the patio, and around the pool, drinks and canapés in hand.

Naomi's heart fluttered when she saw Luca talking with Johan and a group of other guests. He looked unbelievably handsome in black trousers and a white tailored shirt. As though he could feel her presence, his eyes found hers. A gigantic smile lit up his face as he took long strides toward her.

"Amore mio, you look like a dream."

She blushed pink when he lifted her chin and kissed her lips in full view of everyone there. Then, he put an arm around her shoulders and led her and Kerri to the group of friends he'd just left.

Kerri had arranged a wheelchair for Auntie Elsa, who'd found it too exhausting to walk any small distance now. Santina wheeled Auntie Elsa toward the Lapa amidst loud applause from everyone there, including the staff. Following alongside, Chef pushed a small hostess trolley. On it sat the biggest, most flamboyant birthday cake Naomi had ever seen. It comprised at least four layers. Candles covered the top tier. So many candles that one could hardly see any cake beneath it. She could only imagine what it would look like once Chef lit all the candles.

Santina and Auntie Elsa looked splendid in their sparkly tops, just as birthday girls should. Slowly, they made their way through the well-wishers into the Lapa. Once they'd reached their table and were seated, Luca excused himself, went to them, and pinged a knife against an empty wine glass to get everyone's attention.

His speech was short but powerful and heart-warming. He spoke about how lucky he was to have Santina in his life, how she'd been like a mother to him all these years. He said he was more grateful than he had words to express that Santina had found such a wonderful friend in Auntie Elsa. Naomi felt her face flush when he thanked Auntie Elsa for likewise, being such a wonderful mother to her, and for having consented to their marriage.

But when he spoke about how fortunate everyone was to have Auntie Elsa there for this special celebration, the first and last birthday party she'd ever share with Santina, everyone welled up.

The place erupted following his speech. People were congratulating Auntie Elsa and Santina on their joint birthdays.

The mood extended to Luca and Naomi as they received good wishes and blessings on their engagement.

As the wind changed direction, it brought with it the mouth-watering aromas of the barbeques that had been cooking on the other side of the pool. Staff were carrying huge trays with barbequed meats of all kinds to the buffet area in the Lapa. The staff had elegantly displayed a colorful array of salads and other accompaniments to the barbeque. Members of the kitchen staff handed plates to guests and served their requests. On the other side of the Lapa, guests kept the bar staff busy serving wine, beer and soft drinks.

The sunset threw an array of colors on the canvas of the day sky in the west, while in the east, already stars were twinkling against the much darker blue of the night sky.

As the dark of the night took hold, the lights in the Lapa and the pool came on. The fairy lights in the rafters created a starry heaven of their own. Tall outdoor lamps illuminated the patio and the dark areas further away, and the pool had turned into a small lake of light.

Naomi and Luca sat close together at the same table as Auntie Elsa and Santina. Kerri and Johan, and several of Santina's Italian friends, had squeezed in at the table. It was a pleasant, friendly affair, full of laughter and jokes.

Naomi kept an eye on Auntie Elsa in case she became too tired and wanted to take a break from the festivities. But her bright smile and excited eyes absorbed every detail around her. It broke Naomi's heart to see Auntie Elsa was saying goodbye to it all.

Naomi caught Kerri's eye. They seemed to have had the same thought at the same time. The friends smiled at each other. They'd support each other through the storm to come.

When Luca had finished his dinner and pushed his plate

aside, Naomi leaned into him to whisper in his ear. He listened for a moment and then turned to look into her eyes.

"Really? I'm so happy for them. But in that case, it's only fair that people congratulate them, too."

Luca got up.

Pinging a spoon against an empty wine glass again to get everyone's attention, he spoke.

"It seems we have yet another reason to celebrate tonight. I've just learned that Naomi's best friend, Kerri, who is the new manager here at Desert Lodge, has agreed to marry one of the nicest men I've ever met. Johan is the owner of the nearby elephant orphanage, which I hope you'll all visit and support. Congratulations to Johan and Kerri. May you be as happy as Naomi and me."

Luca raised a glass, and everyone in the Lapa followed his example, before launching into another round of deafening applause. Soon, well-wishers swamped their table. They kissed Kerri on the cheek and thumped Johan on the shoulder.

Chef had reappeared, meanwhile. He lit the candles on the cake, while waitresses carrying large trays offered flutes filled with champagne.

Santina pushed Auntie Elsa's wheelchair next to the enormous cake. Once there, it took several minutes for Auntie Elsa to get up, and together, the two ladies blew out the candles on their cake.

In his beautiful baritone voice, Luca sang 'happy birthday.' Everyone joined in and sang in their own time, 'Auntie Elsa and Santina,' or the other way around, which meant that part of the song went on for ages. But through much laughter and jollity, everyone joined in at the end with the usual 'hip, hip, hooray.'

Despite the applause, the flashes from cameras, and the laughter and smiling faces of their friends and family, a sense of poignancy had invaded the happy picture. Naomi and Kerri shared sad smiles but were determined to help make Auntie Elsa's last party on earth the best she'd ever had.

Chef removed the candles and cut the cake into slices, starting at the top tier. Waitresses distributed it among the guests while Santina and Auntie Elsa took their places at their table again. The atmosphere had changed, however. Conversations were more subdued, more reverent, yet still flowing, still cheerful.

The soft sounds of a cappella voices eventually penetrated the babble. Everyone stopped talking to listen to the beautiful songs and voices of the small group of singers from the San tribe. They walked in single file around the tables to stand at the back of the Lapa where everyone could see them. The sound they produced was unusual and unearthly, their bodies swaying to the rhythm inside them. Singing in their native language, no one could understand the meaning of their words. But the beauty and emotion in their voices brought only pleasure. Their singing seemed to be one continuous song. If there were separate songs, no one would have guessed. Their sound affected even those Namibians, who grew up among these ancient hunter-gatherers.

Santina and Auntie Elsa held hands and shared a tissue to stem the tears that flowed from their eyes.

TWENTY-FIVE

The next morning, when Naomi went to meet Luca for their regular early morning swim, the Lapa and surrounding area looked as it always did. There were no signs of the party from the evening before. Either the staff had worked through the night to clean everything, or they'd used magic.

Luca was sitting alone in the Lapa as he waited for her, absorbed in something on his phone. Naomi stood, admiring him for a moment. She couldn't help wondering how he'd managed to look so good so early in the morning. He'd had a shower as his hair was wet and tousled, which heightened his sexiness. That this stunning, amazing man was hers still felt like a dream.

Gratitude coursed through her that they could talk things through and come to a better understanding of each other. She couldn't ask for anything more. Her heart swelled with love for him, for his kindness, his consideration, and for his realness. More than anything, she appreciated how he didn't give up on her, didn't give up on their love, even before either knew for sure how the other was feeling.

Just as she was about to say something to him, the sound of

the doctor's Cessna flying over the lodge made her look up. Luca did the same and noticed her standing there. He got up and went to her, slipping an arm around her waist. His free hand cupped her cheek as he planted a soft kiss on her lips.

He let her go, looking deep into her eyes, a sexy smile lingering around his mouth, his hands warm on her shoulders.

"Good morning, amore mio. You brought the sunshine with you. See...?"

Luca pointed toward the east where pink ribbons of sunrise floated through the sky as it turned into day.

"... sunshine that's replacing my night of missing you."

Naomi smiled at his silly and charming attempt at romance so early in the morning.

She hugged his torso, leaned her head on his chest and gave him a squeeze, instead.

"Let's get to the kitchen. The doctor will be there. He's most probably brought news about Stefan's autopsy."

Together, arms around each other, they walked to the kitchen.

The young doctor was standing by the door, ready to knock, when Luca and Naomi came upon him. Naomi thought it odd he had his doctor's bag in his hand, but realized he might be off elsewhere afterward where he'd need it. He greeted them, his face suitably serious for the news he had to share, and followed them into the kitchen.

The aroma of freshly made coffee met them as soon as the door opened. Staff was already busy preparing refreshments for the sunrise safaris and breakfast in the Lapa for guests who would stay at the lodge.

But the doctor didn't stop. He strode to the door leading to the corridor that would take him further into the grand old house.

An icy hand clamped around Naomi's heart at once. She

glanced at Luca. He took her hand and gave it a reassuring squeeze as they ran down the corridor to Auntie Elsa's room, overtaking the doctor.

When they reached her door, the doctor, who'd had to run to keep up with them, held up a hand.

He was struggling to catch his breath but tried to keep his voice above a whisper.

"Let me examine her first. I'll let you know the moment you can enter."

But Naomi couldn't wait. She had to see Auntie Elsa, had to see she was all right, that she was still alive.

She pushed past the doctor, but he stopped her from opening the door

"Please, Naomi. I know this is difficult for you. I promise I'll let you in as soon as I can. But please just let me help her first."

Naomi couldn't speak, but she could see the doctor was sincere. Her mind was working overtime. What if this was it? What if this was the moment she'd been dreading? She wasn't ready to let go of Auntie Elsa yet. Not like this.

Luca put his arms around Naomi and hugged her tight against his body as he tried to calm her. The trembling in her body lessened somewhat against Luca's warm, secure chest. She felt protected, but for how long? The doctor's demeanor suggested Auntie Elsa had taken a turn for the worst. Naomi wanted to be strong for her. She fought to get herself under control, refusing to shed the tears threatening to fall as her throat tightened.

After what seemed like an hour, but may have been only minutes, the door opened, and the doctor came out. He pulled the door closed behind him trying to make as little noise as possible.

He looked into Naomi's questioning eyes.

"It's as expected. This will be a trying time for all of you.

Auntie Elsa doesn't have much longer, maybe a few days. I've made her as comfortable as I can and administered as high a dose of morphine as I dare. There's nothing more I can do."

Naomi heard his words as though through sand. But his muffled sounds meant nothing other than reinforcing the realization her beloved adoptive mother was leaving her.

Luca put an arm around her shoulders and pulled her closer to him to comfort her.

The doctor opened the door and gestured for them to enter Auntie Elsa's room.

Auntie Elsa sat propped up against her pillows. Her face looked drawn and yellow. She was clearly in a great deal of pain. The doctor had inserted a needle into her arm, which allowed the drip to feed fluid and painkillers directly into her bloodstream. He'd tied the bag with a clear liquid to the nearest post of her four-poster bed above her head, and he'd supplied a catheter, so she didn't have to get up out of bed to visit the loo.

When Auntie Elsa saw Naomi, she smiled weakly and beckoned her closer.

Her voice was a whisper.

"Darling, I'm not doing too well. But please don't be sad. I'm ready to go to my Wouter, and you have Luca…"

Naomi shook her head to show Auntie Elsa didn't need to talk. She sat down on the bed beside Auntie Elsa and took her cold, bony hand in hers. She rubbed her thumb over the back to warm it up, but Auntie Elsa's hand remained cold and clammy. Naomi couldn't trust her voice, so she remained silent, her eyes saying everything she felt instead, telling of her deep love for Auntie Elsa. The two women sat staring at each other, sad little smiles lingering around their lips. There was nothing more to say.

Luca and the doctor quietly left the room so Naomi and

Auntie Elsa could have some privacy, but neither heard nor saw the men go.

After a while, it became clear the painkillers were having some effect on Auntie Elsa. Her breathing slowed, and she closed her eyes. Her face relaxed as the worst of the pain left her body. Naomi made sure Auntie Elsa was sleeping before she got up from the bed and tip-toed out of the room, closing the door softly behind her.

She found Luca and the doctor sitting at the big wooden table in the kitchen, each with a mug of steaming coffee. Both got up as she walked toward them, question marks in their eyes.

"She's sleeping. Thank you for helping her, doctor. What do we do now?"

Luca pulled a chair out for her to sit beside him and signaled Chef to bring her some sweet coffee.

The doctor sat back down, meanwhile, a frown between his eyes as he planned his response.

"There is little we can do. But we can make sure she's comfortable and as pain-free as possible. I've prepared more drips with the right amounts of painkillers. I'll leave those here with Kerri. She's your first aider, isn't she?"

Naomi nodded.

The doctor checked his watch.

"I've called Kerri. I know it's probably earlier than her normal working hours, but I have another patient to get to, so I can't stay."

Just as he finished speaking, Kerri hurried through the kitchen door. Red spots blooming on her cheeks showed the effort she'd made to get here as fast as possible.

Naomi listened to the doctor's words as he explained every-thing to Kerri, but she couldn't take any of it on board. Thank God for Kerri who was immediately alert, taking notes as the doctor spoke so she wouldn't miss a thing later when it counted.

Leaving Kerri with the doctor, Luca and Naomi returned to sit with Auntie Elsa, Naomi's eyes never lifting from her beloved adoptive mother's face. She needed to sear this face into her memory.

Kerri had drawn up a roster, meanwhile, so someone would be with Auntie Elsa every moment of the day or night. She knew it would give Naomi enormous peace of mind. Instructions were to call Kerri and Naomi at once should there be any change in Auntie Elsa's condition.

Each member of staff on the roster accepted their turn to sit with Auntie Elsa while they still had the chance to do so. Naomi supplied Auntie Elsa's favorite books in case she wanted to listen to readings from them. Kerri arranged for a small stereo system and Auntie Elsa's favorite music should she want to hear it. Santina, Luca, and several of Auntie Elsa's friends, who'd remained at the lodge following the party, insisted on being added to the roster.

By the evening, Auntie Elsa, though still in pain, seemed much better again. She was adamant about getting out of bed and joining everyone in the Lapa for dinner, even though she had no appetite. It was a very different affair from the happy one of the previous night. But everyone felt grateful to spend one more evening with this incredible woman.

Afterward, in Auntie Elsa's room, Santina stayed with her, the two friends talking until Auntie Elsa fell asleep.

The other guests stayed in the Lapa along with Kerri and Johan, but Luca and Naomi elected to sit in the guest lounge to have their coffee. It was the first time they got to spend time alone together again since the storm in the desert.

Luca put his cup on the coffee table beside him. With a sigh of contentment, he stretched out his long legs in front of him, crossing them at his ankles. Intertwining his fingers behind his head, he leaned back into the cushions behind him.

"I've been thinking..."

Naomi put down her cup. Her heart was lighter than it had been in the morning after finding Auntie Elsa in so much pain. But she knew her feelings of relief wouldn't last long. Still, for now, the heaviness had lifted.

She smiled at Luca.

"That could be dangerous."

"Dangerous amore? Oh, yes, I see."

He returned her smile. But the frown between his dark eyes remained as he thought of the best way to broach the subject with her. He'd wanted to give her the best. But circumstances seemed to conspire against him. None of his carefully laid plans to woo Naomi and to prove to her how much he loved her had transpired according to his wishes. The doubts she'd accept his proposal had evaporated as they spoke, as they came to understand each other, to know that each reciprocated the other's love at such a deep level.

Now, he'd have to forego another plan. It was clear Auntie Elsa wouldn't long be with them. He wanted to give Naomi the opportunity to have her at their wedding. It was a delicate subject, and the last thing he wanted was to upset Naomi more than current circumstances did.

"Nothing about our engagement has worked out how I'd imagined."

"How do you mean?"

"Don't get me wrong, I had planned on asking Auntie Elsa for your hand, but not in the way it happened. Although, come to think of it, it was a fabulous experience with everyone around us, don't you agree?"

Naomi nodded but stayed silent, waiting to see where his thoughts were leading.

"And although it was more perfect than I could've engineered, I hadn't planned on proposing to you in a truck in a storm in the middle of the desert, amore mio.

Luca sat back up and leaned toward Naomi.

"But now..."

Naomi's heart beat a little faster. Was he about to propose the same thing she'd been thinking?

"... with Auntie Elsa so ill..."

Luca sighed.

Why was this so difficult? They were going to get married, anyway. What difference did it make that it happened now? Yet, he knew it made a difference. They'd only just cleared the air between them. They'd only just got engaged. Neither of them had had time to get used to the idea that their lives would change forever when they said their vows. Was it all too much too soon? How would it affect their future? But now, with Auntie Elsa's imminent death...

"How would you like it if we got married tomorrow?"

Naomi sat in stunned silence for a moment. Even though having Auntie Elsa at her wedding had been in her thoughts, it was a dream that had been slipping away.

"Oh, Luca! Do you mean it?"

Naomi jumped on Luca. He laughed at her excitement and caught her in his arms, pulling her down onto his lap.

"I do."

He kissed her gently.

"I thought perhaps we could have our ceremony in the desert, near the place where you took me to see my first African elephant. Do you remember? The big old bull. That's when I first suspected my feelings for you ran deeper than it prepared me to admit."

Naomi clapped her hands together in front of her mouth.

"That would be perfect. Oh, Luca! But how will we get everything arranged so fast?"

She checked the clock over the mantelpiece.

"It's already gone eight o'clock."

He kissed her again.

"Don't worry your gorgeous head, my Naomi. If our ceremony is just before sunset tomorrow, we'd have most of the day to arrange everything. And this way, many of Auntie Elsa's friends and yours, I presume, are still here to join us."

"That will be perfect."

But a frown remained between Naomi's eyes even as she said those words.

Luca kissed the frown.

"'But' amore mio? I can feel a 'but?'"

"Oh, no. Not a 'but...' I'm just wondering if Auntie Elsa could make it into the desert with us."

"Well, the desert was just a thought. We will do whatever works best for her, si? Even if it means we get married in her room. I don't care where, as long as you become my wife and make me the happiest man in the universe, and your Auntie Elsa can be there to see how happy you are."

Naomi threw her arms around his neck, kissed him and pressed his head to her chest.

"Oh, Luca! You're the best."

She let go of him and sat back.

The frown between her eyes had returned.

"But what about your father? Wouldn't you want him at your wedding?"

"I spoke to him earlier today and mentioned how ill Auntie Elsa was. He said he wanted to meet the woman who'd raised the girl I want to marry, so he's already made arrangements. He should be here tomorrow morning."

Naomi got up.

"Oh, but..."

Luca pulled her down beside him again and gave her another soft kiss on her lips.

"Don't worry, amore mio. Kerri has already taken care of everything for him. You're right. She's a fantastic manager."

LATER THAT NIGHT, alone in her bed, a sudden thought popped into Naomi's head. What about a dress? What would she wear? A wedding dress was a tremendous deal, wasn't it? But even as her mind whirled with the events of the last few days and the thoughts of what was to come in the days ahead, an idea for the perfect dress deposited itself in there, somehow. Auntie Elsa would know...

Early the next morning, when Naomi entered Auntie Elsa's room, she looked so much better despite a yellow tint still on her skin. She was already sitting propped up against her pillows and seemed to be in a good mood.

After the staff member who'd stayed with her all night had left the room, Naomi checked Auntie Elsa had had a good night's rest. Naomi sat down on the bed beside her and held her small, thin hand. It felt warmer than the day before, at least. The warmth of gratitude flooded Naomi's body.

"I have something to ask. Two things, actually."

Auntie Elsa smiled at her daughter, her eyes already consenting to whatever Naomi wanted.

Naomi's smile broadened as she remembered her discussion with Luca the evening before. He'd agreed it would be best the invitation came from Naomi.

"How would you like to be the guest of honor at my wedding today?"

Auntie Elsa's eyes widened in surprise.

"You mean..."

Naomi couldn't contain the gigantic smile that burst forth from her heart.

"Yes. Luca wants us to marry today. We'd love it if you could be there. Would you?"

A frown appeared on Naomi's face as her smile faded, doubt naked in her eyes.

"Could you?"

"Oh, my darling girl. I'm so happy for you. Of course I'll be there. I wouldn't miss it for the world. Where were you thinking?"

Naomi outlined the plan, and Auntie Elsa's eyes glittered more and more with excitement as Naomi filled in the details.

Auntie Elsa was nodding, tears shining in her eyes. Like Naomi, she hadn't thought she'd live to see her darling daughter get married. Now, she could leave this world with even more happiness in her heart.

She smiled at Naomi.

"And the second request?"

"Your wedding dress?"

Auntie Elsa clapped her hands together in front of her mouth, the tears she'd been holding in, traveled down her cheeks.

"Oh, Naomi, that would be so wonderful. You must have it. If it brings you as much joy and love as it has Wouter and me, I couldn't be happier. I couldn't ask for anything more."

Auntie Elsa directed Naomi to where she'd kept the dress in tissue paper in a suitcase at the back of her enormous wardrobe carved from acacia wood. Reverently, Naomi removed it and tried it on. As Naomi was so much taller than Auntie Elsa, the dress fell much shorter on her. But it was a perfect fit.

She twirled around. The cream silk dress hugged her curves and felt as soft as a breeze against her skin. She took it off again and was just about to return it to the tissue paper and the suitcase that had kept it safe for so many years, when she noticed a full lace veil beneath the next layer of tissue paper. It was much longer than the dress, clearly meant to train behind it. But again, because of Naomi's taller stature, the veil fell to her ankles. It was perfect.

She kissed Auntie Elsa and turned to leave just as Santina opened the door. It was her turn next to sit with Auntie Elsa.

Luca had already informed Santina of their plans, and she gave Naomi a tight hug as though she was welcoming her into the Italian crowd.

"I'm so happy for you both, Naomi. Luca deserves so much happiness. And having got to know you a little, I'd say, so do you."

The morning was a hive of activity. Everyone seemed to have something to do and was on a mission to fulfill their duties.

A strange feeling of detachment sat in Naomi's chest, as though she had no part in any of it. She couldn't stay away from Auntie Elsa's room for long and popped in every fifteen minutes to check she was all right.

Luca's father arrived under a cloud of sand as his pilot drove the small plane closer to the lodge. Naomi went with Luca and Santina to meet him.

He wasn't how Naomi had imagined him to be. He was tall, like Luca, but had a much more serious, much sterner demeanor. When he spoke, his voice was a soft tenor, however, which sounded friendlier than he appeared. His smart clothes and gray hair gave him a distinguished air.

The moment he stepped off the plane, Enzo, which he insisted everyone call him, congratulated Luca and Naomi on their wedding. He didn't have Luca's natural charm and warm manner, but Naomi could see he was happy for them both. He held her hand as the small party walked to his suite, Luca carrying his father's bags.

Once he'd settled in, Enzo asked after Auntie Elsa.

As Auntie Elsa was feeling so much better, no doubt her spirits lifted by the excitement of the wedding, she'd asked for someone to wheel her out to the Lapa. One of the regular morning nurses who'd checked on Auntie Elsa helped to disconnect her from the IV to make her more mobile before helping her into the wheelchair and pushing her there.

The sun reflected off the water in the pool, generating light and shade in waves on the buildings surrounding it. Lush green plants and tiny birds helped to create a carefree vacation atmosphere.

Naomi could see how Auntie Elsa would find it more restful out here than staying cooped up in her bedroom all day, even though the room was huge and luxurious.

Enzo was gentle with Auntie Elsa. He sat with her, holding her hand while they whispered together and drank coffee.

Meanwhile, Santina, Kerri and Johan had flown to Windhoek with Luca. Luca, to find wedding bands. The others to look for something to wear to the wedding. Chef and his team were preparing party food. Khwai had commandeered several guards, gardeners and waiters to help set up the venue in the desert. Other staff members were cleaning the safari trucks that were to take everyone to the site for the wedding.

Although everyone was busy, it wasn't frenetic. Instead, the activity around Naomi filled her with a sense of peace. She spent time alone in her room but wanted to spend as much time with Auntie Elsa as she could. She took her things with her and gave them both manicures and pedicures, pampering herself and Auntie Elsa. The two women didn't have to talk, and much of the pampering happened in silence, as each was busy with their thoughts.

Soon, Naomi would be Mrs. Luca Armati. It sounded surreal to her ears, and she couldn't help but feel anxious about what the future held in store for her, especially with a title like that. What would Luca expect of her? Would she be able to fit into his world the way he'd fitted into hers so easily?

She shook her head. It was best to deal with one thing at a time, and today was supposed to be the happiest day of her life. She didn't want to dwell on things that made her feel anything other than happy. All she could think of was how grateful she was Auntie Elsa was still here to witness her wedding. She felt truly blessed.

In the meantime, Chef had prepared a barbeque for lunch. Luca and his entourage had returned to the lodge, hungry and tired, carrying an array of shopping bags. As a result, lunch was a subdued affair, and when they'd eaten their fill, everyone went to their rooms for a short siesta.

But Naomi couldn't sleep. Her thoughts were with Auntie Elsa and with Luca.

Luca couldn't sleep either. He was lying on his bed with his eyes closed, but his mind refused to switch off.

How was he going to help Naomi when Auntie Elsa died? Although she'd attempted to be with them, it shocked him to see Auntie Elsa's rapid deterioration. The doctor was right. Her time to go seemed imminently near.

Luca felt comforted by the thought the doctor would be in attendance. God forbid anything should happen today. It would forever mar their wedding anniversary. He just wanted it to be the perfect day for them all. Sharing this special moment together meant everything to both Auntie Elsa and Naomi. Supporting his bride as much as he could when the time came for Auntie Elsa to leave was his major concern, however.

A sigh escaped his lips.

He rolled onto his side. He didn't want to be thinking thoughts of Auntie Elsa leaving.

Thoughts of happiness should occupy his mind now, the joy

that he's marrying the woman of his dreams. Feelings of being with her, being together, sharing a life, are what should be on his mind, instead.

He got up.

Thinking some exercise might clear his head, he pulled on his swimming trunks and headed to the pool.

To his surprise, Naomi was already there, swimming serious lengths. They were more alike than he'd imagined. A smile curled around his lips as he watched her touch on the side of the pool. She wouldn't be able to miss him as he remained standing there.

Green eyes looked up at him.

"Hi! What are you doing here? I thought you were sleeping."

"I could well ask the same of you, amore mio."

"I needed some exercise."

"Me, too."

He dived over her head into the pool and swam in the opposite direction, knowing she'd race him.

TWENTY-SIX

Khwai had summoned staff to sweep the area under the trees where Luca saw his first African elephant. They'd set out chairs for the guests and laid gorgeous African carpets underfoot to prevent Auntie Elsa's wheelchair, or anyone wearing heels, getting stuck in the sand. Facing the chairs, pink roses from Auntie Elsa's garden decorated an arch made from acacia branches. The entire area enjoyed the cool shade the trees threw against the heat that still clung to the sand, even though it was already six o'clock and time for Luca and Naomi's wedding.

Khwai had appointed chauffeurs for the day, who stopped their trucks at the edge of the carpets to allow their passengers to disembark before driving back to the lodge to collect others.

Auntie Elsa, Santina and Enzo, were last to be collected and sat in the Lapa waiting for Khwai.

Kerri put the last touches on Naomi's hair in her room. Kerri had stopped crying now, but when she first saw Naomi in Auntie Elsa's wedding dress, she couldn't stop the tears.

Naomi had never looked so stunning, so ethereal, so much herself. She was the personification of her soul, contained in one perfect person, the beauty of her heart radiating out to inspire those around her.

For moments, Kerri had stood rooted to the floor, staring at her friend.

"You look... you look... You're so beautiful, Naomi. You look like a princess, or a goddess, or something."

Naomi's happy giggle had sounded like bells.

"Oh, stop it. But thank you for saying I look okay. I was worried."

"Well, you have nothing to worry about, trust me. Except maybe that Luca will be too speechless at the sight of you to deliver his vows."

Kerri had secured the lace veil to Naomi's hair, which she wore in a bun at the back of her head. Kerri had fussed with the veil and teased out a few soft strands of hair to hang beside Naomi's face.

From Auntie Elsa's wedding pictures, they could see she had worn the dress more formally, but with Naomi's minimal makeup and silver flip-flops, Naomi had given the dress a modern twist.

A member of staff had helped to remove the thorns from the seven long-stemmed roses for her bouquet. They'd been tied together with a pink ribbon and now rested on Naomi's vanity table. The pink of Kerri's dress almost matched the pink of the roses and set off the red of her hair.

They could hear the trucks coming and going as they carried the guests into the desert.

When Khwai came to knock on Naomi's door, Kerri handed her the bouquet and followed Khwai and Naomi down the corridor to the kitchen. The last of the staff who had to stay behind to ready the Lapa for the reception formed two lines on either side of the kitchen and applauded as Naomi walked through the door. They squealed and cooed and took pictures.

Naomi exchanged radiant smiles with them and waved as she got into the truck.

Kerri slid into the seat beside Naomi as Khwai started the truck.

When she looked at her friend, she carried a mischievous glint in her eyes.

"There's still time to change your mind and run away."

Naomi grinned.

"Oh, right? Just like you'd run out on your wedding with Johan."

Kerri giggled.

"Okay. Point taken."

Khwai drove sedately so the wind wouldn't have blown Naomi's hairdo to smithereens by the time she arrived at the site.

Even though Naomi had had little time to spend alone with her thoughts, she knew in her heart, she was doing the right thing today. Marrying Luca was a dream come true, one she didn't even know she'd had until she'd met him. Marrying Luca with Auntie Elsa there was beyond anything she could ever have dreamed of, not after her conversation that night with Auntie Elsa when she'd first heard the news of her fatal condition. Dealing with the sadness of Auntie Elsa's death when the time came would have been difficult without Luca. That she was once again going to be an orphan wasn't a thought she'd relished.

But strangely, she never felt less like an orphan. For the first time in her life, she had a family. Yes, Auntie Elsa and Uncle Wouter were her family, too. She never felt like she belonged to them, however. She could never pinpoint why? They were kind and looked after her every need. She loved them, still did, and always would. But it was always there, at the back of her mind, the feeling she didn't belong. But now?

Now she had a family with Luca. It felt satisfying. It felt real. It felt forever.

She could see the site with the guests already seated from far away. As Khwai drove nearer, she made out Luca's tall, straight figure, standing next to Johan and in front, Nick. He looked so different and smart in a suit today, instead of his police uniform. It benefited them when Luca discovered Nick was a licensed registrar and he could arrange the paperwork so they could get married at such short notice.

Khwai stopped at the edge of the carpet, got out and helped down Naomi and Kerri. Auntie Elsa, also wearing pink, was sitting in her wheelchair, waiting to accompany Naomi up the aisle. They knew, given the circumstances, no one would object to this arrangement that flaunted tradition.

The two women shared a tender moment as Naomi bent down to hug Auntie Elsa.

"You look like a dream, darling. I'm so happy for you. My heart feels as though it wants to burst from happiness."

It had worried Naomi that Auntie Elsa might feel too poorly or be too tired to come, but although she was ill, her eyes were bright, and her smile was strong.

Naomi smiled at her beloved adoptive mother.

"It all feels like a dream, doesn't it? I'm so happy you're here with me. I'll keep the memory of this day in my heart forever."

She squeezed Auntie Elsa's hand. To give Auntie Elsa a moment to control the tears brimming in her eyes at the sight of Naomi, Naomi looked up.

Her heart stopped and then galloped at a million miles when she saw Luca. If she'd ever thought he was handsome before, it was nothing compared to the man waiting for her at the rose-bedecked arch. The navy of his suit complimented his coloring even more than black did. He looked like a model who'd just stepped out of the pages of Vogue or some such magazine. His designer stubble showed off his masculine square jaw line. His dark eyes were watching her, a soft, sexy smile lingering on his lips.

When he saw she was looking at him, he shook his head and mouthed, "Wow," as his eyes widened, to show he liked what he saw.

Naomi giggled and bit her lip. No one had ever admired her so openly before.

That's when she noticed the young doctor, dressed in a smart gray suit, sitting near them, a camera in his hands. He was already filming her. Naomi didn't know whether to ignore him, so she smiled at him and waved. Who knew he had so many talents? But just as she wondered if Luca had lent him his equipment, she noticed Gerhard on her other side aiming a serious video camera in her direction. She smiled and waved and was relieved when she saw him wriggle his index finger at her.

Kerri had passed Auntie Elsa a tissue, meanwhile, and made sure her tears hadn't smudged her makeup.

Auntie Elsa took Naomi's hand. Her hand felt small, like a child's.

"I'm ready, darling if you are?"

Naomi squeezed Auntie Elsa's hand and nodded to Kerri, who pushed Auntie Elsa's wheelchair. Naomi walked beside her, still holding her hand. But the moment they moved, the haunting voices of the San singers started the song that accompanied them down the aisle.

It stunned Naomi as she hadn't thought about music for her wedding. She looked at Kerri, who grinned, nodded and winked at her. She grinned back, happy that Kerri had arranged such a wonderful surprise.

A small choir stood under the tall trees nearby.

Naomi was grateful they didn't attempt a rendition of the

traditional wedding march. Their song was the song of the desert, wholly appropriate for the ceremony.

As the three women made their way slowly up the aisle, guests smiled at them and touched Naomi's arm to show their good wishes. It was difficult to return their smiles when her eyes wanted to stay on Luca only. His smile broadened the closer they came to him.

The actual ceremony went by in the flash of a moment, yet everything happened in slow motion. Naomi couldn't hear any sounds clearly. She knew Nick had been talking because she saw his mouth moving. She knew she'd been talking because she could feel the resonance of her voice in her body. She saw Luca saying words and putting a ring on her finger. But it was as though her spirit had left her body.

She knew she'd been smiling because her cheeks ached. She knew Luca had kissed her because she could feel his lips fully on hers. She knew that first Kerri and then Johan had hugged her because she could feel them against her body. She saw Enzo's smiling face. She saw Auntie Elsa's and Santina's tearful, happy eyes as she walked past them. She felt Luca threading her arm through his and holding her hand.

She knew she was happy.

Sitting alone in the truck with Luca as Khwai drove them back to the lodge, sound slowly penetrated her brain again.

Luca was holding her hand, his dark eyes warm and transfixed on hers.

"Amore mio, Mrs. Armati, you are more beautiful than anything I've ever seen. You are my dream come true."

Luca leaned forward. His kiss was soft and tender, yet promised the passion of knowing a life-time of togetherness awaited them.

He smelled exotic and expensive, and as though he belonged to her.

Back at the lodge, the doctor and Gerhard, who'd got there before them, took pictures and filmed them from the moment their truck stopped. Luca helped Naomi down, and together they walked to the Lapa with their photographers in tow.

On Kerri's instructions, the staff had transformed the Lapa into a place that existed only in dreams. They'd used Santina's Murano glass fairy lights again. But this time, they had interwoven the lights and strung it in a kind of gauze that covered the back and the open sides of the Lapa. They'd switched the lights on in the pool and together with the fairy lights, the place looked magical. Someone arty had inserted tons of pink roses into the fairy-light gauze. On each table stood a small bouquet of pink roses. A massive cake, even bigger than the one Chef had created for Auntie Elsa's and Santina's birthday party, stood in the corner. Delicate edible pink roses decorated the cake. It looked too beautiful to eat. Beside it, on a long table, were piles of gifts and cards.

As Luca and Naomi walked toward the Lapa and feasted their eyes on the uber-romantic spectacle before them, they noticed that even the waiters and waitresses had small pink roses stuck to their uniform lapels. A smiling waitress, with a small silver tray, stepped forward and offered them each a glass of Louis Roederer Cristal Brut Champagne, Luca's favorite. They clinked their glasses together before taking small sips, their eyes never leaving each other's. Each could read in the other's eyes, their happiness as the surreal feeling of being in the same dream continued.

Despite the surrounding staff, and Gerhard and the doctor filming them, Luca and Naomi appreciated this moment to be alone together before their guests arrived.

Auntie Elsa, Santina and Enzo, Kerri and Johan, and Nick were first to arrive back. The doctor stopped taking pictures when Santina pushed Auntie Elsa's wheelchair toward the

Lapa. He went over to check on his patient to make sure she was still comfortable. But Auntie Elsa, although tired, smiled him away. Santina wheeled her chair to their appointed places at the bridal table where she and Enzo stayed with Auntie Elsa.

Gerhard continued to film the bridal couple and their guests as the trucks dropped them back at the lodge. It allowed Luca and Naomi to chat with each guest before they went off in their small groups and were replaced by the next bunch as the trucks drove back and forth. Soon, everyone was back.

Chef had outdone himself. The delicate chicken dinner was delicious and satisfying. Neither Luca nor Naomi liked long speeches at their wedding. After dinner, Luca's short, powerful speech to thank everyone for helping to make his and Naomi's wedding wonderful was therefore even more special. But when he spoke of how grateful they were to have Auntie Elsa with them, the atmosphere changed, becoming somewhat soberer. It didn't spoil their celebration, however. After cutting the cake, Chef served slices with the best Italian ice cream Naomi had ever tasted, the music came on, and people danced on the patio.

Auntie Elsa indicated it was time for her to retreat to her room. Santina and Kerri went with her to make sure she was all right, and the doctor followed to check on his patient the moment she was back in her bed.

TWENTY-SEVEN

By the time Luca and Naomi got to Auntie Elsa's room, she sat propped up against her pillows and had a drip in her arm again. Santina sat beside her on the bed and Kerri on a chair on her other side. Enzo, Johan, and the doctor sat on the sofa opposite her bed. Auntie Elsa beckoned for Naomi to sit beside her.

Naomi smiled at Luca, let go of his hand and sat down where Auntie Elsa had indicated. Luca pulled up a chair and took his place next to Santina.

Although Auntie Elsa was smiling, it was clear she was exhausted. Naomi wondered if it was a good idea to have so many people in the room. But before she could say anything, Auntie Elsa, who'd been patting her and Santina's hands on either side of her, turned to Santina.

Her voice was a whisper when she spoke.

"Remember what we talked about? Now is the time. If not now, you may regret it forever. And life is too short for such regrets and for the deep sadness you've carried in your heart for so long, my dear friend. Now is the time for your courage."

At her words, Enzo got up and came to stand between

Santina and Luca, his hands on their shoulders, his lovely tenor voice soft and serious.

"Yes, I agree. It's time, Santina. We have waited too long."

Naomi and the others looked from the Italian trio to Auntie Elsa and back, baffled by the cryptic comments. Luca appeared equally perplexed but said nothing. Santina, whose tears had flowed down her cheeks at Auntie Elsa's words, wiped a tissue over her face, sat up straighter, smiled up at Enzo over her shoulder and took Luca's hand.

Her eyes found Auntie Elsa's.

"You're right, my dear friend. Thank you for giving me the courage to speak finally the words my heart has kept secret for so long."

She turned to face Luca.

"I hope you will hear me out first, before judging me, and if you judge me, you will not do it too harshly."

Enzo, who had remained standing behind them, gave each of their shoulders an encouraging squeeze.

"And I pray you will find it in your heart to forgive all of us, my son."

Santina continued to look at Luca, as though she wanted to will him to understand even before he'd heard the facts.

"Cecilia, your mother, was my best friend. Even as a young girl, she was the most beautiful human being I, or anyone, had ever seen. But despite her beauty, she remained unspoiled. Her wonderful spirit saved her. She drew everyone to her like moths to a flame."

Luca nodded. He'd seen the pictures of his mother as a child and as the woman she became. He'd known the model she'd become. She was the most beautiful woman he'd ever seen, very different from his beautiful Naomi.

Santina continued, encouraged by Luca's nod.

"Who could blame Enzo for falling in love with her so fast?

They were only young, and Enzo would've given her anything. And he did. But there was one thing he couldn't give her. As far back as I can remember, having children obsessed Cecilia. She would laugh and declare she wanted a football team. When she got pregnant soon after their wedding, she was delirious with joy, as were we all for her. But around three months into the pregnancy, she miscarried. She was devastated, and so were Enzo, and everyone who loved her. But there were further complications. She wouldn't stop bleeding, and the doctors had to remove her uterus. That meant she'd never be able to have children of her own. It was a cruel fate that such beauty would never be passed on to her children. Cecilia was inconsolable. Nothing I nor Enzo said had any effect.

"I remember how she'd locked herself in their bedroom and had cried for days. By this time, she was already a well-established model, but she cared not one thing for her modeling career. All our hearts broke for her. When her depression became so severe the doctors were worried she might kill herself, her family came to stay, I seem to remember."

Santina looked at Enzo, who nodded to show she'd remembered their shared past correctly.

"But nothing her family said made any difference. She wouldn't speak to anyone. She wouldn't eat anything. By the time Enzo had the door removed, they'd found Cecilia lying in her own filth in bed. Her eyes were open, and she wasn't crying anymore, but she didn't seem able to hear any of us when we spoke to her."

Everyone listened to Santina's words. A shocked silence pervaded the room as they contemplated the horror of Cecilia's state of mind.

Luca, who'd never heard this part of his mother's history, sat still, his face unreadable as he absorbed the events from the past. He'd been angry with his mother for as long as he could remember for walking out of his life like that. Now, he couldn't help thinking no one knew anyone until they'd walked in their shoes.

Santina's voice penetrated his thoughts.

"Her mother found her one evening. She'd slit her wrists and was bleeding out in the bath. Enzo was beside himself. The ambulance came quickly, and the paramedics saved her. But it was an excruciatingly tough time for everyone, even for me. I hated seeing my best friend going through such pain, and there was nothing I could do to help her."

Enzo squeezed Santina's shoulder in encouragement when it appeared she was finding it too difficult to continue.

Santina swallowed her tears.

"It must have been about a month later when Cecilia finally became well enough again to get up, clean herself, and eat something. By then, she'd lost a lot of weight. She looked dreadful, and modeling was out of the question. She stayed at home, and even though her mother had stayed behind when the rest of her family had returned to their home, she couldn't help Cecilia back to life. Nor could Enzo. No one could. Every morning Cecilia would get up and after breakfast would spend most of the day sitting in the garden, just staring at nothing. The doctor went to see her often. But he declared there was nothing more he could do for her and said he hoped she'd recover in time. We had to be patient with her. But it was such a huge burden for Enzo to carry."

Santina patted Enzo's hand on her shoulder. Tears were flowing down his cheeks as he relived those dreadful days through Santina's words.

"It was then Enzo approached me to ask for my help."

Santina kept her eyes fixed on Luca's face, even as he sat with his head bent forward, listening to her story.

"You must understand I loved Cecilia like a sister. I would

have done anything for her. But she wouldn't respond. That's why Enzo's idea sounded like the perfect solution. He wanted it to be a surprise for her, but decided he needed to get her consent. He tried talking to her for days and days, but she couldn't hear him, or wouldn't. So, when he asked for my help, and I saw it was a way to help save my beloved Cecilia, it was a simple thing for me to agree to. I know it was the way Enzo saw it. There was never anything more in it than our mutual wish to help Cecilia."

Santina sat still for a while. It was clear to the others her words had taken a toll on her.

She wasn't crying anymore, but her voice was muted and had changed timbre from too many tears already cried when she continued.

"After we had confirmation of your conception, Luca, I was the happiest I could ever remember being. I'd have a baby, and this baby would save the life of my dearest friend in the world. Of course, we didn't tell Cecilia about the pregnancy at first. We wanted to make sure there were no complications, that the baby was healthy, and Cecilia could understand what we had done when the time came. That we did it for her."

Santina was silent again. It was her turn to look down, as she collected her thoughts and her courage to continue the story.

"After five months, when I was showing, and Cecilia had put on weight and talked again, we told her. It was the worst day of my life."

Santina appeared unable to continue. Her shoulders shook with her sobs that sounded almost like hiccups.

Enzo stroked her shoulder in understanding and encouragement, even as his tears blinded him. But Enzo's touch seemed to give Santina the courage she needed to continue.

She shifted in her chair and cleared her throat.

"At first, Cecilia just stared at me. Then she stared at Enzo. Then she screamed at us."

Santina's tears ran down her cheeks at the memory, so fresh in her mind still.

"She accused us of having had an affair behind her back. She wouldn't listen. She wouldn't understand it wasn't an affair. We'd done what we'd done out of love for her. Instead, she continued to accuse us of not caring about her, not loving her. It hurt us both deeply that she refused to believe our sacrifice for her. She said she was right to end it all, that this time she'd succeed as she couldn't live with our deception on top of her heartache. Dear God!"

Santina's hand went up to her mouth as deep sobs wracked her body once again.

Naomi got up and offered tissues to Santina and Enzo. Now it made sense that Luca looked so much like Santina. She should have known.

With obvious effort, Santina got her emotions under control, but her voice remained full of unshed tears.

"But in her deranged state, Cecilia became confused. One minute she'd scream at us, threatening suicide, and the next, she'd coo around me, touching my bump and congratulating me. Then, she'd slump into a depressed state again, bemoaning her lot she'd never have children. She never seemed to forget it."

Santina was silent for a few moments as she re-experienced the events in her mind's eye.

"When the baby was born, Cecilia was ecstatic. She seemed to have forgotten she'd thought Enzo and I had had an affair. She accepted the baby as hers. She became besotted with him. But she was never the same again. Her moods and her mind were never stable again. One moment, she'd be the wonderful, enigmatic Cecilia we all knew and loved, and the next, she'd be full of neurosis, insecurities, paranoia..."

Throughout Santina's story, Luca had sat still. His face was pale, his eyes dark as he stared at the floor, his hands helpless in his lap.

Now, his face distorted with anger as he stared, first at Enzo, then at Santina, his voice a growl when he spoke.

"That's why she left, isn't it? She couldn't live knowing you two had slept together behind her back. Oh yes, your intentions were supposedly good, but you still did it, didn't you? And all these years, you'd let me believe she'd left because she'd found some wealthy Greek who could give her a better lifestyle, made her sound like some money loving shallow person. How could you? You've not only betrayed her, but you've betrayed and lied to me."

Luca got up and stormed out of the room, banging the door behind him.

For moments, everyone sat flabbergasted at his outburst, hearing his angry footsteps disappear down the corridor. Then Naomi went to the door.

But Enzo's voice stopped her.

"No, Naomi. Let him go. It's a lot to take in. Allow him to think about it. He's a smart man. He'll see the truth."

Meanwhile, Santina couldn't stop crying. Her shoulders shook, and Enzo continued to stroke her shoulder and arm as he took the chair Luca had vacated so suddenly.

Auntie Elsa held Santina's hand, stroking her thumb across her friend's hand to soothe her.

"You did well, Santina. I'm so proud of you. I'm glad you could tell him at last. I'm sure now you'll heal the heartache in your heart."

Santina sniffed and nodded. Her sobs stopped.

Her smile at Auntie Elsa was weak.

"I could only do this today, Elsa, because of you, your encouragement and the long talks we've had. And yes, you're right. I feel lighter already. Now, I just pray Luca can forgive me."

Auntie Elsa returned her smile.

"Life is so short. Now Luca knows the truth, I'm sure he'll forgive you and love you like the mother you've always been to him."

Auntie Elsa seemed much weaker, as though Enzo's and Santina's ordeal took its toll on her, too. The doctor got up, as did Johan and Kerri. Kerri's eyes looked red with unshed tears, but she said nothing. She went to give Auntie Elsa a quick good-night kiss and squeezed Santina's hand, before she and Johan left, followed by Enzo and Santina.

The doctor checked Auntie Elsa's pulse and made sure she was comfortable and pain-free. Then, he bid the two women good night and left, closing the door behind him.

Naomi remained with Auntie Elsa, holding her hand, as they waited for sleep to claim her. Once Naomi was sure Auntie Elsa was asleep, Naomi left. She took care to shut the door without making a noise. The person next on the roster would be here soon to take her turn to sit with Auntie Elsa.

Satisfied Auntie Elsa was okay, for the moment at least, Naomi's thoughts turned once again to Luca. What a shock Santina's revelations must have been for him. Naomi could understand his reaction. She looked for him everywhere but couldn't find him. Knowing he'd come out of hiding eventually, she went back to her room.

The familiarity of the room clutched at her heart. Her life had taken such turns of late, ones she could never have foreseen. As these thoughts ran through her mind, she rummaged through her wardrobe. Among the many dresses Auntie Elsa had gifted her over the past year, Naomi found a comfortable maxi dress to change into. She laid it on the bed while she took off her wedding dress. It might have been Auntie Elsa's, but now it felt like hers. She hung it outside the wardrobe so she could look at it a little longer before the time came to banish it to its tissue paper and suitcase again. As she turned back to retrieve the dress she wanted to wear, the haven that was her bed caught her attention. She loved her bed, the best gift ever from Auntie Elsa for her twenty-fifth birthday last year.

She looked around the room as she changed into the dress. The lovely dusky pink duvet cover and pillowcases went so well with the grown-up pink walls. That and the beautiful wallpaper on the accent wall opposite her double bed were her favorites.

This room had always been her oasis when things got rough, her castle to retreat to at the end of a long day. It was her little piece of home, where she'd always felt safe. She was grateful for her room, the only one she'd known since moving to Namibia. Auntie Elsa had always allowed her creative freedom to decorate it however she'd wanted. But regardless of whatever transformation it went through–and there were many–Naomi was proud she'd always kept her room tidy, the books arranged in alphabetical order on the bookcase against the wall opposite the window.

She'd have to say goodbye to it, as she had to say goodbye to her life before Luca. Would she ever have such a sanctuary again?

Sanctuary... That's it.

Suddenly, she knew where Luca was. Should she go to him? He had a lot to digest. But she didn't want him to feel abandoned. Not again. Didn't she know what that felt like? Her decision made, she hurried down the corridor.

When she opened the jet's door, she could feel Luca's presence even before she went inside. He was sitting in the back on a sofa, his head in his hands. But he looked up when she walked toward him. His eyes were dark, the hurt naked in them. It almost made her gasp, but she stifled it and went to sit beside him, sliding an arm around his shoulders.

When he spoke, his voice was hoarse.

"I'm sorry, amore mio, for my outburst earlier. What must you think of me?"

Naomi snuggled into his neck but said nothing. What could she say to take away the hurt she'd seen in his eyes?

Luca got up and held out his hand for her to take.

"I can't stay here. Let's go."

"Where are we going?"

"Windhoek. We can stay at the Namib Sands Hotel. I'm sure they'll have a honeymoon suite there."

TWENTY-EIGHT

It came as a massive surprise that Luca could multitask so efficiently. Naomi watched in amazement as he flew the jet, phoned the airport to arrange the Armati for them, and booked the honeymoon suite at the Namib Sands Hotel.

When he'd finished with the phone, she borrowed it to call Kerri.

"Please apologize to everyone for us? We'll see you tomorrow."

Kerri was cool about it, almost as though she'd expected it. She'd already announced it to their guests, who didn't seem to mind in the slightest that Luca had whisked his bride away so surreptitiously. In fact, they thought it rather romantic. There was no need for Kerri to offer explanations. Where would she even begin to explain what was behind Luca's sudden wish to be away from the lodge? It appeared no one else knew Santina and Enzo's long-kept secret.

After Naomi had impressed upon Kerri to keep her informed of any developments with Auntie Elsa, she sighed and sat back in her seat, happy to be alone with Luca on another adventure. Maybe this was what her life would be like from now on?

Luca landed the jet at Eros Airport with expert precision, where the Armati sports car they'd used before waited for them. Ever the gentleman, Luca opened the passenger door for Naomi and made sure she was comfortable before he closed her door. He walked around the vehicle to slide into the driver's seat beside her. Naomi was getting used to the admiring stares the car attracted and remembered that no one could see its occupants inside unless she wound down her tinted window.

By the time Luca pulled up to the hotel, the staff was ready for them but somewhat surprised to find they had no luggage.

The honeymoon suite was massive and lovely. Dark red rose petals lay strewn in the shape of a heart over the crisp white sheets of the bed. Naomi imagined the reason the hotel staff had fashioned their toweling robes into swans was that swans mated for life, a symbol for marriage. Champagne on ice and a cheese board with fruit waited for them on the two-seater dining room table. Gorgeous scented candles placed around the room infused the air with the heavenly scent of honeysuckle. A lucky coincidence, as it was Naomi's favorite.

Luca kicked off his shoes and sank onto the sofa at the foot of the bed. He looked exhausted. Naomi wasn't surprised. It had been a crazy few days and today had been a day of extreme highs and extreme lows for him. She went to sit next to him, leaning her head on his shoulder.

He took her hand and twiddled with her rings.

"This is not how I imagined our wedding night to turn out."

Naomi turned and put a finger to his lips to silence him.

"You've said before, nothing about your proposal had turned out according to your desires, and yet, here we are. We're married. We're happy, aren't we?"

"I'm happy, amore mio, with you. But..."

Naomi turned to face him.

"Luca, please listen to me. I know you're upset about what Santina told you. But think of it this way... I'm on the verge of losing a mother, and you're on the verge of gaining a mother. Surely, you must see, life is too short to be angry with them. I believe Santina and Enzo truly thought they were doing the right thing. Can you imagine their torment through the years? Santina could never claim you as her son, even though biologically, you are. Yet, she stayed and looked after you."

"But they lied. All I can think of is how they've lied and how I'll never find my mother again."

"They didn't lie to you. They just didn't tell you the truth because you were too young to understand it."

"But they allowed me to believe what everyone else thought about my mother. That she left me and... That she was just a... what do you call it? Gold digger, si?"

Naomi touched his face, stroking down his cheek, his stubble prickly beneath her fingers.

Her voice was soft, not wanting to hurt him further.

"But she wasn't your mother, Luca. Santina is your mother."

Luca looked at Naomi as though she had poured a bucket of ice water over him.

"Oh, my God. You're right. That's right."

He got up and paced the room.

"I heard Santina say she got pregnant with the baby she wanted to give my mother to save her life. But I was that baby. How is it I heard the story but didn't hear the truth in it? And you tried to tell me. You said she was my biological mother. But she's more than that. She's been there for me since before my mother left. Since before I was eight. You're right, Santina is my mother. The woman I'd always thought of as my mother,

Cecilia, was no relation at all. She didn't even want me. My father is my father, and Santina is my mother."

A light had gone on in his eyes.

"How could I have been so dumb?"

"You're not dumb, my Luca. You're just used to thinking of Cecilia as your mother. But from the moment I saw you and Santina together, I always thought you two looked a lot alike."

Luca pulled Naomi up and hugged her to him. He swung her around and around.

His delighted laughter resonated through both their bodies.

"So today, not only did I get married to the woman of my dreams. I received the best gift ever. My birth mother. No wonder I've always felt so comfortable with Santina. No wonder she's always felt like part of our family in our home. My God, how was I so blind?"

Luca sat Naomi down and cupped her head in his hands. He kissed her. Soon their kisses became deeper, more passionate. Their breathing became louder until both were panting when they broke apart. Naomi's pupils had dilated, mirroring Luca's as it signaled her arousal.

Luca took her hand and led her through to the bathroom where a large Jacuzzi bath met them. He opened the taps and poured in some bath foam with its delicate scent supplied for that purpose. Then he continued to kiss her and slowly undressed her until she stood naked in front of him. At first, she felt shy, but when he took off his clothes, she relaxed more.

Luca was the most handsome man Naomi had ever seen. Not that she'd seen any naked men before, but she had seen plenty of beautiful toned male guests in the pool, wearing nothing but their swimming trunks. She couldn't help staring at his arousal. It looked so big. Would it fit? She was suddenly anxious. What if they found they weren't sexually compatible?

Perhaps they should have had sex that night in the jet. At least then they'd have known for sure before they got married.

Luca had filled the bath to the brim. He took her hand and helped her in. Then he disappeared, only to reappear moments later carrying the champagne and two glasses. He got into the tub, splashing water all over the bathroom tiles, roaring as he did so. He popped the cork on the champagne bottle and handed her a glass, filling it with the golden bubbles. When he'd poured his drink, they clinked their glasses together. He took a sip, his laughing eyes remaining fixed on hers. He moved closer to her until their naked thighs touched. It sent a thrill through Naomi's body, which became amplified when he kissed her, his mouth tasting of champagne.

They put their champagne glasses on the side of the Jacuzzi as their kiss deepened once again. The warmth of the water, the warmth of the champagne as it made its way down her body and the heat of Luca's kisses all drove Naomi wild. She kissed him back with equal passion, feeling her body open to him.

But Luca was gentle and passionate in turns, taking his time. He lathered some bath gel in his hands and washed her, starting with her arms, her chest, teasing her nipples until they were hard and aching for more of his touch. He washed her back, drawing her close to him. Being pressed against his wet chest was so sensual that Naomi gasped.

Luca got up and pulled her into a standing position before he kneeled in front of her. Then, applying more gel to his hands and lathering it, he washed her stomach and teased her legs apart as he continued to look into her eyes.

When his hands touched her intimate parts, Naomi could no longer contain the moan that broke from her lips. She closed her eyes. Her knees bent as though of their own volition, and she gripped Luca's shoulders. His talented fingers found just the right spot to stroke, and he did so until Naomi felt herself quiver as her release rocked through her body. She'd experienced nothing as powerful before. It took a few moments before she was herself again.

Naomi was just about to lower herself into the Jacuzzi when she realized Luca hadn't finished yet. He steered her over to the side and led her to sit down on the edge of the Jacuzzi. He washed away all the gel from her intimate parts before placing himself between her legs. When his tongue touched her there, she moaned again and held on to his head. He used his fingers and tongue to pleasure her over and over until Naomi was in a haze of contentedness and satisfaction.

But just when she felt it couldn't get any better, Luca got out of the tub, then lifted her out. He carried her to the big super king-sized bed and laid her down on top of the rose petals that released their scent as her body crushed them.

Luca was gentle with her, checking every step of the way she was okay and felt no pain as he entered her. She marveled at his control. He went in slowly, and although at some point there was a sudden stabbing jolt, it lasted mere moments. At his rhythmic thrusts, Naomi relaxed more and enjoyed the sensation of being filled up by him. As his arousal took him beyond the point of return, Naomi watched his face in fascination as he spilled his seed deep inside her. He was more beautiful than she had words to describe.

Naomi didn't remember falling asleep, but when she awoke, the sun was bright through the large windows opposite the bed. In the distance, she saw the dunes of the desert. It felt as though they were beckoning her home. But she resisted and looked around for Luca.

The room was as lovely as she'd remembered from the night before, everything still in its place. Only Luca was missing. His side of the bed felt cold to her touch, which meant he must have been up for a while already. She wanted to get up, but her body felt lazy and heavy from all the loving of the night before. She felt a little sore and, looking down, realized she'd bled on the white sheets.

Shit, how embarrassing. She scooted over to the side of the bed and got up. She wasn't supposed to be on her period, so where did the blood come from? Then she remembered reading that sometimes losing one's virginity could cause a little bleeding. She had nothing with her. Oh well, tissue paper would have to do until she got back to the lodge. She put a pillow over the stain on the bed and went to the bathroom to clean herself.

She could hear Luca's happy whistling before he even opened the door. But it stopped the minute he entered the room.

"Mrs. Armati? Where are you? I've come bearing gifts and food."

Naomi giggled.

"Coming!"

"What! Again? I thought only I had the privilege of being in charge of that now."

Naomi laughed.

"I won't be long. Did you really bring food? I'm starved."

When she entered the room, dressed in a toweling bathrobe, Luca was standing by a trolley of food, a huge grin on his face as he wafted the aromas in her direction.

She couldn't help laughing at his silliness.

The moment he saw her, he pulled a chair out for her.

"Come, sit please, wife of mine."

"You're in an excellent mood this morning."

"Yes, I am. Everything is right in my world. I have the most amazing, most beautiful, most delectable, most delicious, most gorgeous wife in the entire world. What more could I possibly want?"

Naomi grinned at him.

"What about Santina?"

Luca became a little more serious.

"I called her this morning while you were still sleeping. I felt I had to apologize for my behavior last night. She was so sweet, said she understood completely."

Luca kneeled next to Naomi and took her hand in his. His eyes looked up into hers with such sincerity she wanted to kiss away anything that might still hurt him.

"I can't thank you enough, amore mio, for helping me to see the truth that was staring me in the face all this time. I'll be forever grateful to you. I feel blessed to have not just one, but two such amazing women in my life as you and Santina, my dear mother. I'll talk to her properly when we get back to the lodge."

He brought Naomi's hand to his lips and kissed her fingers before getting up and taking his seat opposite her.

"But now we eat, si? I'm starving too. And then I have one more hunger to satisfy before we return."

He wiggled his eyebrows at her, and Naomi burst into laughter, even as her body agreed with him about the other hunger that needed satisfying.

TWENTY-EIGHT

Luca's ability to multitask so efficiently came as a tremendous surprise. Naomi watched in amazement as he flew the jet, phoned the airport to arrange the Armati for them, and booked the honeymoon suite at the Namib Sands Hotel.

When he'd finished with the phone, she borrowed it to call Kerri.

"Please apologize to everyone for us? We'll see you tomorrow."

Kerri was cool about it, almost as though she'd expected it.

She'd already announced it to their guests, who didn't seem to mind in the slightest that Luca had whisked his bride away. In fact, they thought it rather romantic. There was no need for Kerri to offer explanations. How would she even explain what was behind Luca's sudden wish to be away from the lodge?

It appeared no one else knew Santina and Enzo's long-kept secret.

After Naomi had impressed upon Kerri to keep her informed of any developments with Auntie Elsa, she sighed and sat back in her seat. Being alone with Luca on another adventure made her happy. Maybe this was what her life would be like from now on?

Luca landed the jet at Eros Airport with practiced expertise, where the Armati sports car they'd used before waited for them.

Ever the gentleman, Luca opened the passenger door for Naomi and made sure she was comfortable inside the low sports car before he closed her door. He walked around the vehicle to slide into the driver's seat beside her. Naomi was getting used to the admiring stares the car attracted and remembered that no one could see its occupants inside unless she wound down her tinted window.

By the time Luca pulled up to the hotel, the staff was ready for them but somewhat surprised to find they had no luggage.

The honeymoon suite was massive and lovely. Dark red rose petals lay strewn in the shape of a heart over the crisp white sheets of the bed. Naomi imagined the reason the hotel staff had fashioned their toweling robes into swans was that swans mated for life, a symbol for marriage. Champagne on ice and a cheese board with fruit awaited them on the two-seater dining room table. Gorgeous scented candles placed around the room infused the air with the heavenly scent of honeysuckle. A lucky coincidence, as it was Naomi's favorite.

Luca kicked off his shoes and sank onto the sofa at the foot of the bed. He looked exhausted. It didn't surprise Naomi. It had been a crazy few days and today had been a day of extreme highs and lows for him.

She went to sit next to him, leaning her head on his shoulder. He took her hand and twiddled with her rings.

"This is not how I imagined our wedding night to turn out."

Naomi turned and put a finger to his lips to silence him.

"You've said before, nothing about your proposal had turned out according to your desires, and yet, here we are. We're married. We're happy, aren't we?"

"I am happy, amore mio, with you. But..."

Naomi turned to face him.

"Luca, please listen to me. I know you're upset about what Santina told you. But think of it this way... I'm on the verge of losing a mother, and you're on the verge of gaining one. You must see life is too short to be angry with them. I believe Santina and Enzo were honest and thought they were doing the right thing. Can you imagine their torment through the years? Santina could never claim you as hers, even though you are her biological son. Yet she stayed and looked after you."

"But they lied. All I can think of is how they'd lied and how I'll never find my mother again."

"They didn't lie to you. They just didn't tell you the truth because you were too young to understand it."

"But they allowed me to believe what everyone else thought about my mother. That she left me and... That she was just a... what do you call it? Gold digger, si?"

Naomi touched his face, stroked down his cheek, his stubble prickly beneath her fingers.

Her voice was soft, not wanting to hurt him any further.

"But she wasn't your mother, Luca. Santina is your mother."

Luca looked at Naomi as though she'd poured a bucket of ice water over him.

"Oh my God. You're right. That's right."

He got up and paced around the room.

"I heard Santina say she got pregnant with the baby she wanted to give my mother to save her life. But *I* was that baby.

"How is it I heard the story but didn't hear the truth in it? And you tried to tell me. You said she was my biological mother. But she's more than that. She's been there for me since before my mother left. Since before I was eight.

"You're right, Santina is my mother. The woman I'd always thought of as my mother, Cecilia, was no relation at all. She didn't even want me. My father is my father, and Santina is my mother."

A light had gone on in his eyes.

"How could I have been so dumb?"

"You aren't dumb, my Luca. You're just used to thinking of Cecilia as your mother. But from the moment I saw you and Santina together, I always thought you two looked a lot alike."

Luca pulled Naomi up and hugged her to him. He swung her around and around. His delighted laughter resonated through both their bodies.

"So today, not only did I marry the woman of my dreams. I received the best gift ever—my birthmother. No wonder I've always felt so comfortable with Santina. No wonder she's always felt like part of our family in our home.

"My God, how was I so blind?"

Luca sat Naomi down and cupped her head in his hands. He kissed her lips. Soon their kisses became deeper, more passionate. Their breathing became louder until both were panting when they broke apart. Naomi's pupils had dilated, mirroring Luca's as it signaled her arousal.

Luca took her hand and led her through to the bathroom where a large Jacuzzi bathtub met them. He opened the taps and poured in some bath foam with its delicate scent supplied for that purpose. Then, he continued to kiss her and slowly undressed her until she stood naked in front of him.

At first, she felt shy, but when he took off his clothes, she relaxed. Luca was the most handsome man Naomi had ever seen. Not that she'd seen any naked men before, but she'd seen plenty of beautiful toned male guests in the pool, wearing nothing but their swimming trunks.

She couldn't help staring at his arousal. It looked so big. Would it fit?

Sudden anxiety almost overcame her. What if they found

they weren't sexually compatible? Perhaps they should have had sex that night in the jet. At least then they'd have known for sure before they got married.

Luca had filled the bath to the brim. He took her hand and helped her in. Then he disappeared, only to reappear moments later carrying the champagne and two glasses.

He got into the tub, splashing water all over the bathroom tiles, roaring as he did so. Popping the cork on the champagne bottle, he handed her a glass, filling it with the golden bubbles. When he'd poured his drink, they clinked their glasses together. He took a sip, his laughing eyes remaining fixed on hers and moved closer to her until their naked thighs touched. It sent a thrill through Naomi's body, which became amplified when he kissed her, his mouth tasting of champagne.

They put their champagne glasses on the side of the Jacuzzi as their kiss deepened once again.

The warmth of the water, the warmth of the champagne as it made its way down her body, and the heat of Luca's kisses all drove Naomi wild. She kissed him back with equal passion, feeling her body open to him.

But Luca was gentle and passionate in turns, taking his time. He lathered some bath gel in his hands and washed her, starting with her arms, her chest, teasing her nipples until they were hard and aching for more of his touch. He washed her back, drawing her close to him. Being pressed against his wet chest was so sensual that Naomi gasped.

Luca got up and pulled her into a standing position before he kneeled in front of her. Then, applying more gel to his hands and lathering it, he washed her stomach and teased her legs apart as he continued to look into her eyes. When his hands touched her intimate parts, Naomi could no longer contain the moan that broke from her lips.

She closed her eyes. Her knees bent as though of their own

volition, and she gripped Luca's shoulders. His talented fingers found just the right spot to stroke, and he did so until Naomi felt herself quiver as her release rocked through her body. The power of her experience made her dizzy and floppy and it took several seconds before she was herself again.

Naomi was just about to lower herself into the Jacuzzi when she realized Luca hadn't finished yet. He steered her over to the side and led her to sit down on the edge of the Jacuzzi. He washed away all the gel from her intimate parts before placing himself between her legs. When his tongue touched her there, she moaned again and held on to his head. Using his fingers and tongue, he pleasured her over and over until Naomi was in a haze of contentedness and satisfaction.

But just when she felt it couldn't get any better, Luca got out of the tub, then lifted her out too. He carried her to the big super king-sized bed and laid her down on top of the rose petals that released their scent as her wet body crushed them.

Luca was gentle with her, checking at every step she was okay and felt no pain as he entered her.

She marveled at his control as he penetrated her a little at a time until she'd received all of him. At some point there was a slight stabbing jolt, and she gasped, but it lasted mere moments.

At his rhythmical thrusts, Naomi relaxed. The sensation of Luca filling her and stretching her, was beyond anything she could have imagined. As his arousal took him over the edge, Naomi watched his face in fascination as he spilled his seed deep inside her. He was more beautiful than she had words to describe.

***

Naomi didn't remember falling asleep, but when she awoke, the sun was bright through the enormous windows opposite the bed. In the distance, she saw the dunes of the desert. It felt as though they were beckoning her home. But she resisted and looked around for Luca.

The room was as lovely as she'd remembered from the night before, everything still in its place. Only Luca was missing. His side of the bed felt cold to her touch. It meant he must have been up for a while already.

She wanted to get up, but her body felt lazy and heavy from all the loving of the night before. She felt a little sore and, looking down, realized she'd bled on the white sheets.

Shit, how embarrassing.

Scooting over to the side of the bed, she got up. It wasn't time for her period, so where did the blood come from? Then she remembered reading that sometimes losing one's virginity could cause a little bleeding.

She had nothing with her. Oh well, tissue paper would have to do until she got back to the lodge.

Putting a pillow over the stain, she went to the bathroom to clean herself.

Luca's happy whistling came muted through the door before he even opened it. But it stopped the minute he entered the room.

"Mrs. Armati? Where are you? I've come bearing gifts and food."

Naomi giggled.

"Coming!"

"What! Again? I thought only I had the privilege of being in charge of that now."

Naomi laughed.

"I won't be long. Did you really bring food? I'm starved."

When she entered the room, dressed in a toweling bathrobe, Luca was standing by a trolley of food, an enormous grin on his face as he wafted the aromas in her direction.

She couldn't help laughing at his silliness.

The moment he saw her, he pulled out a chair for her.

"Come, sit please, wife of mine."

"You're in an excellent mood this morning, Mr. Armati."

"Yes, I am. Everything is right in my world. I have the most amazing, most beautiful, most delectable, most delicious, most gorgeous wife in the entire world. What more could I possibly want?"

Naomi grinned at him before she spoke.

"What about Santina?"

Luca became a little more serious.

"I called her this morning while you were still sleeping. I felt I had to apologize for my behavior last night. She was so sweet, said she understood."

Luca kneeled next to Naomi and took her hand in his. His eyes looked up into hers with such sincerity she wanted to kiss away anything that might still hurt him.

"I can't thank you enough, amore mio, for helping me to see the truth that was staring me in the face all this time. I'll be forever grateful to you. Now, I'm blessed to have not just one, but two such amazing women in my life as you and Santina, my dear mother. We've arranged to talk when you and I get back to the lodge."

He brought Naomi's hand to his lips and kissed her fingers before getting up and taking his seat opposite her.

"But now we eat, si? I'm starving too. And then I have one more hunger to satisfy before we return."

He wiggled his eyebrows at Naomi, and she burst into giggles, even as her body agreed with him about the other hunger that needed satisfying.

TWENTY-NINE

CHAPTER 29

The sun cast afternoon shadows on the other side of the house by the time Luca landed the jet at the lodge. He taxied it into the hangar.

As it was a Saturday, many of their guests had stayed over, using the wedding as an excuse to take a weekend break. Several people were having afternoon tea in the Lapa while others were still in their rooms recovering from their siesta. A few others were in the pool, cooling off.

Luca and Naomi followed the sound of the many voices coming from the Lapa, knowing it was the best place to find everyone. They weren't wrong. Santina and Enzo were sitting at a table talking with their Italian friends who'd stayed on for a brief vacation following the birthday party, and then the wedding.

When she saw them, Santina got up and walked towards Luca. She appeared hesitant. But Luca excused himself from Naomi, ran to Santina, picked her up and turned around and around with her in his arms as they giggled like teenagers. After he'd set her down again, he hugged her tight to his body, kissing the top of her head.

As she got closer, Naomi could hear his soft words to Santina.

"You're the best mother I could have ever asked for. And I'm so grateful you dared to tell me. Thank you."

He took Santina's hand, and bringing it to his lips, he kissed her fingers, before taking Naomi's in his other hand and leading both women back to the table in the Lapa. Once there, Enzo got up and hugged his son, patting Luca on the back as he did so.

Naomi felt comfortable leaving Luca with his parents and made her excuses to visit Auntie Elsa. As she had received no phone calls to tell her otherwise, she'd assumed Auntie Elsa was all right, but she was keen to see for herself.

Kerri looked up from the book she'd been reading to Auntie Elsa when Naomi opened the door without knocking first. The room felt gloomy. A strange smell assaulted Naomi's nose at once, but she couldn't figure out what it was. Kerri smiled at Naomi and gave her a brief wave. Naomi returned her greeting as she walked to Auntie Elsa's bed. But as she got closer, it shocked her to see how much Auntie Elsa had deteriorated so fast. She seemed thinner, somehow, her skin yellower, her face more drawn, and now even the whites of her eyes were yellow. She sat propped up against her pillows as a precaution against developing pneumonia. A tiny, thin hand laid on top of her duvet, her arm slightly bent and still attached to the drip above her head. Her other hand was under the duvet, for warmth, no doubt. When Naomi touched her hand, it felt icy cold and clammy.

Auntie Elsa smile at Naomi was weak but warm.

"Hello, my darling. I'm glad you're back. Did you have a good time?"

Naomi couldn't think now about her night and morning of carnal pleasure with her new husband while Auntie Elsa had been lying here, dying. She felt tears prick behind her eyes but refused to give in to them.

Naomi nodded. She tried to smile but could feel it was sad and forced.

Auntie Elsa closed her eyes.

"No need to be sad, darling. I'm going to Wouter."

Kerri put the book down. She gestured for Naomi to follow and held the door open for her.

Naomi patted Auntie Elsa's hand.

"I won't be long, okay?"

Auntie Elsa's eyes remained closed, but she nodded slightly to show she'd heard Naomi's words.

Naomi followed Kerri from the room. They walked in silence to the guest lounge where they remained standing just inside the room.

Kerri hugged her friend and smiled at Naomi.

"So? Did you have a good time? Was it everything you thought it would be?"

Naomi blushed pink at the memory of what Luca had done, his tongue in her most private place.

"It was, um... unexpected."

Kerri laughed.

"Yes, that's a good word for it. But you look radiant, so I guess it was more than unexpected. Good for you. I'm so glad it worked out this way. We'd changed Luca's suite into your honeymoon suite, but it was probably for the best to have your first night together somewhere away from here."

Naomi didn't expect such consideration from Kerri, but she should have known her friend would have done something like it.

"You did? I mean about Luca's suite? How lovely of you! Thank you, hun."

"Well, yes. Where else were you guys going to sleep? That's

before you told me you were going to the Namib Sands. I bet it was gorgeous."

"It was."

But Naomi didn't want to talk about her wedding night. She wanted to make sure Auntie Elsa's night was okay.

She became serious.

"How long has she been like this?"

Kerri sighed.

"She started to deteriorate very fast early this morning. The member of staff, who'd been watching her during the night, came to wake me. I've been sitting with her ever since then."

Kerri yawned and stretched.

Only now did Naomi see how tired Kerri looked.

"Well, I'm here now. Why don't you take a break? Go eat something and maybe go back to bed?"

"Thanks, hun. I'm awake now. The members of staff on the roster have popped in, but I've sent them away. Santina has relieved me a few times already. I knew you'd be back this afternoon because Luca spoke to Santina this morning. I figured it was best we stayed with Auntie Elsa today. Called the doctor just before you came in. He should be here soon. He'll tell us how long she still has, but I don't reckon it's much longer, do you?"

Naomi shook her head. Tears pricked behind her eyelids again, but she wouldn't give in to them.

"Thanks, Kerri. You're an angel."

"I love her, too, you know."

The two friends walked back arm in arm. When they reached Auntie Elsa's door, Naomi laid a hand on Kerri's arm.

"What's the weird smell in the room?"

Kerri gave a small laugh.

"One of Santina's friends is a therapist of sorts. She concocted a mixture of essential oils to help aid Auntie Elsa's breathing. Don't you like the smell? I thought it was quite soothing."

"Oh, I see. It's not unpleasant. It's just weird. I've never smelled it in her room before. Does it help her?"

"It seems to."

Naomi nodded.

"Good."

Kerri opened the door and went to sit in the chair she'd occupied before. Naomi sat down on the bed, holding Auntie Elsa's hand, as she did before they'd left.

Kerri read again. Naomi recognized the book. It was one of Auntie Elsa's favorites. Kerri's voice was soothing as she read the words Auntie Elsa had no doubt read herself many times before. Auntie Elsa's eyes stayed shut. Her breathing was shallower. But a small smile played around her mouth as Kerri read, and Naomi knew she was listening to the story.

A soft knock followed by the doctor entering the room put a stop to Kerri's reading. He rushed to the bed. Naomi and Kerri both got up and took a few steps away, to allow him easy access to Auntie Elsa. As was his custom, he asked them to wait outside while he examined his patient. The two friends complied without argument and closed the door behind them. They walked in silence back to the guest lounge.

Chef, who'd seen the doctor on his way to Auntie Elsa's room and knew the drill, got a waitress to serve coffee in the guest lounge where he knew Kerri and Naomi would be.

When the doctor entered the guest lounge almost half an hour later, Naomi knew from his face he was the bearer of bad news. He sat down and ran a hand through his thick, dark hair, a small sigh escaping his lips.

His eyes found Naomi's.

"It's not good news, I'm afraid. Her pulse is very weak. I've made her as comfortable as I could, and I don't believe she's in any pain right now. But I wouldn't leave her bedside if I were you."

They stood when he stood.

Naomi shook his hand.

"Thank you, doctor."

Just as he left, Luca, Santina and Enzo came walking through the French doors. Luca took one look at Naomi's face and went to her at once. He put an arm around her shoulders and gave her a squeeze, kissing the top of her head.

"Come, amore mio, let's go to Auntie Elsa."

On the way, she explained what the doctor had told them moments earlier. Kerri held open the door, and everyone tiptoed into the room to sit around Auntie Elsa's bed. Naomi took her seat on the bed next to Auntie Elsa again, and Santina sat on the bed on her other side. Although Auntie Elsa had closed her eyes, a tiny smile showed she knew they were there, and she appreciated their company.

Kerri hadn't joined them. Naomi assumed she had gone to carry out her managerial duties. But moments later she opened the door again and stood aside, allowing a single file of San singers to enter the room. When they stood at the foot of Auntie Elsa's bed, Kerri retook her seat. She nodded at the singers, and they sang softly. It was a different song than the others they'd sung before. Even though she couldn't understand the words, Naomi knew this was a song of farewell. Everyone seemed to know it.

Santina and Enzo took turns to kiss Auntie Elsa's forehead before they sat down next to each other, holding hands. It appeared holding on to each other would give them the reassurance Auntie Elsa's imminent death had challenged.

Luca and Kerri also kissed Auntie Elsa's forehead before sitting down on her bed. Kerri held Auntie Elsa's other hand.

Luca, who'd come to sit behind Naomi, put an arm around her waist for support.

The speed with which Auntie Elsa left stunned Naomi. While everyone had been listening to the singers, Auntie Elsa had quietly breathed out her last breath. Naomi had felt a tiny shift in Auntie Elsa's hand, and she had known. Only after the singers had finished their song, did she dare to look at the face she'd known so well.

Auntie Elsa's head had fallen to the side, the look of peace clear on her face. She was finally free from the pain that had so tormented her over the past weeks and days. She was finally with her Wouter.

Naomi's tears had come without her acknowledgment. Silent tears that released the sadness in her heart. She'd stayed with Auntie Elsa until the doctor returned a few hours later. By then, Auntie Elsa's body was cold, her spirit long gone to a place where Naomi prayed she would be forever happy. Auntie Elsa certainly deserved it.

When the doctor asked her to leave the room, Naomi joined the others in the guest lounge. Luca got up at once and went to hug his wife close to his body, stroking her back and her hair as he did so, trying to soothe the sadness in her heart. One by one, first Santina, then Kerri, then Enzo, came to hug her. Luca hovered nearby, and when they were done hugging his wife, he put a protective arm around her shoulders and led her to sit down beside him on the sofa. Santina and Kerri had been crying as well and consoling each other. Chef had sent hot, sweet tea and coffee, which they drank while they waited for the doctor to finish what he had to do with Auntie Elsa's body.

It gave Naomi a chance to get her emotions and thoughts in order. The events of the past few days were like a roller coaster. She felt deeply sad, but simultaneously also grateful for the opportunity to be here when Auntie Elsa died. Naomi knew there was a real possibility Auntie Elsa had waited for her to return that afternoon before she'd died. She'd wanted the opportunity to say goodbye to Naomi.

Naomi marveled at the idea that in the space of two days, her life had changed irrevocably. Her beloved adoptive mother was gone forever, and she was on the brink of starting a new life with her husband. Naomi still couldn't get her head around the idea that Luca was her husband. It was real. They were married. Was this how Auntie Elsa had felt when she'd married Uncle Wouter? Hopefully, Auntie Elsa didn't also have to deal with such opposites of emotions. On the one hand, the deadening sadness threatened to send Naomi into despair, and on the other, her joy at being married to the love of her life dictated that she be happy and excited about her new life with him. No wonder she couldn't get a handle on her emotions.

Thank God for Kerri.

Over the next days, Kerri had arranged everything. Auntie Elsa had left a clear Will. She was specific to the last point about what she'd wanted for her funeral. The first stage was easy. Her grave had always been ready beside Uncle Wouter's in the family plot behind the hangar. Naomi remembered going there a few times after Uncle Wouter had died. It was a neat little cemetery surrounded by a white picket fence. Under tall trees, a few others lay peacefully among the grasses there. The graves bore the names of Uncle Wouter, his mother and father, and his grandfather and grandmother. Now, Auntie Elsa would take her place beside her beloved Wouter.

As Auntie Elsa had died of natural causes, the doctor could provide her death certificate quickly. Because the desert heat dictated speedy funerals, they had made arrangements for Auntie Elsa's funeral the following day.

Even though it was a Monday, and many of their guests, who were also close friends, should have left already, they'd elected to stay for the funeral. One stipulation in Auntie Elsa's Will was she wanted no one to wear black to her funeral. She'd been an active member of the church in the nearby village, and they forwarded the information about the attire to them.

A colorful crowd, therefore, assembled at her gravesite at the appointed hour. The vicar stood at the top of the open grave with his bible in his hand. He was the only person dressed in black. Khwai and five of the older guards, who'd known Auntie Elsa the longest, had carried her coffin from her room. Everyone, including every member of the Desert Lodge staff, stood around the grave. They'd used the pink roses that had been part of the fairy light display in the Lapa for Luca and Naomi's reception. The roses had been placed on top of the coffin, so many, they spilled over beyond it. Naomi knew Auntie Elsa would have loved it.

Naomi and Luca stood with Santina and Enzo on one side, and Kerri and Johan on the other.

As blue was Auntie Elsa's favorite color, Naomi had elected to wear her sky-blue dress again. It complemented the blue of Luca's suit one hundred percent. It was the last dress she'd ever wear for her beloved adoptive mother. In her hand, she held one of the long-stemmed roses from her bouquet. When the time came, everyone threw some dirt onto the coffin, and Naomi threw in her rose. The roses on top of the coffin somewhat lessened the sound of the earth as it hit the coffin, but Naomi hated the sound. It reminded too vividly of the dirt she'd heard falling on her parents' coffins so long ago, a sound that still sometimes haunted her dreams.

As the sound penetrated her consciousness, she was again the confused and scared five-year-old standing at her parents' grave sites. On that day, Naomi didn't know what was going on. The social worker had told her that her mummy and daddy were there. But she knew they weren't despite what the social worker had said because she'd looked for them everywhere. The social worker had stayed with her and held her hand. There were many people. Some she'd recognized as their friends, but others were strangers. They'd all looked at her in that weird way, and then they'd cried. She didn't know why. It had all felt like a bad old dream.

Later that day, when the social worker took her to her new foster parents, she'd explained that Naomi would live with them from now on. The social worker had said more things about foster parents - that Naomi didn't belong to them, or something like that, but Naomi felt so numb, she'd barely heard the social worker, and couldn't say anything. Instead, she'd just nodded and sat quietly while the social worker spoke to the young couple who'd looked but not smiled at her. Perhaps her black dress had seemed strange to them? It had felt stiff and unnatural, and she'd fidgeted with the collar that threatened to choke her.

The couple had seemed nice enough while the social worker was there, but as soon as she'd gone, their attitude toward Naomi had changed. They'd stared at her as though she was something at the bottom of someone's shoe, and they'd hardly spoken to her.

Raised voices and slammed doors had accompanied her silent sobs each night in the small, hard bed of her new home. It was next to a newly decorated nursery that had given her the impression they would have preferred a baby and not someone as old as her.

At least she could attend the same school as before. But even there, everyone had seemed strange. They'd looked at her differently. They'd acted weird around her. She'd felt so alone. There was no one she could talk to, even if she'd wanted to. She'd missed her mummy and daddy so much, her entire body ached. She had new parents now. But she couldn't cry in front of them, or anyone. She wouldn't, though the tears always sat in her throat. It was the start of her ability to escape into the books she'd borrowed from the school library.

The heat of the sun and the vicar's voice infiltrated her thoughts. For moments, it felt her two selves, the little girl and the adult Naomi, had blurred into one.

When everyone left, Naomi stayed behind to spend a few moments alone at Auntie Elsa's grave. Luca understood, let go of her hand as he turned to walk away. She sat down on the ground next to the grave. It was peaceful here. She hoped Auntie Elsa was already with Uncle Wouter and she was happy. Naomi cried and talked to Auntie Elsa until only silence and a temporary peace filled her soul.

When she heard the others' voices as the pool amplified them, she got up, said goodbye to Auntie Elsa, and sauntered out of the cemetery, closing the little gate behind her. Sadness sat heavy in her chest, but she knew Auntie Elsa wouldn't want her to be sad. She promised herself when the burden of grief became too much, she'd try to remember Auntie Elsa was with Uncle Wouter. She'd also remind herself that Luca was right. Just because Auntie Elsa had died, it didn't mean they no longer had a relationship. She could feel Auntie Elsa in her heart in the same place she'd always been, where she'd always be. The place Luca now shared.

He'd been so patient with her, she was grateful this was how her life would be from now on. She'd shared the enormous bed in his suite, which Kerri and her team had transformed into a honeymoon suite for them. He'd held her, not suggesting or attempting making love. But later, when she'd relaxed against him, and kissed him, and opened to him, he'd been tender with her.

Naomi sauntered around the corner of the hangar and back to the Lapa.

Chef had prepared tea and coffee and delicate sandwiches. The atmosphere was subdued but not heavy. As people got ready to leave, some local, some getting ready to return to their lives in Italy, Naomi found herself alone with her small group comprising Luca, Santina and Enzo, Kerri and Johan. Quiet calm had descended on the lodge.

Enzo was the first to break the silence.

"Well, I have to get back to Italy tomorrow, but I will be sad to leave such a beautiful place and all of you."

Kerri smiled at him.

"You'll always be welcome, Enzo. Anytime you want to have a break and relax, just call me and we'll arrange your stay here with us."

Enzo seemed anxious, wanting to say something more, but finding it difficult. Santina took his hand and gave it an encouraging squeeze, her sad eyes smiling into his. It had the desired effect.

Enzo relaxed and looked around the small group before continuing.

"I have another announcement to make, but I hope it isn't inappropriate on this sad day when we said goodbye to Elsa."

Naomi found his eyes.

"Auntie Elsa wouldn't want you to think that way, Enzo. She would have been happy to hear whatever announcement you wish to make. And so are we."

He cleared his throat.

"I want you to be the first to know Santina has agreed to become my wife."

He smiled at Santina, and in a gesture so reminiscent of Luca, brought her hand to his lips to kiss her fingers.

Luca was the first to respond.

"That's unexpected."

Santina and Enzo turned to look at Luca at once, question marks in their eyes.

Luca grinned at them.

"Not that I don't think it's a wonderful idea. I'm so happy for you. It's about time that my parents become my parents, don't you think?"

Their smiles said they realized his words were his attempt at making light of the shock he'd tried to hide. It had to have been a shock, they understood. There had been no sign of anything romantic between them for as long as he'd known them, and there had never been. But bringing up the past at Auntie Elsa's deathbed had highlighted how precious, and how short, life was.

Enzo and Santina's love wasn't the passionate love Enzo had shared with Cecilia, but theirs was a deep understanding of each other's hearts and respect for each other that far surpassed the passion so often found in youth. It was as good a basis for marriage as any. They'd been so long in each other's lives they were practically married, anyway.

Everyone got up to congratulate and hug the happy couple. Luca left for moments and came back with a bottle of champagne he'd kept in the small fridge in the honeymoon suite. He got glasses from the bar and poured a glass for each with which to toast his parents.

KERRI TOLD Naomi they wouldn't take on any more bookings after their guests had left. She wanted to get the lodge ready for their new marketing push. Instead, she'd drawn up rosters for the staff to clean every single nook and cranny of the lodge, until it sparkled as new. Only Luca and Naomi still occupied the honeymoon suite.

Meanwhile, Kerri was helping Naomi to go through Auntie

Elsa's stuff in her room. It was difficult to decide what to do with it all. Although tidy, Auntie Elsa had kept everything, including clothes she'd worn in her school days. They could only surmise it must have held some significance, as she hadn't worn it in years. Perhaps it had something to do with first dates with Uncle Wouter?

Naomi was sad, but not nearly as flattened by Auntie Elsa's death as she'd expected to be. Perhaps because she'd said goodbye this time? Probably because they had spent long hours talking before Auntie Elsa had died and had said everything they'd wanted to say. There was no unfinished business.

It helped to find happy memories of the two of them together in photos and school reports and childish drawings Naomi had made when she was little. There were pictures of her mum and dad, and her grandpa and grandma with Auntie Elsa and Uncle Wouter on camping vacations in the desert. There were many little gifts Naomi had given Auntie Elsa over the years for her birthday, for Easter and Christmas. This one room contained an entire life.

Naomi chose several pieces of jewelry as keepsakes and Kerri wanted a few silver candle holders. Most of the stuff went to charity shops. The good clothes went to the church to help with fundraising at their next fete.

Amid the chaos her death had left behind, Auntie Elsa's lawyer arrived to confirm that Naomi was the sole beneficiary of Auntie Elsa's Will. It wasn't unexpected. But the privacy of Kerri's office offered a safe space for Naomi to give way to the tears at the reality that Auntie Elsa had gone. Desert Lodge now belonged to Naomi.

Following the lawyer's visit, and feeling the weight of her responsibilities, Naomi went to sit next to Auntie Elsa's grave to vent her fears and misgivings. It was good to talk these things through with Auntie Elsa.

Several hours later, when Naomi returned to the lodge, she felt much lighter and more optimistic about the future.

Meanwhile, Luca had spent time with Johan at the elephant orphanage. He'd even accompanied the bigger orphans on their daily walk into the desert. But reappeared at Desert Lodge in time for dinner.

The escapades with the small herd always left Luca energetic, sweaty and dusty, and full of stories about the ellies. He was still incensed at the number of elephants being poached and talked about how it almost always happened at night when no one seemed able to stop it. His desire to help resulted in him buying night vision cameras and drones for Desert Lodge and Johan's elephant orphanage. He'd also flown a tutor to teach the anti-poacher guards how to operate the equipment.

———

THE WEEK WENT by quicker than anyone had realized and before they knew it, Friday was upon them. It meant an entire week had already gone by since Luca and Naomi's wedding. As an antidote to the sadness of Auntie Elsa's death, they decided to celebrate their week's anniversary and invited Johan and Kerri to fly with them to Windhoek. Dinner at an authentic Italian restaurant seemed perfect, and one of their Italian guests had recommended a restaurant. The jet and the Armati went down a treat with both Johan and Kerri, neither of whom had ever traveled in such extravagant forms of transport before.

After a sumptuous dinner, the foursome explored Windhoek a little more and ended up in a crazy outdoor type pub for drinks. Above the smell of beer and barbeque and the babble of voices, the obligatory television blared on a wall near the bar. No one was paying it any attention, but Johan did a double take as something caught his eye on it.

"Isn't that Stefan?"

Everyone watched as a newscaster said anti-poachers had found Stefan's body and elephants had trampled him to death in the desert. A short film about ellie Naomi shot by Luca followed the item. When it ended, everyone turned to face Luca.

His shy smile emphasized his joy as the others bombarded him with questions.

"Well, I thought it would be a good way to highlight the plight of the ellies being orphaned because of poachers killing their mothers. I've discovered the reason for the increase in poaching is that people are stockpiling the ivory and banking on the fact that the animals will become extinct soon. That way, they'll be the only ones with the ivory and the richest. It infuriates me."

Johan's voice boomed above the surrounding noise.

"That is bloody clever, Luca, man. Now the poachers will think twice about killing elephants when the elephants might wreak revenge on them."

In the jet, on the way back to the lodge, Luca pulled out copies of National Geographic magazine and gave a copy to each.

Naomi's eyes lit up.

"Oh, Luca, you did it!"

She couldn't be more proud of him.

THIRTY

CHAPTER 30

The light blue sky still carried tiny pinpricks of stars. But they were rapidly fading as the pinks and oranges of the sunrise brushed across them, and the light increased with the birth of a new day.

Luca and Naomi were driving into the desert. He had his eye glued to his camera. She basked in the extraordinary freedom of the early morning breeze against her skin, the desert smells, and the sight of the light fog evaporating before the advancing sun.

When they reached the place they'd been aiming for, Luca got out of the truck and walked around it to help Naomi down. Carrying a picnic blanket and basket from the back of the vehicle, he found the perfect spot. He spread the blanket out on the sand, set down their basket, and poured them each a cup of rich coffee.

Naomi stared at the dunes that disappeared into the distance.

"I'm going to miss this so much."

"We can come back here anytime, Mrs. Armati. Don't you

want to go on a short honeymoon with me, and afterward to see your home in Italy?"

Naomi looked at her husband. He'll always stay beyond handsome.

"Of course I do. I can't wait. I'll go anywhere with you, Mr. Armati. You know that, right?"

Luca nodded.

"And I'll go anywhere with you, amore mio."

Naomi returned her gaze toward the dunes.

"So, do you really think our plan will work? Six months there and six months here? It sounds like quite a long time to me."

Luca sat down and stretched his long legs in front of him, crossing them at his ankles and leaning back against the dune behind him.

"It'll fly by. You'll see. But if it doesn't work for you and you get too homesick, we can always do three months here, three there, then back here and so on. We've cast nothing in stone, Mrs. Armati. I'll be happy to be wherever you are."

Naomi giggled.

"You're too funny. You say that now. But I've seen how focused you are on work."

Luca wiggled his eyebrows at her and patted the area beside him for her to join him.

"I'm more focused on you."

"So, what is your house like, Mr. Armati?"

"You mean *our* house. I hope you'll like it. It's big, and full of marble. But if you hate it, we can move. It's not too far from my dad's house, and Santina lives about fifteen minutes away. Although now they're going to get married, they'll probably sell one of their houses."

Naomi sat down beside Luca and was silent for a moment.

"Can I ask you something?"

"Sure. Anything. You know that."

"I know, but... I don't want to cause you any more pain than you've already been dealing with."

Luca put his arm around her shoulders and pulled her closer to him.

"You won't, amore mio. You can never cause me pain. When I think of you, I think only of pleasure in every sense of the word."

Naomi blushed but couldn't contain the smile his words brought to her lips.

"It's about what Santina said. You know, when she'd told us about what had happened with Cecilia."

Naomi waited to feel Luca tense against her, but when he didn't, she continued.

"What I'm puzzled about is why she stayed with you and Enzo for eight years before leaving. It means she must have forgiven him and Santina. And she must have loved you."

Luca's sigh told of his haunted thoughts around Cecilia.

"I don't think we'll ever know for sure. I want to believe she loved us. She was challenging to live with at times because of her huge mood swings. I remember once she locked me in a wardrobe for several hours for some minor indiscretion. I think she forgot I was in there. My dad let me out when he got home.

"Even if we could ask her, I don't think she'd be able to tell us why she stayed and then why she left. I feel sorry for her. I hope she's found some peace and joy in her life by now. It's so sad, isn't it? Such a waste of life, of love. Cecilia, my father, Santina... Who knew?"

Naomi leaned her head on Luca's shoulder. Together they watched as the sun licked away the cool shadows from the dunes.

Luca turned to kiss Naomi. At first, a tender kiss as an expression of his love for her. But as his passion mounted, his kisses deepened until their hearts, and their breathing was racing, and they were tearing at their clothes to fulfil their craving for each other.

As soon as they were naked, Luca pulled Naomi on top of his aching arousal and holding on to her hips, took part in their mutual pleasure until she moaned again and again.

When he was sure he'd satisfied her, he turned her around. Spreading her cheeks, he entered her. The sight of his penetration, the scent of her, and the sounds of her moistness sent him over the edge, and together, they cried their release. Their voices joined with those who'd left their echo in this barren place, where the dance of life had continued for millennia.

By the time they'd finished their breakfast, although still early, the sun's rays were hot on their bodies.

Luca draped an arm over Naomi's stomach.

"I guess we'd better get back, Mrs. Armati."

She nodded and got up to get dressed, but Luca had other ideas in mind. He found her clothes first where they had scattered them in their haste to get naked. He dressed her, but not in the order she'd do it. They giggled and laughed, and when she had all her clothes on again, she did the same for him.

The journey back to Desert Lodge was bittersweet. The last, Naomi knew, before new experiences in another land would change her forever. But the desert would always live in her heart.

As they drove up to the lodge, a massive truck with seven brand new dune buggies came into view. Everyone who worked at the lodge, it seemed, and a few neighbors were admiring the small vehicles.

Naomi looked at Luca, amazement clear in her voice.

"That was quick?"

"Not really. I'd given the go-ahead the moment we got back from being stranded in the storm. The prototype tested perfectly, and the components for the buggies were already at the factory. It was just a matter of assembly."

Kerri walked toward them, waving, her face beaming with excitement.

"Aren't they gorgeous? Thank you so much, Luca. Your timing couldn't have been more perfect. Now, when our new guests arrive next week, the buggies will be ready to hire."

Luca made a funny smug face, his voice impression that of a sleazy car salesman.

"That was the plan all along."

Naomi and Kerri laughed at his silliness as he helped Naomi from the truck. Together, the three friends walked to inspect the buggies up close, running appreciative hands over the sleek metal. After much adoration, they left the rest of the admirers there and walked around the corner to the Lapa.

Now that no guests were staying at the lodge and Kerri's team had completed the intensive cleaning of the rooms, a calm serenity had settled over the place.

Naomi sighed as she sat down in a chair, facing the swimming pool. It felt good to have the place to themselves for this short while.

Kerri ordered coffee, using her walkie-talkie before turning to Luca and Naomi.

"So, what are your plans? I guess you're still on your honeymoon?"

Luca took Naomi's hand and kissed her fingers, all the while looking into her eyes as he answered Kerri's question.

"Your guess is correct, Kerri. And I intend to take my bride to a place that's even more romantic than this, if that were possible."

Kerri glanced at Naomi, but her friend tried to stay nonplussed.

"Luca has promised to take me to Venice."

Kerri squealed her delight for her friend.

"That's so awesome! It's on my bucket list."

Luca smiled at her.

"Well, when you and Johan tie the knot, he can take you there, si? You can stay at our palazzo."

Kerri's eyes glittered at the prospect.

"Oh, thank you so much, Luca. I'll tell Johan. He'll be so excited. Meanwhile, I'll just have to live vicariously through the two of you."

Naomi laughed at Kerri's silliness.

"Don't worry, I'll Skype you from there."

Kerri grinned at the prospect.

"When are you leaving?"

Luca glanced at Naomi to make sure he wasn't giving away any secrets, but she smiled her consent.

"Tonight."

"Oh, my God, so soon? Well, then you must excuse Naomi and me, Luca. I still have several business details to go over with her."

Luca nodded and kissed Naomi's hand again just as the waitress arrived with the coffee.

Kerri got up and poured Luca a cup, taking the rest of the tray with her.

"I hope that's okay with you, Naomi hun? Sorry to drag you to work during your honeymoon."

"Sure. It has to be done. No biggie."

Naomi got up, kissed Luca, and followed Kerri to her office, glancing behind her and blowing him kisses, which he caught and returned until she disappeared around the corner.

LUCA STRETCHED his legs out in front of him and inter-twined his fingers behind his head as he leaned back in the chair. He tried to remember what it felt like when he'd first arrived at Desert Lodge. Even though it was only a short while ago, it astonished him how recent it was. He couldn't remember what his life was like before Naomi and Desert Lodge.

Okay, he felt they had to rush into marriage because of Auntie Elsa's unexpected illness and death, but he knew in his heart they'd done the right thing. He was glad everything had happened the way it did. Well, not about Auntie Elsa's death. Obviously. But now, somehow, his life made sense.

Gratitude that Santina had had the courage to tell him about his birth and his mother, flooded warmth through his body. How wonderful that his father and Santina were both willing to give up their miserable, isolated existences and give each other a chance. It filled his heart with happiness.

In fact, it was difficult to verbalize how happy he was. It felt like life before it all, before Naomi, was just existence. Now he was alive. He was looking forward to the future with her. He was looking forward to experiencing more of this new feeling that lived inside his body. It was a feeling of belonging. Every-thing was right in his world. He felt content.

WHEN NAOMI EXCUSED herself after lunch to visit Auntie Elsa's grave for the last time before they left, Luca returned to their suite. He never took a siesta in the afternoon but wanted to be fresh for the long flight back to Italy this evening. He almost felt guilty about it until he remembered they'd driven into the desert before sunrise.

Meanwhile, Naomi sat down beside Auntie Elsa's grave. She couldn't help being in awe of how much her life had changed in such a brief space of time. Leaving for Italy, even though not forever, felt like leaving Auntie Elsa, too. Even if she were still alive, Naomi would have felt like this, sad and happy and excited all at once.

Naomi's eyes welled up. She'd miss Auntie Elsa so much.

She sighed.

There was a question she would've loved to ask Auntie Elsa besides wanting to know if she'd met Uncle Wouter again.

Naomi would've asked about change. Why change was something all human beings craved. Yet, when it happened, it brought great fear, often to the point of self-sabotage. Naomi thought it a mystery. She was sure a conversation about change would've been a grand one with her wise, beloved adoptive mother.

As she thought about it and imagined what Auntie Elsa might have said, Naomi decided there and then not to fear change, but to embrace it. It was part of being human, part of life. Everything was in a constant flux of change. Of course it was. When the understanding came, it was not merely a mental grasp but also an emotional awareness that brought a sense of peace.

Despite the many changes in her life, this time, the changes seemed massive. Her new life not only included a new husband, a new family, but a new country and a new business. It could have felt overwhelming. But it didn't. It felt exciting. She felt alive. She felt happy, even as her heart still mourned Auntie Elsa's death.

THIRTY-ONE

CHAPTER 31

By the time the sun threw its long shadow fingers on the ground and over the buildings, Luca and Naomi stood next to the jet, ready to leave. In front of them, the entire staff of Desert Lodge had come to say goodbye.

Kerri, ever efficient, had arranged that the staff walk past Luca and Naomi in single file to allow each person to shake their hands and to give them their messages of goodwill. Khwai came at the end of the long line, his wrinkled face beaming, but tears stood in his eyes as he hugged Naomi and gave Luca an extra-long African handshake. Then, Kerri and Johan gave their last hugs and stood away from the jet, Johan's arm around Kerri's shoulders.

Luca pulled up the ladder and shut the door, while Naomi waved from the window next to her seat. Everyone waved until the jet was too far away to see their hands any longer.

Naomi sighed and leaned back in her seat, putting her head on the headrest.

Luca glanced at her.

"Are you okay, Mrs. Armati?"

She turned her head, smiled at him, and stroked the top of his arm.

"I'm more than okay, Mr. Armati."

At Eros Airport, they changed aircraft. Staff transferred their luggage, and Luca led Naomi on to his private jet. It was much larger and more luxurious than the small Cessna jet he had used to fly to and from Desert Lodge. Naomi watched as Luca performed all kinds of checks and talked to the aircraft control tower. It took about an hour and then they were off. A tiny butterfly fluttered in Naomi's stomach at the thought she was now on her way to her new life.

After they were airborne, she got up and found them something to eat and drink in the well-stocked kitchen at the rear of the jet. She meant to do her bit to help keep Luca awake for the sixteen-hour flight. But when she opened her eyes, Luca was landing at Venice's Marco Polo airport.

Disappointment washed through her she had missed the sight of coming in over Venice.

"You should have woken me up, Mr. Armati."

Luca glanced at her.

"But you were sleeping so peacefully, Mrs. Armati, and you were snoring."

"I don't snore."

Luca grinned.

"No, you just sleep very loudly."

Naomi had never imagined that she might snore.

"Oh, my God, are you sure? Have I been snoring this whole time, and you're only telling me now?"

Luca's grin broadened.

"No, Mrs. Armati, I'm only teasing."

But Naomi wasn't so sure. Knowing Luca, he may just have been polite. She knew Auntie Elsa used to snore when she was tired. As Naomi had been up since before dawn the previous day, she may very well have been snoring. How unsexy! Especially since she'd never heard Luca snore in the time they'd been sharing a bed.

VENICE WAS A WONDER. The moment they alighted, all thoughts of snoring left Naomi's thoughts. The tangy, salty scent of the place, and the humidity on her skin became sensations to appreciate. The seasons were just changing into summer here. Naomi could only imagine how sticky it could get in high summer with the humidity higher than today and tourists cramming the narrow streets. Luca had told her they called those Calle.

The boat that greeted them plowed through the pale water surrounding the city. Naomi's eyes widened as Venice rose higher out of the ocean ahead of them, like a sea serpent rising above the waters. It was a breathtaking sight.

Luca put his arm around Naomi and grinned at the delight on his wife's face.

His family palazzo climbed from the water and towered above the other buildings that surrounded it. He led Naomi inside, where she could not tear her eyes from the intricate paintings on the ceilings. She turned around and around as Luca steered her further into the Palazzo. He was watching her face. He couldn't imagine the impact being here had on Naomi. She'd never been out of Africa before. He understood that Venice was overwhelming, even for Italians who came here on vacation.

He tried to see it through her eyes. The age of the city had to impress, though nothing compared to the ancient desert that had been her home. But Venice was more than a thousand years old. Then there was its otherness, as though being here was being transported to another world, an ancient world of water and marble, art and intrigue, and the ghosts of decadence. Venice had always made Luca feel dizzy with joy.

Their enormous room was on the top floor from where Naomi could admire the canals and other palazzos around them. She'd brought along only a few pieces of clothing. When Luca had suggested she bought a whole new wardrobe for Italy as it would save her flying back and forth with a lot of luggage, it had made sense.

Since it was lunch time, Luca suggested a quick lunch before a short shopping spree. The shops and restaurants closed at three o'clock for the siesta, and only opened again at seven o'clock, Luca had explained.

By the time they returned to the palazzo carrying many colorful bags with new clothes for her, Naomi was bone tired. She couldn't even imagine how tired Luca had to be since he'd flown the jet for those many hours. They headed straight for their bed and collapsed on it without taking off their clothes first.

AS THEIR VISIT to Venice would be for only one week, Luca did his best to show Naomi the Venice he knew, the Venice of his childhood.

Naomi fell more and more in love with the place as it revealed itself to her, as Luca took her to the secret, out-of-the-way places only Venetians knew. That each palazzo contained its own courtyard where lush plants grew, and its private roof gardens where even more plants grew, carried a wonderful romance for Naomi. She delighted in her own little game of spotting the more exotic places that contained these mini oases.

Their time in Venice flew by, and before she knew it, it was time to leave for Modena, her new forever home in Italy.

The evening before they were due to leave, Naomi remembered she'd promised to Skype Kerri from Venice. She texted Kerri to make sure she was available. She was. Luca gave Naomi his laptop and disappeared from the lounge, giving her privacy as she chatted with her best friend.

Kerri spoke the moment she could see Naomi.

"Oh, my God, you look amazing! Tell me everything. Leave nothing out."

Naomi giggled at Kerri's outrageous request. But she tried to give as detailed a description of Venice and their time there, as she could. She got up and turned the laptop so Kerri could see as much of the Palazzo as possible.

"It looks wonderful. You lucky, lucky woman, hun. But you so deserve it. I'm so happy for you. So, you're off to Modena tomorrow. How do you feel about it?"

"Slightly trepidatious. I'll be going to my new life, and I don't know what's expected of me."

Kerri became serious.

"Naomi, hun. No one expects anything of you other than you be yourself. Luca married you, not some version he wants you to become. And Santina will be there. Give her my love, will you? And to Enzo, too. You'll be fine. And if you have any problems, you just call me, okay?"

Naomi felt much better after the conversation with Kerri. She hadn't realized how anxious she'd been about going to her new life and her new home. But Kerri was right. Luca had married her for who she was.

THE NEXT MORNING, as they boarded the water taxi to take them back to Marco Polo airport, Naomi cast one last glance at the city she had come to love so fast.

Luca was watching her.

"We can come back anytime you want, Mrs. Armati. Modena isn't that far away. It will take less than two hours to fly to Bologna. It's our nearest airport. And then just about forty-five minutes' drive from there to Modena. So, you see, we're very close to Venice."

Naomi smiled at Luca.

She was so grateful for his continued sensitivity. He'd been especially attentive to her this morning. She blushed pink when she thought of all the attention he'd paid her.

Leaning over, she gave him a quick, soft kiss.

"Thank you, Mr. Armati. I'll hold you to it."

Luca was true to his word. He flew the jet into Bologna Guglielmo Marconi Airport, where an even more amazing Armati supercar awaited them than the one they'd used in Windhoek. This car was one of Luca's own Armatis. The drive from Bologna took exactly forty minutes by Naomi's reckoning.

As they drove over the rolling hills into Modena, the first thing Naomi saw was the giant silver statue of the Armati logo, which they'd proudly displayed at the entrance to the city.

Luca saw her expression of awe.

"Welcome to the land of Parma ham, balsamic vinegar and the world's most supercars."

"You mean there are more supercar manufacturers here than Armati?"

"Oh, yes, Mrs. Armati. Unfortunately, we're not as exclusive as you might want to believe we are. Maserati, Ferrari, Lamborghini and Pagani all have their factories here. There used to be others, like Bugatti–"

Modena wasn't what Naomi had expected.

She couldn't contain the exclamation that interrupted Luca's listing of supercar manufacturers.

"Wow!"

A medieval city surrounded by lush green countryside, where ancient, neat chimney stacks peeked out over woods more than met her expectations. Farming, it appeared, lived side by side with the advanced industry that several supercar manufacturers brought to the area.

In the distance, Naomi noticed a castle. As Luca continued driving toward it, her nervous glances at him increased. He said his house was big...

Luca saw her anxiety out of the corner of his eye. His grin broadened, but he remained quiet, enjoying teasing her a little. He could almost hear her relief as he drove past the castle. They went a little further up the hill in front of them.

As he came around the corner on the private road, through the trees stood the house he hoped she'd come to call home. A huge three-story stone building, it flaunted beautiful square windows, an impressive entrance and a lovely garden with a fountain at its center.

Luca drove around the garden on the paved driveway and stopped in front of the entrance. Turning to smile at Naomi, he took her hand and kissed her fingers. Then, he got out and raced to help her out of the low-slung vehicle. Together they walked up the steps. Naomi watched as her husband unlocked and opened the door. But just as she was about to walk through the door, he surprised her by picking her up and carrying her over the threshold.

Inside, it was cool at once. A massive double staircase greeted her. He was right. There was a lot of marble.

"Welcome home, Mrs. Armati."

Naomi held on tight to her husband. She knew Luca meant

the building. But for her, it was much more than that. With Luca, she had the family she'd always craved. Now, her heart was full, filled up with love. She belonged to this amazing man, and he belonged to her. Naomi sighed against his chest.

Yes. She was home, finally, in his arms.

FROM ANGELINA

Building a relationship with my readers is the very best thing about writing. So, please feel free to subscribe to my Newsletter - https://angelinakalahari.com/contact/. If you prefer, you can email me at angelina@agelinakalahari.com.

You'll receive occasional email notifications about freebies, new stories and novels, YouTube videos, podcasts, short stories and much more.

The first thing you'll receive upon subscribing, is an exclusive novella called *Diary of Naomi, a Desert Elephant* – it's the story of what happens to ellie Naomi.

Elephants in Namibia are the toughest in Africa. But orphaned elephants are the toughest still. And they need to be.

All elephants must travel great distances to find food to live on and they're renowned for their magnificent memories and deep emotions.

In this novella, discover what happens when they find the people responsible for making them orphans?

HOW TO FIND ME

On my website - https://angelinakalahari.com/ - you'll find lots about books - mine and other authors' books I enjoyed reading. There are videos with readings from my books, short stories and much more just waiting for you to enjoy.

Here are more places for you to connect with me:

Amazon Author Page: https://tinyurl.com/yyxdohld

https://www.facebook.com/authorangelinakalahari/

https://twitter.com/angelinakalhari/

https://www.instagram.com/angelinakalahari/

www.pinterest.com/angelinakalhari

http://www.youtube.com/c/AngelinaKalahari - I'd love you to subscribe to my YouTube channel, too – it's where I post free audio chapters of my books, interviews with other authors and talks about love.

THANK YOU FOR READING UNDER A NAMIBIAN SKY.

If you enjoyed *Under A Namibian Sky*, you might also like the previous, and the next books in the series.

As all authors, I appreciate enormously your short review on Amazon or Goodreads, or wherever you've bought the book, stating why you liked the novel. I cannot stress how important reviews are. They help other readers decide to read it and enable novels like *Under A Namibian Sky* to live in the world.

A percentage of every sale of this novel will be donated to elephant conservation in Africa.

If you've loved Luca and Naomi's story in *Under A Namibian Sky*, then you'll be thrilled by *Love In Modena*, the follow-up novella to that much-loved contemporary romance novel.

"Often I am left with a feeling of 'what happened after' in romance books, and it was really

refreshing to read a follow-up story." – Amazon reviewer.

Naomi has found her prince, her Luca, her soul mate. In Modena, she also found her place in the world with him. But she can't let go of Namibia so easily, not now she's become the new owner of Desert Lodge.

Luca, the heir apparent to the Armati supercar dynasty, understands Naomi's dilemma. Their decision to split their time and responsibilities between the two countries seems like the perfect solution.

Theirs is a lifestyle others can only dream of.

But neither expects that an unforeseen foe in their midst would test their relationship to the limits.

Get your copy of *Love in Modena* today to find out what happens to Luca and Naomi once they leave the desert.

Disclaimer: This novella contains some heat and a happy ending. Don't forget, it's also available in Kindle Unlimited.

***

In the second novel in the *Desert Love* series, ***Heat in the Desert***, we meet Gerhard and Saira.

AN ACCIDENT, A PASSION, A DARK SECRET...

"Heat in the Desert takes contemporary romance to another level - a real page-turner. Trust me - you'll love it!" - a reviewer.

Saira and Gerhard live entirely different lives.

Feisty and ambitious, Saira reluctantly accepts an assignment to produce a TV pilot about weddings at the prestigious, romantic

Desert Lodge. But when the small plane taking her there malfunctions, she finds herself stranded in the desert with sexy, muscular, mysterious Gerhard and his yummy German good looks.

Gerhard is everything Saira desires: he is regal, gorgeous, genuine. She cannot help but feel drawn to him.

Saira might just be the woman of Gerhard's dreams, and now he's found her, he doesn't want to let her go. But there are things in Gerhard's past that threaten to ruin everything...

Explore *Heat in the Desert*, a novel in the captivating Desert Love contemporary romance series, today.

"The way the author describes the characters' emotions stood out for me as it made the story come alive. I could feel everything they felt." - beta reader.

Disclaimer: You can read this novel as part of the series or as a stand-alone novel. It contains some heat and a happy ending. Don't forget, it's also available in Kindle Unlimited.

***

In the next novel, **Starlight Over the Dunes**, we meet an artist and a Hollywood A-lister. Each sought out the desert to contemplate and struggle with their own demons. But the desert is the last place they imagined meeting someone who could be their soul mate. Could they help each other? And will it lead to love?

There are more books to come in the series as I adore writing love stories set in my beloved Namibia. I hope you'll enjoy them as much as I love creating them.

Won't you join me?

MORE IN THE DESERT LOVE SERIES

If you've loved Luca and Naomi's story in *Under A Namibian Sky*, then you'll be thrilled by *Love In Modena*, the follow-up novella to that much-loved contemporary romance novel.

"Often I am left with a feeling of 'what happened after' in romance books, and it was really refreshing to read a follow-up story." – *Amazon reviewer.*

Naomi has found her prince, her Luca, her soul mate. In Modena, she also found her place in the world with him. But she can't let go of Namibia so easily, not now she's become the new owner of Desert Lodge.

Luca, the heir apparent to the Armati supercar dynasty, understands Naomi's dilemma. Their decision to split their time and responsibilities between the two countries seems like the perfect solution.

Theirs is a lifestyle others can only dream of.

But neither expects that an unforeseen foe in their midst would test their relationship to the limits.

Get your copy of *Love in Modena* today to find out what happens to Luca and Naomi once they leave the desert.

Disclaimer: This novella contains some heat and a happy ending. Don't forget, it's also available in Kindle Unlimited.

In the next novel, *Starlight Over the Dunes*, we meet an artist and a Hollywood A-lister. Each sought out the desert to contemplate and struggle with their own demons. But the desert is the last place they imagined meeting someone who could be their soul mate. Could they help each other? And will it lead to love?

There are more books to come in the series as I adore writing love stories set in my beloved Namibia. I hope you'll enjoy them as much as I love creating them.

LOVE BEYOND REASON SERIES - WOMEN'S FICTION

The Healing Touch

How do you live in a world without your voice, without passion, and without James…?

Isabelle spent her career as an opera singer and her life married to an emotionally unavailable man. With the onset of the menopause, Isabelle loses her most precious gift - her voice. As time marches unforgivably on, Isabelle yearns to experience the love and passion she'd always dreamt of in her operatic roles.

Throwing herself into her work, Isabelle finds her soulmate in the least likely of moments. When James auditions for the lead in one of her shows, Isabelle discovers the one thing she has spent her life searching for - him.

But when James unexpectedly dies, Isabelle must forge a new life for herself in a world that is suddenly unfamiliar and forever cold.

Is it too late for her to find the love she craves, or could Angelo be the healing touch to save her fragmented soul?

Inspired by true events, *The Healing Touch* is a mesmerising story of loss, heartbreak, passion and love in many guises.

If you liked The Notebook, then you'll love The Healing Touch.

Explore *The Healing Touch*, the first novel in the captivating *Love Beyond Reason* series today.

"Profoundly moving, delightfully evocative and totally absorbing... reminds me of novels by Nicholas Sparks."

- Mary Anne Yarde, author of the award-winning series The Du Lac Chronicles.

Disclaimer: This novel is written in British English, contains some heat and a happy ending. Don't forget, it's also available in Kindle Unlimited.

***

Next in the Love Beyond Reason Series

Forever and Ever Love

The reincarnated love Angelo Antoniou and Isabelle Cooper share will never give up their yearning for happiness.

In Ancient Egypt, their undying love as a princess and a

high priest, is born. But their love is forbidden, and as she dies tragically, they swear an oath to find one another again.

Eighteenth-century Venice sees them finding each other again, but once more, their love is thwarted.

Now, in present-day London, they find one another once again. But as she's married to someone else, does it mean they still have to fight to be together or can they taste true happiness and fulfillment in this lifetime?

A HUGE THANK YOU

To the best editorial team in the world – Christine, Elizabeth, John, Susie, Julia, Irma, Linda, Judy and Kumi – thank you so much for reading, commenting, suggesting and helping me to create a world in which to escape and to bask for a while.

Without you, this novel would not have become the story it has. I'm grateful you asked all the right questions and helped me to become a better writer.

To Jane Dixon- Smith for the most romantic cover.

ABOUT THE AUTHOR

Author photograph ©www.Bobieh.com

Angelina Kalahari has worked for over thirty-five years as an operatic soprano, stage director and voice teacher around the world.

She received recognition for her contribution to the music, culture and economy of the UK from Queen Elizabeth II at Buckingham Palace.

Angelina has always regarded herself as a storyteller, either through music or through acting and directing. She honed her storytelling skills from a young age, writing and telling stories to her siblings at bedtime. It became a habit over the years. She has many finished novels, children's stories and plays. Her publishing journey as an indie author began with *The Healing Touch*, a Women's Fiction story, based on true events.

Born in Namibia, and having lived all over the world, she currently lives in London, UK, with her husband, her fur cat daughter, a rapidly diminishing population of house spiders and a smallish herd of dust bunnies.

She has recently come to the conclusion that drinking vast amounts of tea holds the key to life.